GENESIS

GENESIS

Published December 2023
Indies United Publishing House, LLC

THIRD EDITION

ISBN: 978-1-64456-688-6 [Hardcover]
ISBN: 978-1-64456-689-3 [Paperback]
ISBN: 978-1-64456-690-9 [Mobi]
ISBN: 978-1-64456-691-6 [ePub]
ISBN: 978-1-64456-692-3 [Audiobook]

Library of Congress Control Number: 2023949506

INDIES UNITED PUBLISHING HOUSE, LLC
P.O. BOX 3071
QUINCY, IL 62305-3071
indiesunited.net

To the women in our lives,
Those who made it this far,
And those who didn't.
May your love shine through us,
Ad aeternum.

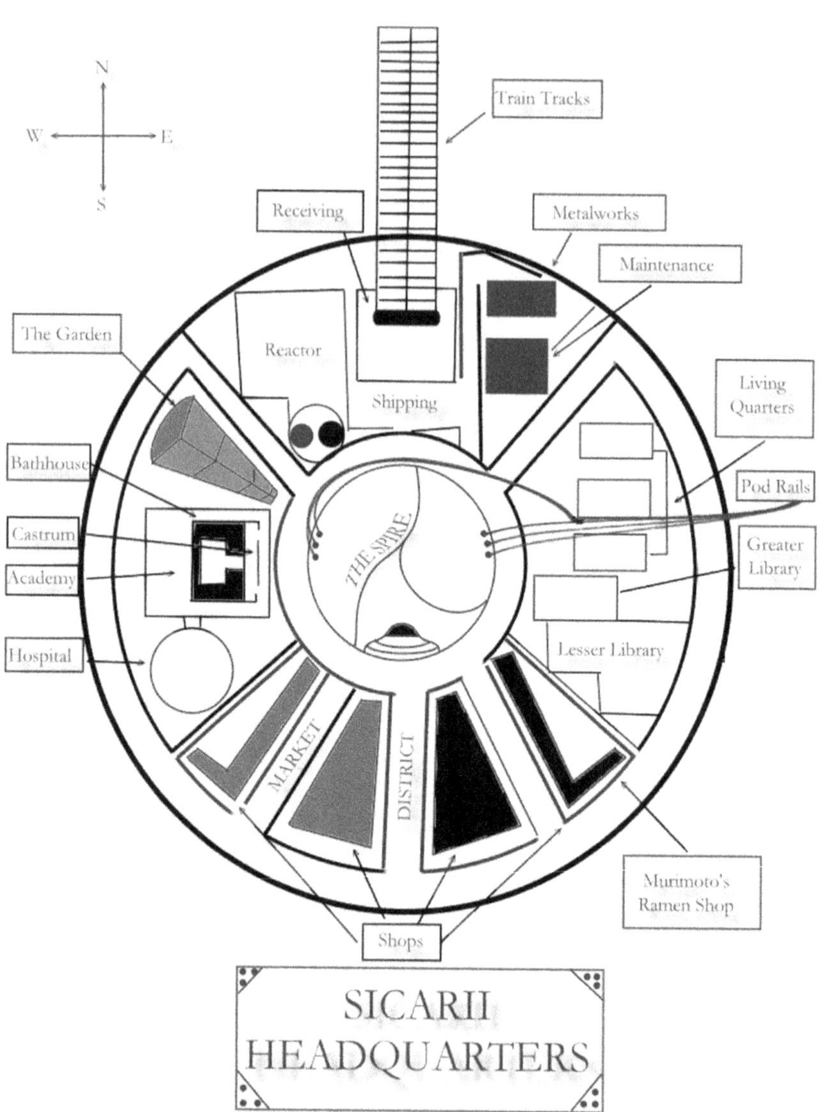

N
W
E
S
Train Tracks
Receiving
Metalworks
Maintenance
Reactor
Shipping
Living Quarters
The Garden
Bathhouse
Pod Rails
Castrum
Academy
THE SPIRE
Greater Library
Hospital
Lesser Library
MARKET
DISTRICT
Murimoto's Ramen Shop
Shops
SICARII HEADQUARTERS

CHARACTER INDEX

The Sicarii

The High Council

Alef (1)
Bet (2)
Gimel (3)
Dalet (4)
He (5)
Vav (6)

The Twelve Squads:

Seraph Squad:

Seraphiel - Leader
Helel ben Sahar - second in command
Metatron
Michael
Jehoel

Squad Three:

Gilroy - Leader
? - Ranger
? - Warden
? - Alchemist
? - Wraith

Squad Four:

Kai - Leader
Tara - Ranger, second in command
Marlowe - Warden
Amina - Alchemist
Piers - Wraith

Squad Nine:

The Black Death Mahta - Leader
Joseph - Warden, second in command

? - Wraith
? - Alchemist
? – Ranger

<u>Non-Squad Sicarii Members</u>

Alphonse - archaeologist, best friend of Kai
Sohei Murimoto - previous Squad leader, owner of Sohei's Ramen Shop
Haley - librarian assistant in the Greater Library
Sofia - bodyguard of the High Council
Verena - secretary of the High Council
Summer - watcher of the Spire's plaza
Dr. Henry Mun - forensic pathologist
Dr. Áñez - medical doctor at the hospital in HQ

Unaffiliated Characters

Black Star - freelance assassin, son of Alexander Stromberg
Maria (White Star) - inventor, mechanic, daughter of Alexander
Stromberg and sister of Black Star
Alexander Stromberg - environmental scientist, bioengineer,
astrophysicist, inventor, father of Maria and Black Star
Sylvia Stromberg (Silver Star) - retired assassin, mother of Maria and
Black Star
Red Star - maternal grandfather of Black Star
Cornelius - purveyor of freelance assassin contracts, financial advisor
Sandy Shores - Italian mobster
Konstantin and Sergei - Russian mobsters
Vadim - Pakhan of the Bratva operating in the New States
Lilian Marshall - ex-soldier and CIA operative
Adrian Blom - head of the Swedish Security Service
The Phantom - ?
Ahmed and Adelina - father-daughter duo who run the Hashround
Haberdashery
Abe Davidson - skilled thief
Elaine - ex-Engineer, inventor

GENESIS

The Lightning Arc
Book One

J. M. Coleman

L. L. Wirtz

INDIES UNITED PUBLISHING HOUSE, LLC

ONE

KAI

On an insignificant rooftop in an insignificant city a steel door burst open from a forceful kick. A middle-aged suited man fell backwards out of the doorway and scurried hurriedly away from the shrouded figure following him.

"What do you want!?" he shouted, unheard by the rest of the world. "I'll give you anything! Money, drugs, women, just please don't kill me!" In the darkness red stared back at him. In that horrifying collusion of parallel and perpendicular lines the man saw only one thing: oblivion.

"Adrian O'Connor," the figure stated, his voice as terrifying as his mask. "On the order of the High Council of the Sicarii you have been sentenced to death."

"No!" the man shouted into the void. "You can't do this!" He moved quickly, but not quick enough to dodge the sword that plunged into his heart, severing his aortic valves and rupturing all four chambers in the process. The man's head fell and the rain began to pour. The blood dripping from the assassin's blade mixed with the water, creating an ocean of diluted ichor between himself and the rooftop. He flicked the blade outwards, spattering the rooftop door with blood like a painter with a canvas. His longsword shone in the darkness, reflecting the lights of The City all around him while revealing the Greek word "θρυμματίζω" (Shatter) engraved on the blade.

"Contract complete," he sheathed his sword and the interior of his mask lit up a brighter crimson than before.

"Voice recognition confirmed," it stated in a cool feminine

voice. "Target eliminated. Funds added in the amount of one-hundred thousand USD."

The young man reached around to the back of his neck and pressed a circular, red-ringed button which triggered a collapse, or rather a dissolution, of his helmet into the space in which the button existed. He looked up towards the night sky. As the rain penetrated the troposphere and fell towards the earth he felt for once, in his entire life, a kind of peace as the water droplets struck his face lightly. The helicopters flying above him broke his peace with their obnoxious rotors that tore through the air like vultures through flesh, and because of this he put his head down, reconstructed his helmet, and began walking forward. Walking towards the ledge, the short, messy-haired killer kept his sights on the helicopters as they headed towards a building on the west side of The City. He jumped across the gap in front of him to another roof and followed them. The boot-like footwear built into his suit pounded ferociously against the wet concrete as he moved more quickly westward.

"Transmission incoming, Kai," his mask stated abruptly.

"Who is it, Eris?" Kai asked.

"It's the High Council."

The High Council? Kai thought. *I highly doubt this is a coincidence.* Kai's thoughts flickered with the endless possibilities of the events that were about to unfold, but no training, no understanding or calculations of percentages and probabilities could make him understand this. "Put them through," he stated.

"Identify," a younger woman commanded.

"Kai. A-Rank Knight-Hybrid. Leader of Squad Four. Assassin under the order of the High Council of the Sicarii." This statement was like clockwork to him. It was stitched into the very fabric of his existence, just like everyone else at the Academy. Name. Rank. Class. Affiliations. Any differentiation ended in death.

"Kai," the young woman said calmly. "Something has happened." She was upset, afraid, and Kai picked up on her emotion immediately.

"What's going on, V?" Kai asked, still sprinting across the rooftops, trailing behind the helicopters. At this height falling meant instant death, but Kai wouldn't fall, he couldn't fall, because the rooftops were his home, as they had been nearly his whole life. So, when he was up there, above the busy streets, above the disgusting swine that were ignorant of their own world, he was okay.

"Kai... it's Alphonse..." His heart stopped. His head fell and he stopped moving, teetering on the edge of a roof hundreds of feet in the air. Any thoughts lingering in his mind fled as pictures and memories of Al began flooding back through him. "He's gone rogue."

A pulse shot through Kai's body. He instantly felt sick, and vomit began forming in his gut. Sadness, despair, and frustration overwhelmed his body and poured out of him like an overfilled jug.

"You'll need the rest of your squad for this one," the young woman said. "He's on the roof of the Empyrion Building. You know what must be done, Kai, and the High Council trusts you'll do it. Transmission over, Eris." The woman's voice cut out and Kai stepped away from the edge and fell to his knees, pressing the button on the back of his neck to collapse his helmet. He began vomiting bile as the shock of his orders overwhelmed him and he hadn't eaten in over two days. *Not Al.* He thought. *Anyone, but Al.* The hard rain beat on his back and head soaking his short, dark, messy hair. He stood up, his throat burning, and wiped his mouth. He looked back up at the same night sky. *Ah, fuck,* he thought. He pushed his hair back with his hand and pressed the same button on the back of his neck, bringing his mask back. The interior of it began glowing a deep crimson yet again.

"Eris?" Kai asked.

"Yes, Kai?" Eris responded.

"Connect me to the rest of Squad Four immediately."

"Right away," Eris confirmed.

"Marlowe," Kai said shakingly.

"Yes."

"Amina."

"What's up?"

"Tara."

"Alive and well."

"Piers."

"Kai! What's up buddy! How are y-"

"Track my position and move on me," Kai ordered, cutting off Piers. "We have a mission from the High Council directly."

"Copy that," Tara responded.

"Affirmative," Marlowe stated roughly.

"On my way!" Amina said excitedly.

"I'm closing in on you now," Piers informed.

Piers arrived first, a fourteen-year-old cloaked boy with shaggy blonde hair and a knack for hacking off limbs with his scythe. "What's up dude!?" Piers exclaimed.

"Now's not the time, Piers," Kai responded.

"My bad, my bad. What happened?"

"We'll go over the mission when everyone arrives." Kai's harshness bothered Piers and his happy demeanor quickly turned sullen as he matched Kai's speed, which was easy enough for him since he was a Wraith. Marlowe was the next to arrive, his thunderous stomp shaking the rooftop below Kai and Piers. Marlowe was a massive, male Pacific Islander with the muscles of a bodybuilder and long locks of curly hair encompassing his head. He was large, but he was fast, unexpectedly fast, which made him even more terrifying as a Warden.

As Marlowe fell into formation Tara joined the fray, her dark brown cloak flapping in the wind and rain. Tara was mild-mannered, strong, and rarely spoke. She was a Ranger, and if she wasn't with the squad she was in the forest hunting with her half-wolf Hastur. Tara's golden hair was braided down to the middle of her back where she tied it off with a piece of string. She was a true warrior and the second in command of Kai's squad. Amina showed up last, a petite girl, eighteen years of age with blueish hair and pale skin.

"Yo!" Amina yelled. "Sorry I'm late!"

"We still have some ways to go," Kai said. "Don't worry." Amina was an Alchemist who wore leather vestments over the standard, black Sicarii suit with vials of poisons and potions in the holsters built into her waist and chest, and two hardened steel daggers strapped to her thighs. She was the medic of the squad, and every squad needed one, but she was much more than that. Amina was deadly with a blade and even deadlier with the toxins she carried around.

"Who's the target?" Tara asked.

"Alphonse has gone rogue," Kai replied. Piers' heartbeat began to race and his face became red. "Damn it..." he whispered under his breath.

"Target location?" Tara responded.

"The Empyrion Building on the west side of downtown," Kai replied. The Empyrion Building was a prominent science and research facility on the west side of The City. Genetic testing and pharmaceutical research were two of the many complex ideas studied by the Empyrion scientists within its glass walls. From the sky, the Empyrion Building looked like an eye, and was referred to as such by most citizens.

"Distance? Amina asked.

Tara pulled out a rectangular piece of metal that fit neatly in her palm and pressed a button on the lower half of it. The metal split horizontally and the two pieces moved away from each other. A thin, reinforced, glass screen began forming in between the two metal pieces until they were six inches apart, where the pieces stopped moving and the screen lit up. In her hands, Tara held the newest line of mobile devices by Trytek, the largest and most powerful producer of all things technologically advanced from artificial reality to military-grade weaponry.

"3.7 kilometers," Tara stated. "At our current speed, ETA is approximately eight minutes and twelve seconds."

"Let's step it up," Marlowe insisted. The five continued flitting across the rooftops, their thoughts on the massive building in the distance, except for Kai and Piers - their thoughts were elsewhere. Alphonse was their friend, Kai's brother, and had been since the very beginning, since their rescue, through the Academy, and up until now. *What happened, Al? Why you?* Kai thought. *Where is all of this coming from?* Alphonse was always a good kid, always bright, always willing to learn. He wasn't the strongest, or the fastest, but he could outsmart just about anyone and he was a hell of a good strategist. If Kai was five steps ahead of his opponents at all times, Al was twenty. He didn't need strength or speed when he could read the minds of his enemies and force their hand.

"We're 1.6 kilometers out," Tara stated. "We should be seeing the perimeter soon."

An explosion on the roof of the Empyrion Building caught their attention and they stopped running. Smoke began billowing into the crisp night air.

"What the hell was that?" Marlowe exclaimed.

Al..., Kai thought. "Split up," he ordered. "Marlowe and Amina, move towards the north side of the building. Get to the roof by whatever means necessary. And Amina," Kai said while unbuckling his sheath, "take my blade. I won't be able to carry it where I'm going."

"You can count on us!" Amina said excitedly while taking Shatter. Marlowe and Amina dashed off quickly onto another building and disappeared in the lights of The City.

"Piers, I need you to create a distraction. Move into the building from the upper floors and do whatever you can to keep the police and their SWAT units away from the roof." Piers nodded his head and moved towards the south side of the building to breach from higher up.

After Piers was out of sight, Kai stared at Tara. Tara was shockingly beautiful by society's standards, but such things mattered not to him. Kai was a soldier, not a lover. An assassin, not a significant other. To Kai, beauty was fleeting and love even more so. The only thing true and honest in the world was Death. Because Death always came for everyone.

"I'll enter through the front door." Kai stated.

"How are you going to do that?" Tara chuckled.

"It's hard to see who's under those black uniforms of Kevlar and cloth, don't you think?" Tara smiled and nodded her head in agreement. "You know what to do, Tara," Kai said, pointing behind him in the direction of a cluster of buildings. "On it," Tara responded, catching a glimpse of the three snipers on the rooftops of businesses at the north, south, and west perimeter of their target location.

Kai smiled a half, crooked smile, hiding this time behind an internal mask. "Thanks Tara. Let's go." Tara smiled back, ignorant of Kai's façade. She moved across the rooftops towards her first target as Kai hopped down the fire escape towards the dank city streets. A few hundred feet in front of him was a roadblock and a cluster of law enforcement vehicles, their red and blue lights illuminating the buildings surrounding them. He moved closer towards the roadblock and saw three SWAT officers directing the westward traffic on a detour that went north around the police line. Kai moved deep into an alleyway close to the walking, talking, traffic lights. A man clad in Hyper Kevlar and a standard issued SWAT uniform began walking towards the alleyway. Kai made noise to attract him further.

As the soldier moved deeper into the swaying darkness, Kai flanked him and locked his arms around the man's neck to restrict his airflow, causing him to lose consciousness within seconds. Immediately, Kai threw on the SWAT uniform over his own suit and pressed the button on his helmet, collapsing it down to just the piece that surrounded his jaw, and placed the balaclava over his own head. Kai put the SWAT helmet on and hid the body and walked out of the alley assault rifle in hand. Across his upper back scrolled the words *SWAT* and *POLICE* in a holographic display of authority.

"Hey! You! What the hell are you doing?" a bald black man with a large mustache and a police jacket yelled in Kai's direction. Kai glanced towards him. "Yeah you! What are you doing? Stop staring at me and get the hell in there!" the man continued to shout. Kai began jogging towards the rest of the SWAT team that was entering through the front doors of the Empyrion Building. He caught up to them and took up a tactical position in the rear.

"Alright men, here's the plan," a man towards the front said, who was obviously the captain of the squad. It was strange to Kai, taking orders from a squad leader after being one himself for over a year. "We're going to move into this building, clear the floors of any late-night employees, which we hopefully won't find, and take out any tangos along the way. Understood?"

"Yes sir!" the SWAT team exclaimed.

"Let's move out then."

The team of well-trained military police moved into the building swiftly, cautiously, and perceptively, and their captain followed them from behind. Their boots made almost no noise against the white, marble floor, and the light coming from the flashlights mounted on the barrels of their assault rifles bounced off the floors and walls, penetrating every crevice of the darkened building. They moved carefully, methodically, like a hivemind, up the stairs to their left and onto the second floor overlooking the lobby. Most of the research labs were underground, so the second floor and above were entirely offices and conference rooms.

As they cleared the second floor they pushed up to the third, unaware of Kai's ferocious presence lurking next to them. Above them came noises drowned out by the hundreds of feet of glass and steel between them and the origin. They stopped at the sign of their commander, Kai included, and listened. A bang. No, multiple. *Gunfire,* Kai thought. The SWAT team moved faster now, closer to the noise, and their leader followed behind Kai. The more floors they moved through, the staler and colder the air got, as if death had infested each and every corner of the building. Fear and doubt began creeping into the minds of the men and women in front of Kai and he could sense it - slight jerks in their movements, hesitations when rounding corners, changes in breathing - they were weak.

As they moved, Kai kept most of his focus on the shadow lurking near them. It crept silently, unheard by the men and women in ballistic vests and armor as well trained as they may be. Kai smirked. *Piers.* Piers placed himself down the hall and around the corner from the SWAT team so that they would see him when they moved up further. The frontrunner rounded first and saw him immediately.

"FREEZE!" she exclaimed. Piers rounded the next corner and the company chased after him. Kai slipped away as their focus stayed on Piers and moved quickly towards the emergency stairs to head towards the roof. He shed the uniform he was wearing and sprinted upwards towards the origin of the gunfire he had heard previously, boots slamming on the concrete steps below him. A glass exit sign protruding from the ceiling lit up the top of the stairs in a brilliant red blaze. He reconstructed his helmet from its resting place and memories of the Academy and Alphonse flooded Kai's mind; his darkness overwhelmed him constantly, but during the Academy Al was always there for him. Their friendship didn't stay as strong once they found their true place within the Sicarii, but Al was still his friend, his brother, and Kai doubted whether or not he could cut down the pale-haired boy that smiled at him so long ago. Fear began overwhelming him and his helmet became a coffin for his mind. His sight began darkening and his body began aching. He heard not the footsteps coming up behind him. A hand fell lightly on his shoulder.

"Kai?" a young woman's voice broke through the silence softly. Kai's hand moved to the knife at his hip and in one swift motion it shifted from its resting place to the throat of a fearful Amina. Her teal hair flew back, and Marlowe stood shocked behind her. "Hey..." Amina's voice trailed off. Kai came out of his trance and replaced the knife at his hip.

"Sorry," Kai said monotonously.

Amina handed Kai his longsword and he buckled the scabbard across his hip. "Are you okay?" Amina asked concerned, quiet, hoping for a glimpse at his true self.

"I'm fine," he responded as he slid his sword out, inspected it, and slid it back in its casing. "The probability of being seen must be minimalized." Amina accepted that her probing got her nowhere and backed off. Kai made eye contact with her, locking her focus on him. "Do you have anything, Amina?"

"Um," Amina fumbled a bit, looking in her satchel. "Yeah, I have a few smoke bombs."

"Good," Kai responded. "Marlowe, I need you to secure the rooftop perimeter. Any witnesses must be killed. Understood?"

"Understood," Marlowe replied.

"Eris, connect me to Piers." Amina realized months ago that Kai tended to speak to Eris kinder than he did his squad mates, and it bothered her greatly. It wasn't due to Eris's obedience, unbeknownst to Amina, because that's not so much what Kai cared about. Rather, it seemed, it was Eris's possible disobedience that drew Kai to her and her always assisting him, even though she wasn't human.

"Right away, Kai," Eris responded.

"Yo," Piers opened.

"Piers, what's your status?" Kai asked.

"Keeping our friends busy and far away from you," he chuckled.

"Good," Kai responded. "Only kill if absolutely necessary. We need to be in and out as quickly and quietly as possible," Kai said kindly.

"No problem, buddy," Piers ended.

"Tara?" Kai asked over the intercom.

"In position Kai. All scouts have been eliminated. I have a clear line of sight on the entirety of the rooftop."

"Excellent," Kai said pleased. "Amina will be laying down heavy smoke so switch to virtual imaging."

"On it." Tara replied.

"Are you ready Amina?" Kai asked.

"Ready."

"Marlowe?"

"Ready."

"Moving in," Kai stated. "Let's get this over with."

Kai kicked in the rooftop door and Amina threw out three metal orbs that rolled speedily outward. The bright lights from the helicopters beat down heavily, so Kai and Squad Four hid in the dark until the smoke would be thick enough to hide them instead. Amina's orbs split up and rolled to different parts of the roof, the first in line to the farthest point, the second to the middle, and the last fifteen feet in front of the doorway, where they stopped and exploded into a thick cloud that, unseen to the eye, had electric currents flowing through it that wouldn't damage organic life, but interfered with electrical systems like the helicopter's infrared and night vision cameras. However, Tara's virtual imaging went past the electrical smoke because it didn't try to see through it, but rather used satellite imaging and artificial reality software to reimagine the area in view. Eris had said during previous missions that the currents in the smoke 'tingled' a bit as she moved through them, but they never harmed her in any significant way.

Kai, Amina, and Marlowe pushed in through the smoke and

moved carefully across the rooftop. Marlowe stayed near the stairs and Amina followed behind Kai further into the smoky void. In the distance, Kai caught the glimpse of a silhouette of a person and as he and Amina moved further in to investigate they watched the same silhouette slide a blade out of the chest of another.

"Wait here, Amina," Kai stated.

"But Kai..." Amina responded quietly. Kai glanced at her seriously.

"I said stay here. That's an order."

Amina backed off and Kai moved in towards the silhouette. As he walked further his boots began sticking to the rooftop and when he looked below him he saw dark red looking right back up. He moved further into the lake of blood and began seeing mutilated bodies around him: arms hacked off, entrails falling out of carcasses, legs hanging on by arteries alone. The scene was grim, even to Kai, and as he moved closer to the silhouette he could hear the chilling sound of metal sliding in and out of blood-soaked flesh.

"Al...?" Kai's voice trailed off and the silhouette straightened and turned towards him. Kai moved closer and could make out the ridges of the clothing hanging off the shadow in front of him.

"Al... is that you?" Alphonse's pale hair broke through the smokescreen and confirmed the fears that Kai held deep inside of him. Surrounding Alphonse were piles of bodies, torn to shreds by the dull, jagged katana he held in his hand. Kai collapsed his helmet to see Al with his own eyes. "W-what have you done?" Kai stuttered.

Alphonse stepped closer to Kai, his face breaking through the mist, piercing Kai's soul with bloodshot eyes and veiny cheeks and brow. Darkness and death invaded Kai's mind as he stared into the eyes of his lost brother and remnants of their life in the Academy came to the forefront. Kai dropped his hand from his hilt and reached out to touch Alphonse's face.

"You know nothing, Kai," Al's voice broke through the silence and cut through the smoke like his blade cut through all those soldiers. Kai retracted his hand and stepped back slightly. Al followed Kai's step with one of his own, maintaining the distance. "Everything you think you know is a lie. Everything you've been told is a lie. Your very existence as you see it is a façade!" Alphonse was screaming now, the veins in his face pulsing with each beat of his heart. "Everything is a lie! You're a lie! Reality is a lie! LIE! LIE! LIE!"

Kai moved in towards Al to calm him down, but Al lifted his beaten sword in front of him. "Stay away from me!" Alphonse screamed. You're not my brother! You're not my friend! You're nothing! You don't even know what you are! You murdered dozens of people for what!? The Sicarii!? On orders!? Alphonse continued screaming at Kai, his eyes getting more bloodshot with each word.

"Al!" Kai shouted back. "You've lost your mind! What happened to you? Why did you do this? These people had families, wives, husbands, and children! They were innocent and you slaughtered them like sheep!"

"And you'll be next," Al responded hatefully, madly, viciously. Kai's face fell and he pressed the button on the back of his neck, encompassing his tear-stained face with his helmet once again.

"So be it," Kai stated sullenly. His brother was lost and his heart was broken.

Alphonse slung his jagged blade at Kai's face faster than he ever could've before. Kai dodged under and struck Al in the jaw with his fist, sending him backwards a few steps and disorienting him long enough for Kai to draw his own blade. The tip of Kai's blade met with Al's chest in a quick slash straight from the scabbard, lightly scratching his skin. Al pushed forwards, slinging his blade wildly in every direction. Kai's eyes followed it with ease and he blocked left, right, down, and up, parrying Alphonse's jagged sword with his upward strike. Kai spun and aimed the edge of his reinforced steel longsword at his brother's waist. Al caught the blade with his gloved hand and wind whipped around them from the speed at which they were moving. Changing his grip, Kai pulled his blade upwards, forcing Al to let go, and cut straight through his shoulder, taking his right arm off in one move.

Al began screaming as blood gushed from his wound. He dropped his blade and struggled violently to stop the bleeding with his left hand. Tears streamed down Kai's face under his mask, his very existence breaking in half. "I'm so sorry Al..." Kai whispered.

"Sleep now." Kai brought his blade downwards and to the right, cutting cleanly through Alphonse's neck. His lifeless body collapsed to the ground and his severed head rolled off to the right. Kai fell to his knees and dropped his blade. His left hand moved frantically to find the button at his neck, and when he did find it he let out a heart-wrenching scream that silenced everything else in existence. The world ceased to rotate, the cars ceased to move on the streets, and the rooftop he was falling apart on top of ceased to exist. He was floating in darkness, just him and Al, and the pain he experienced in that moment was worse than any pain he had felt before. He began sobbing uncontrollably and he put his head in his hands in an effort to contain his sorrow.

"Kai! Kai!" a woman's voice screamed behind him frantically. Invisible hands grabbed him under his arms and lifted him to his feet. They put his left arm over their invisible shoulders and began walking him away.

"Grab Shatter off the ground and pack up the evidence," the woman's voice shouted. "Tara, Piers, get over here now!" Piers' exhausted voice broke through the darkness.

"I'm here, I'm here." Piers began bagging up Alphonse's remains as quickly as possible.

"I'll meet you back at HQ," Tara said through every member's earpiece. "Just go. Get him out of here now."

"Amina..." Kai said faintly, his eyes absent.

"I'm here Kai, I'm right here. Everything's going to be okay," Amina reassured.

I need transport!" she continued to yell over the intercom. The police helicopter circling the rooftop landed and a member of the Sicarii wearing a police uniform stepped out.

"Get in, now!" he yelled over the rotors while keeping his head down.

"We have to hurry!" Amina shouted. "The smoke will be clearing any second!"

Amina put Kai in the helicopter and got in along with him. Piers hopped in next, followed by Marlowe and Alphonse's bagged body and weapon and anything else that would've pointed to them being there. The helicopter lifted off the ground and began flying off, blowing the rest of the smoke over the edges of the rooftop. Amina rested Kai's head on her chest and wrapped her arm around him. He looked out the window at the Empyrion building as the SWAT team that was chasing Piers burst through the rooftop door. Kai closed his eyes and saw only Alphonse smiling at him, just like he did all those years ago. A tear strolled softly down Kai's face and onto Amina as he finally lost consciousness, ending the worst night of his life.

TWO

BLACK STAR

The neon lights on the exterior of the mom-and-pop stores and the streetlamps lit up the slow streets of a small town in Midwest Montana. The Rocky Mountains rose like hands reaching to the heavens and inside a small pizzeria a young man's hands flew rapidly back and forth over joysticks and buttons on an archaic arcade machine.

His attempt to upkeep his brown hair failed and it swept slightly left just over his eyes. His hair was like an anarchic revolution, refusing to conform no matter how many times it was beaten down, just like the owner whose head it sat upon. The hair in his eyes didn't seem to bother him a bit as his focus pushed his sight past its unruliness. His baggy sweatpants fell over his sneakers and his black t-shirt framed his lean, muscular body. His face was narrow with a chiseled jaw and was clean of facial hair, almost like he had never had to shave before. He might have been eighteen years old, but he looked like he could still be in junior high - a common mistake amongst those who conversed with him.

Children poured around the young man, gawking at his finesse and understanding of such an old game. As the game sped up he remained calm, not letting any stress get to him. While the kids were in awe one boy walked up to him and tugged on his t-shirt.

Annoyed, the child asked "Are you almost done mister? We want to play too!" Another child shouted at the skilled gamer from behind. "Hey! You're cheating!"

"Listen," the young man said, "I have to ensure that I get the high score on this thing. I also need to get my 50 cents worth. And besides..." he looked around, "I need to leave my mark on this place."

"What's that mean?" another kid asked.

"It means..." a loud succession of multiple music-like beeps squeaked from the machine, grabbing his and the children's attention as well.

"Ha-ha! You lost!" the 'cheater' kid yelled.

"Aw man," the unkempt man sighed. "That's okay. I think I did well enough." 'NEW HIGH SCORE' the machine flashed at them in a plethora of colors. '273,000 POINTS' The game swiped to the next screen and three underscores appeared in the middle. 'ENTER YOUR INITIALS' the game screamed visually at the crowd. With the flick of the joystick and three button presses three letters appeared on the screen: 'BSR'. The next screen popped up showing the other top four scores with second place, 'ASS', reaching only 10,500 points. All the children began whining and complaining and BSR turned to face them.

"I've been playing this game since before I was your age. If you all keep practicing you can beat my record one day." Behind the counter a heavier, bald and bearded man yelled out to "BSR".

"Hey buddy! You gonna buy somethin' or are ya just gonna play that game all day?"

BSR shrugged. "Sure, why not. Place an order for a pizza and

I'll be back in forty-five minutes to pick it up." He turned away and moved through the crowd of children swarming the dusty arcade machine.

Frustrated and losing patience, the pizzaiolo shouted back as BSR headed out the door, his accent getting thicker by the second. "What kind of pizza!?"

BSR flung his left hand up as he was halfway out, "I don't care, surprise me."

"What's your name!?" the angry old man shouted back one last time, his face redder than his homemade marinara.

"Rick!" BSR shouted back before the door closed behind him.

Rick shivered as the cool night air rolled across his small frame in a hostile attempt to chill him down to his core. "Fuck the cold..." he said quietly.

A man passing him stopped and stared. "Yo dude... it's only 65 degrees outside. It's not cold at all."

Rick looked at him with an empty abyss in his eyes. No words were required. The aura being emitted from the young man was enough. Scared, the passerby turned and began walking quickly in the opposite direction. Rick slung his bag off his shoulder and took out a black hoodie and put it on over his long sleeve shirt. The lamp posts that lined the streets of the small town reminded him of the stories his father told him about his hometown in Sweden. *I need to head north*, he thought. *Hank's cabin should be roughly seven miles out of town. If I travel by foot I should be able to get there in about twenty minutes.* He lightly jogged with long strides until he hit the tree line on the outskirts of the town where he burst into a sprint.

The forest continued to get denser and the shade above dropped the temperature. In the distance he heard a loud knocking. Curious, he traveled up the hillside where he found a frail old man hacking away at a massive pine tree. With every weak strike the notch in the tree deepened and pinecones fell around him, decorating his yard for future pines to grow.

"Need any help, sir?" Rick approached the man. The man was surprised to see someone in his woods, especially a young man like Rick, and so the old man stopped hacking at the tree and set down the axe.

"I don't like trespassers," the old man replied. "But... if you want to help me, I won't stop you."

"Do you trust everyone that easily?" Rick inquired, crossing his arms. "I could rob you or hurt you in some way."

Sitting down, the old man replied again. "No, you don't give off that vibe. Your long hair makes you look like a degenerate, but you don't give off any bad mojo. Also, only an idiot would warn that he is about to attack."

Bad mojo, huh? Rick thought.

"I can tell you didn't come all this way to steal from some old geezer," the old man continued, "unless you're a lot dumber than you look." The hermit pointed towards the axe leaning up against the tree. "Go ahead and pick up that axe and give that tree a few licks."

Let's see if my training has paid off.

The old man walked back to his cabin up the hill and shut the door behind him. Rick stared at the tree, calculating the speed needed to break through the tree with one swing of his leg.

Diameter... roughly six inches. Tensile strength... 14,500 pounds per square inch. 5,000 should do the trick.

With a deep breath, he composed himself and then struck. In one one-thousandth of a second Rick's leg crushed through the tree, toppling it immediately. Wood pieces flew in every direction and the sonic boom from swinging his leg cracked the surrounding trees. The old man opened his door quickly and ran outside.

"What the hell was that?" he shouted towards Rick, seeing the toppled pine.

"Oh," Rick replied calmly, "I think some lightning struck down over there. But I knocked the tree down as well so it could've been a mixture of both." The old man looked up at the sky. It was clear, no clouds, no rain, no thunderstorms in sight.

"Huh..." the old man muttered, confused. "Must've been heat lightning or something..." he trailed off into his own mind.

"Anyways gramps," Rick said, "here's your tree. I'm assuming you needed firewood?"

"Yeah..." the old man trailed off, continuing to look at the sky. He brought his gaze back down and looked at Rick.

"Do you need it chopped up as well?" Rick asked.

The old man stared at him in a trance. "No son, I think I can do it myself. Thanks for all your help. How can I repay you?"

"No need, gramps. Just have a good day."

"Will do, young man. What's your name? Mine is George, just like my father before me," the old man stated, walking towards Rick and lifting his hand.

"My name is Randall," Rick responded, walking forward and lifting his hand as well. "But my friends call me Randy." A handshake commenced between the two men and mutual respect bubbled. "Do you by chance know a man named Hank?" Randy inquired.

"Well, sure. He lives a few miles North of here. I heard he was a real private man, paranoid even. So, I'd tread lightly if I were you," the man cautioned.

"Oh, no problem, sir. I'm his nephew and he's been expecting me, but you're right, he definitely is a private man," Randy paused while thinking. "Well... have a good day, sir!" he withdrew his hand and began making pace back northward.

"Yeah, you too, son, come back if you ever want to do free labor," the old man said as his farewell. By the time Randy got to his destination the sun began to set and the shadow of the trees shrouded him in darkness. He came upon a small cabin where the light emanating from a lamp inside lit up the front porch, and the screams from the cellar reverberated off the surrounding trees, lightly echoing through the empty forest. The night air was humid and the forming dew clung to Randy's clothes like sap to skin.

Inside, a balding man wearing a rubber apron cut deep into the flesh of a man hung from the ceiling by a meat hook. With every cut, every slice, the hooked man shrieked louder and louder.

"SQUEAL PIGGY SQUEAL!" the torturer exclaimed, going on to laugh uncontrollably. Other mutilated bodies hung from hooks, their limbs and genitals strewn across the floor. Gallons of blood covered every inch of the foundation and the torturer himself.

"Why..." the hooked man could barely form words through the pain. "Why are you doing this?"

"You see..." the torturer started calmly, "your people's screams..." he began getting louder, "...bring me pure euphoria!" He sliced away more at the flesh in front of him as it screamed and writhed, attempting to escape. He stopped slicing and pushed the man away from him. Screaming, the hooked man flew across the room, still on the hook, and stopped when he ran into a woman's torso hanging to his left, decapitated and limbless.

"And that's your downfall," a voice broke through the silence.

The torturer whipped around. "Who's there?"

Silence.

He stared into the darkness in the corner of the room. "My name is Black Star," the voice replied. "And you're Hank. Or, at least, that's what you go by these days. You see, one of your little playthings got loose and told your story. Now I don't really care what you do in your spare time, but the issue is that this plaything of yours was declared dead two weeks prior by *you*. This means that you've been taking contracts and not completing them, but still reaping the rewards."

"So? I like to have fun with my toys. What can I s-?"

"You're scum," Black Star interjected.

Hank chuckled. "Looks to me like you came on your own free will Black Star, which means that I can ruin your body with absolutely no consequences at all." His smile widened and he pounced forward towards the darkness.

"I'd tell you to get a different hobby," Black Star retorted, "but I doubt-"

"Shut up!" Hank screamed as he swung the iron hook in his hand through the darkness. Across the room, near the tortured man, cloaked and hooded Black Star stood staring. Confused, Hank turned around. "How did you...?" He leapt back towards Black Star and Black Star parried his hook effortlessly. Hank came back with another slash to the chest, but Black Star grabbed his wrist in the process and swept his leg, pulling Hank down in one swift motion. As his knees hit the ground, Black Star followed with a swift chop to the back of his neck in hopes that the strike would incapacitate him. But Hank fell to the ground, lifeless, and Black Star stared at him. Crouching down, Black Star checked Hank's pulse.

Nothing.

Black Star stood back up and took off his hood, running his hands through his hair in the process. In a moment of panic Black Star yelled. "OH, WHAT THE FUCK!? Not again!" The man hanging from the meat hook looked at him, startled. Black Star met his gaze. "That wasn't... supposed to... every time, man!" His hair was pushed back and curled from being run through by his fingers.

"I guess," the tortured man coughed up blood, "this has happened before?"

"It's a long story," Black Star replied. "Let's worry about getting you down." The hooked man coughed more harshly than before.

"No," he replied. "I've lost too much blood. No matter what you do I won't survive. This is a fitting end for me, I suppose," the coughing continued. "I was always a horrible person. I was greedy, murderous, and loveless. Maybe... through my death I can begin to pay for my sins."

Black Star stared at him.

"Let me die," the man said one final time.

Black Star continued to stare. "As you wish." Instantaneously the room was empty and the man hung in the dim light, alone.

It was night now, and the pizzaiolo began getting frustrated. *That young man is late. What could I expect from a delinquent?* His thoughts were cut short as he began yelling at the children roughhousing around the arcade machine. "Hey, you!" he shouted at a kid. "Get outta 'ere!"

"Kiss my butt, old man!" a tween boy shouted, the rest of the children cheering him on and laughing.

The old man grumbled to himself. *Damn kids,* he continued thinking. Black Star pushed through the door and the doorbell rang viciously. "Hey, Rick! You're late!" the old man shouted.

Black Star shrugged. "I know, I know. I visited my uncle and he kept me longer than I expected. Sorry about that, sir." He handed him thirty dollars. "Keep the change."

"Thank you, son. Just don't let it happen again, eh?" Black Star chuckled. "Yes, sir. I will make pizza a priority." He picked up his room temperature pizza and opened the box. "If you don't mind me asking, what's your name?" Black Star questioned the man while taking a bite.

"Antonio," the pizzaiolo replied.

"Nice to officially meet you, Antonio. You have a wonderful place here." Antonio grinned discreetly.

Black Star smiled and then looked at the analog clock on the wall. *There's a lot of rarities in this place it seems,* he thought. "Well, time for me to go. Nice meeting you Antonio!" Black Star began heading towards the door. Remembering something, he turned around and faced the counter. "Great pizza by the way."

"Come back again, ya hear!?" Antonio shouted.

As Black Star pushed through the door he ran into a posh man wearing a khaki suit, slapping him in the chest with the half-eaten slice of pizza in the process.

"What the fuck?" the suited man said, angered, as the pizza slice fell off his chest and onto the ground.

"My apologies sir," Black Star stated. He took a napkin and began picking off mushroom and tomato debris on the man's white dress-shirt. "I need to watch where I'm going," he continued. "I bet that suit costs more than my whole paycheck."

"Y-yeah," the man was caught off guard, not only from the pizza, but also from Black Star saying almost exactly what he was going to say. "I bet it does, kid. Just... yeah... watch where you're going next time. If I was a less kind man I'd have you pay for this suit."

"I'm really sorry, sir. Thank you for being so forgiving." The man took the napkins out of Black Star's hand and continued walking down the street, wiping vigorously to get the stain out of his shirt. After a few moments Black Star followed, handing his pizza off to a homeless man on the way.

Black Star nodded to the homeless man and passed the pizza off to him. "I don't like olives," he said as he continued walking.

"God bless you!" the homeless man responded with excitement.

Black Star disappeared into the darkness of an alleyway close by and moved towards the church in the center of town. Arriving, he scaled the side of the building to the steeple where he tracked the khaki-suited man as he walked a few blocks. Black Star pulled out his phone. *Excellent, the tracker is working.* Black Star had put a tracking device on the man when he smacked him with the slice of pizza. *I'll wait for him to stop moving and get comfortable in his new location before I make my next move.* Black Star returned to the alleyway from his perch, the darkness consuming him well. The night was still too young for him to turn in.

Black Star decided to travel through town since he was already in the center of it to see if anything caught his eye. Walking down the street he could hear obnoxious cheering before he rounded the corner. When he did he saw a bar, and the cheering was coming from the onlookers of an outdoor volleyball game in the back. The one sure-fire way to get Black Star interested in something was competition. He found it hard not to participate and so Black Star entered, excited for his shot to prove himself. He had finished his work and believed he deserved a break.

The business was mostly outside, so he was able to order without waiting. The man behind the bar was dressed in a black band t-shirt and blue jeans and was cleaning a glass when Black Star walked up. They made eye contact, but Black Star spoke up first. "A White Russian," he ordered. The bartender nodded and proceeded to make the drink. The drinking age in the New States had been lowered after the war due to overpopulation caused by displacement. Money was tight in towns and cities, so any form of income was needed.

The sooner you can destroy your liver and die, the sooner a new person can take your place, Black Star thought.

Black Star was not a fan of loud disruptive groups, but it was these out of character decisions that made him so hard to track. Why would a killer waste his time playing volleyball? Because he was human after all. The bartender placed his drink on the rough, but waxed, wood counter. Black Star handed him cash and picked it up. It was his favorite: a perfectly layered White Russian with cream, coffee liqueur, and vodka over ice. He thanked the bartender and walked outside. He waited patiently for the game to end, watching the regular people do their regular things. Onlookers talked over beer and shots and many others cheered for their friends on either team. Everything was so ordinary, but the best way to hide a wolf was amongst the sheep, and so Black Star finished his drink and entered the next game.

First rule of being in public, Black Star thought, *absolutely no display of power. This is a rule even in the Olympics and other major league sports. For a person to display power would classify as inhuman or supernatural and would be detrimental to society. People would no longer be viewed on the same level. A whole new social hierarchy would be created while the current one crumbled. For that reason you must keep all the sheep in the dark. Coincidentally, it seems, this is also how they prefer to live.*

Black Star entered the court on the team that had lost. The other team roared in victory, which was composed of a four-person party that had been undefeated as of recent, and they made sure to let everyone know by gloating and downing pitchers of golden beer. One player stayed on Black Star's team, but the other two left the court. Two new players joined his team which evened the game out to four versus four. It took another player on his team and apparently a very insistent friend to make that happen. Granted the female friend was a little intoxicated, but she proclaimed to be the "Captain" of the team which Black Star found rather entertaining. The game started with the winner serving, but before the ball was up in the air Black Star remembered a quote from his studies of Sun Tzu's *Art of War* under his grandfather: *"Every battle is won before it is ever fought." And,* Black Star thought, *I've already won.*

THREE

KAI

Kai awoke violently, beads of sweat dripping from his head and torso, soaking the already damp sheets. He gasped for air as he sat straight up, unable to discern dream from reality. Looking around his bedroom his gaze fixated on the large, curtainless window to his right. *It's still dark and raining*, he thought. *What time is it?* He moved his hand to the bedside table on his left, eyes still focusing on the rain, but found no phone when his hand touched the dark wood. He glanced to his left, but his torso caught his gaze first. *Why am I shirtless?* His inner dialogue continued. Memories began flooding back. The squad. The rooftop. Al. His mind began wandering deeper and deeper into the hell that existed within him. Kai threw the sheets off his legs and got out of bed, his bare feet landing softly on the cold hard wood floor of his apartment. He opened his bedroom door and walked into the living room where he found a sleeping Amina in casual clothing laying on his couch, the television on with nothing playing as Kai's gaming system had automatically turned off in the night. He walked around the couch and shook Amina's shoulder, her soft skin playing kindly against his callused blade-wielding hands.

"Amina," Kai said quietly.

No response.

"Amina, wake up," Kai shook her shoulder more aggressively.

"Hmm?" Amina moaned half-asleep.

"Go home," Kai responded.

Amina sat up on the couch and rubbed her eyes, her messy blueish-green hair stuck up in every which way.

"Oh, hey Kai. How did... how did you sleep?" the yawning Amina replied. "Ooh!" she gasped quietly as she placed her bare feet on the cold, wooden floor, her dark painted toenails gathering what little light came through the window. Kai sat down next to her. Amina's eyes were still closed.

"I never sleep well," he said. "And now... with Al..."

"I know," Amina said, opening her eyes and lifting Kai's face up to meet her gaze. "I know it hurts." Amina pulled Kai closer to her and wrapped her arms around him. His face was blank, his mind elsewhere. She was always comfortable around Kai, more comfortable than she was with anyone else, and she spent the night at Kai's apartment on many occasions, especially when work kept them out late as her place wasn't centrally located like his was and her heart was drawn to his like a moth to a flame.

Kai pulled out of the hug gently and stood up. "Go home, Amina," he said.

"Okay..." she responded quietly, upset, hoping that maybe for once he would hug her back or kiss her or pull her hair out and fuck her. Anything, any sort of affection that would make her feel *something*. She wanted him and she just wished that he felt the same. Kai walked around the couch and to the kitchen on the other side. He opened the old refrigerator, the internal light illuminating the dark, one-bedroom apartment, and pulled out a bottle of water. He watched Amina as she faced towards the TV, her back towards him. She pulled off her tank top and Kai could see the scars on her back from the accident in the Academy years prior. She picked up her bra on the floor and put it on, replacing her tank top afterwards. Kai opened the bottle of water and began drinking. She slid off her sweatpants and Kai found himself staring at her black thong as she put on her jeans, left leg first. She sat down on the couch to put on her socks and Kai turned back around and finished off the bottle of water. He turned on the sink, filled the bottle back up, and placed it back in the refrigerator on the same shelf he grabbed it from, dismissing whatever thoughts of desire had flickered in his mind.

"Why don't you upgrade this place, Kai?" Amina asked as she slipped on her mid-calf combat boots. "I know you have the money. You take the highest paying contracts offered for individuals." She zipped the boots up in the back.

"I prefer to live simply. You know that Amina," Kai responded.

"I know... I know..." Amina stood up and slipped on her t-shirt and her black weather-proof jacket. "You've always been strange." She looked at Kai and met his eyes, emotions dancing between them, and then quickly looked out the window before he could see her cheeks redden. "Well, I guess I'm heading out."

"Okay," Kai said quietly. "I'll see you later."

She walked slowly to the door and twisted the brass doorknob.

"Amina?" Kai asked, just loud enough for her to hear him.

"Yeah?" she responded.

"Thank you for bringing me home."

Amina smiled while still facing the door. She turned her head around, still grinning, eyes squinted, and responded, "you're welcome."

"And by the way... where's my phone?"

"It's charging right next to you, silly," Amina replied. She turned back around. "See you later," she said one last time as she opened the door and left, locking it behind her. Kai gave her a key because she was always there, so he figured she might as well have one. He picked up his phone, automatically unlocking it through his touch. The holo-glass screen lit up a bright blue, illuminating the dark apartment. Kai looked at his phone screen uninterested as a notification popped up in front of his eyes:

> NEW MSG: Kai, the High Council orders an immediate debrief on last night's occurrence. Arrive immediately.
>
> -Verena.

Verena was Kai's age and was the secretary of the High Council. She took care of all paperwork, appointments, and contacted every member of the High Council whenever the Council was due to convene. Because of Verena's handling of confidential information her job was for life. If she quit she was dead, but she knew the risks before taking the position.

Kai put his phone down on the counter and walked back into

his bedroom. The hardwood floor pressed coldly against the soles of his bare feet, but Kai felt nothing. He walked through his bedroom door and towards the window that took up most of the wall on the opposite side of his bed. He leaned on the windowsill and stared out towards The City, the bright signs and lights from the buildings and vehicles illuminating his face in an array of colors. *They say*, he thought, *that you can see The City clear as day from orbit. I wonder how true that is?* His mind wandered, flickering between thoughts of Amina, work, and eventually Alphonse. In an instant Kai was back on that rooftop, walking between the corpses, their entrails strewn across the concrete and a lake of blood spreading further and further out from the piles of cloth, metal, and flesh. His thoughts warped again and Alphonse's head began falling from his body as Kai's longsword cut through his neck like a knife through butter.

Kai raised his right fist and punched the wall next to him. *No*, he thought. *No.* He stood up straight and walked across the hall and into the bathroom. He turned on the shower, undressed, stepped in, and immediately stood under the water, letting it run down his face in a last-ditch effort to cleanse his mind and soul. A few minutes later Kai stepped out, dried off, and walked back into his bedroom, opening his closet door to the left of him. He put on a pair of black boxer-briefs, black socks, and slid on his black jeans. He sat down on the edge of his bed, put on a long sleeve shirt and his sneakers, and then stood back up and walked into the kitchen. He grabbed his phone and keys, slid them into his pockets, and walked towards the front door. He took his black, weather-proof coat off the rack, put it on, and walked out the front door, locking it behind him.

His apartment building was old, from the early 21st century, and because of it many of the things that were once beautiful, like the railing of the stairs, the walls, and the doors, were now worn down and rough. Kai didn't mind though. The place was cheap, close to work, and his neighbors didn't bother him. He lived on the second floor, so the only time he ever saw his neighbors was on the stairs, which, ninety percent of the time, was the most unfortunate part of his day.

Kai stepped outside and into the cold and the rain. It was

always cold and it was always rainy in The City, and it seemed to Kai that the cold and the rain were the only constants in his life. And death, death was always there too, of course. He took out a small capsule from his jacket pocket and opened it up, revealing two earbuds that he removed from the capsule and placed in his ears.

Kai took out his phone and began playing his late-night playlist that consisted of lo-fi hip-hop and jazz. The mixture of artificial beats and jazz instruments kept him calm and kept his thoughts away from the darkness inside of him. As he walked down the street towards City Center, pedestrians and cars passed him. Everyone had somewhere to go, something to do, and it always seemed they couldn't get there fast enough. The weather made traffic dangerous, but despite that people never slowed down. *The rain is light tonight,* Kai thought as he looked up towards the sky. He always hoped to see stars, or the moon, or something, yet all he ever saw was the blinding light of holographic women and men standing on top of buildings, advertising sex, food, and cosmetics, and the pink, purple, and blue neon lights that blotted out the night sky.

Kai hated materialism. He hated humanity's obsession with possessions, money, and sex because none of those things ever lasted. Items broke down, money couldn't be taken to the grave, and people cheated, lied, and used their partners day in and day out. Ever since he could remember he thought people were horrible and it was this thought and only this thought that kept him sane in his line of work. To him, he was a servant of Death, a reaper, a cleanser of impurity. He killed greedy businessmen, power-hungry politicians, murderers, rapists, and every other kind of swine that existed on the earth. He had killed more people than he could count and none of them bothered him, none... except for Alphonse. Because despite what the Sicarii ordered Kai didn't believe for a second that Alphonse deserved to die, but he was glad that the order fell on him.

He continued walking, passing his favorite café which was aptly named "The Coffee Shop"; the smell of roasted coffee beans penetrated the night air as he walked past the glass walls, but the rain drowned the smell after he crossed the street, which was always unfortunate. On the days that it didn't rain, or at least stopped raining, the wind would carry the smell of freshly brewed coffee and tea multiple blocks, sometimes all the way to his apartment. Kai had few joys in life, but coffee and tea had always been two of them.

In front of him, Kai could see the blinding lights of City Center, and above it all, piercing into the night sky was Isarcii Pharmaceuticals. The building stood above the rest, watching over the metropolis like a sentinel. As he proceeded towards City Center traffic got heavier; taxi drivers honked their horns at one another all while motorcycles swerved back and forth between them. The recent closure of the blocks around the Empyrion Building greatened traffic in other major areas in The City, like City Center, even at three o'clock in the morning. Fortunately for Kai, he wasn't going much farther. If he could see the lights of the building he knew he was close, so the traffic bothered him less than it normally would've. Moving between cars, Kai crossed the street in a steady stride that made him appear like a phantom. There was no beat in his step, no noise as he moved, except for the movement of water underneath his feet.

He walked up the dozens of steps to the entrance of Isarcii Pharmaceuticals and the doors slid open slowly. He strode across the marble floor and towards elevators that opened automatically, just like the door. He entered and once the doors closed behind him he placed his right hand flat on the far wall. A blue outline appeared around his hand and a panel slid open, revealing what looked like a camera. A faint blue light came out from the opening and moved up and down Kai's face, scanning it.

"Confirm identity," the elevator demanded.

"Kai. A-Rank Knight-Hybrid. Leader of Squad Four. Assassin under the order of the High Council of the Sicarii."

Clockwork.

"Identity confirmed," the robotic male voice stated.

The elevator began descending and continued on downwards for what felt like an eternity. For a moment, Kai was calm, collected, and otherwise emotionless. But, whenever he felt the silence of the elevator, the staleness of the air, and realized that he was finally alone, he fell forward against the wall in front of him, propped up only by his right forearm, and began hyperventilating. He gasped for a release he couldn't find and began crying as his panic attack set in. His tears fell heavily on the floor as he stared blindly at it, and his gasps for air reverberated off the metal elevator walls attempting to suffocate him. His chest burned and a pit formed in his stomach as he realized what he'd done and how he'd torn a hole in his own soul. Kai stood up and punched the elevator door as hard as he could, denting it in the process.

"FUCK!" he screamed at the top of his lungs, not caring for once in his miserable existence if anyone heard him or not. He wiped the tears from his eyes with his sleeve of his jacket and leaned back against the wall, preparing for the damaged door to open. The music never stopped bumping in his ears, but he had just now heard it again as the doors opened and he traded places with a brunette-haired woman, about eighteen years old like himself, who, unbeknownst to Kai, smiled at him softly. The elevator door closed behind him and he stared at the massive, empty stone plaza before him. On his right was a railway with what looked like rounded, separated pods composed almost entirely of glass which could sit up to ten people. He walked over to the first pod in line and the door opened upwards at his approach. He stepped inside, jazz music still beating in his ears, and sat down in one of the seats. As demanded by the blue, holographic sign on the glass at the front, back, and sides of the pod, Kai buckled himself into the seat, and afterwards stared into the dark tunnel before him.

The pod started to move forward and began picking up speed. Rows of lights shone through the mostly glass walls to the left and right of him, illuminating the outside. After a few moments, the tunnel he was in expanded into an open area where the lights of other rail systems flew past him. In front of Kai was Sicarii Headquarters, a bustling mini-metropolis miles underground in a massive cave system, and at the center of HQ stood the massive Spire: a deep black twisted tower that connected to the top of the cave.

All pods entered HQ through the Spire, and as well as being a hub for transportation the Spire was also the center of contract control, record keeping, and monetary disbursement. And at the top, above it all, sat the High Council in their chambers at the connector point between the Spire and the huge stalactite that hung from the roof, surrounded on the exterior by Seraph Squad who stood on a clear platform, watching Headquarters and all its inhabitants in their massive, reflective, armored suits. After a minute or so the pod began slowing down gradually until it came to a halt inside the Spire's Great Hall. Kai unbuckled himself and stood up. The pod door opened again at his presence and he walked out into another massive plaza where five other pod rails, three in front of him and two to his right, sat empty. The pod doors closed behind him and it shot backwards from where it came, disappearing into the void.

Kai turned to his right and began walking towards the white, marble steps that led above. From the arched, white ceiling hung a large, golden, analog clock that read significant times from around the world, which was a rarity as most clocks had been digital since the early 21st century. The Great Hall was dead, as it usually was around this time since most of those doing business within the Spire's walls were asleep, but nevertheless as Kai reached the top a woman behind a wooden desk greeted him.

"Kai, long time no see." Her eyes caught his bruised knuckles from where he had hit the elevator door and matched it with the melancholic expression he wore on his face. "How have you been?" she asked, worried.

Kai took his earbuds out. "Better," he replied.

"Well..." she sighed, "what brings you in?"

Kai pointed upwards with his forefinger but kept the same sullen look on his face.

"Ahhh... I see," the receptionist replied. "I'm sorry to hear that."

"You know how it is, Summer. It's what we do."

"I know. Well... enjoy," Summer said sarcastically.

"Yeah," Kai forced a chuckle. "Will do."

He continued walking forward. Sicarii HQ was massive and expanded miles in almost every direction, but Kai knew it like the back of his hand. He did spend fourteen years here, after all. He took another elevator, this time up to the top of the Spire where the Council chambers were located. Stepping out of the elevator he was met with another familiar face, Verena. She looked over the desk and her red glasses, her dark, tied hair matching her dark complexion, and stared in annoyance at him.

"Took you long enough," she stated, frustrated. "The High Council doesn't like to be kept waiting."

"Yeah, yeah," Kai retorted. "Missed you too, V."

Verena's face reddened, filling with shyness and anger all in one go. She calmed herself and pushed her glasses against her face.

"Kai," she said quietly. "I'm sorry for having to deliver those orders to you. It was heartbreaking. Al was a friend... he was like family."

Kai said nothing and pushed through the doors into the next room and walked to the center. The room was huge, near a hundred feet in diameter. Within the well-lit room stood six, large, throne-like chairs elevated in front of him, with stairs leading up to them, and a crescent-shaped wooden table in front. In those chairs sat five individuals, some dressed in suits, some in everyday clothes, but all wore the stains of blood on their hands. At a forty-five-degree angle to Kai stood a cloaked figure about fifty feet away, with its left foot against the wall and its arms crossed. Their head was staring straight down as if they were sleeping. In the center of the room was a strange indention in the floor in the shape of a small sphere, but Kai deduced it was aesthetic as it didn't seem to be technological, and he had never seen it used or addressed before.

"Kai, nice to see you again," a tall, middle-aged, posh man stated after taking a puff from his pipe.

Alef, Kai thought.

Alef's tamed graying hair was pushed back, gelled and combed to stay should any physical activity arise. His beard was neatly kept and his mustache curved upwards at the ends like the way one would think of a stage magician.

"I wish I could say the same," Kai responded coldly.

"Dalet couldn't be with us today as he had important business to discuss overseas. However, I and the rest of the High Council are present. So, why don't you begin with your arrival at the Empyrion

Building."

Kai went over everything that transpired, from the orders he gave to his squad to the death of Alphonse. The member of the Council he was talking to originally, Alef, led the debriefing and asked questions along the way. Kai finished his story and the room fell silent. Alef sat with his elbows on the table and his hands clasped together in front of his mouth, his unlit pipe sitting carefully in front of him.

"Did Alphonse say anything before or during your altercation with him? Anything strange?"

"Yes," Kai replied. "He kept talking about how everything I knew was a lie, how my whole life was a lie. He kept saying those words over and over again, like a broken record."

"Interesting," Alef replied. "What do you think of this?"

"I don't know," Kai said. "I didn't really have time to think about it."

"No thoughts at all?" Alef asked again.

"Alphonse was my brother," Kai finally said after a long pause. "We grew up together, went through the Academy together. We did everything together. What happened to him?" Kai inquired.

"That's something we can't discuss with you, Kai. We're sorry," an older woman on the Council interrupted.

Kai began getting frustrated. "What do you mean you can't discuss it with me, Vav? He was my closest friend. His final will states that at the time of his death all of his belongings go to me."

"That won't be happening," another Council member said. He was younger, but just as well dressed as Alef.

"Bet is right, Kai," Alef stated. "In the event that an assassin goes rogue, all his or her personal belongings are immediately, and without question, handed over to the leading investigators of the High Council. You know this. Damnatio memoriae is initiated without hesitation, despite the Sicarii member."

"That's fucking bullshit!" Kai yelled, stepping forward aggressively in the same motion. "I killed my friend, on your orders, and I can't even know what was wrong with him? I can't even know why? He slaughtered dozens of SWAT members and while he was bloodshot in the eyes he screamed at me and told me that my whole life was a lie and I can't even fucking know why?" Kai stepped forward again. In an instant the cloaked figure that was leaning against the wall was in front of him, it's hood thrown back from the speed at which it traveled, revealing a bronze woman with long, dark brown, braided hair. Her blade was already at his throat.

"Move an inch and you're dead," the woman whispered in his ear.

"That's enough, Sofia," Alef stated. "Let him go."

Sofia dropped her blade and stepped back, as did Kai.

"Your debriefing is over, Kai," Vav said. "You may leave."

Kai lowered his head and turned around, pulled the door open, and walked out. Without saying a word to Verena he took the elevator back down to the main floor and left headquarters the same way he came in. He turned his music back on and walked back home, passing the same coffee shop he passed on his way there, smelling the same coffee, but not truly smelling it at the same time. When he opened the door to his apartment he put his coat up, took off his boots and after grabbing a drink of water headed directly into his bedroom and laid in bed. He took off his shirt and threw it on the floor, an action unusual for him. He laid in bed staring at the ceiling, recalling memories of his childhood with Alphonse. His mind flickered back and forth between the face of the boy he befriended so long ago and the face of the man he killed, eyes bloodshot, clothes blood-soaked, blade slick and damaged. *Lie. Lie. Lie.* Alphonse said over and over again. *Everything is a lie.*

"I'm sorry, Al. I'm so sorry," Kai whispered softly. Tears began strolling from his face as he covered his eyes with his forearm, until eventually he lost consciousness and everything faded back to darkness.

FOUR

THE PHANTOM

9:52 PM

South Montana

Contract: Shores

A four-door luxury sedan sped down the highway away from the rural city of Helena, Montana in the dead of night. The brisk night air flowed into the car and danced across the face of the khaki-suited man driving. The clouds whipped past as the man exceeded 170 kilometers per hour and after taking the highway out of the city and into the outer neighborhoods he pulled off onto a quiet, dark street where abandoned homes, donned with colorful graffiti, lived in aesthetically pleasing agony. After a few minutes of driving through the ghetto he pulled off into an alleyway behind an old warehouse and parked his vehicle. A man with bronze skin and blonde, razor-streaked hair greeted him as he arrived. His all-black suit matched well with his black loafers and was in stark contrast to the light, pizza-stained suit the driver wore.

"They're waiting for you inside, Mr. Shores," the underling said as he opened the door for the khaki-suited man. Mr. Shores nodded at him and walked through the door and into an entryway that wrapped around the storage area of the warehouse. He proceeded through another steel door in front of him, guarded by another black-suited man, differing from the first only by the paleness of his skin and the length of his black hair, and walked into the main part of the warehouse where he was greeted by a stout Russian man with a thick accent.

"Mr. Shores!" the Russian mobster said as he stood up from his chair at the round table in the center of the warehouse floor, excitement boiling in his demeanor. He wore a white dress shirt unbuttoned a quarter of the way down to show the golden chains hanging from his neck and the mound of hair protruding from his chest. Covering his white dress shirt was a navy suit jacket that matched well with his navy slacks and his black, Italian leather boots. He walked briskly over to Mr. Shores, arms spread wide, and wrapped him in a strong, brotherly embrace. Both men laughed as they let go of each other.

"Konstantin, my friend, how have you been?" Mr. Shores asked.

"Better than you, I see," said Konstantin pointing and laughing at Mr. Shores' pizza-stained shirt.

"Some fuckin' kid barreled right into me on the street, Konstantin. Can you believe that?" Mr. Shores's Italian accent came out in full force as the anger boiled inside of him. "Slapped a hot slice of pie right on my new shirt!" Konstantin placed a firm hand on his friend's left shoulder.

"Ah do not worry, my brother! We will get you a nicer shirt whenever we finish here, eh?" Both men laughed again and began walking back towards the table. To the right of the table was another area of the warehouse, stockpiled with weapons, ammunition, and explosives. Close to the weapons were five cages where trained hounds were held to alert the mobsters of any possible threats arriving.

"Nice of you to finally show up," another Russian mobster said to Mr. Shores as he and Konstantin sat down at the table.

"It'd be nice of you to go fuck ya' self, Sergei," Mr. Shores replied menacingly. Sensing the hostility in the room, Konstantin cut in.

"Comrades, comrades, let's be civil, eh?" his thick accent and boisterous voice cut through the air with ease. "It is time for business, not time to compare our dicks!" He laughed again, this time louder than before. Mr. Shores and Sergei stared at each other, no humor between them. While the men discussed business inside, outside a predator slithered through the dark towards the warehouse.

The bodyguard with the razor-streaked hair stood watching the dark in front of him, submachine gun in hand. He looked left and right down the massive alleyway but saw nothing but darkness past a few dozen feet. It was eerily quiet as well, too quiet, as not even a vehicle could be heard in the distance until a rustling came from his left around the side of the building. Immediately the bodyguard's head whipped in the direction of the noise and he moved towards it to investigate but found nothing. He came back to his position at the door and looked down the alleyway to the left where he saw nothing but darkness yet again. He turned to his right and looked down the alley the other way and saw darkness and two red lights staring back at him. He rubbed his eyes, but when he looked again they were gone. Another noise came from above him and when he looked up there was nothing but the light above the backdoor and the stars in the sky.

"I must be losing my shit, man," he chuckled to himself. "I need some more sleep." He looked back in front of him and towards two red lights staring back from the darkness near Mr. Shores' sedan. He blinked and rubbed his eyes again, but this time the lights didn't disappear.

"Hey!" he shouted, lifting his firearm. "Who's there!? Come out or I'll fuckin' kill you!" The lights inched closer, bringing the darkness with them. The light above the blonde-haired bodyguard began to flicker and sweat began to form on his brow.

"Who are you!?" he yelled.

Silence.

"I said, who are you muthafucka!?" he yelled again, this time his voice was shakier than the last. Before he could blink the red lights were right in front of him and so was a dark figure, only an inch away from his face. The bodyguard tried screaming, but before he could he was struck in his diaphragm with such force that his lower ribs cracked and his breath escaped him. He began vomiting violently and fell dead, face first, into the pool of his own bile. The assailant rolled the body out of the way of the door and proceeded through.

From the perspective of the guard at the inner door it seemed that a powerful wind swung the door in front of him open violently. He moved forward to investigate, shaking while lurching forward, until a slight whisper from above caught his attention. He looked up into the darkness of the ceiling and whenever he did, the darkness looked back. Before the man could scream his throat was slit, and red ichor seeped out as he lay collapsed on the ground. The murderer dropped down from his shadowy place in the rafters and landed on the ground next to his victim.

Inside the warehouse, gangsters were filling crates with guns and ammunition and loading their own firearms just in case something went wrong. "We gotta get these guns shipped out!" yelled Sergei. "The pakhan's courier should be here any minute!"

Back on the other side of the door the darkness knocked. Once. Twice. Thrice. The knocks rang out louder and louder, stopping all in their tracks.

"We're doing business in here!" Sergei shouted angrily. "Poshel proch'!" Another knock - deeper, louder, more violent - echoed throughout the warehouse. The gangsters' hearts began to flutter and beads of sweat began to form on their brows.

Bravery struck Sandy Shores ever so slightly and he called out like his business partner before him. "Who is it?"

No answer.

Sandy looked at Konstantin and Konstantin looked back at him nervously. "Maybe it's the pakhan's courier?" Konstantin asked, knowing the answer.

Silence fell over the warehouse like a fog of terror, penetrating the toughest of men as they began to sweat more profusely. Konstantin looked at one of the men who just finished loading his submachine gun. "You!" he whispered. The man looked back in terror. "Go check it out."

"But boss-" the man began to say before being interrupted by Konstantin.

"Don't be a fucking pussy!" Konstantin whispered angrily. "You're Bratva, yes? So stop being a little suka and go fucking check, or I'll have your balls." The lackey pushed forward towards the door ever so slowly and three more loud, slow knocks filled the warehouse. He looked back at Konstantin and Konstantin urged him on further.

"Hey!" Sergei whispered loudly. The Bratva grunt looked back at him. "If it's anyone besides the courier put a bullet between his fuckin' eyes, eh?" The scared gangster nodded and pushed on until he reached the door. Carefully he opened it, stepped through with one foot, then another, and the darkness ripped him through and the door slammed shut behind him. It took everything in all the gangsters' power to not shit themselves where they stood as they watched their coworker get pulled into the dark. Three more knocks followed suit, just like before and just like before bravery struck Sandy Shores and he slammed his fists on the table, grabbed his handgun from inside his suit jacket, and cocked it.

"This guy is really pissing me off." He looked around the room at the small army in the warehouse and spoke up to all of them. "Now listen here fellas, I'm going to open that door and if you help me kill this fucker I'll double all of your cuts from today. Now it ain't gonna be pretty, but let's kill this fuckin' clown." With just a short speech and the promise of more money, he rallied all the grunts near him and moved towards the door.

Sandy Shores stood to the right of the door and was grasping his gun with both hands near his chest. Two of the grunts opened the door and pushed through. Sandy followed and looked left and then right for any sign of the grunt who was taken by the dark, but there was nothing to be seen. In fact, in the well-lit hallway there was no sign of anyone - no person, no rival gang members, nothing. There wasn't a trace of any blood or any signs of fighting. The hallway was empty as far as he could see, but he felt something, something he had never felt before. The air was thick, like the most humid of days, and anxiety struck him for the first time since this all began. He had been in his fair share of shootouts - rival gangs, police, you name it - but this felt different. Sandy got used to the fact that everyone in a room might be trying to kill him, but this was unlike anything he had experienced before. His gut churned, the hairs on the back of his neck stood up, and a fear he had never felt washed over his entire body.

"I don't see nothing boss," the man on Sandy's left said. "What about y-," a loud clank sounded behind them which spooked the grunt that was just speaking. Sandy turned back to look quickly, his gun raised, and saw only a metal air vent that had fallen from the wall. With a sigh of relief from all three of the gangsters and a thumbs up from Sandy to those inside, he turned back around to continue his search in the hallway and was met with darkness and two solid red eyes the color of blood. Before he could even think about lifting his gun the figure slammed against both of Sandy's ears with whirlwind force, causing his eardrums to explode and his spinal cord to snap, killing Sandy instantly. It slit the throats of the two men next to Sandy without ever revealing a blade, and flitted into the warehouse, past Sandy Shores who was still standing, paralyzed, dead, near the doorway.

The twenty or something men on the other side of the door saw nothing enter the warehouse until the figure, and the darkness it brought with it, was right in front of them. The lights in the warehouse seemed to fade and the dogs in the other room barked viciously, vying to be let out. One of the men to the darkness's right stumbled back and pissed in his jeans.

Is this the grim reaper? he thought, moments before his head came off his body. A second mobster to the figure's left gathered up courage and sprayed bullets ferociously, but to no avail as a deep crimson the color of the darkness's eyes swept up from the ground and stopped the bullets a foot away from what would be the figure's face. It was a courageous, but desperate attempt that left the man without his life as his skull cracked under the weight of a strike that would've crushed solid concrete. The rest of the grunts began to fire, but the same red aura that stopped the bullets from the last mobster stopped the rest of the bullets from the others. The figure moved around the room slaughtering each and every single man who fired upon him, until only two were left: Sergei and Konstantin.

How did he stop those bullets? A human can't do that. Sergei thought. *Superpowers don't exist. Maybe it's supernatural? No, no. There has to be a better explanation. This is only a man.*

The darkness moved quickly in front of Konstantin and he stepped back and dropped his handgun, surrendering on the spot. Sergei, on the other hand, tried to fight back. The red aura that was with the figure struck Sergei like a viper strikes its prey and dragged him closer to the darkness, where the aura formed into a great hand and lifted Sergei to eye level with the figure.

"I'm sorry Sergei, I'm out of here," Konstantin said before running away towards the stairs in the back right corner of the warehouse. The figure refused to give chase and instead let Konstantin go, showing that it had already captured his target. Sergei watched Konstantin flee and then gazed deeply into the crimson eyes of his captor and realized the truth.

This is the face of a demon.

The figure wasted no more time as it had confirmed who Sergei was and it slung Sergei aside, into the concrete wall to the figure's left, killing him on impact.

■■■■■■■■■■■■ ■ ▪ ▪ ▪ ▪

That same night in Rushville, Nebraska a parade filled the city streets with hope and cheer. The wind whipped the clouds east across the city and the New States flag in front of the Rushville hotel flapped in the same direction. The moon was shy that night, reluctant to show its face, but perhaps that was just from the artificial lights that lit up the streets and the floats that moved their way peacefully down them. The floats had been delicately crafted by local artists, the personality of which amazed the children that stood by with bright faces as the floats rolled past. Atop the rolling art displays women and men in costume threw candy down towards the crowd in an attempt to bring the community together for the occasion. The bright-faced children grasped desperately in the air, anxious for the next piece of candy that would satiate their sweet tooths.

In the distance, away from the crowded city streets, the ornate floats, and the lights, the cloaked figure stood hidden on the roof of an insignificant building. Rushville was an old city and just seventy years prior was nothing more than a quaint farming town with a few shops, an inn, and nothing much else. Now, since the war and the revitalization of the States through the success of Alexander, the European Defense Initiative, and the United Nations, small towns like Rushville, the ones that survived the war at least, thrived into small cities with more and more people escaping each day to the comfort of nature and the aesthetic of the humble farming sanctuary.

The creature made its way from the high-rise, through the shadows of the common man, and to a small house in the residential district a few blocks away. A small sign that read "Verner Financial Aid" protruded from the grass on the brown lawn in front of the worn, white house, and passing it the shadow made its way quietly up the otherwise creaky stairs that led up to the porch. It opened the door to the house and shut it quietly, careful not to alert the man talking on the phone in the other room. The front living room of the home was trashed: mostly empty pizza boxes, chip bags, energy drink cans, and crumpled paper littered the matted, carpet floor.

It was obvious, even to this bloodthirsty killer, that it had been a long time since anyone cleaned the house, as it resembled the shelter of a squatter more so than that of a stay-at-home businessman. The figure passed through the living room silently. The carpet harbored the crumbs from meals past, yet not even a corn chip crunched as it crossed. It sidled up against the arched doorway that led into the next room to its right. The figure listened to the conversation and proceeded forward, moving like the darkness to swallow its prey. The man in the room was in a swivel chair with his back turned away from the desk that faced the doorway, unknowing of the presence behind him.

"Yes sir, I have the most competitive prices in the business. Come on by and we'll get a plan set up for you," the obese financial advisor said as he shoveled chips into his mouth. "We'll find a way to get you the money you need to get back on your feet." He turned back around to face his desk and was met with the red glaring eyes of the cloaked figure, barely illuminated by the light of the computer screen.

"Sir, I'll have to call you back. Another client of mine just came in." He hung up the phone and as he did a remnant of his crunchy snack fell from his ratty beard and onto the desk. His balding hair was pulled back in a ponytail out of sheer laziness, as it looked like it had not been washed for as long as his home had not been cleaned.

"Hey, hey," the dirty, fat man said. "Back from the contract so early. I noticed that you and another guy by the name of Black Star signed up for the same contract. I was wondering which one of you would complete it first," he paused to take a shaky drink from his can of Grande Energy Drink.

"I personally had money on Black Star, but a lot of people said you'd get it for sure... anyway, congrats you haven't failed a contract yet. Keep it up and you'll rise through the ranks in no time!" Excitement began boiling within the supposed financial advisor. "See, this was your last D-rank contract as a freelancer. Now, you've gained enough reputation within the system to start taking on C-rank contracts, complete with higher pay and more difficult challenges." The man took a pause to breathe as just speaking began exhausting him. The shadow's eyes were dim, unlike earlier that night, and a quaint, softer aura penetrated the room. There was no bloodlust in it any longer, it seemed, for one reason or another.

"Y'know," the man started, breaking the silence, "there are two things that never change: you never change your mask and you never say anything." The figure remained silent, staring. "Well, I'll not waste any more time. Here is a contract just as covert as you, *Mr. Ominous.*"

This guy's a real wacko, Cornelius, the sweaty recluse thought to himself.

"The target is Trae Zigler. I'll print out an info card for you, give me just a second." Cornelius looked down to the archaic printer, grabbed the card, and when he looked up was met with a vacant room. He sighed. "Man, what a dick," he said as he tossed the card onto his desk with the rest of the junk.

Moments later, the figure moved back to its perch above the small city, looking down on the crowd of cheering civilians during the parade. The wind gusted at high altitude and shifted the clouds above, allowing moonlight to illuminate the rooftops for the first time all night. The phantom was on the move, tracked by the soft light of the moon, and watched the people below go about their lives, oblivious to the other half of the world they lived in. They laughed and cheered, enjoying their pointless festivities, and did their best to forget the corruption of the world for one night. The specter of unknown origin had no use for Rushville anymore and shrunk away into the darkness of the world, its purpose unknown and its goals yet to be fulfilled.

FIVE

KAI

"I have to say I'm rather surprised that you've come here on your own accord."

"I would like to request to see Alphonse's body in the morgue," Kai responded to Alef formally. Kai was knelt on the ground with his left leg propped up and his right knee placed firmly on the floor. Alef put his elbows on the table and brought his clasped hands up to his face in deep thought and his pipe sat smoldering in front of him.

"You're not seriously considering this are you?" Bet whispered. Alef turned to his left and met the young man's gaze.

"Know your place, boy. This is my decision and mine alone. Kai is my responsibility."

"He is our responsibility," Bet said defiantly. "No member of the Council has more control than any other, not even you rabbi."

"You did not find him," Alef retorted in a whisper, "I did... so he is mine." With that Bet returned his gaze forward and closed his mouth.

"I will allow this, Kai," Alef stated after little outward contemplation. "But you are not to remove the body or any evidence from the morgue. Understood?

"Understood," Kai replied. "Thank you for this." Kai began to stand up.

"You're very welcome, Kai, but as you know my decision does not come freely," Alef said quietly.

It never does, Kai thought.

"The Council has another mission for you and Squad Four."

Alef leaned back in his chair and crossed one leg over the other. He settled his clasped hands in his lap. "The target is Adrian Blom, head of Sweden's intelligence agency. Since Alexander Stromberg's death the Swedish government has been doing everything in its power to obtain and control Alexander's research for the benefit of the European Defense Initiative. With the Great War came the death of the United States as the world knew it and the tyranny of the POTUS. As you know, the EDI was the insurer of this death and was formed to invade, destroy, and rebuild the States in order to prevent further mass destruction on their part, which, as you know yet again as a child of the post-war, eventually worked after two decades of death. However, as the Sicarii headquarters is in the heart of the New States and we as an organization could benefit from that research, we must make sure that the Swedish government and the EDI cannot control it. Blom's death must come swiftly, but violently as well. Do you have any questions?"

"Yes," Kai replied, "just one. Why does the Sicarii need to make sure that Sweden and the EDI can't control Alexander's research?" Kai stood with his hands behind his back, attention towards the authority in front of him. "We're an international organization after all. We have eyes and ears in all world governments, especially after the war, so how would we benefit from making sure this information isn't controlled?"

Vav leaned forward in her chair and placed her hands on the table. Her gray hair was pulled into a bun on the top of her head and her glasses slid down the bridge of her nose as she stared down Kai, making sure he understood that the question he was asking was a stupid one. "The Sicarii may be international, Kai, but we are based out of the New States. We must ensure the successful future of the New States and Isarcii Pharmaceuticals. Should either fall we would have to rebuild and relocate again, wasting money, time, and other resources that we do not have."

"Understood," Kai responded. "You can count on my leadership and Squad Four's abilities to see this through."

"Thank you, Kai," Alef stated briefly, emotionless. "Dismissed." As Kai walked out, the leader of Squad Three, Gilroy, walked past him. By making eye contact, the two exchanged more words than if they would have opened their mouths and actually spoke. Mutual recognition of the skill and the prowess of the other was expressed through a single head nod from the both of them. A faint memory flashed in Kai's mind but faded before he could recognize it.

Passing Verena, Kai took the elevator down and exited the Tower District of Sicarii Headquarters. Headquarters was practically a city in its own right, spanning miles of the cavern it existed within. In the center of HQ was the Spire, and around the Spire was the Academy, the Greater and Lesser Libraries, referred to collectively as the Sifriyah, the Castrum, and the Reactor, which powered Headquarters. Everything else was living quarters and places to purchase food, just like a regular city. Those who worked for the Sicarii that weren't members of the Squads lived here day in and day out. They rarely saw anything but the interior of the cave and the lights of HQ, but that was their choice. The High Council didn't stop them from going to the surface, the workers just chose not to out of practicality. Uniforms were provided to them by the Sicarii, but any other clothes they chose to wear had to be purchased on the surface.

Arriving at the front of the Lesser Library, Kai walked through the door and continued down the hallway to his left. As he walked, columns to the right of him separated the walkway from the shelving area of the library. At the end of the open hall was a massive wooden and glass door, locked by a biometric scanner. Kai stood in front of the door and placed his hand on the pad on the wall.

"Identify," an artificial voice demanded.

"Kai. A-Rank Knight-Hybrid. Leader of SquadFour. Assassin under the order of the High Council of the Sicarii." *Clockwork*. The sound of the door unlocking sent Kai into himself. Deactivated locks quickly turned into the memories of swords clashing as Kai became lost in his own mind. Mutilated bodies penetrated through the fog with Alphonse's bloodshot eyes, and with a quick parry and reversal Al's head was rolling across the rooftop once more. As it rolled it created a blood trail behind it which mixed with the ocean of gore already at Kai's feet, bringing Kai's suppressed emotions to the surface. *Lies*, the head whispered, staring at him. *It's all lies.*

A young, distracted woman carrying a mound of books barreled towards Kai, mumbling to herself. Lost, Kai stood unwavering, staring forward as the young woman ran into him, flinging her books everywhere in the process. Instantly, both of them were knocked out of their own trances and began staring blankly at one another, confused about what just occurred. The young woman looked down at the floor and back up to Kai, piecing together how books that were just in her hand teleported onto the hardwood below her.

"Oh!" the young woman said as she realized what had happened. "I am so so sorry! I was in my own head and I was so focused on something else and-"

Kai cut the young woman off. "It's okay. Don't worry about it." He bent down at the same time as her and helped her pick up her books.

"Thank you!" she said, excitedly. She collected her thoughts and the rest of her books. Fumbling to hold the ancient texts in one hand, she stuck her right hand out for a handshake. "I'm Haley by the way."

Kai shook her hand. "My name is-"

"Kai," Haley said. He looked at her, confused, and her cheeks began to redden out of embarrassment.

"I work here in the library and I always hear you with your voice recognition," Haley said to explain herself. She pushed her brunette hair back behind her ear as it fell in front of her face.

"Do you work in the Greater Library?" Kai asked, interested.

"I sure do," Haley replied, her cheeks lightening up.

"That's quite the prestigious job, Haley," Kai complimented. "You must've done really well on your final exams in the Academy."

"Not as well as I'd like," she replied. "But, well enough I guess to get a job here. I would really rather be like my sister: strong, fast, capable, but I'm just better with books I guess." Haley sighed. "C'est la vie."

"C'est la vie?"

Haley smiled. "Such is life," she said, chuckling. "Well, I guess I better get back to work before I get my head bit off. It was nice meeting you, Kai," Haley whispered as she pushed through the door in front of them and walked away.

Kai watched her as she disappeared into the Greater Library shelves and continued on his way towards the classified records vault. Arriving, he placed his hand on another scanner, unlocking the steel door in the process. In the center of the room was the Well of Light, fronted by a steel podium, and as Kai arrived at the podium the Well of Light projected a bright-blue screen into the air in front of him. From the ceiling light poured into the well like water, and the magnificent glow of blue and white light danced on the wall as shadows.

"Show me Adrian Blom, head of Swedish intelligence," Kai demanded. Immediately across the holographic screen flashed countless news articles, records, and other various forms of information on Blom from the time of his birth until now. His achievements and failures displayed in bright blue across the face of the man that would end his life. Family, friends, mistresses and bastards, Kai memorized it all to find weaknesses in Blom's life.

"Give me the city layout of Stockholm and show me the blueprints of the probable locations Blom will deliver his next speech," Kai demanded again.

"Generating... generating..." the Well continued to say for a few moments until the layout of Stockholm, Sweden was presented before him and the probable locations of Blom's speech were marked on it. Calculations were made by the Well to show which locations were more probable than others, but Kai had already made those calculations himself.

After memorizing the information Kai left and went to the morgue inside the Academy on the opposite side of the Spire from the Sifriyah. At the entrance was another receptionist, an androgynous man who Kai did not know and who Kai ignored. Kai walked down the steps in front of him and through the second door on his right. All the bodies in the room were frozen and all had name plates in front of their doors. Kai found disposable gloves to his left and put them on. He found Alphonse's body and pulled it from the freezer that it was resting in. His head had been stitched back on his blueish body and his light shaggy hair was matted from the blood it rolled around in on the rooftop.

"Kai, nice to see you again," an older, Korean man said as he walked through the doors of the morgue and over towards the gloves.

"You too Henry," Kai replied without breaking his focus from Al's body. "Anything you can tell me about the body?"

"Nothing really out of the ordinary," Henry said as he put on the disposable gloves and walked over towards the table. "Wound was clean, organs intact. One of yours?" Dr. Henry Mun asked.

"Yeah," Kai responded, "you could say that." He continued to look over Al's body. "What about his brain? Anything there?"

Dr. Mun picked up Al's records. "No, doesn't look like it. He was perfectly healthy. Ate well, slept well, didn't smoke, didn't drink, only got one tattoo his whole life. He was as healthy as healthy gets."

Kai nodded in agreement.

"Wait..." Kai stopped and looked at Henry. "What did you say?"

"Healthy as healthy gets?"

"No before that," Kai retorted, irritated.

"Only got one tattoo his whole life?"

"Yes, that. Tattoo?"

"Yeah," Henry picked up Alphonse's chart. "One black tattoo of some sort of symbol. Why did that catch your attention of all things?" Henry asked curiously.

"Because Alphonse didn't have any tattoos last time I saw him," Kai said. "Where is it? Show me." Henry rolled Alphonse over onto his stomach and lifted up the hair covering his neck.

"Here," Henry said. Kai inspected the mark on Al's neck and checked his memories for a reference to the mysterious symbol.

Unfamiliar.

"I don't know this symbol," Kai said. "Do you?"

"No," Henry answered. "I've never seen it before. Sicarii bodies come in here day in and day out and a lot of them have a lot of strange symbols, but I've never seen this one before. I just figured it was another kid getting another weird tattoo."

Kai took his phone out and took a picture of the mark. "Definitely strange," Kai said, mostly to himself.

This doesn't really look like a tattoo, does it?

No. Not a tattoo. Something else.

"Thanks Henry. I appreciate your help."

"You're very welcome. Take care of yourself Kai, I know he was close to you."

Kai did his best to ignore Henry's final comment and left.

■■■■■■■■■■■ ■ ■ ■ ▪ ▪ |

"Do you think he knows?"

"He's not an idiot, but no, I don't think so."

"How do you know?"

"Because we'd all be dead."

"But we have Nico and the Seraphim."

"It doesn't matter."

"What will we do if your plan fails?"

"It won't."

"You're weighing the survival of an organization that's existed for thousands of years on the shoulders of a boy. Your arrogance will be the death of you, Alef."

"The decision is one we all made. What you ignorantly call arrogance is simply my trust in the plan. Your fears and frailty cloud your reasoning, Vav. Ascension is upon us and he is the conduit for that ascension."

"Could he really destroy us?"

"He could destroy us all."

■■■■■■■■■■■ ■ ■ ▪ ▪ ▪ |

As Kai entered his apartment building and walked up the stairs the noises from each apartment funneled into the stairwell. To his right, a couple fucking three doors down. Above him, a mother screaming at her child for drawing on the walls. Two floors up, a man playing a video game online with some of his friends.

So much noise, Kai thought. He walked up to his door and

unlocked it, revealing, as he pushed it open, Amina standing behind his couch watching television. She was naked and wet with a towel wrapped around her midsection that covered her breasts and butt. Her wet, blue hair hung down on her shoulders as she brushed it slowly, completely focused on the news in front of her. Kai closed the door behind him and she turned.

"Oh, hey," Amina said, turning back to the TV right after.

"Hey." Kai hung up his coat and walked over towards her. "What's going on?" He looked at the TV.

"Someone slaughtered multiple men in an abandoned warehouse last night. It's all over the news. They're saying it was a drug deal gone wrong, but one guy escaped and was so horrified that he turned himself in. He said everyone was killed by a shadow with red eyes, a phantom that had a red magical hand that came out of his body."

"Do you think it was one of ours?" Kai asked her.

"Not a member of the Sicarii, but definitely an assassin, and a brutal one too. He probably uses some sort of toxin to make his targets hallucinate in order to debilitate them. He's interesting. I would like to meet him one day, I think." Kai squeezed her right shoulder and walked past her and towards the refrigerator.

"Sounds like you have a crush," Kai said.

She stopped brushing her hair and walked towards the bedroom, taking off her towel in the process. "Yeah right. I just think he's fascinating is all."

He watched her. She was beautiful and he knew that, but Kai couldn't appreciate physical beauty the way others did.

A body is a prison for the soul, is it not? And a prison, no matter how ornate, is still a prison.

"Yeah," Kai whispered to himself as he turned back around and took a drink of water out of his bottle. He put the bottle back, closed the refrigerator and walked over to the couch and sat down. He watched the news briefly and then turned it off.

Ordinary people doing ordinary things.
Ordinary.
Ordinary.
Ordinary.

You're ordinary.

Am I?

"Y'know," Amina said as she poked her head around the doorway to the bedroom, "for being eighteen you sure act like you're forty."

Kai looked at her. "What is it they say? Old soul? Blah blah blah," he replied. Amina giggled and went back into the bedroom. She came out fifteen minutes later in black jeans, black boots, and a white shirt. Her hair had almost completely dried and she sat down by Kai who was reading a book on the couch.

"Whatchya readin'?" she asked in a silly manner.

"Nothing really. Just a book I had on the shelf about symbols and sigils."

"Why's that?" she chuckled a bit.

"I went to go see Al today," Kai replied. Amina's smiled faded and she turned more towards him, concerned. "He had what looked like a tattoo on the back of his neck. It was strange. I had never seen it before. But... it doesn't really look like a normal tattoo to me."

"What do you mean?" Amina asked softly.

"It looked more like a burn or a carving. Something damaging." Amina kept staring at him, looking for any sort of emotion on his face and finding nothing. "Anyways, that's why I picked up this book, figured I might find something in here."

"Did you find anything?

"No," Kai replied. "Not surprised. I'll go to the Greater Library a little later and see if I can find something there."

"Yeah," Amina consoled, "that sounds like a good idea." She squeezed Kai and kissed him on the cheek and then stood up. "Well, I'm off! Gotta get ready for tomorrow night. You should get some sleep, Kai. You're going to need it."

"Yeah, will do. Have a good-"Kai looked at the clock.

1:22 A.M.

"-morning I guess."

"You too, love," Amina replied. Catchya tomorrow." Amina walked out the door and locked it behind her. Her smell wisped past Kai and out the door with her.

Huh.

Kai turned the television back on and the news popped back up. He walked into his bedroom and picked up Amina's panties that were laying on the floor.

Every time.

"And now for international news with Ashley Hammel," Kai heard from the tv.

"Adrian Blom, leader of Swedish intelligence, will be holding a speech about the newly discovered research from Alexander Strömberg, the internationally known scientist and entrepreneur who was killed in a fire, along with his family, at his home eight years ago. The speech will be held outside of the newly opened research center in Stockholm, Sweden dedicated to Alexander's work and discoveries."

"Well," Kai said to himself, "I guess that takes care of that. Funny how life works." Kai walked back into the living room and picked up his phone that was sitting on the coffee table in front of the couch.

"Eris." His phone screen lit up.

"Yes Kai?"

"Contact Squad Four. Send them everything I have on Adrian Blom's speech location. Have everyone meet at Tara's place at ten-hundred hours."

"Right away," Eris said.

Kai put his phone in his pocket and grabbed his coat off the coat rack near the front door. He took a deep breath, opened his door, and locked it behind him. He looked at his phone and pulled up the picture he took of the mark on Al's neck and sighed.

Arriving back at the Greater Library, Kai entered through the beautiful wood and glass doors and walked to the back where the oldest tomes were kept. One at a time he pulled them out, carefully skimmed through them, and put them back on the shelf. Nothing. There was no book or scroll of sigils, symbols, and runes, of "magic", demonology, or angelology that within it contained the same symbol Kai found on Alphonse's body. It was as if it didn't exist, as if his eyes had played tricks. The symbol was unlike any he ever saw. And despite Dr. Mun's insistence that it was a tattoo, Kai was unsure. The color wasn't just black, it was more than that. It was too black, too unsettling, and the suppressed terror Kai got whenever he looked at it troubled his very soul. All Kai knew for sure was that the wound wasn't caused by a needle like normal tattoos, but by something he had never seen before. It was like the symbol was melted into Al's flesh, like it had become one with him.

Focus, Kai thought when he realized he was staring off into the distance. He exited his mind and his blurry vision cleared. On the other side of the library brown eyes, lighter than his, were staring back at him.

Eyes? His vision cleared more and splotches of color became brunette hair, fair skin, and well-tailored clothes. Cheeks became reddened and light brown eyes became nervous. Kai's vision came back completely, after no more than a second, and it took him the same amount of time to realize exactly what he was doing. The whole time he was in his mind, in his web, he had been staring at Haley. Her cheeks had become as bright as red spider lilies, and Kai quickly turned his head and put the book in his hand back on the shelf.

SIX

BLACK STAR

After a long night out, Black Star made his way into the forest outside of Rushville, Nebraska, preferring the solitude of the trees and the beauty of nature over the luxuriousness of a hotel. Not that he didn't enjoy the luxury every once in a while, and the relative non-existence of insects, but he needed a change of pace now and then to prevent the monotony of life and fill his life with new experiences. As he traveled deeper into the woods the foliage became denser and his surroundings darkened: smaller trees and dirt ground became thick, tall trees reaching almost a hundred feet in height and the ground became covered in more foliage than anyone could imagine or had probably seen in decades. The darkness of the forest didn't bother him because his eyes adjusted rather quickly, but the bugs chirping all around him did, as it always did. He shuddered a bit at the thought.

After moving ever deeper into the forest, Black Star slowed and picked a smaller tree to climb until he noticed a larger, sturdier tree not far away. He jumped from branch to branch, tree to tree, like the treetops had been his home his whole life. Following his arrival at the perfect tree, he picked a high, thick branch a third from the top, set his bag against the trunk, and laid down, resting his head on his bag. He stretched out as best as he could and peered through the rest of the branches towards the night sky, hoping for a glimpse at the stars, finding only disappointment amongst the clouds. He closed his eyes, but only for a few minutes as a wolf began howling on the forest floor below him. He peered over the edge of the branch to see if he could catch a glimpse but saw only an outline.

That's a big boy, he thought. He looked up towards the sky one last time and as he did the clouds began to disperse, finally revealing the stars he so desperately sought.

I could head home, Black Star thought. *But if I leave, I'll be looking at the same stars I always do.* He shrugged internally. *Might as well stay here, get a fresh start in the morning.* Deciding on his course of action, he gently closed his eyes and let sleep take him.

Around six a.m. Black Star awoke to the chirping of birds instead of insects, the sun shining dimly through the tree branches, and a squirrel jumping from his branch to another not too far away. The wind blew gently through the trees, making them shake slightly, but the trees had been swaying all night long so it didn't bother him at all. Even imagining the worst possible thing that could happen to him didn't bother him at this point. The adrenaline is what he lived for most of the time, even when it came to a minor task like sleeping in a tree.

Danger and fear didn't drive him away from things like it did others - it always pulled him closer as it had since he was a kid. For a moment a memory flashed behind his eyes: a glass bottle, thunder, and a bright blue light. It dissipated as quickly as it came on, and he laid there staring at the branches and sky above him. He awoke feeling refreshed, but unready to get up. He remembered his dreams, as he almost always did, and recalled the dreams he dreamt that brought him back to school once again. The dreams were skewed, as they almost always were, but they still brought back a mixture of feelings both good and bad, laced with nostalgia that melded into bittersweet, hazy memories of a simpler time.

As Black Star thought back he realized his fondness for his younger days. Nowhere else in the world could someone gain so many friends in such a short amount of time, and all in the same place. He felt happy, content back then. He yearned for days like those, days of peace, of contentment, somewhere, sometime, free from the cycle of killing at the least. But alas, he stood up to accept the reality that he had chosen and moved on from his thoughts, as he did every morning.

Is it possible my mind fabricates everything around me in this strange world?

The thought trailed off after a brief moment, replaced with something more presently concerning.

Since I didn't break a sweat yesterday I don't have to go home and change clothes.

In reality, Black Star didn't have a home, only his grandfather's estate off the coast of Japan. It was a place he would return to change and wash himself, but he never stayed longer than a night. The sun began warming his body up and so he climbed down the huge tree, branch by branch, now thinking only about food. Before heading to the home and business of a man named Cornelius in Rushville, Nebraska, Black Star decided to stop by his favorite restaurant: the Hash Round Haberdashery. When he arrived he was greeted with a smile by his favorite waitress in the world.

"Back again, huh?" she said. "And I had hoped we got rid of you," she giggled.

"What can I say? I just can't stay away." He smiled back and then sat down at a booth. The Hash Round Haberdashery was a young business, relative to the age of the city, but the house it inhabited was built at the birth of Rushville in the late 19th century. Because of this the building was built with strong brick and the only changes that had been made in two hundred years had been the mortar on the exterior and the entire interior, as it was now a restaurant instead of a home. Despite the popularity of the restaurant there was nobody inside on that particular day, which didn't bother Black Star at all as alone time was something he always enjoyed.

The lovely waitress brought Black Star a cup of coffee with cream and sugar and sat across from him. "So, the usual again?"

He smiled at her and laughed a bit. "The usual."

"You never change," she said as she got up from the booth.

She's not wrong.

As she began walking towards the kitchen Black Star called out to her. She turned around and met his gaze curiously.

"How about we change the pancake to a waffle?"

She laughed. "Sure. Not a problem hon."

The waitress walked away and Black Star took a drink of his coffee. After a few moments the owner Ahmed, a middle-aged man, came and sat down across from him.

"Back so soon?" Ahmed asked, a smile on his face. "Couldn't stay away from my heavenly hash rounds, huh?"

"I'm in town on some more business, so I figured I'd stop by because I can't pass through without a true breakfast. It's the most important meal of the day."

Ahmed laughed. "You make it sound like an inconvenience to come in! Is that what kids do these days? Just eat on the go?" Black Star took another sip of his coffee and as he set the cup down Adelina walked over and handed him the first of his plates: four strips of bacon and three eggs over medium.

"Thank you, Adelina." Adelina smiled, but said nothing and walked away. "Now, to answer your question, Ahmed: yes, people do like food on the go, but don't change your whole menu to accommodate them. Just add a few breakfast burritos or granola bars or something. If people want good food they'll come to you, but sometimes people just can't fit it in the schedule."

"That's true," Ahmed replied. "But you're different. I bet you'd cross a mountain for this food."

"Ahmed, please, to be fair," Black Star said with food in his mouth. "I'd cross two!" Ahmed laughed and Adelina came back around with the other three plates.

"Here you go! One pancake, biscuits and gravy, and a large plate of hash rounds. Oh! And I'll be right back with some more coffee." Black Star thanked her again, and even though he realized he had received his standard pancake instead of the waffle he didn't correct her and began gorging himself on the food anyways.

"Y'know, I've known you since you were a child. You and your family used to come in here all the time." Black Star continued eating. "Your parents, they were good people." Black Star had no response. Ahmed's phone began to ring, cutting off the awkward situation. "I'm going to grab this call, enjoy your breakfast." Black Star did as he was told and finished his huge breakfast in its entirety along with three cups of coffee.

Times like these I could go to sleep, but obligations keep me up.

Adelina came by and dropped off the bill as Black Star stacked his plates and handed her cash for the bill plus a twenty-percent tip, as always. Ahmed stopped him as he got up out of the booth.

"Leaving so soon?"

"Yes sir. After I'm finished here I got a flight to catch," Black Star responded.

"Back to school huh? How's college going anyways?" Ahmed pried.

"I'm always tired," Black Star said, sullenly, "but that's no surprise."

"A gentleman and a scholar! Y'know," Ahmed said with a smile, "I wouldn't mind having you as a son in law."

Black Star gave Ahmed a questionable look. "I'd have to marry your daughter."

"That can be arranged..." Ahmed said quietly, trailing off at the end. Black Star looked to his right and saw Adelina watching them and his face turned beet red, uncomfortability and awkwardness washing over him.

"Ahmed, I'm glad I stopped by, but I gotta go." Black Star left as quickly as he could and let out a sigh of relief once he got outside. After gathering himself he went to Cornelius's house, only a few blocks away in Rushville. With a brisk walking pace Black Star arrived in just a couple of minutes and passed the "Verner Financial Aid" sign as he walked up to the door. He rang the doorbell and waited for a few moments and then rang it again. Immediately, a tired Cornelius opened the door sluggishly, pushing trash out of the way with his bare feet, toenails unclipped for longer than one would like to imagine.

"Hello, I'm looking to get my life financially in order," Black Star said with a straight face.

Cornelius rubbed his hands across his face and eyes. "Why are you here?" he asked. "It's too early for this and quit acting like it's your first time." Cornelius's gray sweats were stained from food and drink and his greasy face was covered with acne, no doubt from his lack of hygiene.

They passed through the cluttered front room, as they had done many times, and into the back office. Cornelius took a seat behind his desk.

"Why are you here so early?" he asked, rubbing his eyes again.

"Well, I need three more contracts," Black Star responded.

"The lines don't open for another thirty minutes!" Cornelius said, irritated

"Well, that gives me time to talk before I leave. I got a flight at 9."

"Okay. So, you need a new contract?" Still, Cornelius was not functioning properly.

"No, I need three," Black Star retorted.

"Sorry, I'm still suffering from the effects of little sleep."

"I took out one contract," Black Star continued, explaining himself, "followed by another. Then on my way to the next location someone else completed the task for me. Guess I was too leisurely."

Cornelius chimed in. "Yeah, I think the contract you missed is the one the Phantom took. That thing is crazy. Doesn't utter any words and never missed a target. Did you see him?"

"No, he was gone by the time I arrived," Black Star replied. "I saw the aftermath though. It was a train wreck."

"Have you *ever* seen it?"

"I have been in his presence during a passing. He's ominous to say the least. Being around him feels like gravity getting heavier."

"So it's a he?" Cornelius asked.

"I can only assume, but I could be wrong. No one has checked under the hood. No one wants to. That might be it."

"I don't think it's human," Cornelius furthered. "Maybe it's an escaped lab experiment. It kills in a supernatural way. That explains its *need* to kill!" Cornelius got excited, like he made some grand discovery.

"I think that's a little far-fetched," replied Black Star. "Maybe you've been watching too much sci-fi."

"Look at the age we live in! Anything is possible! And it couldn't be human because it doesn't collect the reward. It does it for the hunt. It kills for sport. We need human currency, we need money, but it's currency is blood." Cornelius continued defending his point after opening a Grande Energy Drink and taking a sip.

"Regardless, it's a spooky character. And, like you said, everyone is afraid to look under the hood, but he's good at his job.

He's 13-0, no failed contracts, better than your record."

Black Star sighed, "I don't want to talk about it."

Cornelius laughed at Black Star's short answer. "Oh, don't let that get you down Black Star. You shouldn't compare yourself to something so unnatural. They have power that can't be explained. You have to work with what you have and be happy with it. Holding yourself to other people's standards only hurt you."

"I appreciate the pep talk, but I'm not like others. I hold myself to others standards because I know I can be at the top with them. I just need to work harder and stay dedicated."

"You don't sound as competitive as normal. Usually this fires up your underdog spirit."

"That's because I feel like I'm already at the top. How much farther away could I be?" Black Star asked rhetorically. "Also, I like friendly competition, but that thing doesn't seem friendly."

After a while of small talk Black Star's phone made a notable "*SCHWING!*" as he got a message.

"Hey when you're free, come see me."

"Sorry," Black Star said, "it's my sister. She wants me to give her a visit."

"So, you have a sister?" Cornelius inquired.

"Yeah, she's my older sister. You'd like her. She's like me, but taller and more tech savvy."

Cornelius leaned in, intrigued. "Maybe we can hang out sometime."

"We'll see bud," Black Star replied. "For now, let's just filter through some contracts." A silence washed over the room and a slight awkwardness began setting in. Black Star spoke up after a few moments, but this time in a deep southern drawl in an attempt to lighten the situation.

"Now come on Cornelius, my boy. Let's see what we got here. The world ain't gonna be better off if we don't take no action!"

Stopping the idle chit chat, Black Star and Cornelius began reviewing various contracts, with Black Star doing his best to keep his morals in check, even as an assassin like he was. Black Star wasn't focused on the money, he never was, but what he was focused on was *why* someone had a contract on their head, so he chose them based on that principle alone. In Black Star's mind not everyone that had a contract placed on them deserved to die and not everyone that deserves to die had a contract, so he took it upon himself to pass judgment in the best manner possible.

SEVEN

KAI

Kai woke up, two hours of sleep under his belt and stared at the ceiling fan. It spun slowly, just enough to circulate the air and just enough to help Kai wake up. He sat up on the edge of the bed and began rubbing his neck, staring at the floor for what seemed like an eternity.

So much blood.

The gates of Kai's past opened as he sat there, the morning sun shining on his back through the window. "It's your job," Alef told Kai. "You were built for this. I pulled you out of that rubble when you were four years old after that bomb killed your parents. I saved you and now I need you because you have the potentiality to be the greatest one of us all." Kai ran his hands through his short, dark brown hair and began holding his head.

"Everything you think you know is a lie."

"What's a lie?" Kai whispered, weakly. "Please Al. Please tell me."

"Everything."

"FUCK!" Kai's face turned crimson as he slung his phone against the wall. Wiping the wetness from his eyes he got out of bed and disregarded the buzzing of his undamaged phone lying on the floor.

Tara's house was far outside of The City in the rural parts of what used to be the northern Midwest of the United States. Her half-wolf Hastur stalked the forest surrounding her home, hunting as good wolves do. Tara's home wasn't very large or extravagant. It was little more than a log cabin in the middle of nowhere, just the way she liked it. Had she been born two and a half centuries earlier, Tara probably would've enjoyed life even more, but she was content the way she was.

Kai arrived before the rest of the squad as he pulled up to the house in a light black colored motorcycle: an old pre-war model that was refitted to run on electricity instead of gas and was modified to Kai's specifications. Tara walked out of the front door and onto the porch as Kai collapsed his helmet. Clothed in a gray tank top, blue jeans, and brown boots, her blonde braid fell over her left shoulder and swayed with each step.

"You didn't answer when I called," Tara shouted over the noise of the motorcycle. Kai stepped off the bike and the engine immediately died. "Long night?" Tara asked.

"Too long," Kai replied as he walked up the steps. She opened the door for him, and they both walked into the kitchen, or what Tara called a kitchen. Really, it was nothing more than a small room with an old refrigerator from the early 21st century, like Kai's, and a stovetop oven, also like Kai's. They continued through the kitchen and rounded the corner, where stairs led to the basement.

"I called because Amina, Piers, and Marlowe said they were going to be late. Something with Piers' birthday coming up soon. I don't know," Tara said as they walked down the stairs. In the middle of the dark room was a glowing table-like structure, emanating a blue light. Kai walked around and touched the pad on the far side of it, causing a hologram of Adrian Blom's file to appear before him. He swiped in the air with his hand, scrolling through files and maps as fast as his eye could see.

"Everything here?" he asked Tara.

"Yeah," she replied as she walked over to him. "Everything you wanted at least." Footsteps began sounding down the steps as Marlowe, Amina, and Piers walked in.

"Sorry we're late," Amina said. "This little bugger just wouldn't get a move on." She ruffled Piers' hair and an embarrassed look washed over his face.

"Heh, sorry buddy! I know you hate us being late and all," Piers said as rubbed the back of his neck and smiled his biggest, goofiest smile.

"No worries," Kai said. "Now let's get down to business, shall we?" They all huddled around the table as holograms of Blom and maps of Stockholm projected into the air.

"Target," Kai began, "is Adrian Blom, leader of the Swedish Security Service. It's our mission, as appointed by the High Council, to kill this man in order to warn the Swedish government from hoarding and monopolizing Alexander's research."

"This seems like a one-man job," Marlowe cut in with his gruff voice. "Why does the High Council need all of us?"

"They want us to prove a point. That someone is watching. That someone doesn't like what Sweden is doing with Alexander's research," Kai replied.

"So, they want a show then," said Amina sternly.

"Indeed," rejoined Kai. "So, I'm thinking something flashy. Got any ideas?"

"Show me the layout of the building and the city around it," Amina said. Kai pulled up a satellite image of Stockholm and the new research facility where Adrian Blom's speech was going to be held.

"The building makes a u-shape around an open plaza-like area. Between the two ends of the building is where Blom's podium will be," Kai informed the squad. "Local police forces and a portable K-1 bulletproof barrier should be assumed as present.

"I could make a green firebomb," Amina joked. "I'm sure a flashy green blast of flames would scare the shit out of the Ordies." That's what Amina always called regular people: Ordies. Short for 'ordinary' Kai assumed. He had heard it thrown around assassin circles on the surface. Assassins liked giving names to people who were unaware of the truth and of their work, people who were unaware of the strings being pulled behind their backs. Surface assassins were the same though. Honestly, even those in the depths of Headquarters were the same. No one truly understood the game that was being played, not even Kai.

Perhaps even my strings are being pulled. Kai thought.

"Everything you know is a lie."

"Everything."

"EVERYTHING!"

"Kai, you good?" Piers asked. Kai realized he was sweating and leaning over the table, head in the hologram, and stood back up.

"Yeah, I'm fine. Thanks," Kai reassured his team as he wiped the sweat off his forehead.

"How about this, then," Amina pulled up the map of the building and rotated it, switching from a top-down view to a three-dimensional render of the plaza and the sewer beneath it. "How about we place an explosive charge here," she tapped on the hologram of the sewer behind where the podium would be. "And two more explosives under the ground here and here, where the off-stage police will be standing, directing traffic and pedestrians."

"You're wanting to use the sewer to escape then?" Kai asked.

"Yes," Amina replied. "I feel like that's our safest option. We can be picked up in the Baltic afterwards."

"Brilliant," said Kai. "Straight from evasions class in our third year of the Academy. Marlowe, I want you up on the stage with Adrian. You'll need a Swedish police uniform."

"Understood," said Marlowe.

"Piers, Amina, you two stay in the sewers and wait for my signal to activate the charges. After the charges blow, Marlowe will take out the rest of the police officers, I'll take out Adrian, and you'll wait for our arrival in the sewers. Got it?"

"Got it," replied Piers and Amina simultaneously.

"Tara," Kai said while staring at the newly formulated plan. "I need you in the sky. How soon can you get the L.O.A.D.S. online?" The Low-Orbit Autonomous Delivery System (L.O.A.D.S.) was a Sicarii-operated drone that could be flown manually or remotely depending on the situation. It was used mainly for missions where someone in the field needed to be resupplied. The L.O.A.D.S. was created for use in the Third World War, wherein it would orbitally drop the Archangels onto the battlefields raging across the Earth.

The Archangels, a mercenary group consisting of seven super-soldiers fitted with massive, winged suits, would eject from the drone in orbit, and would plummet onto the battlefield, completely annihilating anything below and around them. Their suits negated all damage they would take from the fall, turning them into a kind of human missile, and the death toll they racked up before even engaging in combat was astronomical. Their suits could withstand direct impacts from missiles, tank shells, bullets, and just about everything else. And once they engaged in combat, that battle was effectively over. Standing around ten feet tall, a single Archangel could destroy a battalion of soldiers in an hour. Their swords could slice clean through three men in one swing, and the boosters on the backs of their suits were like catalysts of holy fire, incinerating those they deemed unworthy in an instant.

"By tonight," Tara answered. "It'll only take me a few hours to get it supplied and in the air." Kai nodded. "We'll need wings."

"I'll load them," Tara said. "Which model?"

"8.3," Kai answered.

"8.3s? The prototype model?" asked Tara, shocked.

"Correct. They're faster-"

"And I can hack them," Eris said aloud, cutting Kai off. "Because they're prototypes, the Wingblade 8.3s don't have a firewall, and most importantly don't have a death wall, so it won't kill me if I try to hack into it."

"But the enemy can hack into it as well," Amina mentioned.

"Correct," said Kai. "But Eris is better." Kai turned to Tara, his face stern as always. "Whenever I give the signal, drop the Wingblades into the water where the drainage pipes meet the Baltic. From there we can take them up to the L.O.A.D.S." Tara nodded and walked upstairs. Kai swiped the hologram away, shutting off the system, and he followed Amina, Marlowe, and Piers back upstairs.

The sun outside had risen to its highest point, bombarding Squad Four and the forest with much needed sunlight. "Would ya look at that," Marlowe said, amazed. He turned around before getting in his car and looked at Kai. "Must be our lucky day."

The sun rarely came out and no one really knew why, but everything changed after the Third Great War. Scientists said things about The City messing with the atmosphere, or weather machines, or even the destabilization of nuclear-powered weapons during the war, but they were all just theories. Perhaps, Kai thought, the Earth couldn't take the sheer amount of blood spilled during the war, but again, not even he knew. All everyone knew was what they could see, and that was rain. It rained all the time. Luckily for Kai, he liked the rain, but seeing the sun every once in a while was nice, even to him.

The next morning, Stockholm was bright. The plaza was crowded with scientists, businessmen and women, stockholders, and civilians. He stood amongst them, a wolf in sheepskin, wearing a black suit, white shirt, black tie, and black shoes. At the nape of his neck was Eris and his helmet, collapsed to forego suspicion. He looked in front of him, towards the stage where Blom would be speaking. On the stage behind the podium and the K-1 barrier stood a row of Swedish police officers, and among them was Marlowe, uniformed in dark blue and a side cap.

"Blom is coming up now," Tara said over their communication system. "Everyone get ready."

Adrian Blom walked up the stage, his short, blonde hair stiff and tamed by hairspray, wearing a navy suit. He waved at the crowd, smiled, and took his place behind the podium.

"Today," he said, "we celebrate a momentous occasion: the grand opening of the Alexander Strömberg Research Facility, here in our beautiful city of Stockholm." Clapping ensued and Kai began walking closer to the front of the crowd. On the roof above him stood five police snipers, watching the crowd and the surrounding area. "With this," Blom continued talking, "we can better not only our country, but the lives of those worldwide." The crowd clapped louder and began cheering as Kai continued moving forward. He looked up and made eye contact with Marlowe who was standing on the stage with five other police officers, armed with assault rifles. Adrian Blom continued talking as scientists, civilians, and businessmen looked onward, entranced at his promises about scientific discovery, new technologies, and government funding.

"With Alexander's research and the support of the brilliant scientists in Sweden," Blom shouted, "we will ensure the future and a brave new world for all!" The cheering and shouting of the crowd rumbled the surrounding buildings and the ground of the plaza.

"Now," Kai whispered. Along with the shouting, an explosion bubbled behind the stage and in the streets to the left and the right of the plaza. If one were to slow time, it would seem that the ground was boiling, the stone melting, and the police vehicles levitating, as the energy from the explosions super-heated the stone and sent it outwards. The police vehicles went flying as they too detonated, and holes were formed in the places that once were covered by concrete, steel, and stone. Kai ran towards the stage as Adrian Blom took cover and the three police officers on stage right began escorting him. Marlowe shot the other two police officers next to him with his rifle as Kai activated his helmet and lunged onto the stage. He pulled out a handgun and shot two of the officers escorting Blom multiple times in the chest as Marlowe shot the third in the head. Blom cowered in fear as Kai approached him, falling down onto the mangled bodies of the police officers that were shot to death.

"Adrian Blom," Kai said calmly. "On the order of the High Council of the Sicarii you have been sentenced to death." Blom whimpered as Kai lifted his pistol and shot him in the head. Kai looked up towards the roof of the research building and saw the bodies of the snipers slumped over the edge.

"Time to move," Kai said. Marlowe followed behind him as both dropped into the hole behind the stage. Amina and Piers stood in the sewers below, ready to kill anyone who dropped through the hole besides Marlowe and Kai. No words were exchanged as Marlowe shed his police uniform and Kai shed his suit and tie, revealing their Sicarii suits. Amina torched the clothes with a chemical compound strapped to her waist that she poured onto the pile.

The four began sprinting through the sewers as shouts reverberated off the walls coming from the police officers trailing far behind them. The sewer was dark and dank. Perspiration dripped off the walls and the smell of human excrement stuck to the stone. Kai followed his team towards the extraction point, and as they were closing in on the exit, he noticed something to his right in his peripheral vision. He stopped and turned around. Now to his left was a small passageway, where a door might've been at some point. An eerie light emanated from the hall and unintelligible whispers, as if someone was talking to themselves, came forth. Kai peered around the corner, expecting to see someone, but instead saw, painted on the wall in what appeared to be blood, a symbol and a phrase:

BEHOLD THE BLACK SEED

Kai fell against the wet, stone wall. He began sweating profusely and shivering at the same time as he looked upon the painfully real symbol above the phrase, the same symbol he had been searching for, the symbol on Alphonse's body.

"Kai!" Amina shouted as loud as she could while still trying to maintain a whisper. "Kai, we need to go!" Kai stood staring, frozen, as Amina ran back for him. She grabbed him and looked the way his eyes were locked but saw nothing more than a damp stone wall.

"Come on!" Amina yelled a little too loudly as she grabbed his arm and began pulling him away. Kai snapped out of his flashbacks and looked at her as if he was seeing a stranger. He looked back towards the wall, and all that was there, yet again, was a damp stone wall at the end of a damp stone hallway.

"Sorry..." Kai trailed off as he began running. Behind them the shouts of police officers and the sounds of drone boosters echoed off the walls as they came up to their evacuation zone. "Commence drop, Tara," Kai ordered. The noises of the ocean became louder and suddenly the smell of the brackish water overtook the smell of the dank sewer. About thirty feet in front of the exit of the sewer, four white, egg-shaped objects fell from the sky with an explosive force, launching water towards the sky.

"Ooo buddy this is my favorite part!" Piers stated excitedly. Every member of the squad looked at him curiously. "What? It's cool," Piers quietly justified himself. Everyone, except Kai who was still thinking about what he just saw, chuckled. They turned around, their backs facing the water, and lifted their arms. From the water burst four white backpack-like objects that slammed against the backs of Squad Four and latched onto them like spiders, connecting to their suits and sending out a blue pulse across the jet-black surface.

"Connected," Eris said aloud. "Deathwall has been set up, we should be free to head out."

"Let's move." Kai activated his helmet and the Wingblades opened up, revealing two thrusters that launched him in the air, his comrades following behind him. Once they reached a higher altitude, a mask came from the Wingblade that covered the mouth, nose, and eyes of Amina, Piers, and Marlowe, in order to prevent them from suffocating. A burst from each of their Wingblades launched them higher into the air and sped them up tremendously. In the distance they could see the L.O.A.D.S., just a black speck in a sea of blue sky and white clouds, but as they ascended the black speck began to form into something more.

At first, they saw a light radiating from the back of the ship, even during midday, which was where the massive engines were that kept the behemoth of a drop ship in the air. As they closed in, what was once a speck now took on the form of a long black rectangle, similar to the blade of a katana, and as they got even closer they truly witnessed the sheer size of the L.O.A.D.S. 610 meters of heat-shields, high-tech weaponry, intelligence hardware, and cargo, kept aloft by five massive engines on the stern and ten smaller engines on the hull, the L.O.A.D.S. was, by all accounts, the largest drop ship in the world. Used mostly for surveillance and supply drops for military units, it now served a different, but equally as important task as it did decades prior towards the end of World War 3.

"We're closing in Tara, ETA two min-"

"KAI!" Yelled Amina. "DRONES!"

"Shit. Everyone fan out! Tara, cloak now! Eris how many are there?" Kai ordered in urgently.

"Five, Kai."

"Begin hacking immediately."

"I already started, but I'm being counter-hacked. It'll hit the deathwall in fifteen seconds."

"How long until you kill the second drone?" Kai was still yelling as he and the rest of Squad Four whipped around in the air, doing their best to stay out of the range of the drones' weapon systems. At the same time, Tara cloaked the L.O.A.D.S. in order to prevent the drones from gaining information on it.

"Twenty seconds" replied Eris, calmly.

"Keep working on it Eris! Amina, Piers, Marlowe are you guys alright?" Kai asked, not only as a captain, but as a friend.

"We're good, Kai!" Amina replied. Kai looked over in her direction and watched her weave effortlessly between two of the drones.

"Yeah, man, don't worry about us!" exclaimed Piers. "Everything's f-WOAH!" Kai jerked his head in Piers's direction as he watched him barely dodge a flurry of bullets coming from one of the drones. "See!" Piers continued as he corrected his altitude. "Everything's great!" Kai shook his head the way a disappointed father would, even though Kai had known no such comfort.

"Marlowe? What about you?" Kai watched as Marlowe weaved around, dodging the drones just as well as the other members of the squad, but he wasn't responding. "Marlowe?" Kai asked again.

"Sorry, sir," Marlowe finally replied, choked up. "Flying..." he paused. "Flying doesn't set well with me." He made a sort of whimper mixed with a gag and Kai remembered that he had forgotten that Marlowe got airsick, and because of this normally avoided flying altogether.

To Kai's right was an explosion, out of which came Amina, who had apparently caught one of the drones with a vial bomb she had created. The drone chasing Kai burst into flames and began falling towards the earth as did the one chasing Marlowe. "Hacking completed," Eris stated.

"Three down, two to go," Kai muttered. "Keep hacking, Eris. Shut off the one chasing Piers." Kai floated in the air, assessing the battlefield. Marlowe came up to his right side and floated alongside him, panting furiously. Kai ignored his exhaustion. The drone chasing Piers burst into flames and fell the same as the other two before it, leaving only the drone chasing after Amina. Piers lined up next to Kai and Marlowe as Amina continued dodging the drone, having too much fun along the way. When she had a good angle, she threw another vial behind her, but it didn't make contact. She looked back, but the drone had disappeared.

"Where'd it go?" Amina asked Kai, nervous. Kai began looking around, as did the rest of Squad Four.

"How did it just disappear?" Piers followed up.

"Everyone be quiet," Kai ordered. "My helmet's targeting system is going haywire. Eris what's going on?"

"I don't know, Kai," I can't find it either," Eris responded.

"Be careful Amina, this thing could be anywhere." Kai called out to her.

"Heh, maybe it got scared and flew away!" Amina chuckled nervously, trying her best to hide her concern. Her teal hair fluttered in the wind as she floated a few dozen feet away from the rest of her team. Her two pigtail buns had fallen down while she was flying, and it was at this time that Kai saw how magnificent she really was. The sun behind her shone brilliantly and transformed her hair into greenish-blue fire as the last drone reappeared in front of her and blew a hole through her abdomen. She began to fall downwards towards the earth, just like the drones before her, and just as they burst into flames so was she enflamed – by a greenish-blue torrent of sun-kissed hair.

"AMINA!"

EIGHT

BLACK STAR

Black Star tossed and turned throughout the night, flipping and changing positions. Trying to fluff his pillow or use his arm as support. Thunder boomed, awakening him, leading to more tossing and turning, this time in an attempt to get comfortable once again. It was still dark out and he knew he had time to sleep, so he pulled the quilted blanket over his head, trapping the heat in and allowing no light to dare meet his gaze. When Black Star awoke again it was around 9 am, which was, for him, sleeping in. But because it had been raining throughout the night and continued raining into the current day, he forgave himself. He looked out the window after getting out of bed and a smile grew across his face. Days like those, where it rained all day long were Black Star's self-proclaimed "lazy days". The weather was gloomy, too gloomy for a man who bathed in the light of the sun, so he took those days as an excuse to do whatever he pleased in the comfort of his own home.

Black Star slipped on a pair of black gym shorts, an old t-shirt, and his slippers that rested at the edge of his bed, one right in front perfectly aligned, and the other which lay haphazardly upside down, a few feet away. He walked to the bathroom and relieved himself, washed his hands, and brushed his teeth afterwards, making sure to brush vigorously for about five minutes, as he wanted to get every single crevice as clean as he could.

When finished, Black Star walked out of his room and down the hall to the kitchen where he began brewing a medium roast coffee. He picked up his phone and began playing music, which, on days like these, happened to be a playlist of lo-fi hip hop and jazz and began working on the dirty dishes in the sink from the day before. Black Star stood at the sink, hands scrubbing dishes with hot soapy water, and gazed out the window in front of him, admiring the beauty of the world. After his coffee finished brewing and he finished washing the dishes, he grabbed an exceptionally large mug with an insignia and names on it, a memory from his high school graduation, and poured his coffee into it. He then added a bit of sugar and french vanilla creamer, stirred it with a spoon, and walked out onto his back porch.

The back porch was composed of Brazilian Cherry wood, also known as Jatoba in many parts of the world and had an awning that covered the single piece of furniture under it: a wooden rocking chair that used to be Black Star's grandfathers. Black Star took a seat in this chair, careful not to spill his huge mug of coffee and stared down at the lake that he had a clear view of. He watched the raindrops dance across the top of the water, splashing up, then back down, inevitably joining as one with the rest of droplets in the lake.

Like the cycle of life. Black Star thought. *We as individuals have our journey down here, to earth, and become one in the end.*

Black Star was lucky enough to not have a demanding physique, and because of that he never had to work out constantly or keep up with some sort of intense regiment. From what he concluded, it didn't really matter whether he worked out or not. He wouldn't get flabby, no matter how lazy he was and how much he ate, which was a lot. He chalked this up to his rapid metabolism, due to his genetics and scrawny ancestors, but he had no concrete proof that was the cause of his physicality. All Black Star really worried about was being the fastest. As long as something couldn't hit him, he didn't care. He still exercised for fun, however, and one could easily argue that his lifestyle was exercise in and of itself, which may have been a reason, albeit a small one, for his pursuit of the lifestyle he led.

Black Star stood up out of the rocking chair, after sitting outside for about half an hour in deep thought, and picked up an iron bar that was leaning up against the wall of the house. The bar was five feet long and thirty pounds and was originally meant for breaking concrete. He stepped out into the rain with the bar and spun it around as anyone would spin a normal wooden staff, knowing that, without a doubt, he would never be struck by lightning. Spinning the staff was routine for him and he spun it in a few different ways in order to not only work his muscles, but to prove to himself that he was still dextrous enough to gracefully handle the weight of the bar for so long. No matter the weather, even in the midst of a storm like then, he always spun his staff and was never once struck by lightning, despite the odds being stacked against him.

The rain finally let up, but the sun still hid behind the clouds. Black Star stopped spinning his staff, put it back where he found it, and finished off his first mug of coffee. He walked inside, filled the mug back up with the rest of the coffee from the pot, and walked into the living room and sat on the couch. He had been itching to play a game or two, so he turned on his favorite role-playing game, loving the idea of creating and playing a character who clearly didn't fit in the world. Doing this always lightened up Black Star's mood and reminded him that he was just a normal guy, despite everything. He also loved the idea of starting out weak and gradually building up strength, learning new moves and gaining new weapons along the way. He liked character development and because of that he brought life to his characters by giving them roles and personalities to follow. For example, one of his characters was named "Chopped Liver" and was a character with outstandingly low charisma, so that when people didn't help him he could respond "What am I? Chopped liver?"

The answer is yes. Black Star thought. *You are chopped liver.* He chuckled to himself.

When playing a game, Black Star would become extremely immersed, often for hours at a time, and did his best to die as little as possible. However, accidents happen, and during one such accident he dropped an explosive device at his character's feet, blowing himself up in the process. But whenever something like that occurred, unlike other gamers, Black Star didn't lash out in rage like a child. Rather he inhaled deeply, cursed under his breath, and closed out of the game. One such accident happened on this particular day, and he responded as he always did.

"That's enough video games for a while," Black Star said out loud to himself. He walked into his room and finished getting ready for the day. He put on socks and shoes, changed his shirt to his favorite "Space Cadet" t-shirt, a popular science fiction television show for kids, and checked his calendar that had a motivational poem for each month of the year.

"Today is Wednesday," he said out loud again. "Only three months and one week left." He looked over at his vintage analog clock hanging on the wall. The clock looked like a black cat, and its eyes darted back and forth with every tick. "And it's only 12:42." Black Star jumped on his bed and lazed around more.

I'll watch a few episodes before I go to Maria's, he thought as he turned on his tv. With that, he watched a few episodes of a documentary on ancient civilizations and religion, of which the civilization of Akkad was of most interest to him.

█ █ █ █ █ █ █ ▪ ▪ ▪ ▪ ▪ |

On the other side of the world, it was a sunny day in a Texan mega-city. It was a true metropolis and grew every single day until it got close to its breaking point only a decade or so prior. Ranches and homesteads that were once surrounded only by trees and green pastures became surrounded by metal and concrete buildings, the fault of which, any historian would say, was due to the restructuring of Houston after its invasion by NATO forces in 2065.

The artillery strikes on the metropolis left craters where buildings once existed, but for the scale of the invasion and the naval raid, Houston suffered less damage than Chicago, Illinois, St. Louis, Missouri, Los Angeles, California, and the US Capitol in West Virginia, all of which were almost entirely decimated due to massive resistance. New York City got the worst of it as hellfire from the skies wove torrents of flame across the surface of the megalopolis and the Archangels slew thousands of United States' soldiers as they moved through the flames, untouched even by the light. Eventually though, even the ranches and homesteads were replaced with condo buildings, and middle-class farmers came to live in condominiums in the heart of a city they knew not.

In the living room of a two-story house in a more suburban part of the city, a loud crash startled a young, female homeowner who was busy in another room of the house. She walked into the living room and saw Black Star standing there next to her chimney, covered in old soot, as the fireplace hadn't been used in quite some time. As she approached, Black Star shifted his stance and leaned against the brick fireplace with one hand and placed the other on his hip.

"Hey, your doors were locked," he spoke up.

The woman gave him a death stare, and although she looked at him angrily, she was unsurprised of his presence there. "My doors are unloc-"

"Okay I didn't try the doors," Black Star interrupted. "What's gooooddd?"

"Trees," she responded questionably. "You doing okay?"

"I'm tired, been doing a lot of running around. Staying busy, meeting new people."

"So, the usual?" she responded. Black Star nodded and knocked most of the soot off him. "You want to talk over some tea?" Black Star responded yet again with no words, but instead put two thumbs up. He followed her into the kitchen, all the while staring at her dirty blonde, shoulder length hair. He could tell she barely touched it, but it didn't look bad so she could go out whenever she needed too.

Did she get a haircut? Black Star thought to himself, examining her hair further. *Nah*, he concluded. *Wait, yes. Her hair was definitely different.* They arrived in the kitchen which was just down a short hall from the living room and the young woman began pulling mugs out of the cabinet.

"I like what you did with your hair," Black Star said. "Short looks good on you."

"You noticed. I'm surprised," she said in response.

"I try to be as observant as I can." The young woman disregarded his last comment and opened another cabinet.

"What kind of tea would you like? I got chai, oolong, green, and sleepy-time tea."

"Chai tea please," Black Star responded.

"You know, in most Asian countries chai already means tea, so it's redundant when people say chai tea," she retorted as she pulled out the tea bags.

"Okay, fair point," Black Star said. "But if that's the case, then when someone wants spiced chai, they say spiced chai chai?"

"What? No, that's stupid. You'd just be saying spiced tea tea. It's redundant."

"Then why does this box say 'Spiced Chai Tea'?" Black Star continued arguing.

"Because to this day, the advertising in the States is still made for idiots," the woman retorted one last time.

"Okay, I concede," Black Star said. "You win."

The tea was ready at this point, so they both picked their mugs up and walked into the sunroom, surrounded by orchids and a hodge-podge of green plants. After a few moments of basking in the sun, the young woman finally raised a question that was eating away at her.

"Are you still doing that thing?" she asked. Black Star could hear her heart race and see the nervousness in her eyes. He watched her for a millisecond, but that was enough.

"Being an assassin...?" he asked, knowing the answer. "Yeah."

Her nervousness gave way to a frustration hidden deep within her. But even though she tried to hide it, Black Star could still tell it was there.

"You haven't found any better opportunities? Are you still going to college at least?" she furthered.

"I am," Black Star responded, "but it's an online class and I only do it for the test, in order to keep my mind sharp. At this point I've come to the conclusion that I can't have a normal job. I'd feel hollow inside."

Not killing people would make you feel hollow? she thought to herself. Despite her feelings on her brother's career choice, she couldn't deny that she was happy to see him doing well.

"How are you, Maria?" Black Star asked.

"I'm doing great actually. Instead of trying to work in the office of dad's company I found that I enjoy the workshop a lot more." Because the world believed the Stromberg family to be dead, Maria had her identity replaced after the events of the her father and mother's assassination. Even though she was no longer White Star-Stromberg, she was still very much a Star and Stromberg in mind, body, and soul, meaning her intelligence and desire for good were far above anything a regular person was generally capable of. She was, for all intents and purposes, a genius, and her creativity and skill with machines led her, despite her endless choices, back to her father's company.

"It's a lot more peaceful this way. The machines don't try to talk to me or flirt with me, which gives me a lot more free time when I'm not dealing with disgusting *men*," she rolled her eyes.

"That's cool," Black Star replied. "Are you seeing anyone new?" He leaned back into the posh chair and let the sunlight hit his face, hiking one leg over the other in the process.

"Yeah, I met a guy about a month ago. He's nice, but not that bright. I suppose I can't expect them to be though."

"How dull we talking?" Black Star asked.

"Like, I can't use words with two or more syllables. He gets confused," Maria said.

"Yeeshk," Black Star said after taking a sip from his tea. "I'd politely cut it off. If you can't be yourself around him, and you have to limit what you say, then it's not going to work out. You can try to stay friends with him, but I don't know how he'd take it. It might be too hard on him, the poor chap."

"You make a good point. I just don't want to hurt him, y'know? Like I said, he's really sweet. He didn't necessarily do anything wrong, and our personalities click, but there's just that intellectual barrier."

"Yes, but by letting it persist and not hurting him now you will only cause further damage down the road," Black Star argued. "The longer the band-aid stays on, the tighter the adhesive sticks."

"You know, for not being in many relationships you sure seem like you know what you're talking about," Maria said.

"From my perspective it just sounds logical," Black Star said after taking a sip of tea. "I don't have to have the life experiences to understand the life experience. I also learn from other's mistakes, so I don't have to make my own." Black Star and Maria stood up at the same time and began walking back into the kitchen, downing the rest of their tea in one fell swoop.

"While that may be true," Maria retorted. "You can't resort to logic in every instance. There may come a time when no matter what mistakes you have learned from others, you still might have no idea what to do. There's a big difference between the conceptual and the actual, bro."

They both squeezed through the kitchen doorway, as neither would let the other go first due to their stubbornness and desire for primacy. They moved to the sink and put their mugs in and then Black Star walked back over towards the door to put some space between them. Maria continued to speak.

"I'm glad you came by to visit, but since you're here I need you to do a favor for me."

"Oh? What service do I have to offer you?" Black Star said with an attitude. Maria strided over to him and got in his face, standing half a foot taller and looking slightly down at him.

"Hey, don't sound snippy with me. I'm doing this for you to begin with! So sound grateful for once in your life."

"Sorry. Oh, how grateful I am to help you, my lovely sister. Better?" Black Star snipped back.

"See, you're getting me all worked up over nothing," Maria took a deep breath. "Quit the smug attitude before I flip a lid. Speaking of being worked up and having an attitude, have you told Jessica about your career?"

"No, I haven't found the proper way to format it so that she won't get hostile about it," Black Star replied.

Maria laughed. "Yeah, I don't think you're going to find a way to say it that won't make her angry. No matter how you word it, she's too smart to fall for your shit. But, back to what I was saying," Maria rinsed out the two mugs from earlier. "You said you wanted me to build you an advanced simulation chamber, something that could generate different atmospheres and environments, and so far, you've funded me with everything I need, even though it was all bartered in blood." Maria made sure to add in that last bit, just so Black Star was fully aware that his lifestyle was displeasing to her.

"But despite what I have received, I still require one more thing: an energy source."

"And what are you thinking?" Black Star asked.

"Menagnetite."

"What's that?" Black Star inquired further.

"It's something Dad came across in his experiments regarding quantum teleportation and space travel. It's an alien mineral from outside of our solar system that has traveled here in small bits through multiple asteroids. It's almost impossible to find and because of this it's the rarest mineral on the planet."

"And how is a rock going to power my simulation chamber?" Black Star asked curiously.

"Because it's very similar to plutonium, uranium, and thorium on Earth, except that it's non-nuclear. I don't have all the details, as I'm no exobiologist, but it's as dangerous and powerful as it is rare."

"You don't have all the information? Impossible," Black Star jabbed.

"Shut the fuck up and go get me my rock," Maria snapped.

"Where is it?" Black Star asked.

"It's in a high-security research facility and military base in Brazil. I have the coordinates."

"You want me to steal from a country's government? Isn't that a felony of some kind?" Black Star joked dryly.

"Steal, yes. So, no killing." She walked towards the basement door and beckoned him to follow.

"Hey, that's a low blow," Black Star responded quietly. "For the record, I don't kill any more than I already have to. I'm not a monster." Maria had no response.

They both made their way down into the basement, which was Maria's office and lab area. She gave him the tour of her small lab and showed him some of her unfinished experiments and old prototypes.

"This research facility is in a military base, like I said, and it's located in the Amazon Rainforest on the western edge of Brazil. They won't take kindly to trespassers, so I have a suit that renders the wearer invisible when activated. You won't even be able to be seen by thermal or artificial reality imaging." Black Star let her finish because he could tell how interested and proud of her own creation she was, but he knew he wouldn't need it.

"That's nice, but I don't want it. Why would I spend all this time developing skills if I can just wear a suit and walk in?" Black Star stated.

"It's not noise-cancelling, dick. You'd still have to sneak."

"Sorry, it's not the same. Besides, I don't like to be unnecessarily slowed down or have to rely heavily on technology."

"Alright, suit yourself. At least take this encryption device. It'll get you through the door. Or do you just want to rely on your skills and kick the ten-thousand-pound blast doors in?"

"You make a fair point. I'll take it. Do you have anything for a fingerprint or orbital scanner?" Black Star inquired.

"I've got that covered. I was able to hack into their systems and put you in without them realizing the breach. I added a fake identity for you, so if you use this," Maria grabbed a piece of technology off her desk and handed it to Black Star, "and hook it up to the terminals then you should get through. They'll catch on eventually, but you should be able to get in and get out before they pin you down."

"No worries. I'm fast," Black Star said, grinning like a child.

"Right," Maria replied.

"Well, looks like you got me covered," Black Star stated after looking over the stuff Maria gave him. "Guess I don't need to prepare."

"One more thing," Maria said. "Take this earpiece too, so I can be your overwatch and tell you where to go in the facility."

"No thanks, I'm going to pass on that. You're taking away the challenge." Maria squinted at him. Black Star insisted on only the location and a map, plus what Maria had already given him.

As they walked back up the steps, Black Star asked one final question.

"What time is it?" he said as he closed the basement door behind them.

"About 7:30 in the evening," Maria replied. "Why?"

"I want to take a nap on your couch," Black Star answered. "Wake me up at 11 if I'm not already up. My body feels a little fatigued."

NINE

KAI

"Have we discovered the origin of the burn on the neck of Alphonse?" asked Alef, the embers in his pipe burning as he held it in his right hand.

"No, we have not," responded Gimel. "From what we've seen, the symbol doesn't exist. I've had my research team on it since Alphonse's body was discovered, and we've found nothing." Gimel, real name Atria, was a thirty-six-year-old Caucasian woman who owned the international technology company Trytek. Through the success of their research and development teams, Trytek revolutionized communication and artificial reality technologies for civilians through the creation and implementation of neural implants. Unbeknownst to the world, Atria led the Sicarii as Gimel, the third member of the High Council. Through her connections, Gimel and her company Trytek, along with the Engineers, secretly developed weapons and equipment, respectively, for the Sicarii.

The Engineers were a separate entity, not beholden to the laws of the Sicarii and the High Council. Formed before the second world war by the United States' government, the Engineers originally consisted of great minds like Robert Oppenheimer and Albert Einstein and were created in order to develop the first nuclear weapon. Over a century and a half later, the Engineers were now an internationally known organization, dedicated to the success and ethical implementation of technology around the world. The relationship between the Engineers and the Sicarii was mutually beneficial as the Engineers used the resources the Sicarii had to build better technologies which they, in turn, allowed the Sicarii to use.

Because of their focus on the ethical use of technology and Robert Oppenheimer's regret for the creation of the atomic bomb, the Engineers refused to build weapons or any other technology that could be used for offensive purposes and refused to assist Trytek in their weapon development for the Sicarii. They were, however, responsible for the creation of the pre-modified Archangel armor and the suits the Sicarii squads wore.

After a period of silence, Alef spoke up. He was sitting in his usual thinking position, hands clasped together in front of his face with his elbows firmly planted on the table in front of him. "Perhaps," he said, "we aren't looking in the right place."

"What do you mean?" asked Bet.

"Fetch Helel." Sofia moved from her place leaning against the wall to a spot in front of the High Council table.

"Are you implying it's magical in nature, Alef?" Vav interrupted, a tremble in her voice common in those who were older in age.

"I do not know," replied Alef, "but Sofia-"

"Yes, sir?" Sofia asked, waiting for orders.

"Find Helel and bring him to us. We require his opinion on this matter."

"It will be done." Sofia said before walking out. A knock on the door to the Council chambers directly followed Sofia's leave.

"Enter," Vav commanded. Verena walked through the door and locked it behind her.

"There's an issue," she said.

"Show us," Alef demanded. Verena walked to the center of the room and placed a small orb into the indention in the floor that Kai had previously deduced was purely aesthetic. In an explosion of color, the room was transformed into the sky and if one looked up, one would've been able to see the L.O.A.D.S. floating above.

"What is this?" asked Dalet.

"It's the Seed of the-"

"No, not that. I know what *that* is," Dalet said, pointing at the orb. "That's not what I mean. What are we looking at Verena? What happened?"

"My apologies, your excellency."

"Continue, Verena," Alef ordered, irritated.

"Right, so an hour ago, at 0530 our time and 1230 Swedish time Squad Four, leader "Kai", assassinated Adrian Blom as was ordered. Following this, the Swedish Police Authority chased the members of Squad Four through the old sewer system of Stockholm, where Squad Four escaped via personal aerial vehicle, named "Wingblades". They were then chased by weaponized military drones."

"And?" asked Alef, still irritated.

"The alchemist Amina was shot." Alef was unmoved, but the rest of the High Council became unsettled, and the air became thick enough to cut with a knife.

"What's her condition?" asked Alef.

"She's alive," replied Verena. "But she'll be out of action for quite some time. The drone tore a hole straight through her abdomen. She's lucky to be alive."

"And lucky my company built nanobots to stitch her back together," stated Gimel. The transformed room began playing like a video recording, allowing the High Council to see all the events that had unfolded during the mission. After witnessing everything with their own eyes, Vav turned towards Verena as she picked the small orb up and caressed it carefully in her hands.

"So, the drone was destroyed by Marlowe and Amina was caught by Kai, correct?"

"Correct," responded Verena.

"What level of knowledge was gained by the Swedish government?" Bet asked.

"It was a level one breach," answered Verena. "Squad Four was seen by the drones as was Amina's face. Due to the obliviation of the recorded existence of the Sicarii squad members, no information was gained by the Swedish government. Purgation and damnatio memoriae will not be required."

"Very good," responded Vav happily. "Less work for us then."

"And less work for our little rogue killer," interjected He, the fifth member of the Sicarii High Council and Director of the Central Intelligence Agency of the New States.

Bet slumped down in his chair and propped his feet up on the table. "Indeed, He. But perhaps it is time for Kai to get back on his feet and do what he's best at."

"I agree," said Alef. "Where is Kai now?" Alef asked, turning towards Verena.

"He is currently on his way back to Stockholm, sir."

"Why is he in Stockholm?" Alef's blood began boiling under his skin. His frustration was evident, and everyone could feel it.

"I'm sorry, but I do not know, sir," Verena replied, eyes glued to the floor.

Alef inhaled deeply to calm himself. "Find him and deliver the order to kill the rogue Gilroy."

"Right away, sir." Verena turned around and left the Council chambers immediately, leaving the High Council to contemplate the situation regarding Amina's punishment.

He spoke up first, expressing his concerns over the situation. After a deep breath, he started "Amina has been a problematic piece in our plan for a while."

"I agree. But she's necessary. Without a doubt her connection to the catalyst is of most importance to our plan," said Vav. As the High Council talked, Dalet sat there, quiet, uncaring of the conversation and uncaring of the decision made.

"Amina will be removed from active duty until she recovers. After she fulfills her purpose, she will be relieved of her position as a member of Squad Four and will be restricted to non-active duty within Headquarters as a medical specialist. All in agreement?" asked Vav. The old woman looked around the room as all nodded in acceptance of Amina's punishment.

"Good," said Alef, taking a slow draw from his pipe. As the smoke crept upwards the center of the Council chamber ceiling opened up, and from it descended a being shrouded in light. As it floated gently downwards, the sound of propulsion filled the room and drowned out all other noises. It was loud enough, even, that if the Council members were to try to converse, they would be unable to hear each other. Knowing this, they stayed silent as their hair and clothes danced with the wind that whipped past them violently.

The sound cut off immediately, and the being crashed to the ground. The light surrounding the entity trickled away, revealing magnificent armor, propulsion engines in the shape of wings on its back, and a ball of white light in the center of the torso. The armor reflected around eighty percent of the light that hit it, making it seem like a miniature star, or perhaps like the armor had been set ablaze, but as the light at the center of the entity faded slowly one could see the detailed symbols and runes covering the armor and the sheer size of the being compared to its surroundings. Standing near ten feet tall, the armored entity's eyes met the gaze of the council directly, despite their seating being elevated from the rest of the room. The wings on the back of the armor folded up as the being knelt in reverence of the Council, fixing its eyesight on the ground in front of it.

"Exit your armor, Helel ben Sahar," ordered Alef. The being stood up immediately and from its helmet down to its knees, the armor split in half and opened up, revealing a Caucasian man with shoulder-length brown hair pulled up in a knot, who was clothed in a specialized Sicarii suit that connected him to the mass of armor he controlled. After he dropped out of the armor it closed back up and its energy core, as well as its eyes, glowed faintly as it stood in an autonomous defensive position behind him. "We have something for you to look at."

"What can I assist with?" responded Helel.

"The dead rogue Alphonse," He cut in, "acquired a symbol on his vessel that is of deep interest to us. We want you to look at it."

"Where is this symbol?" questioned Helel, unsure of whether or not he could assist the council at all.

"Below you," stated Dalet. Helel looked down and saw the symbol projected on the floor. He knelt down and examined every facet of it: the geometry, the possible symbolism, the meaning behind the shape and the angles within and without said shape.

"I know this symbol," Helel said quietly. "Tell me, was it a burn or a tattoo?" he asked as he stood up and faced the Council.

"A burn," stated Gimel, "but a strange sort of burn, like it was-"

"Burnt into his essence?" finished Helel.

"Yes," spoke Alef after taking a puff on his pipe.

"And he's dead, you said?" asked Helel, once again.

"Yes," responded Vav. "Assassinated by the Squad Four leader Kai."

"For the best then," Helel said as he looked once more at the symbol.

"What is this symbol?" Alef inquired further.

"It's not a symbol, it's a seal, and it's called the-"

■■■■■■■■■ ■ ■ ▪ ▪ ▪ ▮ ▮

"Black Seed," Kai said to himself as he stood amongst the ruins of an ancient city in the Middle East, reading Alphonse's journal from the archaeological site at which he had led an excursion team a few months before his death.

December 18th, 2092

We have found Akkad. After years of searching, we have discovered the ruins beneath the endless, hot sand. A marvelous day for the Sicarii and a marvelous day for the world.

December 31st, 2092

Amongst the ruins of the ancient civilization lost to time, we have discovered one of the first temples of man. Filled with artifacts and tablets with citations of deep magicks, the temple was a true cave of wonders. Amongst the walls were carved great symbols and pictures, with phrases unknown to us and unseen before. On the largest wall behind what used to be an altar was a symbol, similar to that of a seed, fascinatingly enough considering the phrase above the symbol stated "Behold the Black Seed" in ancient Akkadian. Similarities between the way in which this "Black Seed" is revered and the Eucharist of Christianity become obvious to the theologian. However, a deep unsettled feeling washed over me as I stood there before that artifact of antiquity, as if death was slowly lurking behind me, as if a sweeping miasma was entering my very existence. It was a deep fear, one I had not felt since I was a boy, an irrational fear, yet a real one all the same.

Unfortunately for Kai, Alphonse's writings stopped there. There was no record of the disappearance of his team, or of the events predating his execution by Kai. It was a dead end, in all senses of the word, as there were no witnesses left alive, not even Alphonse himself. After finishing Al's journal, Kai had proved his theory: that the burn on Al's neck and the symbol on the wall in the sewers of Stockholm were not only one and the same, but that they were real.

"Transmission incoming Kai," Eris said suddenly.

"Who is it?" Kai asked, uncaring as he continued staring at the last entries in Alphonse's journal.

"It's Verena, for the High Council."

"Guess I have no choice," Kai responded coldly. "Put her through."

"Kai," Verena started. "Where are you? Your last known location was Stockholm, but that was an hour ago and we've lost your signal since then. Is something wrong with your tracker?"

"Yeah," Kai responded. Lying through his teeth. "I'm still in Stockholm. Just assessing the situation and making sure no evidence was left behind. I'll get my tracker fixed whenever I return."

"Well go ahead and come back now. The Council has a mission for you," Verena ordered.

"What kind of mission?" Kai asked as he closed the journal and tucked it away in the tan cloak he was wearing.

"It's for you and you alone."

"Who is it?" he asked, still uncaring, still melancholic as usual.

"Gilroy," Verena said calmly.

"Fine. Tell the Council it'll be done."

"Thanks, Kai," Verena responded kindly as Kai disconnected the call without a response.

"Returning to the Well?" Eris asked.

"That's the only move to make," Kai replied, sounding more

exhausted than ever. "The game has just begun and I'm already out of moves."

"Are you going to the Well for Gilroy, or for Alphonse?" Eris inquired further.

"Does it matter?" Kai asked rhetorically. "Either way I won't get the answers I'm looking for." Eris stayed silent after that, as she had no response to what Kai had said.

Kai made his way back to The City, and back to HQ, darkness gripping his heart, his mind, and his soul tighter than before. Alphonse was dead, his only true friend, his only brother, and it was his fault. His parents never existed, as far as he could remember, and the violence that ravaged his childhood followed him into manhood. Everything Kai had loved, he had lost. Almost every friend he made in the Academy had been killed by the time he became the leader of Squad Four, except for Alphonse and Piers, but now Al was gone too, and it was by Kai's own hand that his last friend was taken.

The only father figure Kai knew, Alef, had trained him to be the best, and had shaped him to one day lead the Sicarii by a seat on the Council, but he knew, deep down, that he was nothing more than a tool to Alef, a pawn in a greater game that not even Kai knew or understood. And yet, he was the Council's one and only assassin of assassins, betrayer of his own kind, nicknamed Judas by the rogues, but praised by the rest of the Sicarii. Renown, money, possessions, none of it stopped Kai from the desire of his own death, yet he was too pathetic, in his own mind, to end it himself. So, he kept fighting, kept killing, because there was nothing else he could do.

So tired, Kai thought. *Always so tired.* Eventually, he made his way back to the Greater Library, and walked through those old wooden doors. As he walked through, Haley saw him and smiled and waved at him, but he kept on his way, unwilling to return the favor.

That wasn't nice, Kai.

He continued walking, through the library, into the Well, and back out again after gaining the information he needed on Gilroy, and of course, not finding anything on Alphonse as all information on rogues is expunged from the record system through damnatio memoriae by the record keepers, post-assassination that is. As he exited the Well, Haley came up to him quietly.

"Are you okay?" she asked him, genuinely concerned. Kai looked at her, circles under his eyes, dead in his soul, and responded.

"I'm fine. It's not your job to worry about me, Haley. Thank you though."

"Are you sure you're alright?" Haley questioned again, unbelieving of his words.

"Yes."

"Okay." With that Kai walked away, out of the library and into the streets of HQ. He looked up, towards the ceiling of the cave, where the tip of the Spire met the massive stalactite that hung from the wet rock, where, as all knew, the High Council sat. Around the outside of the chambers, as always, floated three Seraphim in their suits of armor that reflected most of the light that touched them. That's why, people said, Headquarters was always so dark. If there was too much light, the Seraph Squad's armor would stop looking like bright torches and start blinding those who looked upon them.

On the rooftops of the buildings ran groups of Academy students, no doubt training for the world outside. The rooftops were not a necessity, but there was a reason why The City was laid out the way it was. Many of the buildings were grouped tightly together so that the Squads could mobilize more easily without being seen by the populous. The Squads weren't required to use the rooftops, but it made things easier, so the students of the Academy were trained to run across them. Leading the pack was one student, no doubt the head of the class, as Kai had been years prior. Memories of the Academy began pushing themselves to the forefront of Kai's thoughts, so he turned away and left Headquarters as quickly as possible.

Kai left Headquarters through a less known, more secluded exit, in order to avoid contact with anyone. He hadn't slept since the night before Adrian Blom's assassination, so he had been without sleep for around 48 hours and was exhausted. But sleep wouldn't cure his exhaustion because it never did, and he knew that. He ascended to the rooftops because he still carried his blade and wore his suit, so he couldn't risk, and didn't desire, drawing attention to himself.

Alone. Always alone.

Out of the darkness something began falling towards Kai from above, and if he wouldn't have dodged, the weapon held by the falling man would've crushed him instead of crushing the roof Kai was standing on. Kai flung himself out of the path of the weapon and landed roughly ten feet away from where the weapon destroyed the roof. Amidst the rubble stood a six and a half foot, muscular, brown-skinned, bald man, with nothing but boredom in his eyes.

"Gilroy," Kai said as he activated his helmet.

"Judas," that's what we normally call you, right? Kai made no move and responded in no way whatsoever. "I always thought that was humorous," Gilroy said. "Anyways, I figured I'd bring the fight to you and make this quick. I have no resentment towards you, but you're a predator to us and unfortunately, I have to attempt to stop you. No hard feelings, Kai."

"I respect you Gilroy, and I respect your talent. I am only following orders."

"I know you are. While I don't agree with you, or the Sicarii, I understand why you believe you must do this. So, let's not waste time. Fight me, Judas Iscariot, and gain the silver that matters not to you."

With that, Kai drew his blade, and Gilroy lifted his hammer, and the two ensued battle amongst themselves, the rest of humanity unaware of the impact of this war.

TEN

BLACK STAR

Secluded deep in the Amazon, a makeshift research facility lit up the particularly dark night. Deep, violent clouds covered the light of the moon as they thundered and flashed, and the torrential rain soaked everything below. The rain had been coming down for a few hours already, but as far as Black Star could tell no lightning had struck down since he had been there. A large military truck hauling containers and crates tore through the mud, heading for the base, and when it arrived inside of the gated area, Black Star hopped out and continued on foot. He had hitched a ride about a quarter of a mile back, figuring that a ride on the not-so-public transport would be a nice change of pace from running everywhere.

The government had been extremely careful with the alien mineral up to this point. They wanted to continue running tests on it first before escorting it off the premises and risking damage to it and everything around it. With the amount of energy it released on a daily basis, it could be extremely dangerous and could go critical at any point, even though they were sure it wasn't radioactive. Nevertheless, they kept it in the current facility to experiment on it as much as they could before doing anything else with it. Since the structure was temporary, it was composed almost entirely out of galvanized steel and vinyl fabric, which made it relatively easy to climb and was made even easier by Black Star's small stature and light equipment load.

Black Star remembered an outdoor area in the center of the facility from the map that he memorized earlier, so he climbed to the top of the makeshift complex, above the view of the spotlights at the watchtowers, and moved towards the center of the complex. The vinyl roof was slick from the rain, so Black Star stayed cautious as he hopped from one steel support to the next, careful not to step on an unsupported part of the roof, lest he fall through and blow his cover.

Can't go too fast, he thought. *If I use too much force a screw will come loose, a beam will pop off, and the whole section will come crumbling down.* Typically, Black Star disliked masks, but in a situation such as the one he found himself in, where stealth was required, he wore a simple black and white mask, separated by a diagonal line. Black Star found his way to the center of the makeshift complex, and to his surprise was not met with an outside atrium. Rather, there was a metal roof, unlike the rest of the complex, which was covered entirely in military-grade stealth technology.

I knew it would get interesting eventually, Black Star thought. *Let's see what we're dealing with.* Black Star tore a small hole in the roof to the south of the stealthed rooftop and peeked down inside where an empty, well-lit hallway sparkled immaculately like someone had just cleaned it. He tore the hole further and slipped inside, careful not to make a sound, and moved quickly north towards the center of the compound. As he reached the end of the hallway, he peeked around the left corner and saw a man at the end of the hall walking away from him and rounding the next bend with a mop bucket. Black Star dashed quickly to the metal door on the right wall and plugged in the hacking device that Maria gave him. After a few moments the door unlocked and he was met with a standard, empty lab room.

"I know you're here," he said out loud. "You can't hide from me." Black Star began looking around the room quickly, careful not to disturb anything until he found a hidden switch under one of the desks.

"Aha!" he said a little too excitedly. He pressed the button and a section of the wall across the room slid upwards, revealing a descending staircase. Black Star jogged down multiple flights of steps and opened the door at the bottom which led to a large concrete and steel warehouse-like area filled with metal storage containers, barrels, and the like. He saw a small camera across the room and looked around on the ground for a projectile. He found a small screw and threw it as fast as he could at the camera, destroying it in one hit. After destroying the camera, he looked around, and to his right he saw a massive blast door that no doubt led to the outside world, and the truck he had rode in on earlier, parked right in front of it.

I could've just rode the truck the whole way. Black Star thought to himself. *Why does this always happen to me?* He shook his head and walked over to the abandoned truck. He began investigating it and quickly realized that the cargo it was carrying was missing.

Where did you go? Black Star thought. He looked around and saw nothing but mostly empty containers. *You're around here somewhere.* He could smell the pungent odor of the transporters themselves and followed the driver's scent across the room to a small podium with buttons and switches. In the center was a large red button that made Black Star chuckle.

A big red button in a big secret room? How original.

Black Star hit the button and the floor beneath him began moving diagonally downwards and railings popped up around the four hundred square foot platform. Black Star peered off the edge and down into the elevator shaft that lit up as it descended.

I bet I could jump, he thought to himself. He decided against it and instead laid down on the floor. After a minute or so, he stood back up and peered over the edge again.

How fucking far does this thing go down? Jeez. At about that time, the elevator finished its descent and two armed guards stood waiting for the rails to drop. They walked onto the empty platform, looked around, and then one of the men spoke up.

"I don't see anything, control," the shaved-headed guard stated out loud. Black Star clutched to the ceiling of the corridor the men came from and watched them carefully.

"I mean there's no one here. There's nothing. Maybe there was a short in the electrical or something." The two men began walking back down the corridor and Black Star followed, clinging to the ceiling like a spider, careful to dash by the camera's line of sight whenever it was needed, making him quick enough for even those who noticed to not realize what happened. When Black Star truly *moved*, the average human mind couldn't comprehend what it saw, and it made excuses for what it thought was impossible. So many people, Black Star thought often, viewed the world as a coin, as possible or impossible, real or unreal, and it was always one way or the other. So, to the world, Black Star was an impossibility, a blur, a failure of the brain, and Black Star used this to his advantage.

Now to find this "control" the guard was talking about, Black Star thought. He tailed the two men for a bit until they led him to another locked door. The second guard waved his forearm in front of the panel next to the metal door and it slid open, and for a brief moment Black Star could see multiple computer monitors inside, which was enough for him to make his move. He took the opportunity of the opened door, dashed in faster than the eye could see, and took his spot on the ceiling of the control room as a gust of wind trailed behind him.

"Oh shit!" the second guard exclaimed as he shivered uncontrollably. "Who the hell turned on the A/C?"

"It wasn't me," one of the control room operators said. He looked to his left. "Was it you Jim?" Jim shook his head no without saying a word. "Jim says no," the first operator said to the second guard.

"Yeah, we can see that," the short-haired first guard said. "A lot of system issues today." The control room operator shrugged his shoulders as Black Star dropped down behind them. The two guards turned around and readied their firearms as fast as they could, but they fell first. The first operator was next, and after him Jim, and they slept in comfort, slouched over in their chairs unlike the guards whose unconscious bodies were collapsed on the floor. Black Star didn't kill them as these people did nothing to him and probably had families to go home to. Instead, his sleep darts did the trick and knocked all four of the men out before they even knew what happened.

Let's see if one of these cameras has the location of the rock and what I'll have waiting for me there, Black Star thought. He rolled the first operator out of the way and the chair twirled slowly until it lost momentum and bumped slightly into the wall across the room. He got on the console and peeked around through the different cameras in the facility and saw only what he expected: guards, lab assistants, and researchers, all studying various things. He found the area of the facility where they kept the menagnetite, which was, of course, filled with multiple researchers and lab assistants. A couple of guards stood outside of the area so as not to interfere with the researcher's work.

After finding what he was looking for, Black Star hacked further into the system with the help of Maria's tech and found information files on the kinds of things going on in the research facility. He found out that the facility was funded by the Brazilian government, to no surprise, and that the facility tends to deal with things in the world that are considered to be anomalies, keeping other world powers in the dark in order to gain the upper hand. Black Star dug a bit further and found files on a few interesting individuals that the facility had kept tabs on. One such individual was a jewel thief, a petty thief really, who stole just about anything he could get his hands on. No one had any clue how he escaped, and he never had any companions, so in many cases it was as if he vanished into thin air.

Well, I know what I'm doing next once I get out of here, Black Star thought. He gathered the rest of the info on the thief and left the room, breaking the internal access port in the process in order to ensure the door stayed locked from the outside.

Alright, let's go down two levels to the rock. It's pretty sneaky to have such a big facility like this this far underground. I bet this site has been used on more than one occasion. Black Star moved down the hallway to the elevator, but instead of waiting he pried the door open and jumped down the elevator shaft. A few moments of wind gusting around him marked the fall at about thirty feet. Whenever he landed, he looked up and the elevator was above him, coming straight down at him. He quickly pried the next door open and rolled out of the way just in time. As he stood up, he heard people rounding the corner down the hall, chatter and footsteps reverberating off the walls. He was at a three-way intersection, and they were coming from the left, so he took the corridor directly in front of the elevator and hid in a doorway until they passed. He moved back towards the elevator as the door opened and he dashed quickly down the hall where the group of people came from, every step lightly touching the floor.

Now he was, thankfully, on the right path.

After dashing down a few different white hallways, dodging the researchers that were pulling late hours, Black Star arrived at the door to the section of the compound that housed what he was after, and as he did a middle-aged woman's voice came over the intercom.

"There's been a breach. All areas will be shutdown effective immediately until the assailant is captured." With that, the emergency lights in the corridors began flashing red and all of the doors automatically sealed to ensure the safety and capture of the assailant at hand.

Where did I slip up? Black Star asked himself. *Did someone get into the control room?* Black Star tried to reflect, questioning every possibility, but only did so while pushing forwards. He was relieved that he took Maria's advice, so he plugged in the piece of tech she gave him and began overriding the lockdown on the door. Within a few seconds, the door unlatched and opened, and the researchers and guards inside stared at him as if they just saw a ghost. As quick as he could, Black Star dashed across the room towards the containment cell. One of the guards standing next to the cell in the center of the room went to lock it, but Black Star kicked him away, sending a shock of fear throughout everyone else in the room. No one discharged their firearms, as they didn't want to hit their comrades, but before anyone else could even try to stop him Black Star already had the material. He only needed about ten pounds of the dense metal, which ended up being only about the size of his fist, so he cracked it with the force from his hand, snatched it, and flitted out the door, firearms discharging behind him. As he arrived back at the elevator, he heard a stampede of booted soldiers coming for him down the middle hallway, so he hopped in the elevator and as the doors closed they fired towards him.

"He's in the elevator!" one of the guards shouted into his earpiece.

"Affirmative," another guard responded. "We're up here waiting. His exit is cut off."

But while they were waiting for him at the elevator, Black Star was in the stairwell, making his way to the highest possible exit.

What they were chasing was an after-image, a visual remnant created from his immense speed. It's not as if he was never in the elevator, and such a thing was a figment of their imagination, but rather he existed in the space for a brief moment, long enough just to be noticed, but not long enough to be riddled with bullets. When Black Star arrived at the top of the stairs and swung the door open, he was met with the storage area with the blast door that he had started out in. He looked around, bewildered, and tried to rationalize how he had not seen this door previously.

Seriously, every time! he thought. Despite Black Star's keen senses, he tended to miss obvious things like this time and time again, which almost always made his job harder than it needed to be. He looked to his left, and where the blast door was originally was a massive hole. The truck sitting by the blast door was on fire and in ruins, and blood and limbs littered the warehouse.

I don't remember making this entrance, but I'll take it, he thought.

Even though the place was supposed to be on high alert, he didn't see anyone but the bodies in the warehouse. So, he dashed through the hole and immediately sank into the mud a few inches, covering his shoes completely. He pulled one foot out, and then the next, and began running as quick as he could through the mud, weaving between any searchlights that might be trying to spot him. As he left, he wondered why no one was chasing him if the security was on such high alert, but his inner voice was drowned out by the obnoxious sirens that screamed into the darkness of the jungle. Even if they wanted to, the guards in the watchtower wouldn't be able to spot Black Star on such a dark night. Lightning finally struck, however, streaking across the sky and lighting up the jungle for a brief moment, but Black Star was already gone. He had already disappeared into the deep jungle ahead. When the guards did finally arrive, all they saw were his footprints in the mud, water still rippling from where he had stepped. Despite that, they gave no chase.

As he moved outside the fenced area and made it to the jungle, the mud caked heavily on his shoes and legs, each step sinking deeper into the thick sludge. Looking ahead he could see that it was not as deep, and once he reached it, he became untraceable as he jumped up into the treetops and ricocheted from trunk to trunk like a human pinball.

Someone is chasing, no, watching me. Actually, there's a smaller, sharper presence here as well, Black Star realized shortly after leaving the facility. *They need work on containing their aura. I can feel it leaking out of them. But they're too far away to try to engage. Looking back would only let them know that I am aware of their presence. I'll play coy, for now.* Black Star continued dashing through the trees as quickly as he could, despite the wetness of the branches and the muddiness of his shoes.

They don't seem to be together, he continued thinking, *because they feel like they are on different levels. It could be a student and a master... or perhaps...*

Black Star continued dashing through the trees and had little time to inspect each tree branch since his mind was focused on other things. He didn't worry though, and he kept his guard on high alert, but one of the trunks he bounced off was slicker than anticipated, and he began falling, perhaps due to his lack of attention. He hit the ground and slid due to the wetness of the mud, creating a trail behind him, until his momentum came to a stop. He laid there for a bit in shock.

This must be what defeat feels like...

He laid in the rain, stuck in the mud, and hesitated for a moment before pulling himself up and beating some of the mud off his shoes, enough for him to walk evenly on each foot.

"Maria owes me big time," he mumbled under his breath. "Soiling my good clothes..."

As the rain continued to fall, Black Star continued jogging back to civilization, knowing that he couldn't clean himself off properly until he was out of the mud. He was so worried about the mud that nothing else really seemed to matter, because more than anything he absolutely despised being dirty. To Black Star, one of the worst feelings imaginable was having dirt under his nails. On top of the dirtiness, the added weight of mud clinging to his shoes was simply annoying, and the sensation of the mud on his skin made him furious and made him feel like he was coated in a second layer of skin." Despite his frustration, he contained it, even as his shoes made squishing noises on the damp ground. He did his best to block out the noise. He knew he was far enough away from the compound now to slow down, but he didn't want to, as he wanted to get out of his current situation as fast as possible. He continued to think on his previous thoughts before he fell, and his mind moved to the other intruder at the research facility.

Did they have the same idea as me? he thought. *Their intrusion made for an easy escape for me, but that person probably won't have it so easy, and they definitely won't be happy when they find out that a chunk of what they came for is missing, if that is indeed what they came for.*

But, with more questions than answers, which had become a recurring thing for Black Star, he was just happy knowing that it was not him who was directly detected and that his skills were not as dull as he feared. He made his way to the edge of civilization and checked his pocket, just to make sure he still had the menagnetite. He patted himself down, turned out every pocket he could, and true terror fell over him.

"Oh, damn it fell out!" he yelled. Black Star clutched his head as anxiety washed over him. After a few moments, he regained his composure.

New objective! he thought. *Find what was lost.* He began retracing his steps, sure that it must have fallen out around the time he fell. *I'm sure the guards are still patrolling, so I'll have to be extra careful.* He checked his clock for the time.

12:03 a.m.

"Jeez. What a marvelously muddy midnight."

ELEVEN

AMINA AND KAI

Why do you love a man that doesn't love you back?
Because I'm an idiot.
You love him because of his renown.
No.
You love him because of his money.
No.
You love him because of his power.
No.
Then why do you love him?
Because he's beautiful.
But he's broken.
So am I.
But he kills people.
So, do I.
But he's lost.
So am I.
So why do you love him then when you hate yourself?
I don't know.
Why do you hate yourself?
I don't know.
Why do you hate yourself?
I don't know.
Why do you hate yourself?
Because I'm not worth loving. Because I'm pathetic and miserable and selfish and stupid and I'm not worth it!
You messed up.

I know I did.

That's what happens when you try to have fun.

I know.

So then why do you try?

I just want to be happy. I want to smile. I want to be loved.

But you don't deserve to be loved, you said it yourself.

...

You try too hard with him. You know him well enough to know that your body won't attract him.

I know.

So then why put yourself out there? Why show him your nakedness?

Because I want him! I love him! And... I hate myself for it.

You know the Kai you see is not the real Kai.

I know that the Kai I see is just my perception of him and nothing more, but I desire him anyway because I desire who he truly is.

Is that why you touch yourself to the thought of him, despite it all?

...

You're pathetic.

Amina continued laying in the hospital bed, staring at the white ceiling. Her blueish green hair filled with sweat and blood, untamed and wild after being pulled out of her buns by the wind. Tears rolled down her cheeks, but she did nothing to stop them. The pain set in like a burn, and it spread further, as it had continued to do her whole life.

I really fucked up.

The white, glossy door to her room opened, so Amina finally wiped away her tears as a middle-aged South American woman in a white, knee-length lab coat walked in.

"Hi Amina. My name is Doctor Áñez. How are you feeling?"

"Fine," Amina replied, making eye contact with her. "I've been worse."

"That's good," the doctor said, but then paused nervously. "I'm sorry to have to be the one to tell you this, but I have bad news." Amina didn't move, but shifted her eyes back to the white ceiling, unfazed by what the doctor had said. Dr. Áñez hesitated as she scoured Amina's face for any sort of reaction but continued after no such discovery was made.

"When you were shot, Amina, your..." Dr. Áñez took a deep breath. "...ovaries were destroyed. We tried to repair them... and did... but you no longer have eggs. You won't be able to have children, love. I-I'm so sorry." Amina said nothing as Dr. Áñez squeezed her arm. A deep silence filled the room for what seemed like an eternity as Amina lay there, staring at the ceiling, and as Dr. Áñez sat there staring at her worryingly. Finally, Dr. Áñez spoke up. "Let me know if you need anything, sweetie. I'm always here for you." Amina nodded. "I'll leave you be then," Dr. Áñez said hesitantly. She slowly walked out the door and closed it softly behind her. Amina stared at the ceiling for a few more seconds, and then rolled over onto her right side, wrapped her arms around her waist, and cried harder than she had ever cried before.

■■■■■■■■■■ ▪ ▪ ▪ ▪

Kai and Gilroy continued clashing on the rooftop as the crisp night air flowed through them. Both were sweating profusely, and Kai was more aware than he had been in a long time. His muscles were sore from dodging Gilroy's relentless hammer swings because he knew that if he took a direct hit from the hammer, even with the Sicarii suit on, it would shatter his ribcage. Kai hadn't had to catch his breath during a fight in a long time, but he could feel himself gasping for more air with each passing minute.

"Getting tired Kai?" Gilroy asked, a smile on his face. "Come on! Fight me like you mean it!" He lifted his arms slightly in a taunting motion, opening his torso up. "Fear cuts deeper than the sword, but that mask doesn't scare me, so you're going to have to do better than that!"

"Eris... where's the L.O.A.D.S.?" Kai asked, desperately trying to catch his breath.

"It's over the Atlantic, near the ruins of New York City."

"Bring it here," Kai demanded.

"Order sent. ETA five minutes," Eris replied.

Kai charged forward, Shatter in his right hand, and dodged under Gilroy's hammer swing. He launched his left fist into Gilroy's gut and Gilroy responded by bashing Kai's helmet with the end of the hammer staff, cracking it in the process. Kai fell backwards and Gilroy came down on him with a swing of his hammer, which Kai rolled out of the way of, getting back to his feet as quickly as possible. Gilroy swung viciously, and Kai attempted to deflect every swing as best as he could with his sword, but the weight of the hammer destroyed Kai's posture with every sweeping blow.

"I expected more from the leader of Squad Four!" Gilroy said through a flurry of blows. "You can do better than this!" Kai was on the defensive, as he had been for most of the fight, and he struggled more and more to deflect each of Gilroy's vicious sweeps. Kai deflected a swing coming from his right, knocking Gilroy's hammer upwards, and through the opening impaled Gilroy in his left leg, penetrating his armor, shredding flesh and shattering bone in the process.

Kai looked up, and Gilroy smiled, grabbed Kai's blade while it was still in his leg, choked up on his hammer, and shoved it, with one hand, into Kai's gut, knocking the wind out of him. Kai pulled out his blade too late, as a hammer swing from his left caught his ribcage, sending him flying across the rooftop and shattering multiple ribs at the same time. Kai hit the rooftop hard and after rolling, propped himself up on his right arm. Shatter was too far away from him, as he lost the blade in the air, and because of this he had no way to defend himself from the oncoming deathblow Gilroy would soon deliver.

"Kai! The L.O.A.D.S. is above us!" Eris shouted in his helmet.

"Drop... it..." Kai ordered, barely catching his breath.

"But Kai-" Eris began to argue.

"DROP IT NOW!" Kai screamed.

Gilroy flung himself towards Kai and right before landing, was tossed back as an object crashed through the roof and into the building below. Citizens below looked up in horror as smoke billowed out the top of the office building and began fleeing as fast as they could. Police officers that witnessed the scene called for backup and chaos ensued on the ground.

Kai rolled into the hole created by the orbital drop and fell into the room below, where a massive suit of blackened armor was knelt on the ground, it's back opened up. Kai collapsed his helmet and limped into the armor holding his side. The suit closed up around him and the interior lit up red as it connected to Eris who assisted him in controlling its systems.

"Artificial neural link initiated," Eris stated. "Life-support system activated. Injecting epinephrine and morphine now." A needle stuck into Kai's neck and shot adrenaline and painkillers throughout his body, numbing the pain from his ribs and giving him energy to continue the fight. The artificial ribcage in the suit held Kai's own ribs together in order to prevent more damage and Kai let out a scream of pain as the suit fully locked into place.

"Armor of the King initialized. Offensive and defensive systems are fully operational, Kai. You're ready to go." Kai took a deep breath and jumped out of the hole and back onto the roof. Standing eight feet tall, the armor stood above Gilroy by a little over a foot, with the spikes of the crowned head adding only another inch or so to the height.

"Now that's what I'm talking about!" yelled Gilroy, standing roughly ten feet away from Kai. Gilroy pressed a button on his suit, hardening his armor and supporting his leg in order to prevent more damage to it. "I haven't had to lock my armor in years - ever since I was a young man and a fresh captain! That was over a decade ago. You were still running around the Headquarter rooftops during those days, just a child, and now a grown man! Fight me like one, my friend! And let us see if you live up to your name!" Gilroy was more excited now than ever, and it showed on his bronze skin as his laugh lines appeared more deeply, like canyons in the earth.

Kai picked up Shatter and sheathed it in the metal scabbard attached to the Armor of the King. When he pulled it back out the scabbard came with, forming the blade into a much wider, much longer one.

"So, you're the one who wields it, huh?" Gilroy asked, rhetorically. "Well, this just makes the fight all the more exciting!" Finished with the one-sided conversation, Kai charged his opponent, and swept the chunk of diamond-edged steel diagonally from left to right, dragging it across the rooftop to throw rubble upwards along with the blade. Gilroy dodged backwards, but Kai's assault was merciless.

Gilroy was on the defensive now, and as he deflected each incredible blow, he kept smiling and laughing, having the time of his life. Kai's thoughts, memories, and mistakes were pushed to the back of his mind, locked away for now, and the only thing he was focused on was the mission: killing Gilroy. That is what he was ordered to do, and like any good soldier Kai followed orders without hesitation. The mission came before anything: before his life, before his teammates lives, before his happiness and his sorrow.

Kai never failed to complete a mission and that's exactly why he had nowhere else to go but up. Above him was Seraphiel's seat on Seraph Squad, and then finally a seat on the High Council. But none of that mattered to him, not really. He didn't care about power, or success, or money or fame. Kai only moved upwards and forwards in life because he saw nowhere else to go. If Kai wasn't driven by some unknown urge to keep pushing forward, he surely would've ended it long ago.

Gilroy's hammer caught the left side of the armor on Kai's left knee and crushed it immediately. Aiming for the joints in Kai's armor, Gilroy planned to restrict Kai's movements exponentially through repeated bashing of the armor in those areas. With a second unblocked swing, Gilroy crushed the right side of the armor on Kai's right knee. One more swing to either joint would fully damage the armor around one of Kai's knees, causing immense pain and restricting his movement of that joint permanently for the remainder of the fight. Kai swung downwards with a diagonal cut on Gilroy's shoulder, but barely missed him as the excited, bronze man twisted out of the way of the blade, all the while pulling his hammer behind him and launching it forwards with a momentous swing of his massive arms, towards Kai's right knee.

Painfully aware of Gilroy's plan, Kai jolted his leg out of the way, and grabbed Gilroy's face with his left hand. Gilroy brought his hammer upwards with both hands and crushed the armor on

Kai's left elbow, to which Kai responded with a massive kick to Gilroy's torso, easily shattering multiple ribs in the process. Kai's anger and sadness gave way to indifference as his thoughts receded and were replaced with emotionlessness. When Gilroy landed a few feet away, he coughed up blood onto the rooftop and attempted to stand, but Kai was on him again with a shoulder charge, launching him further away and into a generator on the roof. The neon lights from The City cascaded around them, igniting their struggle with hues of purple, pink, and blue. Sparks flew from the generator as Gilroy collapsed on the roof once again, with more pain flowing through his body than he had felt in his lifetime. Kai walked to him and looked down upon his target, massive blade in hand.

"Do you still smile, Gilroy? Or does the taste of death frighten you too much?" Gilroy looked up to Kai with a massive grin on his face and his teeth covered in blood. He attempted to laugh but coughed up more blood in the process. "This ends only one way," Kai continued.

"I know," replied Gilroy as he shot forward, past Kai's immobilized left arm, and towards his hammer that he had lost during Kai's shoulder charge. Because of the damage dealt to the armor surrounding Kai's knees, he couldn't turn quickly, and before he knew it Gilroy was charging back towards him, hammer in hand. By the time Kai turned, Gilroy was on him, and with a twist of the handle of his hammer he ignited the back of it like a rocket, and swung it directly into Kai's helmet, sending Kai flying backwards, through the generator and off towards Gilroy's left. Kai smashed into the rooftop, cratering it in the process, and Gilroy rushed him again, with his hammer behind him to his right, ignited in the back with blue flames. And as Gilroy reached Kai, Kai propped himself up, brought his blade up with his right hand, and cut deep into Gilroy's left side, through his armor, his ribs, and his lung, and flung him away with one powerful, mortal blow.

"Critical engine failure," stated Eris. "Damage sustained by joints and crown at 98%. Armor of the King lock commencing in ten seconds." Eris opened the back of the armor and Kai climbed out, beaten and bruised, holding his side where his ribs had been broken earlier. Sweat and blood dripped from his face and onto the rooftop as he walked slowly over to Gilroy. As he got closer, he could hear Gilroy wheezing, holding on to the little bit of life he had left. Gilroy looked at Kai approaching and smiled, just as he had done before, and Kai stood over him as he attempted to speak.

"This was your plan all along, wasn't it?" asked Kai. Gilroy wheezed again and his voice cracked as he spoke up.

"Yeah, little one... it was." Memories flooded back to Kai, and he re-lived his time at the academy. Training, running, fighting, studying, all of it came back. The nights in the library with Alphonse and Piers, and the incessant jokes Alphonse would make about anything and everything. And, not least of all, the words of kindness and inspiration from the dying man lying in front of him that helped him so long ago.

"You haven't called me that in a long time, teacher," said Kai, compassion in his voice.

"You'd... forgotten... hadn't you?" Gilroy said as he attempted a laugh.

"I've forgotten much, it seems."

"It's..." Gilroy wheezed again. "...to be expected... I suppose."

"Forgive me," Kai said as he crouched closer to Gilroy.

"There is nothing... for me... to forgive. You must forgive... yourself, Kai."

I can't. I can't forgive myself...

"Don't listen... to that voice... in your head." Kai's expression must have changed without him noticing, because now Gilroy was looking directly into his eyes. "My hammer... bring it here..." Gilroy ordered, wheezing even more now. "Perhaps there is... one more thing... I can teach you." Kai retrieved Gilroy's hammer across the rooftop and brought it back to him. "The handle... switch... bottom... open it..." Kai pressed the button on the bottom of the handle, and it opened like a door. A small, rolled, piece of paper fell on the rooftop and Kai picked it up after laying the hammer on the ground. "He's... coming..." Gilroy said shakily.

"Who's coming?" asked Kai, worried.

"Hide... it..." Kai put the rolled paper into the pocket of his jacket. "The answers you seek... are at... your beginning. Find them... and the truth... will set you free..."

"What beginning?" asked Kai. "What answers?" Gilroy smiled one last time as the light left his eyes.

"Everything... is a lie..." With that Gilroy died, and since the beginning of their fight Kai became extremely aware of his surroundings. Police lights surrounded the building and Kai could hear boots pounding on the concrete below him. He could hear engines and propellers in the distance as what he could only assume were VTOLs began closing in on his position.

I'm fucked.

Two bi-copter VTOLs surrounded the building. Their engines roared and the light around them died on their Vantablack bodies as they came in closer. A third VTOL swooped in and hovered on the edge of the roof. The door opened and out stepped a suited Alef, with pipe in hand as always. His wing-tip black shoes clacked on the rooftop as he walked towards Kai and before speaking, he inhaled his pipe deeply, blowing the smoke into the wind.

"You caused a lot of problems this time!" he yelled over the roar of the engines.

"Why are you here?" Kai yelled back. Alef answered only with an order.

"Get in! We'll clean this up." The two other VTOLs descended onto the roof and out of them came people dressed in all black hazmat suits, with a hovering stretcher.

"Take the armor too!" Alef shouted at them. They nodded and moved towards Kai and Gilroy. Kai stood up and grabbed Shatter out of his armor's scabbard and walked towards the VTOL, Alef right behind him. They climbed into it and immediately began flying away towards Isarcii Pharmaceuticals. After a long silence, Alef spoke up.

"What did he say to you?" Kai continued looking out the window and down onto The City. Its lights shone deep into the atmosphere, and he could see advertisements for food, women, drugs, and stores upon many of the rooftops and the sides of the skyscrapers. Even from up here, he hated it.

"He spoke only of his memories of me in the Academy, ones which I barely remember."

"I see. Well, he was a teacher of yours for a very long time and he helped you secure your spot as leader of Squad Four. You must feel upset that you had to kill him." Kai knew what Alef was doing, but he was no fool to fall for Alef's games and he continued looking out the window of the VTOL.

"I feel nothing. I killed him because I was ordered to. I wasn't ordered to feel sympathy for a traitor." Alef grinned as he looked at Kai.

"Good," He lit his pipe once again and began smoking. "Your armor will be confiscated and after the investigation it will be destroyed. Gilroy's records will be expunged from the system and subsequent damnatio memoriae will follow. Speak of this to no one, understood?"

"Understood," answered Kai. But he already had what he wanted, and the information he needed was locked away safe in his and Eris's memories.

Arriving at the roof of Isarcii Pharmaceuticals, Kai stepped out of the VTOL while Alef remained inside.

"Amina's awake!" Alef shouted at him over the sound of the rotors. Kai nodded and began walking away as the VTOL ascended into the night sky and flew off into the distance. After opening the rooftop door, he descended down a dark stairwell and into a room that had only an elevator in it. As he approached it, the elevator doors opened and Kai descended, once again, into the depths of Sicarii Headquarters.

After exiting the elevator in the white-marbled commuter plaza, Kai walked as calmly as possible while holding himself together as his broken ribs began aching him again, proof that his body had metabolized the cocktail of drugs much too fast. Covered in dust, sweat, and blood, the only thing keeping Kai together was the leftover energy from his battle with Gilroy and the small note Gilroy had left him, a note which he had yet to read. He had not opened it, despite it nagging his mind, because he didn't know who was watching. So, Kai trudged on, into the pod, into Headquarters, and walked out of the Spire and into the Castrum which was connected to the south side of the Academy. It was at the Castrum where those who were honored enough to be members of the Twelve Sicarii Squads were permitted to sleep and eat, as well as the place where they stored their weapons, accessories, and Sicarii suits.

Kai entered the Castrum in a sweat and as he began to approach his armor locker he heard voices in the bath house down the hall, coming his way. The locker room was dark, with only the lights from the bath house down the corridor and the small blue lights on each of the lockers faintly illuminating the room. He quickly hid in the dark behind a row of ceiling-high lockers against the wall to his left, clutching his broken ribs, and listened to the conversation they were having.

Their muffled voices began getting louder as they approached their own lockers and Kai could faintly make out who they were by their voices. One was a woman in her early thirties and another one was a man of near the same age, the latter of which had a husky voice that he could only assume to be Joseph's, the second in command of Squad Nine. The woman then, Kai deduced, must be the Black Death Mahta, leader of Squad Nine and the most dangerous alchemist in the Twelve, as the two of them were almost always seen together. There had been rumors circulating amongst HQ that they were secret lovers, but Kai had cared not for their supposed love affair, and because of that stayed out of the childish gossip scene. Joseph's words had been the first that Kai could understand, and it was what Joseph said that bothered him most.

"Gilroy is dead," Joseph said as he and Mahta walked closer and closer towards Kai's position.

"How long ago?" Mahta responded.

"Less than an hour, and it was Kai who did it."

"Kai? Don't tell me Gilroy went dark side on us," Mahta responded shocked.

"It seems so, ma'am," Joseph replied, sullenly. Mahta and Joseph stopped fifteen feet down from Kai, dripping and silent.

"Gilroy was a good man. It saddens me to see him fall so far, Joseph," Mahta said, almost in tears.

"I understand the way you feel. He was a good friend to the both of us," Joseph responded, comforting his superior with a soft, olive-skinned hand on her wet, bronze shoulder. Kai peered around the corner stealthily, assessing his situation in order to find any semblance of an escape route, but found nothing in the process other than Mahta and Joseph's chiseled, wet bodies staring back at him. Mahta turned around towards her locker and dropped the towel covering her. Joseph turned away too, opening his locker door on the opposite side of the row, but left his towel on.

"Joseph," Mahta said as she turned around towards him, causing Kai to quickly go back to his position in the dark, grimacing all the while.

"Yes, ma'am?" Joseph responded, turning as he let his towel fall to the floor.

"Why do I not stiffen you?" she asked, curiously, and almost melancholic, as she stared at his hanging, circumcised penis. She closed in on him carefully and pressed her breasts against his chest softly. Joseph wrapped his arms around her and held her as lovers hold each other in times of need. She rested her forehead on his shoulder.

"I'm sorry, ma'am, but you know I only find intimacy in the bed of someone similar to myself."

"You mean someone with a cock?" she asked softly. Joseph blushed, seemingly ashamed of himself.

"Oh, my love," Mahta said as she lifted her head off his shoulder and stroked his shaved cheek. Do not be ashamed. You are who you are, and I love you all the same. You are my oldest friend and I hate to see you hiding your true self." Joseph smiled at her, and she smiled back.

"Also," Mahta added, with a comically irritated look on her face. "Stop calling me ma'am." Joseph laughed and she did too and at the same time Kai grunted softly as a pain from his ribs shot through his body. Mahta stopped laughing immediately and turned in his direction.

"What is it?" Joseph asked.

"Shh," she said softly, placing a finger over her mouth. "I think someone's here." Kai was stuck, and he knew it. There was nowhere for him to go and if they found him, after what he heard, they may kill him where he stands, and he couldn't take the risk of anyone finding Gilroy's note on him. Wounded as he was, Kai was in no shape to fight, and any attempt at a melee would end in his demise. Kai tapped the button on the back of his neck twice and his helmet closed over his head.

"Activating light refraction," Eris said quietly in his ear. Kai's suit cloaked shoddily, as it had been damaged severely in his fight with Gilroy, but it was enough in a dark room like the one he was in. Mahta closed in and Kai could hear her wet feet tapping softly against the tile floor. She stopped at the end of the lockers, her eyesight just past their edge, and she looked in his direction. She saw him, and he knew it. He was dead.

Mahta looked away, having trouble taking her eyes off him, and looked left and then straight.

What is she doing? he thought, almost terrified.

"I smell you, Rogue Killer," she said in a whisper, quiet enough for Joseph to not hear her. "I don't know why you're hiding, but I trust you have your reasons. Go, while you still can. We will be gone soon." She turned around and walked back towards Joseph.

"I guess it was just my imagination," she said with a chuckle. "All this emotional talk is making me nervous." Joseph laughed as well, and the two of them went back to their lockers and began changing into their normal clothing. Kai darted across the lockers and away from both of them. They finished clothing themselves in silence, grabbed both of their bags, and walked out the way Kai had entered. When they were out of sight and out of hearing distance, Kai let go of his breath and hurried over to his own. He opened the black, ceiling-high door with his handprint and it pushed open. A rack with an assault rifle, two handguns, and a place for his sword and Sicarii suit pushed forth and Kai stepped aside so it could extend fully. Kai's locker was the exact same as almost all the others, except for his weapon rack which was made specifically to his own taste. Kai rarely used firearms but having ones handy just in case never hurt.

All members of the Sicarii, Twelve or not, were trained in the use of melee and ballistic weapons. Those who passed all of their physical, psychological, and scholarly exams at the end of their time at the Academy were given aptitude tests for higher assignment. Those tests decided where students of the Academy should be placed, and whether or not they should be handed over to a Squad recruiter. Those who weren't given over to a recruiter were assigned high positions in the Sifriyah, like Haley, the Spire, the Reactor, the Castrum, or back at the Academy as professors. Those with highly specialized talents, like Alphonse, were sent on missions relating to those talents. Had Alphonse lived longer, Kai had thought, perhaps he would have been a professor or even the leader of a squad like Kai was. Or maybe, he had never meant to be anything more than the best friend Kai had ever had.

Kai's energy dwindled as he took off his helmet and tore his Sicarii suit at the hips, seemingly shredding the fibers that wove it together. This is what the suits did. The jet-black, skin-tight Sicarii suits came in two pieces: leggings with boot-like footwear built in, and a long-sleeve top that stretched to the chin of the wearer, protecting them from neck to toe. When both pieces were worn, the threads of each wove together to form a single, seamless, protective armor that stopped projectiles and possible damage that would be caused by blunt-force and slashing trauma. The suit was like a second set of muscles and looked like it too. The black strands woven throughout the suit imitated muscle fibers in their look, giving the wearer a much brawnier appearance if nothing was worn over it. When running and jumping, the suit acted like muscles, stretching and compressing to give the wearer a small boost to their speed, height to their jump, as well as minimal shock absorption should they fall a little too far.

Now naked, Kai could inspect his damaged body further. His left side, from shoulder to hip, was a dark purple: a sign that Gilroy may have shattered more of his ribs than he had liked. His knees and arms were bruised too, though not as bad, and his hair was caked with blood on the left where Gilroy had struck him with his hammer. Kai, still holding Gilroy's note in his hand, hobbled down the hall slowly and after what seemed like an eternity found himself in the bath house. The steam from the fragrant waters rose gracefully and swept themselves into his nostrils, clearing his mind and helping him think more clearly. After checking to make sure there was nothing or no one watching him, he unraveled the scroll-like note and read it slowly.

After reading, Kai dipped into the pool and sunk low, covering his head with hot water, and let the paper note dissolve in the process. The blood from his hair leaked out and turned the water almost pink around him, but it was swept away as a filtration device pulled it and the paper bits in. After his bath, his bruises seemed to have lightened, perhaps due to the waters in the bath, but his mind was even heavier than before. Gilroy's note deeply troubled him, but he had no clue what it meant. It was the exact same with Alphonse's writings.

Everywhere Kai went, every clue he thought he found was just another dead end, or so it seemed. He walked back over to his locker and after drying off, put on his street clothes which consisted of black slim jeans, black form-fitting sneakers with white stitching, a charcoal-colored t-shirt that clung to his muscular shoulders and chest and hung loosely down his torso, and his black, high-collared, weather-proof jacket. He gathered his helmet and suit top and bottom and placed them in a green canvas duffel bag that he grabbed before closing his locker. His stomach roared at him, demanding food, so Kai walked to a five-stool ramen bar a couple of minutes away from the Castrum and sat down alone at the bar.

"I'll be with you in just a minute," the shop owner said while stirring a pot of broth, not looking at who entered under his well-lit, steam-filled roof. Kai didn't respond and had no need to look at the menu on the wall in front of the shop owner as he always ordered the exact same thing.

"Humans are creatures of habit" he remembered Gilroy saying to the class during a combat-training session in his second-to-last year at the academy.

Even me, I suppose, Kai thought sullenly.

The shopkeep turned around and looked at Kai, his eyes growing wide at the sight of him. "Kai!" he yelled, excited. "It's been too long! How have you been?" The bald, fifty-year-old Japanese shopkeep wiped his hands off on the towel hanging from his apron and reached out his hand to shake Kai's. Kai met him in the middle, and they shook strong like men do as Kai answered his question.

"I've been better, Murimoto-san. How's business?"

"Please call me Sohei, Kai," Murimoto said, his forehead wrinkling in the process. "We've been friends too long for all the formalities. I'm not a squad leader anymore. But business has been alright: not too bad and not too good. People these days rarely care for fresh food when medicine can give them the nutrients they need. It doesn't seem right to me. The human body needs food. But... what do I know?" he shrugged, almost sadly. "I'm getting too old for all this I think."

"I feel the same way," Kai said as he took off his jacket. "Nothing beats real food, and nothing comes close to comparing to your tonkotsu ramen."

At that, Sohei Murimoto, the gentle, but serious man, smiled. "You're too kind to an old man like me. This one's on the house, with chashu, negi, and egg, just the way you like it."

"Thanks, Sohei," Kai replied with a hint of a grin. "It means a lot." Sohei turned around and began preparing Kai's ramen as Kai thought over Gilroy's note in his mind.

> *"Lilac death in the ruins of old joy,*
> *Will bring you back to the love you lost,*
> *Amidst the storm's bite."*

I don't understand, Kai thought. *I never understand anymore.*
Or perhaps, the other voice of his said, *you never did.*
After a few minutes of being stuck in deep thought, Sohei turned back around and handed Kai his bowl of ramen. The scent of the pork broth, green onions, and ginger filled Kai's nostrils and lifted his spirits, even if only by a little, but a little was just enough to give him the courage to raise his bastard of a problem to another.

"Sohei," Kai said hesitantly. "Can I ask you a question?"

"Of course," Sohei responded, eyes locked on Kai's.

"Alright, well," Kai started, "what do you think of whenever you hear the phrase 'ruins of old joy?'" Sohei grasped his chin with his left hand and began staring at the floor. After a few seconds, he answered.

"Figuratively, I think of past loves, ones lost to time."

"And the ruins would be memories of those loves?"

"Hai," Sohei responded.

"What about literally?" Kai furthered.

"Literally?" Sohei asked, curious. After seeing Kai's serious look, he pondered again. "Literally, I would think of an abandoned area where a person or many people would find or rather gain joy, like an amusement park or an athletic stadium."

Kai continued to prod Sohei's mind. "Are there abandoned areas like that anywhere in The City? From before the Sicarii rebuilt it?" Sohei thought long and deep, but after a minute or so arrived nowhere.

"Not that I can think of off the top of my head. I'm sure there's plenty of places like that in The City, but a city as huge as the one above our heads is hard to wrestle with," he chuckled. Kai sat thinking, his hands clasped in front of his face, with his elbows on the table. Every time he went into deep thought, he found himself like that. And every time he found himself like that, he changed because it reminded him of Alef, his liar of a father.

"Tell you what," Sohei said in reaction to Kai's aura of disappointment. "If I think of anything, I'll give you a call. Sound good?"

"Yeah, sounds good," Kai responded as he picked up his chopsticks.

You need to see Amina.

I need to sleep, he responded to himself in his mind.

"Itadakimasu," he said under his breath as he took a bite of the first meal he'd had in almost two days.

TWELVE

BLACK STAR AND THE PHANTOM

Curitiba, a Brazilian city renowned for its culture, was the civilization that Black Star arrived at after reacquiring the menagnetite, but before taking it to his sister in the New States, as he wanted to finish all the business he could before returning home. He was in Curitiba looking for Abe Davidson, as he had found records of Abe's thievery while he was in the research facility the night before. In a way, Black Star was scratching the Brazilian government's back for scratching his, a fair trade in his mind even if they didn't feel the same way.

Black Star had been researching Abe's previous jobs in order to understand the patterns Abe followed. This led Black Star to a jeweler who he believed would be the next hit on Abe's list. Black Star sat patiently on the second story balcony of a restaurant across the street from the jewelry store, waiting for the thief to make his move. He sipped on his bottle of water, with an empty plate next to him, wearing casual clothes with his dark gray bag slung on his back. After a few minutes, he noticed Abe exit the jewelry store wearing jeans, mid-top tennis shoes, and a plain dark green v-neck t-shirt.

This was Abe's schtick, Black Star thought. *Steal items before anyone can realize, walking out of the store casually so as to not raise suspicion. Most likely a magician turned petty thief.*

Abe walked down the street, pockets lined with gems, and Black Star watched him like a hawk. Abe looked both ways and then took one look at Black Star, still sitting on the rooftop, and darted the opposite direction. Black Star was motionless, still confused, bottle of water still at his lips.

Did he notice me? Did I stick out too much? While Black Star pondered where we went wrong, he saw another person in pursuit of Abe. The man wore a dark purple cloak with an extra high collar that covered the lower half of his face and was very obviously in the business of hunting men. Abe and the purple-cloaked man took off down the street while the oblivious pedestrians struggled to process what passed. They felt only a gust of wind but never gave it a second thought as they were busy people moving through their everyday lives. After seeing that people were not focused on him, Black Star was relieved.

These guys are fast. Unnaturally fast. I can't let them get away. This is my one chance for a real challenge, Black Star thought.

Black Star began giving chase after the two men. The thief made a right, jumped on a bus bench, and grabbed hold of a fire escape. The man chasing him climbed up the side of the brick building, using the lips and windowsills available, eventually transferring over to the fire escape as well.

Is he leading him to an open area, or just trying to escape? Black Star thought to himself. He was following shortly behind, bounding upward between the building they were on and the one next to it by leaping from wall to wall, carrying the momentum with him. They all took separate paths, Black Star noticed, and he thought that perhaps it was due to a sense of pride they all possessed - the pride to not follow in others' footsteps.

Abe arrived on the rooftop first but tried to get further away as he had spent this long avoiding conflict. He didn't want to start now, so he jumped to another building behind them. The purple-cloaked man caught up to him and tackled Abe in mid-jump between the two buildings. Black Star arrived at the top of the first building just as the tackle had transpired and watched in fascination.

Abe and his tackler rolled on the concrete of the next roof as they hit it hard, and Abe kicked the man off him as they rolled. They both stood up and engaged in hand-to-hand combat, as Abe knew he couldn't escape this time, and Black Star continued watching in awe that another person had joined the hunt, as it is rare for two people to be hunting the same person at the exact same time. Based on watching Abe's handling of the fight, Black Star concluded that he had no refined technique, which meant that he had no teacher, and thus wasn't as big of a problem as the purple-cloaked man whose technique was nigh flawless. Abe threw a punch at his assailant, which was redirected, and another which was caught.

It was then that Black Star jumped in, surprising the other two men. He let them choose the pace of the fight, as he always did in order to gauge the strength of his opponent. This time, the man's right hand was caught by Abe, and Black Star went to kick the man in the face, but the man used his left hand to catch the kick, causing Black Star to lose his balance. He caught himself with his hands at the same time that Abe landed a punch to the man's face, stunning him and releasing Black Star's leg in the process, as Black Star twisted and kicked both of them in the jaw, sending them flying backwards.

Abe recovered quickly and attempted to run away once more but was tackled yet again by the purple-cloaked man before he could gain any speed. Abe pushed him off and sprung back to his feet at the same time that the man swept his right leg towards Abe's legs. Abe jumped over the leg sweep and launched a fist forward, which the man evaded. Black Star hopped in once again and threw a chop at Abe that was easily blocked. The cloaked man charged Black Star, seeing him as a nuisance, and went for a gut punch. Black Star dodged over the man's head and ended up behind him, but the man was already charging Abe. Black Star launched himself towards Abe and kicked him mid-air, sending him flying a couple of meters away.

A normal person would've easily been knocked out by such a kick, but Abe seemed unfazed. Black Star landed, rolled, and transferred his momentum into a strong, spinning kick at the cloaked man. Amazingly, he caught Black Star's kick, and held on to his leg and slung him at Abe. Black Star collided with Abe, who had just got back to his feet, and the cloaked man charged both of them, throwing punch after punch at Abe who was desperately trying to dodge, all while keeping an eye on Black Star.

Abe frantically dodged the strikes and waited for an opening before retaliating with a single, strong punch of his own, which was stopped by Black Star. Now, he and the cloaked man were one-on-one yet again, and he began striking at him quickly, like a snake trying to kill its prey. The man took up a boxer's stance and began dodging quickly left and right, and whatever strikes of Black Star's he couldn't dodge, he swatted away. On his last strike, Black Star went for the man's jaw to disorient him, but the man grabbed his forearm and pulled him in for a headbutt. Not wanting to take the man's headbutt in full force, Black Star launched his knee upward into the man's gut, but it was all a part of the man's plan to get him closer to him, and the man slung his elbow in full force into Black Star's eye, sending Black Star backwards and stunning him more than he'd like. His eye watered uncontrollably and stung horribly as he tried to keep it open. Yet again, Abe tried fleeing, but the cloaked man grabbed him and continued to engage him. Abe understood he was outclassed, but had a slight speed advantage, so he did his best to evade until he got his one opening.

Black Star closed his wounded eye and stood up. *It's time to end this before I miss my shot*, he thought. In a blazing speed Black Star was right in between them and grabbed both of the swings that had been thrown. Tired of the menage a trois, a vial rolled down the inner sleeve of the cloaked man and into his hand. He threw it on the ground, and it burst into a massive cloud of noxious gas. It hurt when inhaled and acted as a muscle neutralizer, but the most dangerous thing about it, however, was the fact that the gas was transparent.

Black Star knew immediately what had happened, as the smell overtook his nostrils, but it was still too late. Black Star dashed away as quickly as he could in order to catch his breath as his lungs flared and burned. Abe, on the other hand, took the brunt of the gas before he could move away, and collapsed on the ground, his eyes bright red as he heaved. He was disoriented and could no longer escape. The cloaked man walked over to him, grabbed him, and snapped his neck, and just like that the fight was over. The gas quickly dispersed, leaving no scent or trail of its use besides the shards of glass on the concrete rooftop. Black Star was impressed that he didn't get the kill, and that a person with enough skill came out of nowhere and stole the contract right out from under him.

After all, Black Star had to show respect to the one who bested him, so he walked over to shake the man's hand while the man let Abe's loose body fall to the rooftop.

"Congratulations sir, you got the best of-" Black Star stopped. He lost all train of thought and his hand clenched up and turned into a fist that he launched at the man's face, as a long-buried rage boiled to the surface. The feeling had been buried for so long, along with the memories that accompanied it, that it had almost been forgotten, but the man caught the punch and spoke up.

"What happened to the friendly attitude?" he asked as he lowered Black Star's arm and stepped back.

"You deserve far worse than that bastard!" Black Star shouted. The man was still unaware of what happened to cause Black Star to change so drastically, so he stepped back a few more feet and took off his cloak. He was a dark-skinned man with a small gas mask on and had chains wrapped around his chest.

"Are you sure you want to do this?" the man asked.

Without thinking and without a weapon, Black Star charged the hunter, which allowed the man to play him like a fiddle. Once Black Star got within combat range, the man jumped back again to see how affected Black Star's senses had been by the noxious gas. On top of the neurotoxin, Black Star had a million things running through his mind, rage being first and foremost. All of these negative effects had him operating at less-than-optimal capacity, but even so he charged at the man once more. Feeling his muscles tense up with every step, he threw one punch at a significantly slower pace than normal. The man wrapped Black Star's arm in chains and then Black Star kicked at him, falling into the man's trap yet again, and in an instant both of his legs had been wrapped as well. The man leg swept him, and Black Star fell on the rooftop, uncontrollably stiffening up in the process. In just a few seconds from the first punch, Black Star had been detained completely. The man laughed as Black Star fell to the ground with only one arm free.

"Hey, you made it ten steps kid. That's pretty good." The man finally looked directly at Black Star's face, and memories came flooding back to him. He remembered Black Star's father and he smiled widely as it all became clear to him.

"Oh, this is great. This is too good. We've been looking for you," he chuckled some more. "Tracking you. For YEARS with no luck. Then, out of all places, out of all situations, we meet like this. I'm not a man of faith, but this is miraculous, perfect."

Black Star's face didn't seem to change much, even though his eyes were locked on his captor with the intensity of a thousand suns.

"Don't look at me like that. This is our reunion. I haven't seen you since you were what, nine?" The man kept laughing. "After all the years of having a contract on you they finally removed it, only for us to meet now." The man crouched down and got closer to Black Star. "Whatever god is out there must be looking out for you because I only kill for money, so consider this your lucky day. While I have you here though, I might as well gather as much data on you as possible." The man pulled out a small knife and took a thin slice out of Black Star's neck and put it into a vial he had hidden in his vest.

"I guess this makes it my lucky day too. Keep the chains, they're a gift. And oh, you might want to head to an apothecary or something." Black Star was both embarrassed and infuriated and tried to shout through his numb mouth as the man disappeared into the bustling metropolis of Curitiba, leaving Black Star with nothing but the chains, the gash on his neck, and his own thoughts.

I knew that man. I could never forget him. That was my parents' killer. After all these years I had accepted that he died, and that I should just move on, and continue my life not dwelling in the past no matter how painful it was. I still searched for answers to find the ones responsible for their death. But when I couldn't find him, I accepted that I would never discover the truth. When I saw him though, I couldn't control myself? That was the man who single-handedly changed my life. He took away everything precious to me and I could never forgive that, no matter what excuses he had. My father was one of the greatest thinkers of our time. When the world was bleak, and resources were low, he was there and he never gave up, even when people laughed at him. He was a hero. My mom was a hero. I guess this suppressed rage could only be bottled for so long. A tear fell from Black Star's left eye.

I had the opportunity to make things right. He was right in front of me, but when I punched there was no force behind it. Am I outclassed that bad? Am I truly weak? The blood stopped running from his neck, proving to be not as serious of a wound as he had thought. His pride hurt more than any wound he had received. He took a few deep breaths as tears rolled down his cheeks and gathered himself.

I haven't slipped up like that in a long time, he thought. *Why couldn't I put force behind the punch though?* Black Star reflected for a bit before coming to a conclusion. *Of course. I couldn't kill him because we have unfinished business. Even though I wanted to, I couldn't let my anger get the best of me*, as if Black Star had forgotten that he had been paralyzed by the man's neurotoxin. *Self-consciously I knew that. I finally have the opportunity to get the answers I have long waited for. After all these years of lying awake questioning his motives, I can finally ask him. If I would've acted brazenly, I would continue to live in regret.*

Thinking about all this actually brought a smile to his tear-stained face. These questions had haunted him for years, and now Black Star finally had the opportunity to get answers. For once in his life, he wouldn't be left in the dark. Still entangled, Black Star accepted the embrace of the chains as he couldn't move even if he wanted to. The blood on his neck began to dry and his vision faded to black as he lost consciousness.

■■■■■■■■■■ ■ ■ ▮ ▮ ▮ ▮

The dark night brought in a hazy fog. The air was getting colder as the months grew long, and a local priest at a church in Salt Lake City, Utah had been doing everything but being a fatherly figure. A priest is a person who should be known within his community for doing what is morally right, but this priest had been stealing from his own parish, his own people, who trusted him and yet who he betrayed for riches. People had heard rumors of other terrible deeds, but those who spoke up were paid hush money so that he was able to continue his facade.

From a bit of research, it was discovered that he had killed and replaced the last pastor, which otherwise would have been quite obvious to just about anyone. But with the technology of the late 21st century, a good bout of plastic surgery made him look almost exactly the same as the previous priest, even down to the freckles. If he hadn't acted strangely, or had any evidence found against him, no one would have noticed. Who he was before was a mystery, and no evidence pointed to any life prior to the one he had currently. He probably needed to escape his previous situation, so that's why he killed Father MacElroy and replaced him. This imposter, luckily, could be dealt with freely. His motives and his plans after impersonating the priest were yet to be discovered, and if all went according to plan then they never would be. Oftentimes, churches would pay for a residence for their priests to live in. With this being a rather large church with a quite generous community, Father MacElroy had a rather modest house on the church property, that was, however, larger than most priests.

It was late one night and crickets chirped, owls hooted, and the impersonated Father was getting ready for bed. As he was brushing his teeth, he heard a horrible scratching on his bathroom window where moonlight flooded in and met his gaze. He jumped a bit and walked out of the bathroom, foam running from the corners of his mouth. He turned his porchlight on and peered out the window, noticing a fat opossum who had just been feasting on his trash like a banquet for a king.

"Just one of God's creatures," the Father sighed with relief.

Then a rapping came from his kitchen, a rhythmic rapping,

Tap. Tap. Tap. Tap. Tap. Tap.

Questioning what it could be caused his mind to run wild. Every door was locked, every window was closed, but only so many things could create a constant beat like the one he had heard. He walked into his dark kitchen and seeing nothing he turned around and was met with two, bright, blood red eyes that pierced his soul. The eyes judged his life and everything that built up to this moment. The priest's heart sank, but he still had fight left in him, even though he had never had to deal with the supernatural before.

He carried holy water with him and threw the vial in front of him. It was a direct hit on the silhouette that was intruding on hallowed ground. The glass shattered into small chunks and a quick smile grew on the priest's face. When he realized it had no effect, the man was consumed by fear. The Phantom used his right arm, the only arm evident, and pushed the clergyman to the floor. The priest started to shake and his heart began to pound as panic set in. He jumped up as quick as he could and ran towards the front door, fidgeting with the doorknob until he finally yanked it open and sprinted, in his pajamas, toothpaste still in his mouth, to the doors of the church. He was an older man, so the short run already had him out of breath, but he ripped open the church doors and ran into the pews and collapsed, tired and heaving, trying desperately to catch his breath. He tried to collect his thoughts, but no matter what he did he couldn't think rationally.

A demon shouldn't be able to step on holy ground, the father thought. Yet when he peeked over the pews, he saw the Phantom waiting patiently for the man to look him in the eyes, like it found joy watching those lesser than it being consumed by terror. At its mercy, the pastor fumbled over himself and tried to scoot back deeper into the pews, knowing he couldn't outrun it. Perhaps he was trying to look pitiful, in hopes of being left alone, but it didn't work. His perception of the Phantom began to warp and alter. What originally looked humanoid now began altering its shape, stretching out in different directions as if it was trying to spare one the tragedy of knowing what was under the cloak. The impostor Father MacElroy could only describe what he saw as tentacles or something far worse underneath the cloak. Then, it spiraled and twisted upwards in an inorganic manner. As he watched the Phantom's body churn, his stomach churned, and he began to tremble and sweat uncontrollably as acid began forming in the back of his throat. The creature towered above, stretching up to the stained-glass ceiling in a horrendous form. The cleric stood in awe in the midst of the pews, terrified as he gazed upon a true horror.

Is this the demon's true form? he thought. He tried to make sense of reality, but all he could see was his greatest fear. It twisted from where it was and snatched the priest by the head and lifted him up in the air. The priest could still see the Phantom's red eyes, and perhaps those were now the only soothing aspect of the encounter. As he hung there, suspended by the darkness, a swarm of wasps poured out of the twisted dark and covered the body of Father MacElroy completely, stinging him over and over again, forcing their way into his clothes and in every hole of his body. He was pelted to the ground by insects as they poured down his throat like honey with wings. They hummed rhythmically, creating something beautiful out of something truly disgusting.

The man was sure to die from the venom, if not from the insects forcing their way inside his body. Though as hard as he tried to grasp reality, he couldn't understand what was happening. True reality set in, but the impersonated priest was long gone. The Phantom had not moved a step once entering the church, and Father MacElroy lay on the floor, lifeless. The man had merely imagined his worst nightmares, as his body was clean and unscathed besides his heart which had burst.

The ominous figure wasted no time lingering around, and so it disappeared into the darkness as quickly as it had arrived. The night was still young, with plenty of opportunities, and even though such a thought is terrifying in and of itself, the Phantom seemed to have some sort of moral guidance and intelligence enough to work the system, even though it had no use for man's currency.

It reaped the benefit from killing others, or perhaps it served someone else. Either way, it seemed to act independently, passing its judgment on others by killing or striking fear into them. It fed off the energy of terror humans released at the end of their life, and so it had the upper hand on all its targets and sat comfortably at the top of the food chain. The Phantom was a reminder that there was always something better, more dangerous, more terrifying. The word of the creature had spread throughout the world by this point, but not everyone believed in such magnificent stories. Those that didn't deserved a personal demonstration, and so the Phantom came to them and struck the faith of fear deep into their soul.

Life has value. But as simple of a saying as that is, most people have forgotten it. That's why underground dog fights exist, and why so many shitty people pay to watch them fight. These animals have been beaten, malnourished, and neglected, and the only praise they ever receive is when the crowd cheers as they kill their brothers and sisters. These foul people will take any animal to fight another, such as chickens, but despite the popularity of cock fights, dogs still bring in the most money.

On one particular night, some of the onlookers had captured a pack of sickly dogs and instead of taking them to get euthanized they brought them to the warehouse to fight for the enjoyment of others. And once the fights were over, the vile humans went home to their families and continued their disgusting lives as if they had done nothing wrong, leaving the ringleader of the bunch to clean up the mess and prepare for the next show.

Sure, he fed all the dogs as a reward for living another day, sometimes. But other days he would simply "forget". To the Phantom, these people were the most disgusting and were the ones that deserved the most terrible kind of death imaginable. They believed that they were superior to all other creatures and because of that they meddled with the lives of the creatures they believed to be below them, disregarding all the feelings the poor animals could be experiencing. These kinds of humans lacked empathy and deserved no sympathy from the Phantom. Having no way to comprehend how the animals they mistreat felt, these people needed a reminder of the food chain and exactly where they lie on it. Foolish people think they are the apex predator when they can barely even grasp the concept of power. The world is vast and mysterious and that is something the close-minded would never understand.

The warehouse was well lit and the ringleader was opening the cage to the first dog. It was common for the hounds to bark and whine, hoping to escape their prison. These noises, however, were deep growls, an audible example of the fear of their future. The feeling of being watched washed over the man, showing his level of perception even though the Phantom made no noise. The Phantom's red eyes burned and its aura tore through the air and passed through the man's body. He was perceptive and brave as he stared down the Phantom and raised his pistol. Even while trembling he had the ability to overcome the pain in his stomach and he opened fire on the ominous figure with his full-auto handgun, which was capable of shooting fifty rounds every two seconds. All the shots hit and he knew it. The Phantom was a bucket with water spewing out across its body. But the Phantom was unaffected, as if the bullets passed right through it. And when the ringleaders realized this, he ran.

He turned his back to the Phantom and fell over, like he had been tripped by something. Nothing was there and yet the man could feel pressure around his legs constricting them like a snake. The pressure became greater and greater, and he screamed as he felt and heard his bones crack. The man looked behind him, towards his shattered legs, but he was met with the empty room. Then the door in front of him unlocked and opened and he saw the Phantom crouched on top of the cages facing him, as if striking a pose for its own amusement. The doors of the cages had been opened and the ravenous dogs darted out of them, racing to see who could get to the immobilized ringleader first. The man could see the hunger in their eyes, but could do nothing about it, and the dogs, starving and salivating, came upon him and tore his flesh. His eyes popped out of his skull as the force of a dog's bite crushed bone, and another tore out his throat at the same time. Two more dogs tore at his stomach as they clawed their way through him. The man screamed, until the blood from his torn-out throat suffocated him and muffled the sound of his life being taken from him.

From the time the man thought he had pulled the trigger he was already under the influence of the Phantom. The man had never shot and his legs were never crushed. None of it was real except for the outcome. The Phantom left the door open for the canines, unknowing of where they could go, but knowing that anywhere was better than the prison they were held in. The Phantom left the room and left the door open to the outside world. In a matter of minutes, after they had finished their meal, the dogs ran off barking into the night and the whole perimeter was vacant.

THIRTEEN

KAI

Falling.

Falling.

Falling.

Amina's hair seemed to burst into flames as the sun kissed her green locks while she plummeted further and further down towards the earth. The wind whipped past her as she began picking up speed and the blood from her abdomen created a macabre trail in the sky for Kai to follow as he chased her down. He had tossed his longsword Shatter towards Marlowe and began diving through the clouds in hopes that he would reach her before she hit the ground. He engaged the thrusters on his Wingblade and launched himself faster, hoping, praying, he would catch her.

I'm almost there.

I'm almost there.

He saw the water behind Amina rushing up to greet them as he broke through the clouds. He was only inches away from grabbing her, but inches were miles when you were only seconds from splattering against the ocean waves. His fingertips brushed her foot, then her ankle. Kai grabbed as quickly as he could, pulled up, and engaged his thrusters as quickly as possible, slowing them down, but not enough. Knowing what was imminent, Kai got under Amina and wrapped his arms around her, and as they hit the water with tremendous force, Kai woke up to a thunderclap that shook his apartment walls. Unfazed, he stared at the ceiling, shirtless, pantless, and covered in sweat. He looked through the bedroom door and towards the television, where the holographic screen displayed the time in a pale red.

8 A.M.

Four hours? Is that all the sleep I can get these days?

He tried sitting up and was immediately reminded of the ribs he had broken in his fight with Gilroy the night before. He winced but pushed through and got out of bed anyways. It was storming outside and the sky was gray and overcast. He could hear the cars on the streets honking at each other as the rain pounded down all around them, rushing, he had assumed, to get to work before all of their supervisors fired them. Rushing, he had thought, to their pointless jobs to pay for their pointless things, just to die at the end of it.

At least they think they're in control. At least they don't live with the knowledge that they're being herded and used like sheep.

After staring for a moment, Kai diverted his attention away from the massive window in his bedroom and towards his closet, where he found a pair of black jeans and a black, long-sleeve thermal shirt to match the cold, wet weather. Pulling the shirt down over his bruised torso was more of a chore than he would've liked to admit, but it was nothing compared to the pain he felt deeper inside himself, the pain that he ignored, or at least attempted to ignore. Kai walked barefoot to his refrigerator, pulled out his water bottle, and took three swigs from it before replacing its cap and putting it back where he found it. The water soothed his dry throat and he found comfort in the cool hydration it provided for him every morning.

"It's always the little things, Kai," Alphonse had once said. *"Hold on to them and you'll be okay."*

Kai put on his socks and boots slowly, as his broken ribs were still aching him, and afterwards grabbed his jacket that he had thrown on the couch after arriving home early that morning. He put it on, grabbed the duffel bag with his suit and his damaged helmet, opened his door, and stepped out in the hallway at the same time a woman, dressed in blue jeans, brown boots, a cream-colored sweater, and a worn, blue scarf stepped out of her apartment. Her blonde, bobbed hair fell gently on her old scarf, and she met Kai's gaze with surprise. Kai quickly turned around and locked his door. She had already done the same, so while Kai was locking his door, she walked towards the stairs behind him.

Please don't talk to me, he thought. *Please.* Kai had never been good at talking to people because he didn't understand them and never had the opportunity or the desire to. So, when someone passed him on the street, or in the apartment, or anywhere else, he just kept his head down and hoped that they wouldn't have the desire to talk to him either. The blonde-haired woman walked past him, her eyes tired and mostly hidden behind her bangs.

"Good morning," she said quietly as she passed him.

"Good morning," Kai said, matching her volume. As she walked down the steps, the smell of her perfume penetrated him, and he stared at her as she walked away.

Flowers.

Kai waited a few moments for her to exit the apartment building, picked up his duffel bag, and made his way down the steps as well. He exited the building and walked across the street to the old concrete parking garage where he parked his motorcycle. The apartment building Kai lived in and the parking garage he parked his motorcycle in were two relics of an age long gone, remnants of the war that had struck The City before it was what it is now - before the Sicarii rebuilt it for their own purposes. They had survived the bombings, the small nuclear explosions from failing robotic systems, and all-out war, but were left scarred, scorched, and ridden with wounds where bullets had dug deep into the concrete.

Despite what they had been through, they still stood, and like the others around The City that had survived the war, they were considered to be landmarks of life before it had disfigured them. But despite their disfigurement, they were protected - one such landmark being the old football stadium only a few blocks away from Isarcii Pharmaceuticals. Kai pulled black, faux-leather gloves out of his evergreen canvas bag and pulled them on. He did the same with his damaged helmet, pulling it on over his head. The crack to the face had disabled all the internal systems connected to Eris, but the basic functions like the artificial reality overlay remained intact, allowing him to still see while he had it on. He strapped his bag to the back of the seat and then swung his leg over and held on to the bike long enough for it to register that it was him. A red, holographic screen appeared between his hands.

"Access code required," it stated in a robotic voice.

"7477", Kai responded. The screen turned into a ring and began spinning quickly clockwise. After a few moments, it vanished, and words appeared where the circle had been.

"Access granted," the voice said, and the screen showed. Kai twisted the handle towards him and revved the engine. He walked his motorcycle backwards, and then took off once he was able to, speeding down the ramp to his right and out of the old parking garage and onto the wet, paved road. He took the busy streets out of City Greater and onto the lifted highway that wrapped through and around the lesser and greater provinces of The City, spanning the one-hundred-mile diameter of The City in its entirety. As he hit the outskirts of downtown, he sped up, pushing his vehicle easily past 320 kilometers per hour and drove deep into the lesser provinces. The lesser provinces were only considered to be "lesser" due to their less elegant appearance and the little amount of money flowing through them, but where they lacked in high-tech skyscrapers, extravagant lights, and five-star restaurants, they made up for in beautiful culture, strong people, and passion. It was there, in the heart of the lesser provinces, that Kai met a young girl by the name of Elaine who he regarded, despite his access to all the Sicarii's resources, as the most brilliant inventor he had ever come into contact with.

Kai slowed down and merged right, taking the off ramp down to the regular streets. The sky was still overcast, the day still gray, and as he drove down the wet roads from the early morning rain he passed abandoned homes, prostitutes, a group of men fighting, and more liquor and recreational drug stores than he could count. After the fall of the United States most recreational drugs were legalized as the European Defense Initiative was starved for money and the Sicarii needed a way to control the populace.

Harsher drugs like methamphetamines and heroin were still illegal, but the charges for possession and distribution were vastly reduced. Besides these, only one other recreational drug was illegal, but this drug differed from the others and law enforcement handled it more strictly than any other drug ever produced. Possession, consumption, and distribution of the drug resulted in prison time with a subsequent death sentence. It was with this drug that the Sicarii controlled much of the weaker populace of the New States, as they were the ones who discreetly produced the dangerous and rare drug, unbeknownst to most of the world and to their own, besides the High Council itself.

On the street, the drug was called Sunshine, but it was actually a bastardization of one of the chemicals created by Alexander Stromberg called CNSU-23, which was the twenty-third iteration of the Central Nervous System Unifier, a chemical originally created to unify the processes of the brain and spinal cord in order to send it into a permanent overdrive state. Alexander was hired by the Sicarii to complete this project, but after the failure of the twenty-third iteration and the birth of his youngest son, Alexander quit working for the Sicarii, a decision which led to the eventual assassination of him and his wife by the Sicarii. The recreational version of the drug produced by the Sicarii could either be taken via eye dropper or injection directly into the central nervous system, usually by needle, through the temple and into the brain, or most commonly into the spinal cord. Since the recreational drug was not the perfected version of the CNSU, the effects weren't permanent and the "high" lasted from a few hours to a few days, depending on the way in which the drug was disseminated into the central nervous system. Those who were considered to be upstanding members of society and not junkies usually took the drug via eyedropper and only took it in small quantities, as large doses of the drug could blind users and destroy vital brain functions. Those who injected the drug were those who believed they could not live without it, or actually could not live without it, and the drug allowed them only to function on the basic level that non-users could function.

For those who weren't extremely addicted to the drug, it provided them with a connection to the world that negated nihilistic tendencies, depression, and disconnection from the real world. On top of this, the drug heightened brain function, increasing physical and mental capabilities of those who took it. Because of all the positive side-effects of the drug, it was commonly used by those who worked in the fields of artificial reality, especially if said workers were inside of AR programs for long periods of time.

Symptoms of increased AR exposure left people depressed, nihilistic, and possibly destructive as their brains had problems discerning whether or not the world in which they existed was real at all. Sunshine cured this, for a short time, and became popular amongst all people as a way to better connect with the world and those in it. However, extended use of the drug left people worse off than they would have been and caused those who took it frequently to exhibit violent reactions to otherwise normal situations, leading to destruction of property, others, and self. Because of the destructive capabilities of the drug to the self and society, the law of the New States, implemented by the European Defense Initiative and created by the U.N., forbade the use, distribution, and creation of the drug in the New States. This, of course, led to the international distribution of the drug on the black market, leading the U.N. to illegalize it worldwide.

Kai parked his motorcycle outside of a small, abandoned warehouse and walked to the steel overhead door in front of him and knocked on it. A voice came over an intercom above him while a camera to the right of the door stared at him.

"Who is it?" a deep, masculine voice asked over the intercom.

"Kai," Kai responded directly.

"Why did you come back?" the intercom asked, anger brimming in the voice of the person behind it.

"I need your help, Elaine."

"What did you DO?"

"I need repairs," Kai stated again, unfazed by the voice's anger. The overhead door jerked up quickly and a teenage girl with a pink, pixie haircut wearing a white sports bra, dark green cargo pants, and black boots stepped out quickly and came at Kai in a violent manner. She gasped as she saw the damage to Kai's helmet.

"You son of a bitch! What did you DO? WHAT DID YOU

DO TO MY GIRL!?" She ripped the helmet off of Kai's head and rotated it in her hands to get a closer look at it. A horrified expression came across her face.

"Oh my god. Oh my god oh my god oh my god." She looked up at Kai with tears in her eyes as she pointed a finger in his face. "You're lucky if I can even fix her."

"I'm sorry Ela-,"

"Sorry doesn't cut it. Not this time Kai. You're supposed to be careful with her. These repairs are going to take me forever." Elaine put her head down and walked back inside with Kai's helmet.

"Bring your bike in. You didn't damage that too, did you?" Elaine asked, still pissed.

"No, I didn't," Kai answered. Elaine huffed and Kai hopped back on his motorcycle and drove it inside. Elaine shut the door behind him. Inside the small warehouse were computer systems, half-finished inventions, a bed, an old, remodeled refrigeration unit, and all the other necessities for living quarters. She carried Kai's helmet over to a desk with four computer monitors, old models from the 2070s, but the last non-projected computer monitors ever produced, and therefore sturdier, cheaper, and easier to repair than the more sophisticated models, and placed his helmet on her diagnostics table next to her desk. Elaine removed Eris's core from the helmet and inserted it into one of her computers before plugging in cable after cable to hidden ports in the helmet's disfigured shell. Kai walked around the small warehouse and gazed at the failed inventions, broken tech, and other bits of things scattered about. After some time, Kai spoke up.

"How long have you been living here, Elaine?" She gazed up briefly to meet his eyes, and then looked back down at the monitor screen before responding.

"A few years, give or take. Time doesn't pass the same in here as it does out there."

"What do you mean?" Kai asked, curious.

"In here, I'm free. I do what I want, when I want, as long as I want. I work on my projects, eat when I want, shit when I need, and sleep when I can no longer stand. But eventually, it gets boring. And that's the problem with freedom, Kai. That's always the problem with freedom. It's boring. Because without restriction, without rules and regulations, without laws, we have so much and yet so little that we can't even comprehend which one it really is." After a moment of silence to gather his thoughts, Kai spoke up again.

"Better to be free than to be controlled, I would like to think."

"We would all like to think that Kai," said Elaine sympathetically. "But tell me this: if you were floating in a void, free of regulations, free of laws like gravity, free of all things except for yourself, would you be happy? Would you even know what to do in an endless void where only you existed? Would there even be anything to do except float there?" Kai had no response.

"But hey," Elaine continued. "At least you're *free*." She chuckled to herself. No words were spoken after that, not for at least an hour, until Elaine was finished with her diagnostics.

"Alright," Elaine started. She walked over to Kai who was sitting on her couch, across from her television in the back of the warehouse. She sat down on the side closest to her and faced towards him, propping her leg up on the couch with her hand resting on the back of it. "She took on a lot of damage," she continued, "but overall, I think she'll be okay. Her core is intact, and her shell can be repaired, with time. The blunt-force trauma the shell suffered compacted a lot of the hardware which burnt the AR overlay chip. I'm surprised you could even drive over here with that thing on."

"I guess I trust your creations even more than you do," Kai smirked. "How long do you think it'll take to repair?"

"About 48 hours. Can you work without her?" Elaine asked sympathetically.

"I can, but I don't want to. She's helped me more than most understand. Even though she's artificial, she feels more real than anyone else." Kai put his elbows on his knees and held his head in his hands as he stared at the concrete floor below him. Elaine slid closer to him and put her arm around his shoulders.

"But what is *real* anyways, Kai?" she said quietly. "Is *real* what you can see? What you can smell? What you can touch? Is *real* what you can feel in your heart, or think about in your mind? What is reality but something that plays with our senses and touches our soul?" Kai sat up and looked at Elaine.

"Do you believe in the soul?" he asked sullenly.

"If I did, would it make my question any different?" Elaine retorted.

"I suppose not," Kai said. "Either way, she's come to be a friend."

"As I had hoped when I created her," Elaine said with a smile. "You need more."

"As do you," Kai replied with a chuckle.

"But Kai," she said as she got up. "That's why I have *you*." By the end of the conversation, they were both smiling, and Kai was walking out with his motorcycle after saying his goodbyes while Elaine stood at the button to close the overhead door behind him.

"Thank you, Elaine, for everything." Kai said.

"No need to thank me. She'll be done in no time. Just make sure you come back and get her!"

"Will do," Kai said as he put on the spare motorcycle helmet Elaine gave him. Elaine shut the door behind him as he drove off, back towards the city, back towards his apartment, and back towards Sicarii Headquarters, where the High Council sat at the top of the Spire, overlooking their killing machine.

■ ■ ■ ■ ■ ■ ■ ■ ■ ■ ■ ▪ ▪ ▪ ▪ ▪

"Your pet is causing problems again, Alef," Vav said in an irritated tone. "The other members of the Council don't agree with the relaxed attitude you've been taking with him." Alef said nothing as he stared across the room at the massive door that led into the Council chambers, his hands clasped in front of his mouth.

Vav continued, "The Council has decided unanimously that should Kai and his squad cause any more problems for us like they have on their last two missions, we will have a contract placed on each member. We cannot risk exposure like we did in Stockholm or like we did last night."

Still, Alef said nothing.

Gimel spoke up next. "We have not been exposed since the

slaughter at Masada over two-thousand years ago and we won't let it happen again." After a long pause, Alef straightened his posture and faced the other members of the High Council.

"Where is Jehoel?" he asked calmly.

"Jehoel is laying low, as she has been for quite some time," responded Gimel.

"Have you told her about your decision?"

"It's irrelevant," said He.

There was another long pause before Vav spoke up again.

"We know that Kai retrieved something from Gilroy before the latter's death, Alef."

"And you think that I was unaware of this fact? Whatever was retrieved was destroyed. Seraphiel has searched everywhere for clues and has found nothing except that Kai had a conversation with Sohei Murimoto, one of the food vendors and previous squad leaders at Murimoto's shop here in Headquarters. When questioned, Murimoto stated that Kai had asked him about the phrase "ruins of old joy", but there was nothing else."

"We must find the information that was exchanged in any way we can," Gimel said, frustrated. "We must not let this get out of hand." With that, Alef stood up out of his throne behind the elevated, crescent-shaped table. His slightly wrinkled hands were shaking, unbeknownst to his fellow Council members. He quickly but carefully pulled out his pipe so as not to raise suspicion of his condition, lit the dark herbs inside it, and inhaled as he normally did. His hands shook less now, and he set down his ornate wooden pipe on the equally as ornate wooden table and pressed a white button protruding from its underbelly. Almost as quickly as he had pressed the button, Verena walked in through the doors on the other side of the room. Gently, the hooded Sofia raised her head and looked at Verena, who made eye contact with Sofia and shuddered ever so slightly with fear. Sofia put her head back down and assumed her unmoving position leaning up against the wall to the right of the High Council table from the entrance. Being the only member of the High Council standing, Verena addressed Alef directly.

"How can I assist you, Your Excellency?"

"Summon Seraphiel immediately." Alef said without a pause.

"Right away, sir." Verena quickly turned around and left the room. The other Council members stared at Alef, save Dalet who was absent from this meeting, but instead of looking back he kept his eyes forward, lifted up his pipe, and re-lit it with his gold-plated flip lighter. Not a minute later, the top of the Council chambers opened up and the leader of the Seraphim dropped onto the floor below. His suit was similar to the rest of his brethren, except his core burned red like a dying sun and his armor was scorched from years of battle. Seraphiel's warsuit opened up in the front, just like Helel's, but instead of a lean, brown-haired man, out stepped a blonde-haired boy.

"Hello, Nico," said Alef with a grin.

The boy's face was emotionless, but pristine. He wore no black Sicarii suit like the rest of the Squads or like the other members of Seraph Squad, but a high, Mandarin-collared, gray, long sleeve coat with black, ornate buttons down the center, gray capri pants made of a similar fabric to his coat, and black textured boots that met close to his pants, with only an inch or two of white skin showing between.

"Hello, Alef," Nico replied. The High Council was shocked, as they had never seen the true visage of Nico, but Sofia wasn't. She was on edge, like a feral cat being approached by a perceived predator. She was no longer up against the wall with her hood up, but standing still facing Nico, with furrowed brow and weapons at the ready. Nico turned his head toward her.

"Hello, Sofia," he stated in a monotone voice. He turned his head back towards Alef and walked forward. Sofia was still frozen in place.

"What do you want from me, Alef?" Nico asked without expression. Nico's casual demeanor with a member of the High Council angered Gimel, and with a rage she burst out of her seat and smacked both of her hands on the table.

"How DARE you speak out of turn! You are speaking to a member of the Sicarii High Council! I would have you executed for this!"

Alef turned towards the red-faced Gimel and addressed her sternly. "Calm down Atria. Nico and I have known each other our entire lives." Gimel was befuddled.

"Known each other your entire lives? This boy is sixteen at most!"

"This *boy*," Alef stated, "Is as old as I am." He took another long pull from his pipe. "Your eyes deceive you. You are speaking to a man three years older than I am, a man who fought in the Third World War and a man who has, since the war, been the leader of the Archangels and the Seraphim who took their place." Shocked, Gimel sat down and all thoughts the rest of the Council members had were long gone.

"Now that we are free of disruptions, I have a task for you Nico. Rather, I have a problem," Alef said while smoking his pipe. Nico stood with his arms crossed, a blank expression across his face.

"Leader of Squad Four, Kai, has been assumed to have acquired confidential information from the recently assassinated and ex-leader of Squad Three, Gilroy. This information, or remnants of this information, may have been leaked to Sohei Murimoto, ex-leader and current owner of the ramen shop down the street from here. Find out what Murimoto knows at any cost but be quiet about it." Nico nodded his head, climbed back into his suit, and flew upwards out of the Council chambers. Alef turned back to the rest of the High Council. "The information will be found. Notify Dalet of Seraphiel's mission and the existence of this information." Alef turned away from the table and walked down the long hallway behind where the High Council sat, and to his chambers where he would retire for the night. Without saying a word, Vav, He, and Gimel disappeared, as they always did after the Council meetings, their seats filled with nothing but the projectors that allowed them to attend the conferences while still in Shanghai, Washington D.C., and Trytek Headquarters, the latter being located somewhere near the Rocky Mountains in Colorado. The last member left in the room was Bet, who stood up and walked down the same hallway as his teacher, but instead of turning left at the end of the hall towards Alef's chambers, he entered the elevator to his right and took it to the helipad on the roof of a skyscraper a couple of miles away from Isarcii Pharmaceuticals.

FOURTEEN

BLACK STAR

A new day had come. The weather was gloomy and the sun desperately attempted to break through the clouds as Black Star returned to knock on his sister's door. The dried blood was still on his neck as he never made an attempt to clean it off. What had happened to him in Brazil still affected him and in some way he left a part of himself back there on that rooftop. He no longer carried himself with confidence like he used to. Maria opened the door a few moments after Black Star had knocked.

"Hey, I'm glad you're back. Come on in," She was happy to see her brother back safe. They walked into the living room and she took a seat on the couch. Black Star took a seat in her "pope chair", which was an ornate, tall, backed chair that he had nicknamed for fun.

"Black Star! What happened to your neck!" she asked quickly as she lunged over to him to inspect. His hair may have been long and unruly, but it wasn't long enough to cover the mark.

"I got bested. He didn't kill me, but he left his mark on me."

"A killer sympathized with you?" she asked, surprised as she looked at the wound.

"Well, I guess he had no business with me. He toyed with me because I wasn't worth killing," Black Star replied.

Maria stopped herself from getting angry and restrained herself from pestering him with a million questions.

"Well," she began, "medicine isn't my field of choice, unlike our sister, but you definitely need to get that cleaned up before it gets infected!"

"No, no, I'm fine," Black Star said quietly, waving his hand left and right. He opened his bag and grabbed the menagnetite and gave it to her. "Maria, I have to tell you something."

"What is it?" she asked hesitantly.

"I found our parents' killer. It was the man who did this to me... who-" she immediately jumped in and cut him off. She tried to avoid conflict but couldn't any longer.

"Damnit Black Star! I know where this is going! I told you to leave that shit in the past!" she yelled.

"I know, I know. I'm sorry," Black Star said, defeated. "Up until this moment I did keep it in the past, but when I saw him I lost control. Just seeing him made me forget everything. All I could think about was making him pay."

"If you were sorry you wouldn't have done it. This isn't a game. You just picked a fight with a professional. Can you understand how childish that is?" she asked, still fuming.

"I know I can beat him if I stay calm," Black Star responded. "But he needs to stay alive just long enough for me to get some answers."

"Absolutely NOT!" Maria yelled. "Let. This. Go. Dad did shady things! I hate to admit it, I hate to have to tell you this, but good people don't get assassinated!"

Black Star stood up. "I'm sorry you feel this way. I was hoping that if anyone understood it would be you. Father only did what was best and he may have made mistakes, but we all do. I know he had good intentions."

"He experimented on you!" She sighed. "But you're right. We all make mistakes, so go make another. Go get yourself killed because you want petty answers, because you want to believe in conspiracies over facts!"

"I'm sorry you feel differently, but I cannot let this go," Black Star responded calmly. "This is my way of doing good. By killing people like him it stops them from hurting others. I do it to prevent any kid from having to feel the way I did, to go through what I had to go through. Even if I get my hands dirty it's worth it in the end."

"I think you should go," Maria responded. "If you're not going to listen then I'm not going to talk." In just a couple of minutes, her joyful mood had turned sour like an overripe lemon.

"Alright, I'll see you later." Black Star took his leave and walked out the door. He opened up his phone while walking down the street and checked his bank account.

I'll make him an offer he can't refuse. I'll use all my money if I have to. Every penny saved.

A memory of past disputes surfaced in his mind as the words "go get your answers" swirled in his head.

I want those answers and then I want to see the light leave his eyes. It was foolish of me to think that Maria would be happy. Maybe granddad was right. Maybe my sister has too much of Dad in her. That kindness has turned into weakness. To be honest though, am I really strong enough to take him? Even if I prepare it might not be enough. He killed Mom. Am I really stronger than her?

Black Star passed through the metropolis. Even though it was overpopulated, the air was clean and pure. The sky was covered in both dark and light clouds with small patches of blue peeking between. The sun wasn't visible, but its light still radiated faintly across the world. He walked aimlessly throughout Houston for almost an hour until he passed a park. Hoping to find some peace and tranquility amidst the boisterous city, he entered and found a grassy knoll. He laid down, using his bag as a pillow, and stared at the duality of the world manifested in the clouds above.

I wish I didn't have any obligations so I could just watch these clouds all day. Then something occurred to him looking back on yesterday. *He said I didn't have a contract on my head anymore, so I'm free for the first time. I can finally watch these clouds and not fear that someone is watching me.* Black Star pulled his phone out of his pocket and began playing a bit of symphonic music in an attempt to soothe his aching mind. The music began to play and he set his phone on his chest. *So how can I be more free than ever and yet feel more empty and alone than I ever have?* A bit of anger began festering within him as his thoughts moved once more to the man that distorted his life. *He better not say he killed them just for the money. I hope for his sake he has a better answer than that. A higher-.* A frisbee hit his right knee, knocking him out of his trance.

"Sorry about that! Can you pass it back?" a teenage boy yelled across the park to Black Star.

"Sure," Black Star said, just faintly enough for the boy to hear him. He stood up and tossed the frisbee with his left hand and the disc flew in a straight path until it skewed left slightly and hooked right before reaching the boy, hitting him directly in the hands.

"Thanks man," the teen said as he ran back to his friends.

Black Star laid back down and returned to his thoughts. *Do I need to do any more training before I fight him? Even if I was in a weakened state from the overwhelming emotion, taking me down isn't easy. The way he moved one-on-one was completely different than the fight with Abe, so it's safe to assume he was toying with me. But how much of it was toying? Did he ever get serious? He's experienced, that's for sure. I couldn't read him in the slightest. He never once had a slip up or flare up in power, even for a moment, so I really am going in blind. I'm kind of excited for this moment. It feels like my whole life has led up to this point. This could be the end of me, or a new genesis, either way it's worth it to know I didn't let our family get walked over, that I stood up for what I believed in even to the end.*

The clouds he had been watching darkened further and moved directly above him. Rain began to fall in slow, fat drops. And even though he was starting to get wet, Black Star had no desire to move or get out of the rain. He let the rain fall because he wanted to feel something, *anything*, for the first time in a long time. He shut his eyes and continued to lay in the grass until he eventually fell asleep, only to wake up a few minutes later as he couldn't calm his mind enough to gain any sort of respite. Normally, Black Star's numbness let him enjoy life for the most part - it allowed him to joke and have fun and actively engage in the world, but he was never truly happy. He wasn't sad either, just indifferent, which was enough for him. But now, the negatives outweighed the positives and so his numb peace left him.

A song ended and a new one began, this one more beautiful than the last. The passion of the orchestra resonated with him and the funk he was in immediately deteriorated.

What am I doing moping around? he thought. *No one, not even I, wants that. This is my opportunity. I should be excited. It's bittersweet to say, but... I'm finally going to get my revenge. Every skill I've acquired, every kill I've made, would be in vain if I didn't do this. He is the one who set me down this path. I need to beat him at his own game and then I can be free to forge my own path. Before I do that I need to talk to Cornelius. He can help me find out who the assassin really is. But I have one more time-sensitive stop before I can go there.*

Black Star jumped up and approached the teenagers playing frisbee who were only a couple of years younger than him. They started packing their stuff up as the raindrops fell harder.

"Hey," Black Star said. "Are there any train stations in town?"

"Uh... yeah," one of the boys responded. "Go down this street to the pharmacy, take a left until you see Bridgeway Street. You'll see the train station from there."

"Thanks for the in-depth directions, kid. You really know your way around." Black Star put up his hand and waved goodbye as he walked away.

"We're almost the same age," the kid said quietly, bewildered, as Black Star disappeared around the corner of the street.

Black Star jogged through the city streets heading south. Unlike most people who rode the train, he had a different plan in mind, as he didn't want to pay for a ticket. He took the stairs up to the station, hopped on a nearby fence while no one was looking, vaulted onto the roof of the train station, and once the train began moving, he hopped on its roof. Under normal circumstances, Black Star moved like everyone else. But when he needed to truly move, he preferred to release his speed in short bursts to conserve energy. It was less taxing this way and much more efficient. The speed and brevity of his dashes allowed him to slip by most people unnoticed.

As the railcar began moving, Black Star looked at a sign on his left and saw that the train was heading the opposite way that he needed to go. "Oops. Wrong train," he said aloud. The train began accelerating quickly and, in a few moments, the one Black Star was supposed to be on would be passing him. He could see it ahead, barreling towards him, so he waited, just for a moment, and then jumped on the other train as they sped past each other at roughly 350 kilometers per hour. Black Star slid a bit, as the railcar was wet from the rain, but most had blown off at the speed it was traveling.

After the train had stopped at the station, it continued on its rails throughout the evening until it arrived at Black Star's next destination in the heart of the Midwest. This place was the pinnacle of life after the War and was so large that it spanned through multiple states. Immediately after the surrender of the New States to the forces of the European Defense Initiative, many neighboring metropolises came together, multiplying revenue and tax allocation to accelerate educational programs and put the new mega-city on the forefront of technology and economics.

Many refugees were created due to the war, and most found their home in The City, and those men and women that were strong enough became laborers in the neighboring communities and The City was built on their backs. As the spectacle grew, the only name it was referred to as, and what eventually became its official name, was "The City". So Black Star, on his way to The City, had time to think of his situation and had time to be patient, as he didn't want to rush into things like he did on the rooftops of Curitiba. As he entered The City, he awed at the skyscrapers that rose to the heavens like the Tower of Babel. The architectural genius to create something so large was boggling, and their height was magnificent to some, like Black Star, but disorienting to others who were used to solid ground.

The Midwest had always been known for its rapidly changing weather, moving from rain to sun in a matter of minutes and from below freezing temperatures one day to boiling the next. But with the assistance of climate change over the course of the 21st century, it became more extreme. That, added with the nuclear fallout due to the weapons systems in the Third War, caused, Black Star assumed, the gloomy overcast and high amounts of precipitation throughout the year. So, this particular day was unfamiliar to the locals, and was incredibly hot, with not even a single cloud to protect them from the sun. Simply, the air was humid and miserable, even to Black Star.

Unfortunately, this made Black Star's task a little more troublesome than it needed to be. He was well acquainted with scaling the outside of buildings, but these buildings were made almost entirely of glass, so the surface was sleek and hard to grasp, which meant little leverage for Black Star. The building he was scaling felt molten, like his hand would melt if he stayed in one place for too long, but he always loved overcoming adversity as it always made victory sweeter.

Black Star's destination was a meeting in the highest level of a corporate office away from public interest. He had accepted a contract that was to take place at a dinner meeting between two company owners, so he made his way to the top of a building across from where his target would be in order to get a clear view of the environment.

I should have brought some water, he thought.

As Black Star arrived on the rooftop he pulled a small box out of his bag and opened it up. Inside was a collapsed bow, made of fiberglass and high-grade aluminum - a more primal weapon in the times he lived, but still one of the most effective. The bow was silent, unlike most other ballistic weapons, and had a much higher skill ceiling, both of which attracted Black Star to it. Black Star preferred simple weapons, as always, and was never keen on having the most advanced technology at his disposal. Granted his bow was still above and beyond the original stick and string variety, but its purpose and function still remained the same.

Meanwhile at the target building one of the businessmen by the name of Luke Fitzwater, the owner of the building, was waiting for his partner to arrive. After about half an hour the sun had descended in the sky and there was a knock at Mr. Fitzwater's door. His partner, C.M. Pueter had arrived, and the two men shook hands firmly at the door.

"Is there a problem?" Mr. Pueter asked. "Why is there no drink in my hand?"

Mr. Fitzwater laughed. "Well, I planned to treat you to dinner first."

"Some service you have here, Luke. Where's this dinner you're talking about? I don't see any food either." Mr. Pueter chuckled a bit.

"My chefs are the finest, I promise you. They're just running a bit behind. I accept full responsibility." The two men moved to sit down at the comfortable chairs in the suite.

"No, no, I understand. You gotta dress the cow up and make it feel pretty before you cook it! Haha!" Mr. Pueter was the kind of man that laughed at his own jokes and wasn't at all ashamed about it either. A few moments and a bit of chit-chat later, another knock sounded throughout the apartment. Mr. Fitzwater stood up and opened the door, and a couple of servants came through with food for the partners. The aroma was more intoxicating than any scotch Mr. Fitzwater had to offer, so the two men, excited for their dinner, moved to the balcony where a table and two chairs were as the servants set the food down and poured some water.

"Why pick today to eat outside? It's been uncharacteristically hot today in our beautiful city," Mr. Pueter asked.

"My balcony doesn't get much use due to the constant rainfall and gloominess," Mr. Fitzwater responded. "And look, the sun is setting so we'll have a gorgeous view."

"Mother nature is fickle, Luke," Mr. Pueter replied. "That's why man created controlled environments."

For Black Star, this part of the job could be the most agonizing. Waiting for an opening, watching the two men most likely talk about the dullest of things, it was enough to make him heavy-eyed. But he had to stay alert for his opportunity, even though watching them eat such a fine steak meal made him jealous. He couldn't hear the conversation, and he was awful at reading lips, so he ad-libbed their talk to keep himself entertained. The sun was behind Black Star and much lower in the sky than it had been previously, so the roof had begun cooling off drastically.

The two men finished their meal and Mr. Fitzwater grabbed his expensive scotch and crystal glasses and proposed a toast for the new direction of the company.

That's my cue. No wind blowing. Looks like fate is smiling on me.

Black Star readied his bow and before they could clink the glasses, he shot the first arrow and immediately strung another one as the first tore through Mr. Pueter's skull and pinned him into the wall. The crystal glass shattered on the ground as Black Star let loose his second arrow that whipped through the air right past Mr. Fitzwater, scratching his forehead just barely, but enough to make him bleed terribly, as forehead cuts bleed worse than almost anywhere else. He looked in the direction of Black Star, raised his glass, and took a sip as the blood began running down his face. Black Star nodded, even though Mr. Fitzwater couldn't see him, and Mr. Fitzwater ran out the room yelling for his servants.

The contract had been placed on Mr. Pueter by his own partner, as the two had opposing views for the future of the company. Mr. Pueter sought to outsource the entire company, which would have left thousands of families jobless. Mr. Fitzwater had come to know all his employees by name and made a promise to fight for them and their families. Not everyone could be a CEO, but that didn't mean that those regular women and men couldn't have a nice life and live in some degree of luxury. Mr. Fitzwater understood after so many millions piling in his bank that the number became meaningless to him because he could sire no children. He knew he couldn't be buried with his money, so he sought to give it to those who needed it, and made his employees lives infinitely better for it.

Mr. Fitzwater knew he couldn't poison the food because he would be suspected more than anyone else. He needed to make it look as though the assassin tried to kill them both, so that's why Black Star fired the second shot and purposely missed. Black Star's contract was complete and he could finally leave The City and go to Cornelius's. The reward for this contract would be nothing more than icing on the cake for Black Star as he took great joy in ridding the world of another corrupt businessman. He collapsed his bow, put it back in its small box, and put that box back in his bag. He walked to the edge of the building and looked down as his heart sank and then skipped a beat. It was like he was looking down at a rushing sea, spooking even he who could fall great heights like a spider or squirrel. He looked back up at the sunrise to his left and smiled at its beauty.

A gift from God.

So, he took a deep breath, looked back down, and jumped.

FIFTEEN

KAI

"You shouldn't be here." The dry wind whipped across the sandy dunes around the excavated city of Akkad and through the black robes of the figure in front of Kai.

"I need to find answers. I need to find the truth behind the Black Seed. I need to find the truth behind what happened to Alphonse." The cloaked figure moved from in front of the steps that led down to the temple face and Alphonse's notebook.

"The truth will not set you free Kai. It will kill you. This will make you an enemy of the High Council." An unkindly darkness covered the face of the person standing off to Kai's side. Not even the sunlight reflecting off the sand gave Kai any glimpse at the visage underneath as he walked past. He stopped again before starting down the steps and turned his head toward his adversary.

"I've never cared about my life. Ever since I can remember my life has never been my own. I've killed hundreds of people and I've done horrible things for the Sicarii. I never cared about myself. I never cared about others. But after Alphonse everything changed. I've always hated myself. But now, I can't even stand to look at myself in the mirror. I look down at my hands and all I see is his blood. I dream and all I see is his head rolling around on the roof of that building. I've... been too long in this world. But before I go, I want the truth."

"Then it is the truth you will find," the cloaked figure responded.

Kai turned away one last time and continued walking down the steps, light in hand, and moved his way deeper into the darkness leading to the temple front. Once there, he turned on the generators scattered about to bring light to the excavation area. The lights illuminated the temple front, and once again he stared down the Black Seed carved into the temple face. To the right of the excavation area was the table where Alphonse's journal was originally, and in a deep corner, shrouded by darkness, was the hole in which he hid the journal so no one would find it. He knew the High Council would send someone to find the journal and to uncover what they could, but he didn't know who and he didn't know when. The Council wouldn't risk reburying Akkad, as they had been searching for it for too long, but it wouldn't be long before they sent another team, just like Alphonse's to continue the excavation.

Kai took Alphonse's journal and put it in the backpack he was carrying on top of his desert clothes. He moved into the temple slowly, with his own personal light raised, as not even the light from the excavation lamps could penetrate the thick darkness held within. The columns holding up the ceiling were beautiful, inscribed with ancient Akkadian and decorated with visages of people, bull-men, great warriors, and mammals with the wings of birds and faces of men. Kai crept slowly further through the darkness until he reached steps going up, leading, he assumed, to the altar. He climbed the steep steps, light still in hand, and after climbing much longer than he anticipated he reached the top where the stone altar stood, where on top of the altar sat absolutely nothing. He looked around for some clue, for some sign of anything, some answer to the writings in Alphonse's journal, to the Black Seed, to what he saw in the sewers in Sweden, but there was nothing. It was a dark, stone temple, filled with nothing but memories of an ancient civilization lost to time. Defeated, Kai walked down the steps and towards the light of the excavation lamps outside the temple. His thoughts began to wander and his hope began to fade.

The answer was that there wasn't one. And he was right, it has killed me.

Slowly, whispers of death filled Kai's mind, and thoughts of self-annihilation overtook him. His sorrow overwhelmed him and the whispers grew louder as he dropped the light and collapsed to the lightless, stone floor, tears rolling heavily down his cheeks. He screamed and pounded the floor, truly unleashing, for the first time in his life, all the pain he had felt from the time his parents had died to the night he killed Alphonse. He was broken, and it wasn't by blade or fist, explosive or gun, but by the loss of everything and everyone he had ever loved. As his tears dripped to the floor and his fists pounded heavily upon the stone, the dust and sand coating it moved away, and through his hazy vision, clouded by tears and darkness, he saw it plain as day: the Black Seed.

Pain shot through Kai's skull, and he screamed as the whispers grew louder in his mind. Memories flooded back to him, those of recent and those from long ago, ones that he couldn't remember, that he shouldn't remember. Alphonse's head rolled across the ground as it screamed at him, morphing into the face of Alef pulling Kai out of the rubble of a home. A blue light flashed in Kai's mind's eye and matter disintegrated into ash, transforming into his parents, their faces filled with love and happiness and their white lab coats cradling him with tender care until their faces melted, their flesh peeled from their bones, and their clothes were turned into dust. They yelled each other's names as well as a third that rushed away with the roar of the ever-changing revelation of corruption. Kai screamed as visions of ancient people cannibalizing each other rushed into him, ichor and viscera shredding between their broken teeth. Another rush hit him, as if heavy, cold, dark ocean waves were taking him away, and he saw a teenage boy slaughter his family and eat them bit by bit. Kai could feel his mind ripping apart at the seams and his head pounded like never before.

NO! NO! GET OUT OF ME! Kai screamed inside himself, lost in an ocean of devastation as the Seed forced its way deeper into his memories.

STOP! NOT THERE! NO! NO! The Seed dug deeper inside of him, and memories of the Academy, Alphonse, and his sorrow flooded back. Deeper and deeper it penetrated, revealing the bones of a past hidden behind a wall of traumatic devastation.

"I SAID NO!" Kai screamed out loud, finding enough reprieve to desperately get to his feet. His light was nowhere to be found, and he couldn't see the excavation lamps outside the temple to lead his way. He stumbled aimlessly around, grasping hopelessly at the darkness until he found the wall with his hands, and behind the dust and sand found unending carvings of the Black Seed. He stumbled around and collapsed to his knees one last time, clutching his head with both hands as he stared at the stone below. A flickering of light, like that of fire, illuminated the floor in front of him and he looked up desperately in hopes of salvation from someone, but he was met instead with the Black Seed, towering above the altar, illuminated like the setting sun.

With one final shriek his ego was penetrated and the infection of the Black Seed spread throughout his mind, revealing - annihilating, revealing, annihilating, in an endless ocean of destructive revelation. In an instant he was carried away in the sea of chaos until he was a child again, four years old, standing in the living room of his childhood home, crying. His parents rushed to him and tried to console him, but his tears kept coming even if he didn't know why. The room around him began brightening and he could make out the sound of faint crackles whispering through the air. The sound became louder and the light became brighter, terrifying him even more than he already was. His parents were scared too, he could see it on their faces, but his tears began blurring his vision, no matter how many times he tried to wipe his eyes. The paint began peeling off the walls and pieces of furniture ignited around the three of them. His parents began shouting over the crackling at one another.

"John!" his mother yelled. "What are we going to do?" His father looked towards him and smiled and then looked back towards Kai's mother.

"There's nothing we can do, my love." At first, his mother looked terrified, afraid of what was to come, but after just a brief moment of weakness she smiled and accepted reality and held the hand of her husband and the father of her child. Kai's parents came towards him and wrapped their arms around him and held him tightly. His parents turned towards each other and kissed one deep, final kiss.

"I love you Lillian," his father said to his mother.

"And I love you, John," his mother replied. They both turned towards Kai, with tears in their eyes.

"We love you so very much, son," his father said.

"We will always love you. Never forget that my darling," added his mother. They held Kai one last time and Kai cried sorrowful, terrified tears that burned as they moved down his face. And then, with a flash, everything disappeared and his vision went black. Yet again, he was in an ocean of dark infinity, but this time the turbulence had gone away and he was left instead floating in the never-ending dark. Above him, or in front of him, he was unsure at this point, the Black Seed floated - in the air, in the ocean, he did not know, but it was there, staring at him, corrupting him.

"What are you?" he asked it calmly as he floated in nothingness. The Black Seed pulsed with a dim, dark light, and Kai stood up from the cold, stone floor and looked up towards the altar one last time, where no Seed, no light resided. His cheeks were stained with tears and his Self was thoroughly raped by a force greater than himself.

"Nzhurmiwa," he said in a whisper. Kai turned around and walked out of the temple the same way he had come in, but this time he left vulnerable and with the truth about Alphonse, himself, the Black Seed, and the thing behind it all. He slogged back up the steps that led out to the desert and after being blinded by the light of the sun checked his phone and noticed he had a voice message from Murimoto that he had received while down in the temple. He played it immediately.

"Kai, I was thinking about that riddle you told me and it made me realize something. Now I don't know about the latter part of the riddle, it makes no sense to me, perhaps that's because it's for you, but the part that struck me was 'ruins of old joy'. I don't know how literal the riddle is supposed to be, but there's only one place like that in the City and that's the old football stadium downtown, the one that was converted after the war into a graveyard? That's the only thing I could think of so I figured I'd let you know. Anyways, don't forget to stop by again soon and get some more ramen. This old man is always open for you. Oh, also, if you need any more help on this matter I suggest visiting Haley in the Greater Library. She might have more answers than me."

After hearing Sohei's message, Kai knew exactly what he had to do and where he had to go. At this point, Kai knew that his death wasn't far off. The High Council had to be on to him and no matter his rank they wouldn't stand for the actions he'd taken, or the ones he would take in the future. And yet, fear did not reach Kai. Not after what had just happened. Memories that he never lived, that he never knew from a time long ago were trapped in his mind, unable to escape, torturing him with every passing second. The corruption had seeped into his soul and he was diseased in a way no doctor could heal.

Kai took a commercial airline back to the New States, unlike his earlier travels using resources he had gathered over his time at the Sicarii. He had no reason to hide and since the Sicarii were on to him already, as he had assumed, he had no way of hiding even if he wanted to. Luckily, commercial airlines were just as fast as most private forms of travel, so he reached the New States in a little over an hour. His mind was silent from the airport to the elevator leading down to the entrance of Headquarters, until it finally spoke to him.

What do you think you can do?

Kai ignored his mind, the adversary residing within him, and pressed on. As the pod flew down the rail towards the Spire he saw a flash of fire light up the market district. The pod came to a stop and he ran out towards the south end of the subterranean city. As he moved in the same direction of Murimoto's ramen shop, the Spire Guard ran past him, their armor, similar to that of SWAT armor on the surface, was composed of a lightweight metal and Kevlar chest piece with holographic signs on the front and the back. The way this armor differentiated from the SWAT armor on the surface was that it was reinforced with the nano technology that composed the Sicarii suits, so it not only protected the Guard, but made them faster and stronger as well.

"SPIRE GUARD! MOVE OUT OF THE WAY!" the frontrunner yelled as he and his team moved past Kai and residents of HQ and rounded the corner of the street. Kai rounded the corner as well and saw Sohei Murimoto's shop in flames. He ran forward a bit and saw Sohei's bruised, lifeless body pinned above the storefront, flames licking at his heels. Panic set in and Kai backed away slowly and hid in a dark alley not too far off. After his experience in the temple ruins he had not been in control of his mind, and his thoughts and memories were not entirely his own. He was scared, broken, but he still knew what he had to do.

Kai pushed his panic down, got up, and walked to the Sifriyah in an effort to find someone he never really knew and never really planned on knowing up until now. As he walked through the wooden and glass doors of the Greater Library the smell of old books penetrated his soul, and had the events in Akkad not happened perhaps he would've sat down and enjoyed a few. But he could not, for his mind was not his own, not anymore. The library was empty, as it almost always was, and on the far side of the shelves, near the entrance to the Well, stood Haley, brunette hair tied in a ponytail, light brown eyes focused on returning old books to high-tech shelves.

Kai began walking towards her. She looked up as he began walking and met him halfway. She saw something was wrong. She saw that Kai, despite his usual melancholic demeanor, was worse than she had seen him before.

"Kai wh-"

Kai raised his finger to his mouth to shush her. He got closer to her before he spoke up.

"They're watching. Sohei Murimoto is dead. We must keep quiet," he whispered.

"You look horrible, Kai. What's going on? Sohei is dead? What happened?" The questions flowed from Haley like a waterfall.

"We can't talk here. Do you live in The City?" Kai asked.

"Yes," Haley replied.

"Do you know the Coffee Shop?" he inquired again.

"Yes."

"Meet me there in three hours. Does that work for you?"

"Yes," Haley stated again. Kai nodded and walked away, out of the library and onto the streets of HQ, where he was met with Verena, standing, waiting for him.

"The Council requests your presence, Kai. They await you in their chambers."

Is this it? Kai asked himself.

"Understood," Kai replied. Verena escorted Kai into the Spire and to the elevator. Silence ensued.

Is this where I die?

Does it matter?

No, not really.

But what about Haley? Amina? Marlowe? Piers? Tara?

They know the risks. Their lives are not mine.

No, but you affect them, surely. Do you not care for them at all?

I do, in a way. I am their leader, but I am not their friend. Friends die, or worse I kill them. It is best to keep them at a distance, for their safety and mine.

So, you've made up your mind then?

Yes. If I die here, that'll be okay. It's what is owed for the sins I've committed.

The elevator door opened and Verena stepped out first, followed by Kai. She opened the massive wooden doors leading to the Council chambers and shut them behind him whenever he entered. Sitting in front of him were only five members of the Council, eyes locked on him as he stood at the doorway, Dalet's seat empty. Gimel spoke up first.

"Come forward Kai. We have something we must discuss." Kai stepped forward, past the indention in the floor and stood in place, glancing over at Sofia leaning up against the wall. "You've been aggressive, disloyal, and stubborn as of late," Gimel continued. "And if it were up to me and me alone, I would've had you executed where you stand. Soldiers like you are problems, but the results you produce are next to none, not even Mahta stands at your level."

He spoke up next. "Your work with Gilroy was reckless, but phenomenal. Your mess was cleaned up and the media was fed falsified information that the generators in the office building failed and exploded."

"We know a message was relayed from Gilroy to you in his dying hour," Bet said. "What was it?"

Kai hesitated to answer but spoke anyway. "It was a riddle."

"A riddle?" Vav asked.

"Yes," Kai stated.

"What did this riddle say?" Vav inquired further.

"Lilac death will bring you back to the storm." Vav looked at Alef who put down his bellowing pipe and crossed one leg over the other as he leaned back in his chair.

"We have two final missions for you, Kai," Alef said. One is a full-squad operation, hunt-and-capture, no kill. Why is none of your concern. We will cover the details in a moment. The second mission will be your final one. There is a seat open on the council, and we wish for you to fill it."

Kai was stunned.

"This may come as a surprise to you, Kai," Vav began, "but the Council feels that you would be best suited at the head, where none can tell you how to think and feel, or what to do. With this, your friendships will be terminated, your Sicarii records expunged, and your existence annihilated. Do you understand?"

Kai nodded, still shocked.

"Damnatio memoriae is not only reserved for rogues, but for future members of the Council as well. Your possessions will be taken, your apartment will be gutted, and you will be gifted with more than you can possibly imagine. Your funds will be endless and you will be free to pursue anything to your heart's desire, including the mystery surrounding the death of Alphonse, your late brother in arms."

"Why... me?" Kai asked. "Why? I never asked for this."

Alef spoke up again. "You're an asset that of which the Sicarii has never seen before. You're fast, strong, intelligent, and your skills as a leader, even in the face of trauma and pain, have allowed you to lead your team into a year's worth of success, barring the incident with Amina, who is, fortunately, recovered. It might be wise for you to visit her." Kai nodded again.

"Now for your mission, Kai," he said. "We will give you the details here as the Well of Light does not have any information on your target. Your target is a woman who lives in The City that goes by the name of Lillian Marshall."

Lillian.

LiLLIAN
LILLIAN!

Kai's brain screeched at him, darkness swirling in his mind, memories igniting and annihilating in milliseconds. He collapsed to the floor and grabbed his head. Sofia moved away from the wall and became attentive towards Kai.

"Is everything alright, Kai?" Alef asked.

"I'm fine, I'm fine," Kai reassured. "Just a migraine."

"Go to the medical ward and get that looked at after this," Alef ordered. "You took a hit from Gilroy in your battle, didn't you? You should've seen a doctor immediately."

"Okay," Kai stated, knowing full well the headache wasn't from the hit he took during his fight.

"Getting back to it," He said, "Lillian Marshall is an ex-soldier and CIA operative who is putting her nose where it doesn't need to be. She is cybernetically enhanced and has been since taking an almost direct blast from an IED in New York City back at the end of the Great War. She's in her fifties now, but she fights like she's twenty, and her enhancements can be blamed for that. She has artificial limbs, with retractable blades in all of them."

Gimel took over where He left off. "On top of this, she has a state-of-the-art neural processing unit created by my company, Trytek. This unit isn't on the market and has only been given to those in a very high position that are in regular combat situations, like Lillian."

LILLIAN!

"Even if you could kill her Kai," Bet said, "don't. She has very valuable information, both within her body and mind that we need. Capture her and call for transport."

"Understood," Kai said.

"There is no information on Lillian Marshall in the Well," Gimel said, "so we will be giving you this information chip that should give you everything you need in order to hunt her down." Gimel handed the black and gold, square chip to Sofia who walked over and handed it to Kai.

"This should slot directly into the port on the back of your helmet and should meld with the nanobots that compose your helmet so that you can still use the dissolution feature. I have had my top engineers construct it."

"Thank you," Kai said. "Should I retrieve Amina for this mission?"

"Yes," Alef stated. "You'll find her in her room in the medical facilities. Whenever you complete this task, we will go over the final mission for your ascension. You are dismissed."

Kai nodded and walked out of the Council chambers and past Verena, who winked at him from her desk as he stepped into the elevator and turned around. The doors closed and Kai started hyperventilating

This isn't good.

This isn't good.

The High Council? Me? No. No. This can't be happening.

The elevator stopped and Kai walked out, head pounding. He walked slowly to the medical facilities and then to Amina's room. When he arrived, Amina was still in bed facing away from the door. He opened the door and walked in, but Amina didn't move.

"Amina..." Kai began. "It's time to go."

Amina looked towards him with tear-stained cheeks and sat up hesitantly. He walked over to her, helped her up, and helped her get dressed.

"You never... came to visit me..." Amina trailed off.

"Yes, I did," Kai responded. "I'm the one that brought you here. I stayed by your side every day until I knew you were stable."

"Why...?"

"Because what happened was my fault. Because I'm your leader."

"Because you care about me?" Amina asked.

"Yes, Amina. Because I care about you." Kai responded. Amina smiled and put her boots on and stood up.

"We have another mission," Kai said.

Amina looked at him and then looked back at the floor. "We're toys Kai. Pawns. You know that, right?"

"You can't say that here," Kai whispered in her ear. "They're watching."

"I don't care," she whispered back. "I've given up everything for them and look where that's left me. I have nothing. And now..." Tears welled in her eyes.

"Now what?" Kai asked.

She stood up. "And now I can't even have kids," Amina whispered as she walked towards the door.

Empathy overtook Kai and he went over to Amina and hugged her. She cried in his arms for what seemed like an eternity, and he held her through it all. Afterwards, they took a pod back to the City and Kai took her to his apartment, where she laid down in bed and went to sleep. Kai looked at the time on his clock and saw that he still had half an hour to spare before his meeting with Haley, so he turned on the television. He flipped through the channels until he found something that piqued his interest.

"In international news," the woman on the T.V. said, "a Brazillian government facility was attacked by terrorists last week. Military police and government investigators are unsure of who or what attacked them, but the attack left the side of the building damaged from an explosion and the terrorist group stole something from the facility, although the Brazillian government refuses to say what. This has been the late-night news with Evelyn Johnson. Up next, Zach Rawson's pop culture segment with "Did actor James Hampton get a nose job?" With that Kai turned off the T.V., uncaring of pop culture, drama, gossip, and all other forms of social absurdity.

Kai stood up and walked over to the far side of his living room where a window looked out onto the busy street below. He saw his own reflection staring back at him, faintly, like a watermark on the world, and it was the first time in a long time that he truly looked at himself. His eyes were heavy and the dark circles under them were darker than they'd ever been. His form was a mystery, a shroud, a burden. Kai snapped out of his dark thoughts quickly and walked over to the front door, closing his bedroom door on the way. He grabbed his coat, checked his jeans and shoes, and walked out.

Outside the Coffee Shop, he saw Haley sitting at a table by herself in one of the corners where the glass front met the brick interior. From an outsider's perspective Haley looked okay, like there weren't a million things running through her head. But Kai could tell, he had been there before. She was *terrified*. He walked in and over to her and a sigh of relief came over her as he sat down.

"What's going on Kai? What happened?" she asked desperately.

"Sohei is dead and in his last message he told me to find you."

"Find me? Why?"

"I don't know. Were you two friends?" Kai asked.

"I guess you could say that. More of a frequenter of his shop than anything else." Haley chuckled, embarrassed. "Sohei did enjoy the library. He came by quite often to visit and to read some old religious texts, I think. What about you?"

"Sohei was always a mentor of sorts to me," Kai said. "I met him in the Academy when I was a young boy and I remember whenever he decided to open the ramen shop. He was a good person, or as good of a person as an ex-squad leader can be." They both nodded in agreement.

"I found Sohei when the Spire Guard did and he was staked into the brick wall above the shop front."

"...Staked?" Haley asked, bewildered and horrified.

"Yes." Kai stared her down as she realized what that meant.

"There's only one group I know that has the strength for something like that," Haley looked deep into Kai's eyes. "The Seraphim."

"Exactly my thought," Kai said.

"But why?" Haley asked, confused. "Why would the Council send a member of Seraph Squad to kill Sohei? What did he do?"

"It was my fault," Kai confessed. "As I'm sure you know Haley, I'm a squad leader."

"I know," Haley replied, "but prove it." She smiled.

Kai smiled back through his lifeless demeanor. "Kai. A-Rank Knight-Hybrid. Leader of Squad Four. Assassin under the order of the High Council of the Sicarii. Your turn."

Haley laughed a bit. "Haley. C-Rank Wraith. Scribe of the Greater Library under the order of the High Council of the Sicarii."

"A Wraith, huh?" Kai was surprised.

"Just like my sister," Haley replied. "Except she's a lot better than me. But get back to what you were telling me about Sohei."

"Right," Kai said. "I was contracted with killing the leader of Squad Three, Gilroy, after he went rogue. After he ambushed me on the roof of an office building right outside one of the secondary entrances to HQ, and I defeated him, he gave me a piece of paper with a riddle on it." Kai looked around the store to make sure no one was listening in. For the most part, this late at night, the twenty-four-hour cafe was mostly dead.

"I couldn't figure out the riddle on my own, so I destroyed the paper and brought the riddle to Sohei, who couldn't figure it out either. Well, earlier today he sent me a voice message that gave a possible answer to the first part of the riddle," Kai stopped. "Before I go any further, I want to tell you this: I don't trust you. I don't know who you are and even if I did, I wouldn't trust you. I don't trust my own squad mates except in combat. But Sohei trusted you, it seemed, and I trusted Sohei more than anyone else. What I've told you so far is knowledge the High Council does not possess, as far as I know. When Alef first asked me about Gilroy, I lied to him. Then, just an hour or so ago, the Council asked me directly what message Gilroy relayed to me and I told them a piece of the riddle, but not anything that they could learn from. Because I told Sohei the riddle, the High Council had him interrogated and killed. At least, that's what I believe. So, you can either run to the Council and tell them what I've told you so far and be rewarded, or you can stay, listen, and risk your life by helping me."

Haley looked at Kai deeply and sincerely. "You're brave for telling me this, despite the repercussions to yourself. I will not tell the Council, Kai. But the road you walk is a dangerous one and the chances of this ending well are slim to none. If you open this door, you will not be able to close it."

"I'm not brave," Kai retorted. "I'm careless. No one dare look beyond that door with reasonable sense because they fear what they must lose to see the other side. I simply have nothing left to lose."

"There is always more to lose, Kai," Haley responded. "Always. Now, tell me the riddle."

"Lilac death in the ruins of old joy/ Will bring you back to the love you lost/ Amidst the storm's bite. Sohei said in his message that 'ruins of old joy' made him think of the old football stadium downtown that was converted into a graveyard."

"That's exactly what I was thinking," said Haley. "And 'lilac death' would make sense."

"Why?" Kai asked, curious.

"Because all of the gravestones are lit up with purple neon lights."

"I guess I know where I have to go then," Kai said. "Thank you, Haley." Kai began to stand up when Haley stopped him.

"Wait, Kai, before you go," Haley pulled out a piece of paper and a pen and wrote something down. "Here's my number. Call me if you ever need anything. I live just a few blocks away from here so I can meet almost any time. And please, be careful."

"Will do, Haley. Thanks again."

SIXTEEN

BLACK STAR

In a modern style penthouse the morning sun pierced through the windows that overlooked most of The City. The living room was well lit, and the white walls absorbed the rays of the sun beautifully. A door opened and a man walked out of his bathroom in a towel. His dark skin glistened from the steam and his muscles pulsated as he walked into his bedroom. He tossed his towel into the basket and put on a dark purple robe, as dark purple was his favorite color. The short locs on the top of his head remained unmoved as he walked to the kitchen to get a cup of coffee. The coffee machine was programmed to start its process at 10 a.m., an hour and a half after he normally woke up. This gave him time to work out and take a shower every morning before the machine ground the beans and created a hot, blonde roast for him.

A ringing came from a small panel on his living room wall. He walked over with his cup of coffee and looked at the screen. It was a number he was unfamiliar with, but he answered it anyway.

"Hello?" the man said.

"I'm looking for a man who goes by D?" the voice over the phone said.

Shocked, but intrigued, D decided to play along, as he knew a regular person wouldn't know his title or his connection to the High Council.

"Yes, this is he. Who is this? And how did you get my number?"

Black Star was laying in his bed, his phone in one hand, paddle ball in the other. "I had a friend help me search online," he began.

"We only had a few leads and filters to go on, but I knew once I found your face I'd get more information. I persevered and searched through thousands of pages to find what I could. This is Black Star, by the way."

"Impressive," D replied. "There shouldn't be any information on me out there. What do you want from me Black Star?" D asked as he leaned up against his wall and sipped on his black coffee.

Black Star got up from his bed and began walking around his bedroom. "I have a contract for you worth ten million, if you're interested."

D swallowed his coffee and coughed a bit. "That's a pretty penny, so why not do the contract yourself?"

Black Star set down his paddle ball and walked over to his Space Cadet bobblehead on his dresser and started fidgeting with its jiggling head. "Because I'm the target."

"You're placing a contract on your own head?" D asked, surprised.

"Yes," Black Star replied.

"So, you want me to kill you?" D inquired further.

"If you think you can. You didn't seem interested in talking last time we met, so I figured I'd sweeten the pot for you."

"Oh shit," D said, a bit of excitement boiling in his voice. "You're that kid from Brazil, Alexander's son. I don't know why I didn't make that connection sooner with your bizarre name."

"So, are you up for the job Mr. Businessman?" Black Star asked.

"Depends," D said. "How impatient are you to die?"

"I can wait a bit," Black Star responded. "But don't keep me waiting too long. I've been looking forward to this."

"I can meet you tomorrow evenin-"

"Perfect!" Black Star said, cutting D off. "I'll send you the coordinates. I want this to be special." D, unamused, demanded respect even off the clock, especially from a child.

"That won't work. You need to accommodate me and let me finish talking. I can meet you tomorrow evening at the abandoned Red Fizz factory. It's in old Chicago.

"Alright," Black Star said. "I don't think it would be as aesthetically pleasing as what I had in mind, but I'm easy to work with. Also, you don't have to get snippy with me. Technically, I'm your employer.

D, recognizing the wit of Black Star mixed with the smart-ass attitude sighed and took a deep breath.

"You got it sir. I'll see you tomorrow," D replied.

"Oh, you can drop the formalities, bud," Black Star said, trying to get under D's skin. "I'll be there around six." Black Star hung up the phone and D took another sip of his coffee.

I don't remember being that arrogant as a kid, or that eager to prove something.

After the display in Curitiba D wasn't concerned with Black Star, so he purposely suggested a close location to himself, so he didn't have to go far out of his way for such a quick contract. The next day D was there first, waiting and looking at the war-torn ruins of downtown Chicago in the distance while smoking a cigar. Storm clouds rumbled above and lightning struck not too far away. After a few minutes, Black Star appeared behind him on the opposite side of the rooftop, wielding a hu tou gou, or hook sword in each hand.

"You're here early," Black Star said. "Why is that?"

"I had to check for traps. I wasn't going to blindly walk into the battlefield," D replied while smoking his cigar, facing away from Black Star.

"Wow, I'm hurt. You think I would ensnare you? I want to win from my skill, not from cheap tricks."

"I didn't think you would, you're old school. Most assassins don't settle scores with a duel anymore. Back in my day it was used to battle over territory though." D paused to puff from his cigar again then turned to face Black Star. "Do you still think this is a game?"

"Would you believe me if I said it's the only way I can take this seriously?" Black Star replied.

"Should I believe an impulsive liar?" D retorted.

"Valid point, so let's get more serious."

"Really? You get serious?"

"I've got a lot of questions," Black Star stated. "Questions that keep me up at night. What made you kill my parents? Was it money? Power? Did you have a grudge? Was it worth it? Did any good come of it?"

D blew out smoke and threw the cigar down on the rooftop, it's cherry still intact. "That's a loaded question. Power, money mostly. But that contract got me a promotion. I'll admit that not many benefits came to the rest of the world, but it was a crucial operation in the business world. To be honest, your father would have died years prior if your mother hadn't spent so much time protecting him. But I had no grudge against them other than the grudges I carried from those who gave me the contract. Good men don't live long, kid."

Black Star looked calm but was boiling on the inside. "I was afraid I wouldn't like your answers. You chose to kill them for petty reasons."

"We're assassins. We're all petty," D laughed.

"Just like that cigar, let's enjoy this slow burn," D said as he removed his coat and showed his vested, muscular torso wrapped in heavy chains with a small 20-kilogram ball at the end. He removed the chain, unwrapping it from his torso and began spinning the ball slowly in his right hand that was covered in a leather gauntlet that ran up to his elbow. He dashed towards Black Star who reacted immediately, and they met around the middle of the rooftop. D slung the dense ball quickly towards Black Star, which arced like the frisbee he had thrown back to those teenagers, and so predicting the curvature in a split second he jumped backwards, dodging the ball, and launched himself forwards with a kick that was blocked by D's free arm. Black Star placed his hooks on the ground as his kick was blocked and used the force, and D's arm, to launch himself into the air above. Black Star came down with his hooks attempting multiple slashes, but all were blocked by D's outstretched chain as sparks flew around them in the evening air. Black Star landed on the ground and lept towards D again, deflecting D's chain from above with one hook and slashing with the right. D dodged backwards as Black Star attempted to kick, but D deflected the kick with his forearm as he slung the steel ball towards Black Star's head. Black Star ducked and caught D's chain with his left hook. Because of his position, he couldn't dodge the kick to the gut, so D delivered it with brutal force and in one swift motion to put some distance between them. Black Star released his hook from the chain he had caught.

"You brought these hooks to counter my chains, didn't you?" D asked through a smile.

"Twin hooks have many uses," Black Star replied, "and your chains kept me at bay in Brazil. I didn't want that to happen again. But I'd use them regardless of your choice in weapon."

"A preference huh?" D said, intrigued. "Do you think you have enough experience with those to take me down? Or do you think your bloodline is enough to stop me?"

"If I wasn't confident in my ability I wouldn't be here!" Black Star yelled as he charged D again, slashing twice vertically and once horizontally. D dodged the blades and guided them away with the palm of his hand as they passed. He was cool and collected, as if time was moving in slow motion.

"I think you would've fought me whether you were confident or not," D said as he continued dodging the flurry of blows. "You see it like I do: one person gets victory and the other gets to rest well. Regardless of the outcome, you're happy." D countered a blow and went for one of his own, but Black Star dodged. He continued speaking as the two danced through chain and sword. "That's why you were willing to put a contract on yourself. You don't care if you die. You don't think you have any other purpose in this life other than revenge." D smirked as if he had Black Star figured out.

Black Star jumped back and began twirling his hooks around himself, contemplating D's words. Even during breaks like these, Black Star continued to move, making small movements like spinning weapons in his hands in order to keep his physical and mental momentum until the fight was truly over. After a moment, he spoke up.

"You're right. I wouldn't be burdened anymore if I die. But right now, I have more of a reason for living than you." D began spinning the long chain above his head and then to each side, elongating it slowly until he slung it downwards at Black Star, carrying the momentum he had generated. Black Star moved out of the way, and the blow crushed the concrete on the edge of the roof. He looked behind him and realized he was too close to the edge of the roof. Even if he fell, he wouldn't be harmed seriously, but it would put him in a weaker strategic position, and a weaker strategic position meant death in the world of the assassin. Black Star dodged to his side again as the ball crushed the concrete below him. The chain came at him as D yanked it back and he pinned it to the roof with one of his hooks, rolling in the air as he dodged over it. Black Star took the moment to look around and noticed that slowly but surely, D had been chipping the edges off the rooftop and crushing certain places over and over again.

He's trying to take me off balance. I need to get him off this rooftop. Black Star thought. *For some reason, rooftops feel like his home.*

"Are you ready to turn things up a notch?" Black Star asked D.

"It's your contract. I'm ready when you are, boss." D said with a smile. Black Star picked up his second hook, giving D his chain back. He twirled his hooks around him and began picking up immense speed as he did. D wrapped his chain around his leather-bound right arm to shorten it and began spinning the 20-kilogram ball. Black Star dashed forward, faster than D had ever seen before.

Straight at me again, huh? D thought. *This kid never learns.* When Black Star was in hook's length of D he redirected and dashed right, seemingly sliding across the roof, and flanked D's weak side and slung his right leg as fast as he could at D's side. D raised his left arm to block the kick, but at the same time noticed one of Black Star's hooks coming for his opposite side.

Shit, D thought. *This is gonna hurt.* D caught the blade with his chain and leather wrapped right arm but didn't have the strength to take the kick from the left. The kick went straight through his block, cracking both his radius and ulna, and

sent him flying off the edge of the roof and onto the lower rooftop below. In mid-air Black Star was on him again and when he attempted to grab D, D punched him in the face with his right arm. Black Star took the hit, and as both men hit the lower rooftop they tumbled in separate directions. Black Star recovered quickly, rolling and transferring his momentum into a handspring that had him back on his feet in a second. D, on the other hand, struggled getting up after he rolled, as he couldn't put pressure on his broken left arm. Black Star wasn't one to kick his opponents while they were down, so he allowed D a breather before he continued the fight.

As D stood up, he realized the ball at the end of his chain was gone and he laughed.

"A one-man pincer attack huh? God damn that was a good move, kid," D said. "Who taught you that?"

"I guess in a way you could say it was from my grandpa, or my mom. Maybe a movie?" Black Star answered. "Or maybe it was just me."

"You're a better fighter than your mom. I'll give you that," D replied.

"Why didn't you kill me in Brazil and end this?" Black Star asked, his rage pent up inside him, begging for answers. "Did you want to prolong my life so we could meet again and you could see how I've developed?"

"You're smart, Black Star," D began. "You know the answer. I had a contract on your parents. They died, you lived. When we met in Brazil, I considered you a lost cause that wasn't worth pursuing. Simply put, you were pathetic."

"And now? Am I pathetic now?" Black Star inquired, spinning his hooks again.

D laughed. "That has yet to be determined."

"Brazil was a casual passing," Black Star said. "This. This is our true reunion, and I hope you're enjoying it."

"Whatever," D said, readying himself for round three. "If you keep talking, I'll spark another cigar." They both chuckled a bit under their breath because they realized they were more similar than they had thought. But despite their similarities, they both knew that one must die, and one must live.

The two assassins ran towards the middle, and before they met D lowered himself and spun his chain as he spun his body. Black Star took the opposite route and jumped over D, who caught Black Star's foot with his chain and yanked him down. Black Star landed on his chest and rolled quickly, just in time to dodge D's knee drop. D recovered as well and slung his chain at Black Star again, who ducked under the chain and pinned it into the rooftop again with one of his hooks.

Predictable, D thought, but whenever he went to yank the chain in an attempt to take the hook from Black Star, Black Star quickly grabbed the hook with his left hand and broke off what he could of the chain. With one broken arm, D moved in closer and in an attempt to disarm Black Star. He grabbed his wrist as Black Star swung his hook, but the plan failed, and Black Star, knowing his enemy stood no chance against him, twisted out of the grab, kicked D away, and in a flash cut straight through D's right shoulder, severing his arm.

"Fuck," D said as he looked at his arm on the ground and then fell backwards onto the roof.

"You know," Black Star began as he stood over D's body, wiping his slightly bleeding nose in the process. "Sometimes having something to fight for is just the edge you need."

"Don't be modest," D replied. "You were the better fighter. You were stronger, faster, and a better tactician. Your motives don't matter. You beat me, man. Don't put your victory under others. You won from your power alone..." D took a moment to catch his breath as the dark ichor ran out of his shoulder. "This is a cutthroat business. We don't honor death like we should. But you, you're different. You remind me of me when I was younger. So, do me a favor if you could. There's a lady I've been sweet on, can you let her know what happened?"

This could be a trap to get me to go somewhere, but he's the one who signed the contract. Even if it was a trap, they wouldn't get credit. It could be a bluff, but I think he's actually genuine, Black Star thought with intrigue.

"I'll do that for you, but only as a 'good riddance' to your reign. It seems like a simple request."

"Oh... ah-ah-ahaha..." D's groan turned into a chuckle at what Black Star had said.

"What's so funny?" Black Star asked.

"You're stupid, you know that? My reign? I'm just a pawn, kid. All you did was defeat me, but not who I work for. You tried to cut the head of the snake off only to find it was a hydra. What a fool..." D's eyes fluttered as he began losing consciousness due to blood loss. Black Star saw and kicked him in the side.

"Ow," D said, his eyes shooting open.

"I want answers," Black Star explained himself. "You're not

allowed to die yet."

"Kids man..." D muttered.

"Tell me more," Black Star insisted.

D obliged. "Go ahead, continue to fight this never-ending battle. But if you keep giving into that darkness you will have created something far worse within you. You'll never find the peace you're searching for. Bear that in mind Black Star. Just know I don't hate you. Everything up until now has been strictly business."

"You're pretty talkative for a man on his deathbed. I feel like I'm playing some cheesy game."

"You're the one that kicked me awake," D said, irritated. "But I have some things to get off my chest before I pass. Atone for my sins or some shit. I achieved great wealth and social status in my life. I even loved my job in the beginning. But in the end, none of it brought me happiness. Fuck!" D yelled as blood continued running from his arm. "Look where it brought me - to the mercy of a kid." He stopped again to catch his breath. Black Star could tell that he only had a few minutes left in him, as his skin was turning pale and the light in his eyes began to fade.

"We're greedy and lustful by nature, but does that make us bad people?" D asked. "It's the only way we know how to survive. You can't change that. You can't change the innate instincts of humans. Not that it matters to me. Here in a moment, I'll be free of my burdens. If you're willing, let me pass in peace. But if you want to squeeze my life from me, I can understand."

Black Star watched him and thought about it for a moment, but somehow found remorse within himself for the man who ruined his life and murdered his parents. "D," Black Star spoke up. "What's your real name?"

"Jermaine," D said softly. The blood pumping out of his wound slowed, his eyes faded, and he died as Black Star knelt down beside him.

"Sleep well, Jermaine," Black Star said, closing his eyelids.

I guess I'll go see Cornelius again. He's the only person who somewhat understands my situation. Black Star took one last look at the man that had haunted his dreams and turned his life upside down. Yet all he could see now, despite the pain and suffering he caused, was the man Jermaine, unhappy and alone. *Parents are meant to teach you morals*, Black Star thought. *At least I got that from them. Wait. He never told me where his lover lived! Was he just messing with me up until the end?* Black Star thought for a moment and then came to a conclusion. *Oh well. It doesn't matter.*

Black Star took off his bloodied t-shirt and changed it out for a gray v-neck with white, horizontal stripes. After changing out his clothes, he folded both of his hooks which allowed them to fit in his bag easily. He hung over the edge of the building and pushed off it and landed back on the ground and rolled to reduce the strain on his feet, letting the shock absorb into a much larger surface area than just his ankles. After walking a few moments hunger overtook him, and he began thinking desperately about food as his hands shook. Due to the fact that he used so much energy in such a short amount of time, Black Star required nourishment in order to gain his energy back. So, he took a granola bar out of his bag and ate it while he walked. After arriving in a local town on the outskirts of The City, he saw a sign for a small soup shop on the street called "Helga's Kitchen", complete with a drawing of a steaming bowl of soup next to it. He followed the signs to the shop and stopped out front of the old, run-down shack. *Jeez*, he thought. *I hope the food is more appealing than this.* There was a standing sign next to the walkway that had been written on in chalk.

TODAY'S SPECIAL: FRESH CLAM CHOWDER
HOURS: TUESDAY-SATURDAY: 10-6.
SUNDAY AND MONDAY: CLOSED

Black Star took note of the sign and walked in, where a kind, heavy, middle-aged woman greeted him. "Hi hon! Come in come in. I don't bite unless you taste good," she giggled as her silver-streaked hair stuck to her sweaty face. "Take a seat wherever you like. You just missed the rush." The woman was getting ready to close, as it was a little after six, and so Black Star looked over the menu after he took a seat at a booth.

"Do you have the clam chowder ready?" he asked.

"No hon, unfortunately I'd have to make some. It would take about 20 minutes," she said, obviously exhausted from a hard day's work.

"That's okay," Black Star said, aware of her exhaustion and his as well. "Don't worry about it. Is the beef stew good?"

"Oh yes honey! People often wonder what's more hearty, me or my stew!" She laughed a kind, warm laugh, like that of a mother.

"I'll take that please," Black Star said, emotionless. She nodded and disappeared back into the kitchen. After a few moments, she popped back out with a huge bowl of steaming stew.

"Careful," she warned. "It's been warming in the pot all day, so don't burn your mouth." Black Star wasted no time blowing on the food and immediately began digging in, finishing off the double serving in minutes. She came back to him after he was finished, surprised that he had eaten it all so fast.

"I guess I don't have to ask how it was. I'll take your ravenous eating as a compliment! Honestly, I think you woulda ate just about anything I put in front of ya," she said.

"You're right," Black Star agreed. "I probably would've eaten just about anything, but don't let that make you think it wasn't delicious." He picked up the bowl and slurped out the remainder of the broth, warming up his insides.

"Thanks for the meal, Helga." Black Star tore off half of the napkin and used it to wipe his mouth. He took the other half, folded it, and put it in his pocket. Then he pulled a $20 bill out of his bag, slapped it on the table, asked her if she accepted cash, and then told her to keep the change.

"Have a nice day young man," she said.

"Have a terrific Thursday," Black Star replied as he walked out of the shop and towards his next destination. He still had a slight hunger, but he knew if he ate too much he would fall asleep, so he had gotten used to never being full over the past couple of years. Black Star pulled out his phone and sent a message to Cornelius, letting him know he'd be swinging by later that night. He never worried about showing up randomly at Cornelius's, as the guy never got any sleep anyways, but he decided to send him a message, nevertheless.

I never thought he'd become such a good friend, Black Star thought. After that, Black Star took a taxi to the nearest train station as he was too exhausted to run, and then took the vactrain from The City to Helena, Montana.

Later that evening, around 9:00 p.m., Black Star arrived at Verner Financial Aid. He was lucky enough to see the sunset on the drive over, but by the time he arrived at Cornelius's it was dark. He knocked on the door and after a minute Cornelius answered but could only open the door halfway as trash blocked it from the other side.

"Hey, you made it safely," Cornelius said. "I assume all went well?"

"Kind of," Black Star replied. "It was a hollow victory. That guy wasn't calling the shots after all. So, I only stopped *him*, but it's still progress."

"Well, do you feel any better now that you got your revenge?" Cornelius inquired as they walked the neat path between the trash and into the living room.

"A little bit. I have solace knowing he can't harm anyone else, and I feel good knowing I did what my parents couldn't, but I've come to realize it doesn't create a better world," Black Star said as he sat on the couch. Cornelius started up his game console.

"Isn't that your mantra though? If you kill all the people who plant seeds of corruption only flowers will bloom," he said with a smug, but joking attitude.

Trying his best not to smile, Black Star replied. "I can't help but feel like I've said that to you one too many times. Either way, you are right. That is the big plan, but apparently the seeds of corruption are far deeper than anticipated."

"What do you mean?" Cornelius asked

"Well, he said that his organization was like a hydra with many heads. A part of me wasn't ready for that. I kinda want to call it good and stop. I got what I wanted out of it. He also told me I'm no longer being tracked so I'm free. This might be my only time to get out of the business. Maybe we should let the corruption win, you know. Accept the world for what it is and quit trying to change it..." Black Star trailed off and Cornelius was shocked to hear such a pessimistic response from him.

"That sounds like quitter talk if you ask me. Black Star, look at me." Cornelius wasn't known for being a serious man, but he hardened his voice and began talking sternly as Black Star looked up at him.

"Look, you don't quit when odds are stacked against you. That's not who you are. I know right now it seems like you are trying so incredibly hard, but barely making a dent, but you're doing so much more. You give people like me hope! I'm scared Black Star. I'm scared I might look at someone the wrong way, or say the wrong thing, and it's over for me, and I know no one will bat an eye. I deal with a lot of assassins and they're all the same greedy, egotistical fools. You're different. You care how things affect the world. You get so close to corruption and you don't let it affect you. You're like Icarus, flying so close to the sun, but your wings refuse to melt. That's your secret ability. So, you can't let the corruption win. You are not fighting this battle just for yourself. You're doing this for everyone. For the people living in fear. I'm sorry you have to do it alone. A lot of us are too weak and would only get in the way. But that's what you do Black Star. You bear the pain to ease others like me! I believe in you, because if anyone can do it, it's you." A tear fell from Cornelius's eye as he ended his monologue. He had been holding it in for a while, Black Star could tell, and he finally came clean.

"You're right, man. It was selfish of me to think I should just quit because I got what I wanted. This picture is so much more than just me. Thank you for showing me that." Cornelius patted Black Star on the back.

"That's the spirit! So, what's your next step?" Cornelius asked. Black Star leaned back against the couch and thought about it for a moment before responding.

"I need to step up my game further - do even more contracts. So many that I get their attention, forcing them to place a contract on my head. Then, when they show themselves to me, I'll cut off their heads all at once."

"Aren't you worried you might be pushing yourself a little too hard?"

"I guess we'll find out. You can't fire me up like that and then extinguish my flames!" Black Star said excitedly, throwing his hands into the air. He took a moment to breathe and then kept talking. "But enough about me. How are you doing bud?"

"Me?" Cornelius asked, surprised that someone was asking him about himself. "I'm doing fine. I got more contracts than I can hand out, so business is great. I even got some new games on my PC, so I've been staying preoccupied."

"Have you been getting out at all?" Black Star asked.

"No, didn't you hear me? I got new PC games bro. Besides, no one wants to hang out with me." Cornelius replied.

"Well, to be honest Cornelius," Black Star started as Cornelius handed him a controller. "I can see why. You need to take care of yourself more. Take a shower more often too. And clean up your place. I'm your friend man but smelling is my weakest sense and I can smell you."

"I'm happy how I am right now," Cornelius retorted. "I've gotten used to the loneliness and I don't have anyone to clean up for. Though I suppose I could work on my hygiene."

"Well, the place isn't too professional, but I'm happy if you're happy. Enough deep talk man. Let's play some games. I wouldn't mind being preoccupied for a bit." With that, the two friends started up a game and played well into the night, laughing and sharing drinks as they beat boss after boss.

SEVENTEEN

KAI

"Here she is." Elaine presented the repaired helmet to Kai, along with a medium sized duffle bag. "Good as new."

"Thank you, Elaine. What's this? And what do I owe you?" Kai asked.

"Your survival," she responded. Kai looked at her curiously.

"Don't look at me like that. You know what I mean." Elaine pointed a finger in his face. "Don't die on me." Elaine grabbed his head and began inspecting it. "And get a haircut. You look like a mess."

Kai chuckled as best as he could. "Yes ma'am."

"And there's a surprise in the bag. It's for your suit. Let me know how I did. Now give me a hug, you existential idiot." Kai hugged Elaine and then climbed on his motorcycle.

"Will do. See ya later," he said as he put on his helmet. Elaine nodded and closed the garage door. The interior of Kai's mask lit up, and the deep crimson of the interior washed over his face for the first time in three days.

"Hello Kai," Eris said.

"Hello, Eris," Kai responded. How was the nap?"

"Refreshing," she said. "A little taste of death every now and then is healthy, don't you think?"

Kai didn't respond. He turned on his motorcycle and began driving back towards City Center.

"What happened to you while I was gone?" Eris inquired.

"Nothing to be concerned about," Kai answered.

"Nothing to be concerned about? Kai your vitals are all over the place. When was the last time you slept? Ate? Your neural activity is entropic. I'm surprised you're functioning at all. You should be in a medical facility."

"I'm okay, Eris, really."

"Whatever you say, Kai," she replied. "How's Amina?"

"Amina is out of the infirmary. She's sleeping at my apartment."

"And how does that make you feel?" Eris asked.

"I don't know," Kai responded. Eris fell silent. After a few minutes, Kai spoke up again.

"I have something for you." He took the microchip the High Council gave him out of his pocket and slotted it in his helmet. "It's from the High Council - information on a Lillian Marshall, our next target."

"Let me take a look," Eris said. After a minute of silence, Eris spoke up again.

"Kai, this woman is dangerous. And not just the normal kind of dangerous. Her enhancements make her the perfect killing machine: hidden weapons, titanium bones, artificial nerves, enhanced neural processes, you name it."

"We'll be fine," Kai said. "Recall Squad Four and have them meet me at my apartment." Eris said nothing and when Kai arrived at his apartment building, Tara, Marlowe, and Piers were standing outside waiting for him. Kai collapsed his helmet as he approached, and a look of worry came over Piers' and Tara's faces.

"Are you okay, man?" the fifteen-year-old Piers asked.

"Just a long day yesterday, but I'm fine. Let's head inside." Kai opened the door to the pre-war apartment building and his squad followed him up to his place. He smelled his neighbor's perfume again, *flowers*, but ignored it and went inside where Amina was sitting on the couch watching TV.

"Amina!" Piers yelled as he ran towards her and practically jumped on her.

"Ooh!" she grunted as he fell on her. "Hey buddy what's up?"

"How are you? Are you feeling any better? Are you still a part of the squad?" Piers berated her with question after question, showing, even more so than his affection, the fact that he was still a child.

"I'm good," she said. "Feeling a little under the weather still, but as far as I know I'm still with you guys." She looked towards Kai hesitantly and he nodded. Amina smiled and Piers stood up.

"We have a mission, don't we?" asked Tara.

"Yes," Kai said. "Eris has all the intel, so to keep confidentiality you'll all have to wear her. Is that okay with you, Eris?"

"Of course," Eris responded. Kai removed the pad from the back of his neck and gave it to Tara first. After the information was gathered by all, Amina returned Eris to Kai, who placed her back on his neck.

"Does everyone understand the mission?" Kai asked. Everyone nodded.

"So how are we going to go about this capture?" Marlowe asked in his gruff, but quiet voice. "I'm sure I have the strength to restrain her, but someone is going to have to knock her out at the very least."

"Given the fact that she has prosthetic limbs," Kai said, "we should be able to remove them without serious damage to her life."

"That's where I come in, I hope," Piers cut in. "I haven't had any real action in *forever*."

"I was thinking the same thing," Tara said.

"Alright then, Piers, it'll be your job to remove her prosthetics. Make sure your blade can do the job," Kai ordered.

"Don't worry, Kai, I got this," Piers reassured him.

"So, we know where she is," Amina spoke up softly, "but we don't know how to trap her. Any ideas?"

"Lillian won't want a fight," Kai said, "so I think it's most likely that when presented with overwhelming odds she'll try to flee. In her mind, if she can get away she can live longer to expose the truth of the ties between the NS government and the Sicarii. There's a smaller building next to her apartment. Marlowe and I will attack her in her apartment and force her to flee out of the window and onto the rooftop below. We should be able to capture her there."

"I can set up tethers on the corners of the rooftop beforehand to trigger whenever she lands on the roof," Amina stated. "We should be able to lock her down that way and then Piers can remove her limbs."

"And I'll set up on a rooftop across the street and hit her with a tranquilizer of some sorts whenever she's in position," Tara added.

"Good," Kai said. "We'll set up at 11 p.m. and hit her at midnight." Everyone nodded in agreement and Tara, Piers, and Marlowe left. Kai sat down on the couch next to Amina who was still in her tank top and sleep shorts, with a blanket wrapped around her shoulders. They sat there in silence for a while, until Amina leaned over and kissed him on the cheek.

"I'm going to go lay down before the mission," she said. "Come get me if you need anything."

"Okay," Kai said as she stood up and walked into the bedroom. Kai laid down on the couch and watched the TV for a moment before looking up and staring at the ceiling. After what seemed like an eternity, he let darkness take him, and his thoughts were annihilated by the quietness of the void.

When Kai opened his eyes next, it was dark, and he was left with a strange tingling in his body and a faint memory of flesh peeling from bone, but that quickly subsided. He sat up and looked at the time.

9:30 p.m. the clock read.

I think that's the most sleep I've gotten in a long time, Kai thought. He stood up and looked in towards his bedroom at Amina who was still asleep. He walked over to his refrigerator, opened it up, grabbed his water bottle, and drank the remainder of the purified water in it before washing it out and filling it back up in the sink. He looked around his apartment for a moment and realized, possibly for the first time, just how *empty* it really was. Kai had a couch, a TV stand, and a TV and that was it. No tables, besides the one in his bedroom, no pots or pans, no plants or other decorations. He had *nothing*, and for the first time in his life he felt disturbed by it. After what felt like hours but was no more than a minute, Kai went and woke up Amina and they left together to meet the rest of Squad Four at the Castrum.

The way to HQ was quiet. No words were exchanged between Kai and Amina as both of their minds were long gone, captive by the darkness that had dominated them. Eventually, they reached the Castrum and inside, the lockers, where Kai had come to wash away his sins not long ago. They entered and met Piers, Marlowe, and Tara who were already naked and putting their Sicarii suits on. Marlowe's body was hard, dark, and chiseled, and heat poured off his flesh like hot coals. His hair was thick and curly and covered every inch of him. Tara's body was perfect, like the rest of her. Her breasts were well-formed and muscular and she had strong dark nipples that stood in stark contrast to her olive skin. Her muscles were defined over every inch of her body, and she was more fit than even Kai himself. She looked like Athena or Artemis, a perfect warrior-goddess, save for the brutal, jagged scar that ran from her right hip to her left shoulder, of which Kai knew nothing about. Piers was... a boy. He was fifteen now, and the body of a man was slowly coming to the surface. His face was hairless still, but his jawline was stronger than it had been at the beginning of last year, Kai had noticed, and he had grown just slightly taller from his previous 5'3 height.

Kai looked away from his teammates and approached his own locker. He placed his hand on the jet-black surface and it opened, revealing his firearms and Shatter, placed in its sheath and on the rack, and his suit pieces hanging on the door. He stripped naked and placed his clothes inside and Amina did the same. They both walked to the bath house and stepped into the waters, as was required before any mission. In order to strengthen the members of the Squads and keep their suits clean, a bath in the Castrum bath house was necessary before and after every mission. The waters were special, and they seemed to strengthen, clean, and even heal Squad members to some degree. Maybe it was just the intense heat, or maybe there was something in the water - Kai didn't know and at this point he really didn't care. His curiosity left him in Akkad and he feared he would never get it back.

Amina and Kai sunk deep in the waters and stayed away from each other until Amina stood up, water dripping down her naked body, clinging to the hair light brown hair between her legs, and sat down next to Kai.

"I'm sorry," she said quietly as she stared at the far wall of the bath house. Kai turned and looked at her and she looked back, tears welling in her eyes. He could tell that she was trying her best to hold herself together. "I'm sorry for fucking up the mission. I'm sorry for forcing myself on to you. I'm sorry for being a needy, stupid, emotional bitch," she began to cry. "And I'm sorry for being me." The tears rolled down her face as Kai watched her break down. She pulled her knees to her chest and sobbed into her wet thighs.

"Amina," he said. She looked up at him through her tears. "You have nothing to apologize for." She cried more and he wrapped his right arm around her and held her close. "You are amazing, just the way you are. You're beautiful, intelligent, dedicated, and stronger than you know. And it's not that I *don't* want you, it's that I *can't* want you. Not only because I'm your superior, but because it's just not in me and I'm sorry. You are a wonderful person Amina, and I know that this life is harder on you than anyone else, and I'm sorry for that too. I wish you could get out, and I hope you do one day, somehow." Amina continued to cry as Kai held her. Thoughts of compassion and images of intercourse were replaced by blood, death, and memories, both from himself and not, and his mind darkened once again.

"We must go," he said to Amina. "It's time." Amina nodded and stood up with Kai and they both walked out of the bath house and back towards their lockers. Marlowe, Tara, and Piers had already walked outside, so Amina and Kai were left alone to dress and equip themselves as necessary. Over her suit, Amina put on her leather vestments to store her vials and afterwards she put on a black backpack where she stored the tethers she would set up on the rooftop.

Over his suit, Kai put on his black, weatherproof, high-collared jacket and he affixed Eris to the back of his neck. He grabbed Shatter and affixed the sheath to his left hip and a handgun to his right with an extra clip of ammo as well. Amina and Kai closed their lockers and walked outside the Castrum where they met the rest of Squad Four. Marlowe wore nothing over his suit except for his axe which was held in place on his back. On Tara's left forearm was a metal gauntlet, stretching down over the back of her hand, that she used to prop up her rifle. On her back was her rifle, equipped with an artificial reality scope and tranquilizer rounds, on her left hip was a short sword, fashioned after a Roman gladius, but made of a much stronger metal than regular iron or steel, and lower down on her thigh was a pistol, the newest military-grade model from Trytek.

Piers was covered in a Vantablack cloak that, at night, made him just about impossible to see. Despite his age, Piers was the top Wraith in his class and graduated early with Alphonse and Kai, whom he saw as both mentors and friends. Piers was the fastest member on the team and would be tasked with ambushing Lillian Marshall and removing her prosthetics with his diamond-edge scythe, which he had folded and placed under his cloak and across his lower back.

"Everyone ready?" Kai asked. His squad nodded.

"Let's move out then," he ordered.

An hour passed and the trap had been set. Tara awaited the arrival of the target as she sat to the north, across the street on the roof of a building a few stories higher than the building she was watching over. Amina and Piers waited close by, on the west fire escape of the building where they had set the trap, waiting for the moment to strike. Marlowe stood outside of Lillian's door, waiting for the signal from Kai who stood on the roof of a building to the east, across from his target's window. It was midnight and Lillian Marshall sat in shorts and a tank top, on her couch, watching TV when Kai activated his cloaking device, sprinted, and jumped across the rooftop and into her window. Lillian stood up immediately, her salt and pepper hair falling partially out of her bun and readied her firearm that was sitting on her coffee table.

"Show yourself!" she yelled. Kai tackled her and launched her against a wall. She discharged her firearm and missed Kai by a hair. Marlowe busted through the door and charged for Lillian, who, when faced with a near seven-foot-tall, hulk of a man and an invisible enemy ran for the only exit she could: the window on the west side of the building. She jumped out of the window and landed on the roof below, where she was immediately seized by the four tethers that shot from the roof corners. Panic began setting in and the blades in her shins and arms popped out and began tearing at the metal tethers. Piers and Amina flanked her from behind and Piers unfolded his scythe and took it to her left arm, severing the metal at the shoulder joint. He did the same with her left arm, but she tore through the tethers at the same time and headbutted Piers, knocking him back. Kai and Marlowe jumped down on the roof at the same moment Lillian loosened herself and Tara missed her tranquilizer shot.

"Tara," Kai said worried. "I need you to make that shot."

"I'm trying my best, Kai." Lillian began charging Amina who readied her knives. The first tranquilizer hit and knocked Lillian off course just enough so Amina could dodge her attack. Lillian rebounded quickly and attempted to flee when Tara hit her with a second tranquilizer. She slowed down and collapsed to one knee. Kai and Marlowe began walking towards her. Piers cut off both of her legs and she lay limbless on the ground. Her eyes began to flutter from sleepiness and Kai crouched over her and dissolved his mask.

"Lillian Marshall, by the order of the High Council of the Sicarii you have been sentenced to entrapment and interrogation," Kai said monotonously. At that, Lillian lost consciousness, and Kai called for a pickup from Sicarii HQ. After about five minutes, a VTOL police aircraft came and hovered outside the roof. A squad of police officers set up a police line around the perimeter of the building and another moved into the apartment building from the ground to search Lillian's apartment and interrogate any witnesses. Marlowe carried Lillian into the aircraft and Kai and the rest of the squad followed him. The doors closed and Squad Four took to the skies. After about five minutes, the VTOL landed on the top of the same building that Kai had landed on with Alef not too long ago. A medical team with a stretcher and He were awaiting them when they arrived.

"She's undamaged I hope," He yelled over the engines of the VTOL.

"Only her limbs were severed," Kai responded. "She was shot with two tranquilizer rounds, but she seems to be in stable condition."

"Well done, Kai," he said. "This has found you great favor with the High Council." Kai nodded and the unconscious Lillian Marshall was whisked away into the building. "Follow me. The

Council requires your presence." Kai looked back at his team who were calmly awaiting his next order.

"Our success today is something to be celebrated. You are dismissed." His team nodded and Kai turned back around to face the blonde, shaggy-haired member of the High Council as the members of Squad Four were airlifted away from the rooftop. Just moments later, another aircraft picked up Kai and He and took them to an indiscriminate rooftop a few miles away from where they were at.

Kai stayed behind He as they stepped out of the vehicle and took an elevator from the roof and down directly into the Spire. Generally, no one besides High Council members took this elevator, so Kai was surprised that He took him this way. After descending for a brief time, the elevator opened up to a blank, dark hallway. At the end was an ornate, wooden door and in the center of the hall was a perpendicular corridor that led to the left. Kai and He took this hall and entered the Council chambers from the rear, with only Dalet's seat sitting empty. All eyes were on him as He took his seat and Kai walked down the steps to his right and in front of the High Council.

"Kneel, Kai," Vav ordered. Kai knelt, his right knee on the floor, and gazed up towards the Council.

"Your ascension is nigh," Alef stated after setting down his billowing pipe. "You have one last mission, of which we will discuss with you momentarily."

"As always Kai, your success is astonishing. You handled the Lillian Marshall situation very well and for that we applaud you," said Vav, her elderly voice trembling as always.

"Your relationship with Amina, however," Bet spoke up, "is rather concerning."

"She means nothing to me," Kai stated. "I assure you. The nature of our relationship is purely platonic."

"We hope so," responded Bet. "Because where you are going, she cannot follow."

"Your work was invaluable for the NS government as well, Kai," He stated. "Lillian Marshall was a national threat, and you overwhelmed her with your physical and mental prowess."

"Thank you, I am fortunate to have an excellent team," Kai replied. Alef took another hit from his pipe and set it back down.

"You may rise, Kai," Alef said. Kai stood up and crossed his arms behind his back, the sheathed Shatter hanging at his side. Your final mission will be your most difficult one, and even though you will have your team for it, I fear they will not be of much help," Alef said. Kai looked at him puzzled.

"From what I understand, you have taken great interest in the work of Alexander Stromberg, correct?"

"That is correct," replied Kai.

"Then have you ever heard of the name Black Star?" Alef inquired further.

"Yes, I have. I remember when I was younger, when Alexander died he had a wife and three children that died in the fire along with him. The youngest boy's name was Black Star."

"That is correct, Kai," Alef stated. "But the High Council has come to learn that Black Star was not killed in that fire." Kai was astonished.

"The son of Alexander lives?"

"He does," replied Alef, "and that is something we cannot allow." Kai's astonishment turned into worry.

"Why?" he asked.

"Because the fire that killed Alexander and his family was no accident. We had him killed. We burned his life to the ground." Kai took a step back and anger rushed into him.

"Why!? Why would you do that? Alexander worked for the world! He worked for peace and prosperity!"

"Alexander worked for *us*, Kai," Gimel stated. Emotions flooded through Kai and the void screamed at him from within. He collapsed and yet again the veil of illusion was lifted from his eyes. The Black Seed penetrated his psyche and berated the boundaries of his ego, eating away at his perceived reality.

NZHURMIWA

"Stand, Kai," Vav demanded. Kai stood up and faced the High Council yet again, sweat dripping down his face.

"Black Star has taken the mantle of assassin and has been searching for answers about his father and, even more so, about us," Alef continued. "His prowess with weapons is unmatched and his speed and strength are unnatural. It is likely that Alexander perfected his serum that he worked on for us and injected it into his own son, giving him superhuman strength and speed, ensuring the success and eventual proliferation of his bloodline."

"What would you have me do?" Kai asked.

"Kill him," Alef stated. "He is a threat to the Sicarii and the High Council and to all the work we have done to ensure that Alexander's research can be best used for the good of the Sicarii and for all."

"It will be done," Kai stated monotonously.

"But beware, Kai," Vav began. "He may have abilities that seem unnatural, or supernatural even. He is well above and beyond anything Lillian Marshall or Gilroy ever were. No rogue, corrupt politician or businessperson will compare to him. He is unmatched in every single way."

"Understood," said Kai.

"Now for the details," Alef said before taking another puff out of his smoldering pipe. "Black Star is after a man named Vadim, one of our contacts in the Russian Bratva. Because of his ties to us, Black Star will, very soon, hunt down, interrogate, and assassinate Vadim. We know this because we placed the contract on Vadim's head and we placed it for freelance assassins. Because of his skill and search for answers, Black Star chases contract after contract, fueling his lust for knowledge and without a doubt, his desire for the hunt."

"You wish for me to stop this assassination then?" Kai interjected.

"No," Bet stated. "Vadim is a loose end and he must be burned away. Let Black Star kill him and trap Black Star after." Kai nodded in acceptance of the order.

"Use whatever means possible to kill Black Star. Do not attempt to capture him. Do not attempt to immobilize him. End his life and erase the threat without hesitation. Do you understand?" Gimel ordered.

"Yes, my liege," Kai responded while bowing.

"Good," Alef stated. "Only after the success of this final mission will you be ready for your ascension. You will find Vadim and Black Star in the abandoned Hotel Francesco in the remnants of the old city. You have two days. You are dismissed."

EIGHTEEN

BLACK STAR AND THE PHANTOM

Black Star opened the door to his sister's home. It was unlocked, as Maria knew he was coming over. She had just finished eating and so she was putting up her leftovers in the kitchen. Black Star walked through the small hallway and into the kitchen and began speaking once he saw her.

"Hey Maria. I'm sorry where we left off, but I need your help."

"Oh, you need my help? What could that be for?" She avoided eye contact with him and her sarcasm cut through the air like a knife through butter.

"Well, I need some advice more than anything. You know, I've had this dream of stopping corruption, but with my last encounter I found out just how hard it really is. I wanted to stop, but my friend told me I can't stop because he believes in me. This whole time I thought I was doing it for me mostly and because of that I was able to stay relaxed. Because I was going at my own pace I wasn't nervous. Now I find out that I have multiple people depending on me and I feel like I have the weight of the world on my shoulders. All these people depending on me is new and I don't like this anxious feeling. This pit in my stomach is eating at me because I don't know what the right answer is. What should I do?"

"You put this on yourself," she said as she closed the fridge and finally looked at him. "I told you not to get involved. You can fight corruption some other way. Become a politician, a law enforcement officer, something, but you chose this path instead. You chose the dark path of killing and now you must walk it. You're like the guy who wants to dig through the other side of the Earth, from

America to China, except you don't know you have to go through the Earth's core and it's getting hot. You're worried, scared even, but it's too late to turn back." Maria didn't seem to be in her typical outgoing, helpful mood, but it was no wonder why. But even though she was in a terrible mood, and Black Star was the cause, she couldn't leave him alone. He was her brother and she loved him, even though he messed up constantly. Her best quality, to him, was her ability to forgive.

"So, the only way out is forwards," Black Star said. "Therefore, I'll pursue this goal, even with the additional weight. But now I have no leads. The person I thought was the ringleader had nothing for me. Now I still have the same goal, but even less information to go off of. It's like I'm even further from my goal than I was originally."

Maria nodded and left the kitchen. Black Star followed her throughout her house as she walked into the laundry room, continuing the conversation the whole way.

"So how do I know I made the right choice?" he asked her.

"You don't. You won't know until the day you're judged." She began grabbing clothes from her dryer to throw into the basket for clean clothes.

"So, what if I'm just a deranged psychopath trying to justify his murders?" he inquired further.

"You could be. But you shouldn't look at yourself in that light. In cases like this there is no right answer as far as I can tell. You're just picking the lesser of two evils," Maria responded.

"Well, what would you do? Killing has become the largest tool in my arsenal," Black Star said as he leaned up against her washer.

"I'm sure you know that if you stop now, everything you've done up to this point is meaningless. I'm not saying you should keep killing, but this is *your* mess to clean up." They walked out of the laundry room and up the stairs. "I'll support your decisions because I know you won't listen to anyone and you'll just do what you want," Maria continued. "Just please, please be more careful," she stopped to look at him. "I hope you understand the severity of this. We don't have much of a family. I don't want to lose you." She took the basket of clothes and walked up the steps. Black Star followed behind and smirked as they walked down the hall and entered the second door on the right. She put the basket on the bed and began folding her clothes.

"Wow, you care about me?" Black Star asked jokingly.

"Yes, you forced me to say it. I hope that helps you understand. I don't want to lose you. Your life isn't meaningless and it's not just something that can be thrown away. It would affect a lot of people. It would affect me more than all. But I know you can handle yourself. I just pray you can handle yourself as well as you think. You have a big dream, but if anyone can do this it's you."

"Aw," Black Star said. "You're giving me the warm fuzzies. Seriously though, I'm sorry I never took how this made you feel into consideration."

"Yeah, whatever," Maria said. "I *am* the most in touch with my emotions of the family, but I still prefer our silent understanding. If you know we love each other you don't have to say it, but you really needed to hear it."

Black Star took a seat on her bed and grabbed her comforter and cuddled up under it. He continued watching her fold clothes for a moment and then he spoke up again. "Can I hear you say it one more time?" he smiled. With a blank expression she looked over to him and without skipping a beat while folding she answered.

"You ruined the moment and I will hurt you."

"No, please don't! I'm fragile!" Black Star said as he pulled his head under the covers. He could feel her stare burning a hole into him. He peeked his head out and muttered under his breath. "You're not as relaxed as you look."

"I'll be more relaxed when you leave," she retorted.

"Yikes, okay, guess I'll see you later." Black Star slinked off her bed and slowly inched toward the door. He opened it and looked back at Maria.

"Hey Maria," he began as he stopped in the doorway.

"Hmm?" she hummed without looking.

"Thanks for talking with me."

"No problem. It's what older sisters do. If you want some pasta, it's in the fridge."

"Thanks," Black Star said. "But I don't have an appetite." He turned back and started heading down the stairs. Maria didn't respond, because she couldn't find the right words at the time, but that simple gesture of Black Star declining food was enough to show that he was uneasy, harboring doubt, sadness, and a deep darkness within himself. Things that he and most people dealt with daily, of course, but it was rare for it to affect him so much that it was evident to those around him. For others, he mostly remained a closed book. But this time, the trials of life seemed to have broken his spirits. Black Star closed the door to Maria's house behind him, and as he did his sister dropped the shirt in her hands and a tear rolled down her cheek.. He was back on the streets of Houston and as he walked he started scratching his neck. He felt acne that had newly formed and sighed as he ran his fingers through his hair, letting it lay how it fell.

Man, this stress is causing my acne to come back, he thought. *And that just stressed me out more. Why can't the answers be simple?* He looked up at the evening sky touching the buildings and saw a crow pass by overhead, coasting on the strong winds. Black Star could have turned his back on his goal, but he would have only delayed the inevitable and would've forsaken the world around him. He knew what he had to do, even if it was daunting. Even if he did all the heavy lifting he couldn't let the world crumble around him in good conscience. It's what he, and his father, both thought was worth fighting for. He thought back and remembered something his father had said to him.

"If something must be done, you might as well be the one to do it because you'll get old and decrepit waiting on others. Don't do it for the credit, do it because you want to. Let that be recognized. Your future is clay and all you have to do is mold it."

However, Black Star's future was a little more complex than a clay bowl, but the same principle still applied, he supposed. Black Star related to the crow above him, drifting in the wind, only flapping his wings after long intervals. As he walked through the city, he noticed the streetlamps turn on as the sun bade farewell to that side of the Earth, watching the darkness grow stronger and stronger. The streetlamp's light warding off the empty darkness on his path led him to a revelation - he had been wandering in the dark, alone on his journey, nothing to illuminate his way. This made it hard for him to decipher the right path and made the temptation of darkness all the more tantalizing.

"You get so close to corruption and you don't let it affect you," he remembered Cornelius saying. *I wish that were true,* he thought.

He could feel himself slipping into it. And although he fed the darkness from time to time, he always seemed to control it. Seeing the streetlights reminded him of his friends and family. His own light could only reveal so much, but with his friends and family to light his path, to ensure he didn't stray too far, he knew he would be okay. Their love for him protected him from the darkness that enveloped him. He had his own light, but each day more and more of it was consumed by the writhing dark. Another revelation hit Black Star and he smiled.

I'm in a dark dungeon walking down a path to the boss room. My friends are the torches that light my way!" The bird flew out of view. *Sometimes it's nice to let the wind take you, but the wind won't always take you where you need to go. That's why we have wings. The next step is the same as the last. It feels like I'm not moving, but that's what it means to have a long-term goal. It feels stagnant, but you need to brush that feeling aside. When you walk through a blizzard, you can't see anything. It all looks the same, but you know the steps you are taking. Focus on your other senses and take one step forward. One at a time. One step closer to the finish line. That's why I won't give up. Even if I can't see, even if I can't hear, even if I can't feel, I am aware. I have taken a step and I will make another. I won't stop.*

■■■■■■■■■ ■ ■ ▪ ▪ ▎ ▏

Over the years, one of the things that had not changed were the laws on international waters. Out there, everything was legal as long as you didn't get caught. The law enforcement of surrounding countries only operated up to two hundred miles or three hundred and twenty kilometers from the shoreline. Past that, the seafaring vessel's laws were those of the country it originated from. But if it originated from no country, then it was faced with no laws.

Out in the deep water of the ocean, the full moon glowed and reflected off the face of the waves. A massive yacht, owned by an extremely wealthy man was the only thing that could be seen for miles. He often threw parties on his pleasure craft where anything was allowed. Some nights he hosted auctions where he sold sex slaves, refugees, and children, and other nights he hosted blood sports, where losers ended up dead and orgies where semen, discharge, blood, and all other body fluids ended up covering the yacht from stern to bow. This guy proved time and time again that he could put a price on human beings and make them do whatever he pleased.

While the attendants were inside having a good time, an ominous shadow lurked on the boat. It's a mystery how it got on the ship in the first place, as it did not board with the other guests. But no matter how it got there, it was there, and it wanted blood. The auctions, like the one on that particular night, always ended in a soiree, which was just an excuse for the partygoers to get extremely intoxicated, but such a thing did nothing but help the Phantom even more.

On the bow of the ship, the Phantom crouched, moving silently, hoping to look through a window and see the status of the others inside. As it approached the window muffled voices and off-beat steps were heard. In a single leap the Phantom was able to make it to the next level and grabbed onto the railing before climbing over in order to survey the balcony. A lone man was walking towards him but killing this early could result in someone finding the body or getting suspicious where the individual went. The Phantom's hesitance was, more than anything, proof that he wasn't a bloodthirsty animal. Since the Phantom decided it was best to leave the man, he clung to the side of the ship and allowed the man to pass by. He was clearly a guard, although only on a superficial level since there was little need for a guard in the middle of the ocean as the owner of the pleasure craft had paid off the surrounding pirate clans.

On the level below, the Phantom could hear the conversation of the people he heard walking previously. The party seemed to have just begun, but one of the partygoers below had already had his fill, and a woman was guiding him to the railing so he could purge the toxins inside. The Phantom climbed over the railing after the guard was out of sight, uncaring of the story the drunken fool below had to offer.

It moved quietly, pursuing the guard that had just passed, and the guard, unaware of anyone following him, rounded the corner of the ship and walked up steps that led to the bridge. The captain of the ship stood and watched out towards sea, drink in hand, as his officers stood at their posts. Since the ship wasn't moving there wasn't much for the men to do, so they relaxed as best as they could while being in the middle of nowhere. One of the seamen read a book, another scrolled through news sites on his phone, and the captain stood there contemplating what his life would finally be like once he retired. The guard walked past the bridge and down another set of steps, but the Phantom had reached his destination. The steps leading up were metal, but no sound came from them as the Phantom moved, as though it floated above the world. It opened the door to the bridge slowly, and the heavy metal groaned every inch as it slipped in somehow unnoticed.

The captain felt a draft and looked over as the door creaked open yet saw no one enter. A simple oddity like this one, however, wasn't enough to make him uneasy. Sailing the seas had made him a rugged man and he was too close to retirement to be scared of the wind. He walked over to shut the door when he felt a sharp pain in his chest. It was quick and unfamiliar, and he felt a warmth coursing down his body and into the seam of his pants. He looked down to see a bloodied stain forming in his white shirt and a blood-covered hand sticking through him, grasping his heart. He dropped his glass as the Phantom tore his heart out, like plucking an apple from a tree, and his mouth fell open, but no words came out as there was no expression for what had just happened. The captain collapsed, and his final moments were spent wondering what he had done wrong as he stared at the beheaded bodies of his officers in front of him.

The heart continued to beat for a few moments in the Phantom's hand until it stopped, and after losing interest it dropped the heart on the floor. Since this mission was in a completely different environment than it was used to, the Phantom knew it called for a different approach. They were out in the middle of the water, nothing, no one in sight for hundreds of miles, and with the captain gone there was no communication off the boat. So, the Phantom let loose. No stealth. Only death. It could let carnage ensue. It left the door open and moved to the lower levels where the attendants of the soiree were enjoying their time. Climbing down the side once more, it passed in front of a porthole in the door in front of it and observed the prey ahead. It watched them all dance and drink, like they had no care in the world. They felt untouchable, it knew, but they wouldn't feel that way for much longer.

The Phantom walked through the door as any human would. One by one, it caught the attention of the partygoers, as a cloaked figure undoubtebly would. It was a spectacle amongst the high-class folk who awed at it as it passed by. The owner of the yacht was eating an hors d'oeuvre towards the front of the room, across from the Phantom, and spoke into the microphone next to him.

"Hey look! Someone forgot to mention it's not a costume party!" he finished off his snack and began laughing. The rest of the crowd laughed as well at the expense of the Phantom. A server passed the Phantom, balancing glasses of red wine on a platter, and continued walking past for a brief moment as the Phantom gouged his throat with one quick strike of its thumb. As the server collapsed, and everyone began screaming, the Phantom picked up the platter and slung it at the owner of the craft who had made the joke, who continued to stuff his fat face with hors d'oeuvres until his head came off his body.

People were in a panic trying to rush out the door, but the effects of being in the Phantom's presence overtook them, and its aura began affecting their vision. The room swirled and churned, worse than what waves and alcohol could produce. Most experienced the room melting and the doors sealing up. Those that didn't just shrieked in agony as their minds tore apart. They had become trapped in themselves and many that tried to resist the horror clung to the walls of the room in desperation, looking for what used to be the exit.

One of the women clinging to the wall looked back and

instantly regretted it. She saw her friends, people who had taken pleasure in the slavery and abuse of others and had thought of them as property, receive the punishment for their sins. They were powerless as the Phantom leaped from one person to the next in a scatterplot fashion, snapping and slashing necks, spraying blood around the room in an unholy cleansing. The horrified woman followed against the wall and fell through a part of it. She was on the outside now and didn't realize she had found the doorway as she couldn't even begin to comprehend anything she was seeing.

Inside the room, people were falling over each other trying to get out. The few guards that had arrived were just as terrified, and the guard from earlier tried in a desperate attempt to shoot the Phantom, but instead only managed to spray a magazine of bullets on the horrified guests, shredding body and bone as he did. The Phantom stood in the middle of the chaos as red appendages came from under its cloak, a tentacle for every person, and in a twisted roller coaster it grabbed hold of the remaining survivors, some by the legs and others by the body, gripping tighter those that struggled, and it pulled them close. The tentacles began spinning, gaining momentum and stretching away from the Phantom. Faster and faster, they moved and the guests, already terrified, had been stricken with a fear that they had never felt before. Some of their hearts burst, others began to laugh, and as the maximum velocity was achieved the tentacles disappeared and the rest of the guests splattered against the walls of the room, coating everything in blood, brain, and bone. Just like that, the ball was ruined. The tables and chairs were destroyed, but the Piano Trio No. 2 in E Flat by Franz Schubert continued playing overhead, and it was the only relaxing part of the night.

After the massacre, the Phantom passed the woman who had been driven insane outside the door and killed the remaining non-slave survivors besides her on the ship. Afterwards, it went back to the bridge, activated the emergency beacon, and fired a flare as a distress signal so that the nearest navy would know something was wrong. They would free the slaves, find the maddened woman, and give the tortured souls a chance at a new life. The oppressors, the Phantom thought, had received what they had in store for them.

Unfortunately for the world the night had only begun, and more judgment needed to be dealt out, like an angsty magistrate ready to throw down the gavel on the guilty. This judge, however, had no jury, and may God have mercy on any person who set foot in its court. The Phantom traversed like a dark shadow, undetected by anyone at a speed that could hardly be recognized. It was on a spree like no other tonight, moving from contract to contract, city to city, almost like it was going for a record. It left a massacre throughout the New States and afterwards made its way to its final destination. It arrived at an airplane hangar just to kill one man. Vadim was his name, and with as much blood that was on Vadim's hands this moment was inevitable.

On top of the hangar stood the ominous figure looming over its final target. Vadim was talking to another man, and from the Phantom's view within the lingering dark they were both incognito, so the Phantom couldn't discern who was who. The Phantom grew impatient watching the men with their petty talk, and as its impatience grew they sparked up a pair of cigars as if they had no plans of stopping their conversation anytime soon. Knowing very little about Vadim, there was no way for the Phantom to tell who was who. It couldn't kill them both, as its story must be told, lest the world forget its great works. Its impatience overwhelmed it and the specter descended from the hangar, wind gusting around it, and landed on top of one of the men, smashing his skull into the concrete and splattering his brains across the ground. The other man backed away and shouted obscenities as he dropped his cigar. The Phantom looked down at the busted head and back to the man moving away. It had killed the wrong guy.

The man was still corrupt, but it wasn't his time to die. The Phantom made a mistake, which was one of the few pains it could feel. It looked up and Vadim was a hundred or so feet away as he had been running while the Phantom contemplated its mistake. The Phantom was about to give chase, enjoying the game of cat and mouse, but before it could move, it heard muffled cries coming from inside the hangar. For a moment, the hunter felt compassion, and hearing the cries of someone in distress piqued its interest. It opened the hangar door and stepped in. In the dark in the center of the hangar was a woman tied to a chair. She was beaten, bruised, and scared, and had obviously been through more trauma than she could have ever imagined. The Phantom crept towards her on all fours, like it didn't know how to properly approach someone. Its blood red eyes that normally glowed bright began to fade. The poor woman was more scared of the Phantom than the person who had captured her, so she screamed and wriggled trying to escape. The Phantom reached her and slowly removed the tape on her mouth as she struggled against it. After it removed the tape it started working on the restraints. The woman was too scared to make out words so she began crying, unsure if the worst was over or had just begun. After a few deep breaths she tried to speak.

"Pl-please. Please don't hurt me." The Phantom looked up and then back down as it used its claw to cut one of the restraints. "Please say something so I know I'm safe." The Phantom looked at her again and cut the final restraint. An audible "click" was heard by both, and as it was a violent explosion overtook the both of them and the woman splattered. The blast was massive, enough to damage the surrounding hangar, and came from a plastic explosive taped underneath the seat of the chair. It had been Vadim's plan all along to play on the sensibilities of his stalker - save the victim and the victim dies along with whoever did the saving. It was, if anything, a symbol for Vadim's response to the Phantom's plans. The woman was bait, waiting to be destroyed like a pawn in chess. The Phantom didn't expect the blast and couldn't escape in time let alone save the woman at all. It was slammed against the hangar wall and knocked unconscious, and its cloak was scorched. Luckily the cloak was strong and it protected the Phantom from most of the heat of the blast.

Police sirens woke up the sleeping dark who came to on a pile of broken boxes. It was still holding on to the woman's hand, or rather the hand was holding on to it, as it was the only piece of her that survived the blast. On top of destroying its cloak and knocking it out, the explosion had damaged its mask, which cracked and fell off as the figure stood up. Underneath was not the face of a demon or an otherworldly creature, or even a specter of the past. It was a familiar face, covered in sweat and shrouded by shaggy brown hair.

It was the face of Black Star.

Black Star put his hand over his face as he came to, grasping for the reality that had been annihilated by the blast.

"My mask... it's destroyed," he muttered as he pulled the woman's hand off his wrist and set it down. Bits and chunks of her were everywhere and the smell of death mixed with the smell of smoke and flame was so horrendous that he started to gag. It was as if he was experiencing his first bit of carnage for the first time all over again. Coming to his senses in this state was a wakeup call for him. The untimely scene left him confused in his surroundings, but he knew he needed to flee. He picked up the shattered mask off the ground, and on the inside, broken but true, was the Black Seed. He dropped it.

Having an ego with that mask was a mistake. It was causing my personality to diverge. I was so eager to change the world I couldn't wait. Picking people off slowly wasn't enough to offset the immense amount of corruption. I killed and killed and then realized too late that the corruption never went away. It went into me. That bastard D was right. I created something far worse within myself. Black Star stumbled through the rubble, clutching his head as he continued to think.

There's always duality in man and the mask exploited that. I let myself slip too far in that persona and it became a part of me, but never again. Before Black Star could continue, the sirens grew louder. He had to make a swift exit out the back, hiding along the shadow line and avoiding any lights. His mind was shattered, but nothing was hurt more severely than his pride. He had been too careless.

Vadim was smart enough to have a backup plan and then called the police to his hangar. I doubt that he has this planned everywhere he goes. He must've been tipped off.

He took his burnt cloak off and turned it inside out, revealing metal buttons and zipper pockets. He slung the bag over his shoulders and even though it was burnt to a crisp it still held true.

How foolish I have been, Black Star thought as he slunk into the shadows. *For a little bit I thought that by having friends I was somehow immune to the corruption, but I was corrupt from the beginning. The moment I donned the cloak and killed someone I became an assassin. The moment I killed more than the specified target I became something far worse. Maria was right. I was right. There's something wrong with me. I'd be lying to myself if I said I wasn't proud though. It was working on people. I was making a change. They would see the Phantom and think, 'I can't turn into that. I can't be that. I can't get involved with that. If that's my adversary, I'll stay home.' But the sacrifice I made was my humanity. I claimed to be in control, but as I look back on what I did it got foggy. Was I ever in control? I tried to create a certain mindset when I wore the mask, to protect myself... foolish!*

Black Star stopped and leaned against a wall as he clutched his head. "What... what have I done?"

NINETEEN

THE HIGH COUNCIL

ALEF

Alef stood amongst the rubble of the collapsed building as dust circulated in the air. His team of heavily armored soldiers swept the broken building, scouring it for any survivors. Their weapon-mounted flashlights lit up the dark and penetrated the unnatural dust cloud that had been created when the building collapsed after the missile strike. Alef walked slowly, careful not to scuff his handmade, leather dress shoes or dirty his tailored suit. Afterall, what kind of man would allow himself to get dirty or damaged? After a few moments, Alef came across a person lying face down in the dust. Very carefully, he used the sole of his shoe to roll the person over, confirming that the rogue he was searching for had been exterminated.

"The target has been eliminated," he communicated through his earpiece to his team. In the same moment, a woman rose from the ash and pointed a handgun at Alef. Energy surged through him as his gaze met hers, and in an instant her body was riddled with bullet holes as the soldiers mowed her down.

"That was the last of them sir," one of the masked soldiers said as he walked up to Alef.

"Good," Alef said. "Gather your men and head back to the transport. I have more pressing matters to deal with."

"Right away sir," the soldier responded. He gathered his men as Alef had ordered and they moved towards the high-speed VTOL that awaited them outside the rubble. A few hours later, Alef arrived at the Spire and to his study behind the ornate wooden door at the end of the Council chamber hall. Inside, light flickered against the book-lined walls and wooden floor, originating from the fireplace at the other end of the room. A large, leather chair sat facing the fireplace and a wooden desk sat in the middle of the room. On the desk was a lamp, a stack of books, a black prism towards the edge of the desk facing the door, and a scroll from the written Torah of which he was composing a commentary on. On top of the bookshelves that lined the walls were glass boxes, each with its own artifact, spanning every age of human history. There were bones from the Neolithic period, weapons from the bronze age, scrolls from classical antiquity, and more, all of which led to the conclusion that Alef was, if nothing else, a cultured and extremely wealthy man.

Alef walked towards his desk and sat down, turning on his lamp in the process. The black prism on his desk lit up and a holographic screen appeared above it. He touched the screen and began calling Verena. She picked up immediately.

"Yes, sir?" she asked.

"I would like to speak to Nico," Alef stated.

"Nico isn't here at the moment, sir," Verena responded.

"Find him," Alef ordered. "I'll be waiting in my study."

"Right away, sir," Verena responded. Alef ended the call and rolled up the scroll on his desk and clasped it together. He walked over to a rolling, wooden cart near his fireplace and poured himself a strong drink in one of his beautiful, crystal glasses. He took a sip as his hand began to shake, and then lightly packed herb into his pipe and sat down in his chair, staring at the fire. He lit his pipe and, as he had for decades, inhaled the herb deep into his lungs. The shaking in his hands began to fade and he exhaled deeply. For almost an hour Alef sat in his chair, sipping his liquor and smoking his pipe. He was silent, and his mind equally so, until a rapping at his door broke the silence.

"Enter," he spoke loudly. The door opened and Nico walked through wearing a black t-shirt, gray chinos, and black athletic shoes.

"Why have you summoned me, Alef?" Nico asked in his

monotone voice. "It's my day off."

"Tell me, what does a soulless soldier like yourself do on your days off? Hunt rats?" Alef smirked.

"My interests run deeper than you can imagine, Alef," Nico retorted.

"I'm sure they do, my old friend," Alef took the final sip from his drink. "Pull up a chair, we have much to discuss." Nico picked up the chair from the desk and moved it over to the fireplace, angled towards it like Alef's. "Dalet has been killed by the prodigal son of Alexander."

"Do you wish for me to hunt him down?" Nico asked.

"No," Alef responded. "Not you and not yet. The Council and I have tasked Kai and Squad Four with this."

"This is Kai's final challenge then, before the ascension?" Nico asked.

"Yes, it is."

"And if he fails?" Nico asked again.

"Then Black Star will take his place," Alef responded. "Either way I will have a conduit."

"You mean the Council will have a conduit?" Nico questioned further.

"I *am* the Council," responded Alef, a smile on his face.

"Then the time is nigh," Nico said. "I will ready the Seraphim."

■■■■■■■■■■ ▪ ▪ ▫ ▫ ▏

BET

The nightclub was dark, lit up only by the flashing lights and naked holographic strippers above the dance floor. Bet sat in the VIP corner, arms wrapped around two different women, hands cradling one of each of their tits under their dresses. One was kissing on his neck, her fake pink hair falling over his shoulder, while the other drank down her fourth mimosa. The red velvet lounge sofa he sat on belonged only to him, as did this nightclub and half the other nightclubs and bars in The City. Bet may have only been twenty-five, but he owned more of the night life in The City than any of the gangs. His turf was indisputable and the gang lords found that they served him more than the other way around.

Unlike Alef, Bet didn't like getting his hands dirty so he paid his way to the top, keeping his suits clean and his hands bloodless, or so he thought. But there was more blood on his hands than some of the gang lords that ran The City. Bet brought his hands back to himself, despite the bemoaning of the women he owned, and sat up. He took a drink of vodka as the woman on his left sat up after him and slid her hand into his partially unbuttoned shirt and began rubbing his chest.

"What's wrong, hun?" she asked, more worried than horny.

"Don't worry about it," he said before downing the rest of his drink. "Go dance, both of you. I want to be alone." Both of the girls got up and moved towards the dance floor, obeying his command. Bet leaned back against the couch, crossed one leg over the other and sighed. He thought back to his childhood years with contempt. His father was a lawyer for celebrities and was, by all standards, a good father. His mother was a stay-at-home mom and took care of him and his sisters and was, by all standards, a good mother. His parents were Catholic, and he remembered going to Church every Sunday and being the only person who absolutely despised it. *Why would I want to sit in this boring building and speak to the sky*, he remembered thinking as a boy. He hated it all, and especially hated his parents. Now, he was still uncertain about the existence of God, even after being taken under the wing of Rabbi Alef, and he still hated his family, even after they died in that plane crash. *Good riddance*, he remembered thinking.

His parents were wealthy, well-known, and well-liked, so whenever their plane went down the whole world knew. And according to the entire world the whole family died, including their son Matthew. But whenever Matthew crawled out of that fiery wreckage, his family's bodies scattered in pieces and charred to a crisp, a middle-aged man with a goatee and white-shocked black hair was waiting for him. Medics rushed to assist the boy and armored soldiers stood at the man's side, ready to kill anyone or anything on that mountain top should their master give the order.

Matthew and his whole family died that day and the rest was history. Now, with a seat on the High Council, Bet had more power, more money, and more pussy than he had ever wanted, but he wasn't satisfied. He was never satisfied. And the only thing standing in his way was the rest of the Council.

A fat, bald, tan man in a black suit approached Bet as he sat deep in thought. Hearing the footsteps, Bet raised his head up off the back of the sofa.

"What is it?" he asked, irritated.

"You have a caller, sir," the bodyguard yelled over the music as he held up the phone. Begrudgingly, Bet took the glass rectangle and brought it to his ear.

"Who is it?" he asked, still irritated.

"It's Atria," the woman over the phone said. "Come to my office. I have information for you." Gimel hung up the phone.

"That woman, I swear," Bet said. *Fine,* he thought as he stood up from the couch. "Call my driver," he said to the bodyguard. "I have a plane to catch."

■■■■■■■■■■■ ▪ ▪ ▪ ▪ ▪

GIMEL

"Took you long enough," Gimel said to Bet as he walked through the door and into her office. Gimel's office at Trytek was a modern wonder, shaped almost entirely out of reinforced, military-grade glass locked together by small junctures of steel.

"I can see you've upgraded since last I was here, Atria," Bet chuckled.

"I try to stay modest," she said with a smile as she stood up, her black blouse matching her red pencil skirt and black heels perfectly. Atria walked over to Bet and kissed him gently. "I've missed you, my darling," she whispered to him.

"And I you," Bet said with endearment. "But you have information for me, yes?"

"Yes," Gimel responded. "Sit. Someone will be joining us

momentarily." Gimel sat back at her desk while Bet took a seat in one of the glass and steel chairs in front. After a few minutes of chatting a call came in.

"Here we are," Gimel said. "We can finally get started." Two holograms appeared around the table: one to the left and one to the right, projected by the room itself. The one on the left was He, and the right, Vav.

"Surely this is important, Gimel," Vav stated, her voice as rugged as her skin. "I'd hate to be wasting my time."

"You're both in secure areas, I hope," Gimel stated. Both Vav and He nodded in agreement.

"Good," Gimel said. "Alef is up to something and it doesn't include us." Bet gave a concerned look to Gimel.

"What do you mean?" Bet asked.

"Yes," He spoke up. "Enlighten us."

"Wednesday at 0100 hours Trytek began picking up encrypted chatter originating within Headquarters. As of this morning, the signal is still bouncing around HQ and The City."

"Get to the point," Vav stated.

"The chatter seems random, but the encryption isn't Sicarii and each time the signal bounces it always pings back to the same place."

"And where's that?" He asked.

Bet looked at Gimel again who looked back at him, worried. "Alef's study," Bet said quietly. Gimel nodded in agreement.

"This is troubling," Vav stated. "But I'm not surprised. I have known Alef since he was a boy and this behavior isn't unlike him."

"What do you mean?" asked Gimel.

"Power. The boy wants power. And he'll do anything he can to get it," answered Vav.

"Then we must prepare," said He. "If this information is true, then Alef's plans must be close to their fruition."

"That's not all," Gimel spoke up. "Nico has been moving around more than usual and his relationship with Alef makes Nico's loyalty to the High Council questionable to say the least."

"Nico is loyal to Alef and Alef alone - something I realized as my rabbi's student," added Bet. "If Nico is moving, the end is closer in sight than we think. We must move quietly and quickly if we are to get out in front of this."

"I agree," said Vav.

"As do I," said both He and Gimel.

"Kai's coronation will be taking place in two days. We must assume Alef's plans will come to fruition then when we all take our seats at the table. Without a doubt, he will seek the ascension for himself, " said Gimel.

"I will ready Isarcii Pharmaceuticals," Vav stated.

"The CIA and the Prime Minister are loyal to the High Council and the New States. I will make sure our movements are legal and offer whatever support I can," He furthered.

Gimel and Bet looked at each other, worry in their eyes. "Bet and I will ready the full force of Trytek," Gimel said. "We must make sure that Alef doesn't succeed." The Council members nodded in agreement and the holograms of He and Vav disappeared shortly thereafter.

"I fear this will not go as well as we hope," Bet said.

"As do I, my love. As do I," responded Gimel.

■■■■■■■■■ ■ ■ ■ ■ ▮ ▮ ▎

HE

He ended the troubling call with the other members of the High Council and stood up from his desk in the CIA headquarters near Washington D.C, buttoning the top button of his navy suit jacket along the way. The sun shone through the glass wall to his left and so he walked over and looked out to the trees surrounding the building. After a few moments in thought preparing himself, He walked over to his desk and paged his assistant.

"Nabhij," He said as he pressed the button on his desk screen.

"Yes sir?" a young man answered on the other side.

"I need to see the Prime Minister immediately," He ordered.

"I'll set the meeting and call the shuttle immediately, sir," He's secretary said. He moved back towards his desk and sat down and took a sip of his black coffee. A pinging sound came from his desk, so he touched it and a holographic screen appeared in front of him. He swiped up on the screen and an email from one of his higher ups appeared.

> Damien,
> I need the agency's intelligence budget documents from '92 immediately. They're already late. The House and Senate are waiting.
>
> Albert Zolnowski,
> Director of National Intelligence

He swiped away the message and turned off the screen at the same time that Nabhij walked into his office.

"Your shuttle is ready, sir. The Prime Minister will see you now."

"Thank you, Nabhij. While I'm gone, send Mr. Zolnowski the intelligence budget documents from '92. He's on my ass again."

"Right away, sir," the secretary said. "Enjoy your meeting."

"Ah, yes, it'll be a blast I'm sure," He said sarcastically. The walk to the shuttle was short and when he arrived at the landing platform the solid black, flying vehicle sat with its door opened like a wing, waiting for him. A short-haired man with tactical gear and a submachine gun stood off to the side, ready to enter the vehicle after his boss. He entered and his shadow followed. The ride to the White House seemed shorter than the walk to the shuttle itself, and once he arrived he stepped out to a swathe of guards and the Prime Minister herself, Dr. Zainab Abdallah.

"Damien, it's good to see you," Prime Minister Abdallah said graciously as she shook He's hand.

"It's good to see you too Zainab," He responded with a smile.

"Come, we'll talk in my office," she said. The walk to the Oval Office was brilliant, as always. The white walls did nothing less than sparkle and the red carpet made one feel like royalty, even the likes of He who was closer to royalty than anyone else he was walking with. After a short walk, He and Prime Minister Abdallah arrived at the Oval Office and sat on the cream-colored couches to discuss the business at hand. Zainab poured them both a stiff drink and sat down across from him.

"So," she took a drink out of the crystal glass. "Is this a matter of national security or a house-call from the Sicarii?" she asked.

"Both." He took a drink as well and held the glass in his lap as he crossed one navy suited leg over the other.

"Please do explain, Damien," Zainab demanded.

"A member of the High Council, Alef, seeks to betray the rest of us."

"Alef? He's the older gentleman, correct? The veteran of the War?" Zainab inquired.

"Yes. He's always been rather secretive, and I think we will see the fruit of those secrets very soon," He took another sip of his drink. "The Council is preparing for a coup."

"And you think this will be big enough that it will affect the structure of the New States?" Zainab asked further. For a moment, they both paused and stared at each other. "Of course you do, that's why you're here." He nodded in agreement. The Prime Minister set down her drink and stood up and walked towards the window behind her desk.

"Fuck," she whispered angrily, careful not to worry the guards that would be listening outside the door.

"I would suggest you evacuate somewhere remote, in case we fail and Alef's plans stretch further than just the domination of Headquarters," He said, taking yet another drink. "Call your wife and your kids and take them somewhere safe, my lady. Whatever happens, the New States needs its Prime Minister."

"What cards does he hold?" the concerned Prime Minister asked as she walked back over towards the couches.

"As far as we know, he has at least one of the Seraphim working for him, if not more. He may have loyalists in the Squads as well."

"One of those Seraphim are worth a thousand soldiers," Zainab stated under her breath. "How can I help? What will stop this coup from taking place?"

"Our defense must be covered up and redirected in order to ensure the secrecy of the organization. The actions the High Council takes must be made legal on the Congress floor. If it doesn't, our course of action will not succeed."

"It will be done. How long do we have?" Prime Minister Abdullah furthered.

"Two days," answered He.

"Two days!?" she yelled as quietly as she could. "You know those politicians! How am I supposed to pass this in two days?"

"If it can't pass in the given time, it must pass by the time our movement is finished. We will be in position at midnight on the 17th."

"Fine, I'll do what I can. In the meantime, I will retreat."

"As will I and the rest of the Council, until the day of, when we must take our seat at the table."

■■■■■■■■■■■■ ∎ ∎ ∎ ∣ ∣ ∣

VAV

"Grandma! Grandma!" Two little twin boys ran towards Vav as she walked through the doors of her grandson's estate in rural China. "We've missed you!" one of the boys said. "Yeah! It's been foreeeevvverrr!" the other boy added. "Where have you been?" "What have you been up to?" The two little boys bombarded Vav with questions as she continued smiling and looking down at them. And just as she was about to answer their barrage of questions, their father rounded the corner.

"Boys don't bother your great grandmother," he ordered in a light-hearted tone while he held back a chuckle. Go bother your mom instead."

"But daaaaaadddddd," the boys said in unison.

"Go!" he demanded again, more serious this time. The twins huffed and then ran off into another room.

"Hi grandma," the man said as he gave Vav a hug. "How have you been?"

"I've been busy, as always," she said still smiling. "But I am so very happy to see you."

"We're happy to see you and we're glad you could be here for the boys' birthdays. They've been talking about you and your stories ever since you were here last time."

"I remember when you were their age you were just as excited as they are now," she replied as they began walking towards the room the twins ran off in.

"And I'm still just as excited every time I hear them. You never told me how you came up with those famous stories of yours, even though you said you would tell me when I grew up," her grandson looked at her with fake irritation on his face.

"A storyteller never reveals her sources," Vav said shaking a finger at him. As they came to the next room, Vav tightened her grip on her cane as she stepped down the two steps into the living room, where the twins and their mother were playing with toys on the floor. The mother stood up and greeted Vav as she walked in the room.

"Dana," Vav said, her voice shaking. "It's so nice to see you."

"I'm really happy you could be here, Lin," Dana said as she hugged Vav.

"You're taking care of my boys, aren't you?" asked Vav. Dana chuckled.

"You know I am, grandma. And I always will."

"Good," Vav said. "Someone has to take care of this family when I'm gone."

"Where are you going now, grandma!?" one of the boys yelled. She walked over to him and rubbed his head.

"Nowhere yet, I hope. But when I do it'll be somewhere very far away."

The other boy spoke up. "When you go will you come back? Will we see you again?"

"I hope one day," she said endearingly.

"Awwww..." the boys said together, sadly.

"Don't worry about that now, little ones," Vav said. "You have something more important to focus on."

"What's that grandma?" one of them asked.

"I have the most wonderful story for you two," she said with a smile as the boys' eyes lit up in an instant. "It's about a man with *very* special powers."

TWENTY

BLACK STAR

I was young and I thought I was making the adult choice. To be so young but have such a strong desire to change the world, I was ready to face everyone at once and I even had the power to do so. I thought that my willingness to kill was my resolve. My personality was to never waver, never falter. But somehow, somewhere, my view became skewed. My path stayed straight, yet my end point was continually shifting downwards. Proof of my determination? How naive was I? That lady died from my actions! I told myself I wouldn't fall into the darkness, but that I would control it. My perception was off. I was already standing in it, practically consumed by it. I pretended like having friends protected me from evil. I must have been drunk on fairy tales and childhood dreams. This was my warning. I'm lucky to have had the wakeup call. Black Star continued thinking as he moved his way through the alleyways of The City.

Vadim is an emissary of the Bratva, a pakhan, a leader. According to the contract, he's currently located here in The City in an abandoned hotel somewhere. I failed at the hangar, in more ways than one, so tonight is my final chance to upset his business here. I won't allow him to leave until he's paid for the way he's been pushing Sunshine, a bastardization of my father's miracle. I need to search quickly to find the Hotel Francesco. Under normal circumstances and due to his strong will, Black Star wouldn't have fallen prey to the effects of the Black Seed. But because he kept feeding it, it blossomed within him until the roots of corruption buried themselves deep in his bones. With the destruction of the mask he stopped the spread of the darkness, but it was a darkness that could never be annihilated as it made a void within himself, a void that not even God could touch.

My arrogance was almost my undoing, he thought. *I was so confident that I was in control that I hadn't realized what was truly happening.* Black Star zipped through The City, moving through the shadows, untouched even by the neon lights from the holographic advertisements on buildings and rooftops. The rabble were unaware of him, even as he came within a few feet of them. The dark surrounded him, as it did the Phantom. But this time he wore no mask, only the bag of Black Star. He was changed now and was neither his old self nor the Phantom. After searching for an hour or so in the edges of downtown he located his target building. He didn't have long to prepare, but neither did Vadim. The dissolution of his shadow had happened only a few hours prior, so Vadim hadn't been at the hotel very long before he arrived. He climbed to a rooftop across from the hotel and took his bag off. He checked inside to see what equipment he was working with - things he carried just in case, but rarely ever used.

Man created machines to increase work over effort, he thought, as he pulled an electromagnetic pulse emitter from his bag. *Another gift from my lovely sister.* As well as the emitter, he found a few shurikens, a smoke bomb, a crushed granola bar, and some bandages. His stomach growled, because being hurt drained more energy than anything else and forced his body into repair mode. Being as thin as he was and having limited body fat meant that he had little energy stored at any given time. His hands trembled just by rummaging through his bag. He opened the granola bar and pieces of it fell on the rooftop as he ate it, hands still shaking. After finishing it, he turned the bag inside out, put his cloak on, and pulled the hood over. He hid the smoke bomb and shurikens within his sleeves and hopped down into the alleyway that separated the two buildings.

Let's get this party started, he thought. He placed the EMP emitter on the wall of Hotel Francesco and after arming it, an invisible pulse was sent throughout the building that knocked out all electronics, including the weapon-mounted flashlights of the guards inside. One by one the lights on each of the floors went out, from top to bottom, and Black Star moved into the lobby unnoticed.

The moonlight shone through the small windows on the opposite wall of the entrance, illuminating square sections of the carpet flooring of the abandoned hotel. Broken technology and furniture from the early twenty-first century littered the room, creating interesting shadows that drew the attention of Black Star for a split second as he entered. Black Star focused his sight on two men that were hanging around the windows, talking, laughing, and sharing a joint.

Damn, Black Star thought. *If I were here on different matters, I may have joined them.*

Their thick Russian accents split the air and as Black Star neared them he could feel the heat radiating from them. He could almost taste their body temperatures rising from the entertainment they received from one another.

"This is why I hate working in abandoned places," one of the mobsters said. "No one pays the damn electric bill!"

"That's why they give us flashlights, the cheapskates!" the other responded. "And these don't work either!"

Black Star watched the two men as they walked back to their designated posts. The larger man tossed what was the rest of the joint out the west facing windows of the recently shut down hotel. They moved slowly, begrudgingly, back towards the heavy, wooden, double doors at the entrance of the hotel lobby. Black Star crouched behind the worn maroon couch in front of him to stay out of sight. Just by placing his hand on it, Black Star could tell that the couch was extremely uncomfortable, meant for "entertainment" purposes only. He cringed at the thought. To the east was a corridor with four elevators, two on each side, and a stairwell at the far end. A single, rotating camera was on the ceiling, but was destroyed when Black Star triggered his EMP.

He picked up a piece of glass strewn on the floor from the shattered glass-topped table in front of the obviously uncomfortable sofa. He threw it across the lobby and into the hotel restaurant, where it struck a small pot, just as he had intended.

"What was that?" the smaller mobster whispered, startled.

"It was probably just a rat. What are you scared for?" the heavier mobster chuckled.

"That's a big fucking rat then," the small man retorted nervously. It was obvious to Black Star that the smaller man wasn't cut out for this job and was probably here because his bigger friend talked him into it. The Bratva definitely wasn't for the fearful or faint of heart, as it had become the most feared mafia in The City after pushing the weaker gangs out. The small man moved to investigate and raised his submachine gun in the process.

They've been waiting for me alright, Black Star thought. He moved quickly and delivered a swift chop to the back of the man's neck, knocking him out immediately. This alerted the second guard who stood a few feet away and turned quickly at the sound, gun readied. As he turned around he saw no one, only the body of his comrade slumped over on the ground. Then he heard footsteps behind him and his vision went dark as Black Star delivered a chop to the back of his neck as well, knocking him out like his friend. Black Star left them alive because they were grunts. Based on what he saw they probably didn't even make their own decisions. From what he gathered from Vadim they were more pawns for him to discard. Their goals probably didn't even align with the rest of the hierarchy. As far as he knew, they were just a couple of thugs trying to make a quick buck.

Hopefully when they awaken they'll realize that they're in the wrong line of business, Black Star thought as he opened the door to the stairwell and moved up to the second floor. When he got to the top of the steps, he quietly opened the door and slid his way into the next corridor, observing the fine paintings that had been ruined by years of neglect. On each side of the hallway were doors that led to rooms, and as he passed them he heard a voice coming his direction from down the hall. He moved into the closest room, darkness surrounding him, the streetlights pouring in the window only illuminating the desk on the far wall. The small room seemed nice, he thought. The guard passed and Black Star slithered through the doorway and moved in the direction the guard came from. The hallway veered right to a medium-sized barroom where a large window on the far wall illuminated most everything in moon and streetlight. One of the two guards in the room was behind the bar, digging through bottles and making one hell of a racket.

"Can you believe they just left this whiskey here to age for me?" He laughed as he held two bottles in the air. A shout came from down the corridor that Black Star came from.

"Hey, we've got an intruder!" the guard that had previously passed him shouted from down the hall. Black Star realized his mistake and knew he shouldn't have let that guard pass him so casually.

Guess I'm still kind of out of it, he thought to himself. He rolled from the wall of the corridor to behind a ratty chair and then crawled to an end table nearby. *They know of me, but haven't noticed me, so I'll just stay out of sight until I have an opening to the stairwell.* As Black Star was thinking, a door opened next to him and another mobster stepped out.

As the man stepped through he began to speak. "The power is out, so I couldn't... shit!" The man cut himself off as soon as he saw the cloaked Black Star hiding next to him. Black Star immediately pulled him into the dark, even though he was a bulky man and over six feet tall. He wrapped around the gangster like a snake and constricted him, choking him with his arms and forcing the air out of the man's lungs with his legs. The guard behind the bar took a swig of whiskey and set the bottle down.

"I got this," he said too confidently. He grabbed an old-style RPK light machine gun that he had set down underneath the bar. He pulled the trigger and did his best to manage the recoil as he sprayed bullets toward Black Star. The flash of the barrel ignited the room in violent yellows and oranges, contrasted from the cool white light streaming in from the window. The bullets shredded Black Star's cover and tore into the unfortunate guard that he had just choked out. Black Star moved, as quickly as he could, and he felt the momentum behind him as he dodged each bullet individually.

Damnit.

This guy has chosen his path and he walks it with a smile. I can't save him. Bullets trailed Black Star as he moved towards the center of the room where a coffee table sat with a flower pot on top of it. He leapt off the coffee table, rotated in mid-air, and threw one of his hidden shurikens at the trigger-happy gangster who stopped laughing, let go of the trigger, and fell to the ground dead as the shuriken struck him in the skull. The force from the throw had cracked his skull and the shuriken dug deep, shredding his frontal lobe like a chainsaw. Black Star landed, rolled, and even through all of that the pot on the table he leapt from didn't move a single inch. Black Star moved towards the other gangster as the one from down the hall joined them, and Black Star knocked his gun upwards as he attempted to fire it, causing the guard to open fire on the ceiling. Black Star followed this by launching his elbow into the man's nose, breaking it, and disorienting him further. The guard from down the hall had her submachine gun raised, but Black Star was already in motion and grabbed her as a meat shield while the previously disoriented man fired in their direction. He grabbed the pistol off her hip as he carried her across the room and shot the broken-nosed guard once in the chest and then once in the head. He dropped the pistol and the woman's body and muttered to himself.

"Using guns is too easy," he said as he surveyed the room for any other potential threats. After sweeping the rest of the corridor he moved towards the staircase. Realizing he forgot his shuriken, he walked back over to the man behind the bar, plucked the shuriken out of his skull, and then wiped the blood on the man's thick green cargo pants. During this time it occurred to him that more guards might be coming down the steps after hearing the gunfire, so he sought an alternate route. He moved into one of the hotel rooms and broke the locks on the window. He opened it, stepped out onto the windowsill and shimmied over a bit.

I don't think anyone would mind if I skipped a few levels, he thought. He was up two floors now, about thirty-five feet, and he could see the neon lights of The City reflecting around him. The purple, pink, blue, and red lights were beautiful, and they mesmerized him as he scaled the side of the building. Between every floor was a small brick ledge, and so Black Star used that as leverage as he propelled himself higher up the building. He didn't want to take this path originally, but now that he had been found out he didn't have much choice if he didn't want to take the risk of getting shot.

No matter how fast I am, he thought, *the chance of me dodging thousands of bullets is slim to none.* About three fourths of the way up the building was a balcony, and so he sprung up to it, using his arms and legs to propel himself off the wall and up. Luckily for him the balcony was closed off, so the guards on the inside couldn't see or hear him, but he could hear them.

"Did you hear someone enter the building?" a concerned guard said.

"What the FUCK do you think those gunshots were? Fucking FIREWORKS!?" another guard shouted back. "Of course, there's an intruder! We even got confirmation over the radio!"

"So... do you think they got him?" the slower guard inquired further.

A third, more feminine voice entered the conversation. "It doesn't matter. If anyone comes through that door unload on them. Our job is to protect the Pakhan at all costs. As long as no one gets any further, we've done our job." The rally speech calmed the others down and they continued to secure the perimeter. Black Star could hear them moving about as their boots clacked against the floor. He moved up one more floor and realized that he could go no further, even though he still had two more floors to go. Everything above was a flat surface that not even he could climb, lest he made much more noise than he wanted to. Next to him was a flagpole with a tattered U.S. flag flapping in the wind, sticking out from the building roughly eight feet. The moon shone strongly on him as he moved along the outside of the building and he was thankful for it as it lit his way. What he was not thankful for was the wind that tore through him, as it not only chilled him to his bones, but it reminded him of his last encounter with Vadim. His mind flashed back to that moment, standing on the top of the hangar. It was hazy in his mind as if it had been a dream.

I was sent to kill him, and I tracked him to an old hangar before he arrived here at Hotel Francesco, hoping to take him out early. He was making a transaction from another man, and I was watching from above. They were both bald, and from the top I couldn't tell them apart as they were shrouded in darkness. I had to guess. Left or right. Who was Vadim? I jumped down onto the man on the right and crushed his skull in the process. I killed the wrong guy. Of course, Vadim fled. I was going to pursue him, but I heard screams from inside the hangar. She was tied to a chair in the center, but I didn't see the explosives under her. She was scared of me. I remember cutting her restraints, but most importantly I remember the feeling of what I wanted to do. I had to resist it. I barely resisted it. I cut the final restraint on her bloodied wrist and the urge to kill overtook me. I wanted to kill her. I needed to kill her. I had to take a deep breath and as I did the explosion hit me, blasting me back and obliterating her. The smell... God that smell. I get nauseous even now just thinking back on it. Was I not in control of my own body? I suppose I had never been around someone so helpless at that stage of bloodlust. I almost couldn't resist it. I don't know if I could have. My mask was destroyed and I remember seeing something inside, but I don't know what. I don't understand why I have gaps in my memory. Everything's so foggy. I have a photographic memory, which has positives and negatives, but I should still remember everything, every horrible detail. What's happened to me? No matter what, Vadim has made an enemy of me tonight.

Black Star took a deep breath and came back to reality. He found himself tightening his fist as his anger overtook him. He took a moment to focus while still on the flagpole. He took one last look down, at the concrete hundreds of feet below him, and then made his jump to the balcony. He was like a cat, silent, sneaking, but deadlier than anyone could possibly imagine. He climbed into the window and onto a catwalk that wrapped around the whole floor. The top two floors of the building had been gutted, to Black Star's surprise, and Vadim had set up shop there. The burgundy curtains on the windows flapped in the wind and the room was lit dimly by the light of the moon. Black Star stood there, crouched down, and observed the room while he could. From what he saw, it looked very similar to a loft. There were mannequins on the upper level where he was - some were bare, others had top hats and scarves. The lower level had boxes stacked everywhere and as far as Black Star could tell this is where they were pushing Sunshine from. In the center of the room was Vadim, sitting at a desk, facing a door across the room covered in plastic explosives, detonator in hand.

Fucking prick, he thought, disgusted at the fact that Vadim had manipulated his father's successes to subdue the population. He jumped over the railing and landed quietly behind Vadim. Black

Star walked towards him slowly. Vadim thought nothing of the possibility that someone could scale the entire building, even though he had been met with a supernatural darkness only hours before. Perhaps he was tired or too frazzled to think straight. Black Star moved towards Vadim's ear and whispered into it gently.

"Who are we waiting for?" he asked. Vadim jumped and let out a yelp like a scared child. It was a peculiar sound coming from him, as his hard, but round gut, bald head, short beard, and deep Russian voice shouted everything but that. It was a comical scene, but Black Star had no time to laugh. As Vadim jumped back out of his chair and turned around, Black Star drew back his fist and released a ferocious punch straight into Vadim's jaw, no doubt cracking it in the process. Vadim fell to his knees and dropped the detonator.

"That was for the woman you killed," Black Star said. "So you could have a few extra moments of life with me."

"She was a pawn," Vadim chuckled. "And so am I." Unpleased with the answer, Black Star kicked him in the face, breaking his nose and shattering his left orbital bones. Vadim let out another shout, this time much deeper and much more in line with his aesthetic. Vadim laid on his back, nose broken and face bloodied as Black Star looked down on him.

"You have committed acts of terrorism," Black Star said. "You've harbored illegal weapons and sold dangerous drugs. You've ruined people's lives. For that-" Uncontrolled laughter from Vadim interrupted Black Star.

"Oh, save the speech! You are a killer, just like me. Don't come here all high and mighty with your self-righteous bullshit." Vadim spit out blood and continued as his face began to swell. "You thought you could play the system, *ditya*, but I got news for you: the system played you. Other assassins have known about your lies. They're tired of you taking all the contracts, sticking your hands in everyone's cookie jar. You destroyed the balanced trade. You will be joining me in hell!"

"It's been nice talking to you," Black Star retorted. "But your time is up and I have to get going. Your operation is over." Black Star revealed a hidden blade under his cloak and used it to pierce Vadim's heart.

"They'll... find you..." Vadim said as life drained from him.

"Rest easy," Black Star replied as he wiped his knife off and stood up. Looking around the room for any other exit upwards and finding nothing, he walked to the door covered in explosives.

What could I have done to save him? he thought. He walked through the door and entered into a stairwell. The left went up to the roof and the right went down into the rest of the building. *That's my escape*, he thought and then proceeded up the stairs. *Man, I really need to get something to eat.* His thoughts continued as he walked out onto the rooftop. *I could really go for some hash rounds right about now. I wonder how Ahmed and Adelina are doing.* Black Star felt a drop land on his head and he looked up. *Jeez. Rain too? This night just keeps getting worse.* In just a few moments the rain went from a drizzle to a downpour and Black Star jumped from Hotel Francesco's roof to another and began running west.

By all accounts it was a rather beautiful night. The rain was annoying to Black Star as he was wet and cold and had not had real food since his stew at Helga's Kitchen. But the lightning streaking across the night sky made him smile as he ran faster and faster, careful not to slip up and go tumbling off the rooftops and onto the street below. Black Star was fascinated by the layout of The City as the rooftops seemed much easier to traverse than normal cities.

It's as if these were built for running, he thought. *I can move a lot quicker here than I ever could anywhere else. Damn this feels nice.* His stomach grumbled. *Ugh. Need food. Tummy angry. Energy low.* He felt like a robot that was running on low battery. He jumped from one roof to the next and after running and jumping for a few minutes he heard an unfamiliar noise. A regular person couldn't have heard it, as the rain and the sounds of the busy streets would have drowned it out, but he did. It was a click, and he could feel something coming at him fast from a rooftop below. He turned in mid-air and barely dodged a tether that shot past his face. More followed and he dodged all but the last one which caught him around the ankle and slammed him on the roof below.

I'm getting slow, he thought, his pride damaged from being caught in such a ridiculous trap. He stood up off the wet rooftop and looked at the tether wrapped around his ankle, attached to the edge of the roof. *This is advanced,* he thought further. *Did it sense me? I was moving pretty fast so it must be automatic because no regular person would have the reflexes to catch me, even at a fraction of my top speed.* As he was looking the tether over, a large, long-haired dark man, a young blonde-haired boy, and a green-haired, pale woman all wearing similar outfits dropped onto the rooftop from a slightly higher one. The black, skin-tight suits they wore slightly resembled muscles and barely caught any light. Across the street, even through the rain, Black Star could hear someone loading a magazine and pulling back the charging handle on their rifle. From the sound, he could tell that the rifle was rather advanced as well, and that it was heavy enough to take him down should he take a direct hit from it.

"Who are you?" he asked as he stood there, no longer paying attention to the tether as he already decided he couldn't break it with his speed as he was now.

"He's early," the large man said to the other two.

"What should we do?" the boy asked.

"Follow protocol," said the woman with her green hair in two tight buns. "We've been trained for this. Kai will be here any moment."

"Is Kai your leader?" Black Star shouted. His three captors were shocked that he could hear them, but they didn't respond.

"Tara, take the shot! He can hear us somehow. Do it now!" In a flash, a bullet ripped from the barrel of the woman across the street. Black Star dodged, putting the tether between himself and the bullet, and the bullet shredded through the diamond-lined tether and exploded in the process. The smoke was quickly whisked away by the rain and wind and Black Star unwrapped the torn tether from his ankle.

"You don't want to do this," he warned them. The large man with the long locs pulled a hand axe from behind his back and extended the handle so he could hold it in two hands.

"Should we wait for Kai, Amina?" the young boy asked the green-bunned woman as he pulled out a folded scythe from under his cloak and unfolded it.

"If we don't move now he'll get away Piers," said Amina in response as she drew two daggers from her leather vestments that covered her suit. Tara set down her rifle, ran, and leapt across the street and rolled as she hit the rooftop they were all on.

"We have to do this," Tara said as she drew a handgun from her hip and a short sword from the other. "Squad, formation B. Marlowe, on me." Marlowe collapsed his axe to just a one-handed grip and moved forwards towards Tara. The young boy Piers stood behind them and Amina, the green-haired woman, stood behind Piers.

"One last chance," Black Star said as he began stretching. "Don't do this. Let me go. I don't want to kill you." Unfazed by his threat, Tara and Marlowe charged him and Tara fired her handgun as she ran. Black Star slid back and forth on the roof, doing his best to minimize his energy output as he barely had any as it was, and dodged each bullet that came at him. They moved much slower to him, and he could track them through the air with relative ease like he had done in the hotel. From his left came Piers, faster than Marlowe and Tara, and jumped up and over him in an attempt to cut off his head. Black Star, of course, redirected Piers and launched him away, feeling an interest in the young boy grow as he did. Amina flanked his left as Marlowe and Tara rushed in and threw a handful of daggers before her two squad mates got in the way. Black Star dodged those too with a simple handspring and twist in mid-air that avoided the swing of Tara's sword towards his legs at the same time. Marlowe came down strong with his axe as Tara's swing missed and Black Star redirected it with his hand, like D had done to him, and then twisted and kicked both Marlowe and Tara in the face, sending them backwards and stunning them in the process.

Piers was on him again in an instant, moving much faster than the others and smiling all the way. Black Star dodged the fury of calculated slashes as he twisted and spun every which way, keeping almost constant eye contact with Piers as he did.

"You're good kid, but not good enough. Not yet. Stop this and walk away. You have your whole life ahead of you. Don't throw it away," Black Star said, genuine concern for the boy's life in his words.

"You talk like an old man," Piers laughed. "You're like four years older than me, max!" Piers chuckled some more as he moved in for another flurry. Tara and Marlowe came up again and as they did Black Star grabbed Piers's wrist, shattered it, and flung him across the roof towards Amina by it, hoping to take out two birds with one stone. Amina caught Piers with an audible *THUNK!* and laid him down on the roof as Tara and Marlowe danced around Black Star, hoping to lay even a single hit on him. While they both swung away at him he kept watch of Amina and Piers, the former of whom was pouring a liquid on the latter's arm. Tara raised her handgun and began shooting at Black Star between slashes, hoping mostly to hit his leg or his foot in order to take him off balance.

She's firing point blank without putting her team in danger, Black Star thought. *This is coordinated well. They've practiced this formation a lot. I'm impressed...*

Tara was unsuccessful, however, and as she shot Black Star ripped the slide off her pistol and threw it off the edge of the roof. Around the same time, Piers was back on Black Star, anger burning within him. It had only been seconds since he saw Amina pour the blue liquid on Piers's arm, so Black Star was taken aback by the quick recovery. Piers attempted, yet again, to somersault over Black Star, using him as a springboard for a setup to attack. But yet again Black Star saw it coming and used Piers's momentum against him to fling him away.

This time, Black Star had thought, *I'll launch him onto the roof behind me and get him out of the fight.* But there had been no roof behind Black Star, as he had quickly realized, and Piers fell roughly forty stories and splattered against the ground, bone and flesh fragmenting on contact.

Oh shit, Black Star thought.

Amina rushed over to the edge of the building they were on and saw the silhouette of the young boy smashed on the ground and let out a wail that no one should ever have to hear, as they were the cries and screams of a woman's heart torn in two. She left her team alone with Black Star, and whenever she turned around she realized her mistake as tears swelled in her eyes and hatred poured through her veins. Tara swung at Black Star after Marlowe had missed yet another attack.

Black Star redirected her blade and impaled Marlowe with it. Letting go of the gladius, Tara stepped back, and when she did Black Star tore the blade out of Marlowe and cut upwards through his right shoulder, sending his arm and axe flying. Black Star kicked Marlowe away, picked up the axe, and despite Tara's best efforts to dodge, he cleaved halfway through her, from left shoulder to right hip, and then dropped the bulky weapon as Tara's lifeless body fell to the ground, her organs spilling out as she hit the wet concrete. In a matter of seconds, most of Squad Four had been wiped out and Amina stood at the edge of the roof with more hatred in her heart than ever, staring down a true monster.

Her pale, green hair had fallen partially out of her buns as she watched her squadmates die and she knew she was the last defense before Kai arrived. She opened the pockets of her leather vest and pulled out several small vials filled with every color of liquids imaginable and clutched them in her hands.

Hurry up, Kai, she thought. She charged Black Star and threw the two handfuls of vials at him, peppering the rooftop with multicolored smoke. The smoke burned his eyes and he dashed out of it, but as he did Amina launched knives towards him from within the smoke. Black Star dodged as he barrel rolled through the air, but as the knives flew past him, they exploded and smoked out the roof around him. He could feel his skin crawl with whatever was in the smoke, so he dashed out yet again and straight into Amina as his eyes began to water and he began to cough. Amina slid and attempted to trip Black Star, who jumped over and used her as a springboard to get away. They both recovered and Amina came at him again, launching smoke vials at the ground near him. He managed to catch a few of them, but there were too many, and the rest of the rooftop was now covered in an unnatural rainbow-colored smoke.

I guess this will be a bit more challenging than I expected, Black Star thought as he closed his eyes and held his breath. He was listening for Amina now, but she was quiet, as a good assassin should be, and it was obvious that she was in her element. He was curious, however, as to why she could breathe and see just fine, despite the toxic smoke in the air. When Amina was a few feet away, Black Star heard her step, and he dodged the swings from her daggers just in time as they trimmed off a sliver of his hair. She disappeared back into the smoke and Black Star continued to listen. The cloud surrounding him was thick and it made his skin itch. It irritated him, as the mud had done in Brazil, and he wanted to be free of the smoke skin he wore. Amina came at him again and she was too close for him to dodge this time, so he grabbed both of her wrists and kicked her. She stepped back and he gave chase, moving faster than he had against any of the other squad mates. He spun and kicked at her again and she dodged, just barely. But Black Star, more than anything, was trying to dissipate the smoke with his speed rather than kill the target in front of him. He continued after her, sliding, flipping, and jumping, kicking all the while, hoping to disperse the toxic cloud and debilitate Amina at the same time.

He's not on the offensive like he seems, Amina thought. *These aren't wild swings. He's using the whirlwinds to change my environment, carrying the momentum with each spin. This isn't good...*

She dodged what she could, but took a couple of hits along the way, no doubt breaking her bones in the process even through the strength of the Sicarii suit. She kept blocking and when Black Star went to kick again she took the final vial in her pocket that she had grabbed in between dodges and threw it towards the ground between them. Remembering his fight with D in Brazil and feeling that the smoke had dissipated, Black Star opened his eyes, caught the vial, grabbed Amina by the throat and smashed it in her face. She screamed as the glass shattered and the toxic liquid blinded her and melted her skin.

"I'm sorry," Black Star said with guilt and grief in his heart. "I didn't want this. I didn't want to kill that kid. I told you to stop." The skin on Amina's face continued to smoke as it boiled from the acid. She cried and screamed, but eventually all of her pain went away as the acid melted her nerves and seeped deep into her. As she stopped screaming, a man dropped behind them onto the rooftop, and Black Star looked over his shoulder at him.

"K--Kai..." she croaked.

TWENTY-ONE

KAI

Kai sat inside The Coffee Shop in a big leather chair in the corner opposite from the door. He stared out the windows as the rain poured down on The City streets, heavier than it had in a very long time, and drank his hot, caramel-noted coffee sip by sip. His mind was burdened, more than it had ever been, but no matter how burdened he was this little cafe helped him and felt like home. When he was alone, the smell of coffee drifting along the brick walls and wooden floor gave him a taste of what it was like to truly breathe, even though he had known no such luxury in his life. And today, of all days, he needed it most. He was nineteen now, one year older than yesterday, but he knew it changed nothing. It never did. It was the first birthday without Alphonse, without someone to bother him about it all day long even though it annoyed him. His mind drifted along the sad current, through memories of Al and his life since he was a boy.

He remembered when Alef had found him, rescued him, he had thought, from a collapsed building. He remembered starting the Academy and on the first day Alphonse came up to him and said, "We're friends now", even though Kai, at four years old, didn't know what a friend really was. Alphonse had stuck to Kai like glue and helped Kai through loss, pain, depression, and just about everything else. As they moved further into the Academy they met others: Amina, Piers, Verena, Benjamin, Noor, but then Noor died, Amina got hurt, and the world grew a whole lot darker. They grew up and became soldiers, all of them fighting for a spot on the Twelve. Kai was top of his class, followed by Verena and Alphonse, and whenever they graduated Alphonse became a researcher, Verena became the secretary to the High Council, and Kai got placed in Squad Nine under the Black Death Mahta, who was nothing if not a perfectionist.

Now, he was the leader of Squad Four, soon-to-be member of the High Council, and he knew, deep down, that he deserved none of it. He didn't deserve the titles, the money, the awards, or the kindness. He didn't deserve friends or family or power. Alphonse was dead now and had been for about six months, and Kai, his one true friend, had killed him. Kai's hands shook as he took a sip of his coffee.

I'll never forgive myself, he thought.

His thoughts whisked him away yet again, this time back to being the leader of Squad Four. Amina, Piers, Marlowe, Tara, they were all his responsibility, and whether he deserved it or not they were all his friends and they were the only family that he really had. He had to do everything he could in order to ensure their survival and success. He had to make sure they had a good leader after he was gone. He had to make up for his mistakes somehow. And Amina... his thoughts whisked away once again, this time into the deep rabbit hole of his relationship with her. Her face flashed through his mind, and she was falling, wounded, through the skies above the ocean, just like she had fallen, wounded, at the Academy when they were younger. And both times, just barely, he caught her.

She loves you.

...

Do you love her?

I don't know.

Amina was the most brilliant Alchemist Kai had ever met besides Mahta and in a lot of ways they reminded him of each other. Mahta was just older and... harder. Amina made him laugh, even when he didn't want to, when only Alphonse could ever do that, and she was stronger than she ever knew, stronger than Kai himself, he often thought, which wasn't saying much. And she was *beautiful*, God was she beautiful. Her eyes, her hair, her laugh, it touched Kai in a way that was unknown to him, a way he didn't quite understand. She loved him, he knew, but he didn't know what that meant or how that felt so he kept her at a distance because he didn't know what else to do. Kai took another sip of his coffee and kept staring out the window at the rain.

After Kai killed Alphonse, everything changed. Alphonse was the last light left in the world, the last hope for the future of humanity. He wanted to carry on Alexander Stromberg's idea of a better tomorrow for everyone, and he hoped that he would find something through excavation and research. But all he found was the Black Seed and something deep and dark slumbering in the ruins of Akkad. It drove him mad, Kai had realized, and Kai could feel it doing the same to him. He didn't know what it was, but it felt like a disease, like something had seeped deep into his bones and was eating away at him from the inside. He could feel his mind slipping, and the darkness would take him from time to time. It grew stronger every day, and he didn't know how much longer he had until he was like Alphonse. But unlike Alphonse he bore no mark of the disease, which was one of the one thousand questions created by the answers Kai found in the dark of the temple.

The darkness churned within him and took him to Sweden, back in the sewers, back when he *knew* he had seen it. *Why there?* he thought. *What's there?* He didn't know. Maybe, one day, he would find out, but the cost, he was sure, would be far too great. He remembered shooting Adrian Blom in the head on that stage. He watched his brains splatter against the ground. He didn't care then, but he did now. He remembered his first kill as leader of Squad Four, Allison Kingley, and how he slit her throat as she sat in her luxurious office, late at night after getting off the phone with her husband and child. He remembered Adrian O'Connor, the businessman he had killed right before Alphonse. He could still feel the resistance as his sword moved through O'Connor's flesh and pierced his heart. He remembered Yuto Ito, a Japanese civil rights activist who he killed in front of his friends. He didn't care then, but he cared now. So many deaths and more, all by his hand, and for what? He remembered Gilroy, his teacher, laying on the ground in front of him...

It was just another year, he thought. But it wasn't just another year, and he knew it. This year had changed him, forever, and he knew that if he survived the next one and took the seat on the Council, he would never be the same. Kai finished his coffee, stood up, and walked over to the bar where he placed the mug so the barista on duty wouldn't have to walk around the bar to get it after he left. He grabbed his coat off the rack, put it on, thanked the barista, and walked through the wooden door and out onto the street corner. The awning above the door blocked the rain from drenching him, but he didn't care about getting wet, so he stepped out in the storm anyways. The thick raindrops berated his coat and the bottom of his Sicarii suit and bounced off, as both were weather-resistant. He put in his earbuds, played his lo-fi playlist, and began walking down the street to his right and continued reflecting on his life. Eventually, his thoughts moved from Alphonse to his squadmates, who would begin setting the trap for Black Star in a few minutes.

Marlowe, Amina, Tara, Piers...

Their faces flashed in his mind as he remembered them.

They deserve a better leader than me.

His thoughts moved away from his squad and back into the temple at Akkad, where he had been torn open from within. He remembered the cold, the darkness, the *movement*. He would never forget it. The thing that spoke to him from within, through ideas, Nzhurmiwa, he would never forget it either. Not because the memory couldn't fade, but because it wasn't a memory, it was an experience, a never-ending actualization of emptiness that followed him even in his sleep. The waves crashed against him, even now, and he didn't know how long it would be until he drowned.

After ten or so minutes, Kai arrived at his destination and peered up at the concrete building. He took out his earbuds and walked through the massive archway in front of him and after a few moments he was back outside, the rain pouring down on him once again. He stopped and looked around at the holographic neon purple gravestones that surrounded him, taking in their multitude, their beauty, and their loneliness. He went up the steps to his right and began walking amongst the sea of purple light, amongst the memories and sorrow that clung to the stones. He searched the names, each one heavier than the last, trying to find something that stuck out, something that the Sicarii didn't want him to find.

What am I looking for Gilroy? he thought. *Who am I looking for?*

He walked all the way around the old stadium until he had reached where he started and he went up another level. Still yet, after another trip around, he saw nothing but the flowers loved ones had left. It was still raining, just as hard as it had been, and the water ran down the steps like a river. He circled back around and went up to the fourth level still, unable to find anything. He had been there for an hour, his hair was as soaked as it could get, and he knew that the time to meet up with his squad mates was drawing near, so he decided that after he finished this round he would leave and come back another day. He continued walking in front of the holographic neon gravestones, reading and reciting each and every single name in his head as he walked by.

David.
Angela and Leonard.
Kristen.
Sarah.
James and Anthony.
Krishna and Avneet.
Liza and Jae-Sung.
Seth.
Haruto.
John and Lillian.
Yekaterina.
Ya'aqob.

Kai stopped as the realization crashed against him, freezing him in place. After a second or two, he stepped back a few feet and looked at the names in front of him as the shock set deep into his bones.

Here rests John and Lillian Aletheia,
Survivors of the War.
Saviors of the World.
Lovers of the Stars.

Kai's eyes glazed over as tears rushed to the forefront. He fell on his knees and cried like he had in the temple. His sorrow ran out of him through water and through water it was washed away, living forever in the earth below. He thought he could not feel this pain ever again, but he clutched his chest anyways and whispered to his parents anyways.

"I'm so sorry... I'm so sorry..." And even though he knew not what he had done, he apologized anyways, for he knew that it was by his hand they had been slain, and by his hand that he had slain so many others after them.

"Now I am become Death, destroyer of worlds."

And for the first time in his life, he looked up at the sky, pleading to God by action, and was answered only with the thunder, lightning, and rain. The tumultuous deep began whisking him away, clawing at his mind, begging for his soul. And as he descended into the depths of annihilation, a voice called over the sound of the downpour.

"Kai, where are you? It's almost time."

Shit! He got up as fast as possible, springing into action not through thought, but through instinct, forgetting the place he was just in.

"I'm on my way Amina!" he yelled as he sprinted towards the entrance to the stadium opposite of where he entered, tears still running down his face. "I'll be there in ten!"

"Make it five, Kai. Black Star should be here in fifteen."

"I'm on it!" he yelled again. Kai wiped his eyes and sprinted as fast as he could and touched the button on his neck to materialize his helmet. "Eris, I need to get to Squad Four as quickly as possible. Show me a path!"

"Right away," Eris said. A few seconds later she spoke up again. "Take the fire escape up to the roof on the building in front of you. Our fastest path will be the rooftops." Kai did as she said and climbed to the roof where he took off in a sprint, as fast as his body and suit could move. The wind and rain whipped past him as he hurdled across rooftops and vaulted over generators and air conditioning units with ease as he propelled himself further and further towards his goal. The buildings became older and harder to navigate as he continued to move east towards the designated rendezvous. He could see the building off in the distance. Six minutes is all it took for him to arrive at his destination and when he finally landed on the building he was met with lakes of watery blood, the torn bodies of his teammates, and a cloaked man holding Amina in the air by the throat.

"K--Kai..." Amina choked out. The figure looked behind his shoulder and saw Kai and let Amina go, her limp body slumping on the rooftop.

"This damn rain," the figure said under his breath. "I can barely hear anything." He moved away from Amina. "Who are you?" he asked aloud.

Kai moved closer to her while keeping his eyes on his target. He passed an impaled, armless Marlowe whose light had left his eyes and the body of Tara, which had been almost completely cleaved through, no doubt by Marlowe's axe that lay next to her which was coated in blood and sinew. Kai crouched down by Amina and touched her bloodied hair. Her eyes were white as snow and her face was mangled.

"I knew it was you..." she said in a whisper. "I can't see you, but I knew. He used my own acid against me. Kai..." Amina began coughing and Kai wrapped his arms around her and propped her up. Blood spewed out from her mouth and onto her chest. Kai collapsed his helmet and looked at her with his own eyes, wiping her mouth with his coat in the process. "Kai there's... there's something wrong with him."

"What do you mean?" Kai asked quietly, still keeping an eye on his target.

"Black Star... he's... like an animal. He moves like a snake, like a cat, and he could hear us, even through the rain. He used all our weapons against us..." Amina trailed off.

"I should've been here sooner," Kai looked around. "Where's Piers?"

Tears welled up in Amina's blinded eyes. "He threw him off the roof Kai... I... I watched him fall... I... I..." Anger boiled in Kai, but he pushed it down. For now, he pushed it down.

"I'm sorry Amina. This is all my fault."

"No," she said bluntly. "No. It's not. Kai, we..." she coughed again, hacking up more than just blood. "Ohhh fuckkk..." she groaned. After a few moments of pain, Amina continued. "We chose you. We accepted you. I know you weren't close with... with Tara or Marlowe and I know you pushed Piers a-a-away after Alphonse died, but they never held it against you. I..." she took as deep a breath as she could. "I never held it against you."

"I don't deserve you, I never did," Kai said, fresh tears replacing the ones he shed earlier.

"I love you," Amina said, her voice getting shakier by the second. "I've always loved you." Tears began rushing down her cheeks. "I'm scared Kai. I don't want to die. Please Kai. Please. Please don't let me die." Amina's words tore through Kai like razors, but he held it together as best as he could... for her.

"You're going to be okay," he lied to her. "Everything is going to be okay."

"Please, Kai. Please," she said desperately as she clung to him. "Please kiss me."

"Amina, I..." Kai was taken aback.

"Please. Just once. Please." Kai paused and then leaned over and locked his lips with Amina's. They felt different than he thought they would, but better than he could have ever imagined. He felt her life, her love, pour into him steadily. Black Star looked away. After what felt like a lifetime, Amina let go and slumped back down.

"Exactly how I imagined," she said with a smile. Then she sighed the deepest of sighs and the breath of God left her. Kai cried again, even when he thought he was out of tears. He laid Amina down and pressed the pad on his neck and began unzipping his jacket as his helmet came over his head. He let his jacket slide off his shoulders and onto the rooftop next to Amina's body, revealing his sword attached to his back. He grabbed the handle and pulled it down to his right hip, revealing the overlay that melded with his suit, and the sheath that was connected to the overlay rotated as he pulled. Once at his hip, he pulled it towards him, and the sheath rotated forward and Kai drew his sword like he normally would. Afterwards, the sheath snapped back upwards, and fused back with the overlay of his suit.

Thanks Elaine.

"I didn't want to kill them," Black Star said. "And I don't want to kill you. Let me go."

"Black Star, son of Alexander Stromberg. By the order of the High Council of the Sicarii I sentence you to death."

"The Sicarii, huh?" Black Star retorted. "Maybe you do have some answers after all."

"Your pride will be the death of you," Kai said, tears staining his cheeks underneath his mask.

"And your loyalty to this Council will be yours," responded Black Star.

TWENTY-TWO

KAI AND BLACK STAR

Kai and Black Star stood a few dozen feet apart, but their goals were miles away. Kai readied his sword and brought the hilt up to his cheek with both hands, blade pointed at his enemy, his left side facing forward. Black Star stretched every muscle on his body at the same time, starting with his arms and moving down to his legs. Kai studied Black Star, the way he rotated his shoulders, cracked his knuckles, and stretched his hamstrings as he pulled his bent leg behind him, one at a time, with each hand. The cloak was large, most likely meant for a bigger person Kai had thought, and because of this Black Star's hands were often concealed in the sleeves, something of which Kai also took note. Black Star spoke up between his stretches as Kai held his position, Shatter pointed at his target's heart.

"This Sicarii, look how they discarded your team. And you. Do you even know what you're fighting for? What was their sacrifice for?" Kai had no desire to answer, and really, more than anything, Black Star's voice bounced off him and faded into the night. Black Star bent over and picked up Tara's bloodied gladius off the ground, as Marlowe's axe was too heavy for him to use properly.

I would've preferred that boy's scythe, he thought. *Too bad.* Black Star spun the blade around and studied it for a bit. He hadn't had the chance earlier whenever he killed Marlowe, so he figured now would be the best time as Kai waited for him patiently. Kai was still standing, unmoved, unburdened, facing Black Star. Black Star finished spinning the blade around and held it down to his side in his left hand. The two assassins moved towards each other slowly, methodically, the intent to kill surging throughout their bodies. They rotated around each other counter-clockwise as they moved closer to the center of the building. Black Star knew he would win, it was impossible for him to lose, but he also knew that he had to keep his guard up just in case.

I might be low on energy, he thought, *and he might be fast or strong or whatever. But no matter what, I'll beat him. I still have cards up these sleeves.*

Kai watched Black Star as they moved around each other. Shatter gleamed magnificently in the light of The City, reflecting hues of purple, pink, and blue.

"Any information, Eris?" Kai whispered, his helmet masking his voice from Black Star's listening ears.

"Yes, but you won't like it," she replied. "This guy is dangerous, Kai. *Really* dangerous. I don't know if you can kill him." Eris had been gathering all the intel she could on Black Star as Kai watched him stretch. Satellite imaging had tracked him around the world, as long as he wasn't moving too fast, and so Eris could see clearly his fight not only with Squad Four, but with others as well.

"I'm not worried about killing him," Kai responded. "He just needs to be stopped, whatever that means. He can't learn about the Sicarii. He can't be allowed to kill anyone else."

"I don't know, Kai," Eris said, unsure for the first time since Kai had known her. "I'm not a human and this guy scares *me*. But he seems to favor his legs. I can't imagine he'll use the sword for much more than parrying and a few quick kill shots. He's acrobatic and quicker than Gilroy or Lillian Marshall. Go for his legs and you might be able to slow him down enough to get a few good hits in on him. But remember Kai, this guy is fast, so fast that he disappears from sight if he moves quick enough. The Sicarii satellites can't track him at that speed, so he has to move faster than any aircraft ever created."

"That's impossible," Kai said as he edged closer to Black Star.

"It's not, Kai. I've watched him do it. I don't know how he does it, but he does."

"Either way, he can't do it here. Generating that much energy in that short amount of time would destroy everything around us. He couldn't pull it off. His speed is still a problem, so I'll need your help Eris. Track his movements so I can focus on his legs between parries. Can you do that?"

"I'll try," said Eris.

"Good. That's all I need." Kai and Black Star were a few steps from each other so Kai twisted his wrist, feinted for a pierce, and then rotated his blade and came down towards Black Star's left shoulder. Black Star parried, stepped to the side, and retaliated with a slash of his own that Kai parried perfectly, sending Black Star's blade back towards him. Kai swung Shatter methodically, gracefully even, but the force behind his swings were anything but. The power of each swing was dangerous, Black Star could tell, and it only took a few parries and pains from the metal-on-metal reverberations for him to realize that he should start dodging instead.

They aren't just fast, Black Star thought. *There's raw power behind them too.*

Kai continued the barrage, and between every few swings went for Black Star's legs. The two of them weren't moving very much, except for the parries and dodges, the former of which rang loud throughout the night air, so they stayed mostly in the center of the rooftop. Black Star evaded a blow directed at his head and moved to Kai's left in order to get behind him, but as Black Star dashed, Kai moved, and blocked the attack targeting the small of his back. Black Star came upwards with Tara's gladius as Kai turned and swung downwards, and the two clashed in the middle, the blades booming as they bounced off each other. Knowing he wasn't going to win the fight with his strength, Black Star flipped away and quickstepped backwards to put some space between them. Both Kai and Black Star inspected their blades for damage as that last hit had met edge with edge. To both of their surprises, no cracks had formed along the edges, only a few nicks here and there.

"Who are the Sicarii?" Black Star spoke up, still desiring answers. "Who, or what, is the High Council?"

"Kai," Eris spoke up. "This guy killed Dalet."

That's why the Council wants him, Kai thought. *Or is it something more?*

The rain continued to berate The City, and the pools that had formed on the roof, mixed with the blood of Squad Four, reflected the lights around them just like Kai's sword. The torrent without reflected the one within and the darkness within Kai churned like a sea in a hurricane.

"Come on, bud," Black Star spoke up again. "At least say something!" But Kai refused to give his opponent the satisfaction, so instead he raised his blade in front of him ready for another round. Black Star shrugged and charged, hoping to turn the momentum from the dash into a stronger attack than normal. Kai could tell that he was moving much faster than a regular person could, even with a Sicarii suit, but Eris could still track him, so Kai wasn't worried. Black Star came at him quickly and transferred the momentum from his dash into a spinning kick. Kai moved quickly as the kick slid past in front of him and shoulder charged Black Star to take him off balance. Black Star dodged under Kai's shoulder and carried the momentum from the kick into a leg sweep and Kai responded by flipping over Black Star, dragging his blade across the concrete roof and wrenching it upwards to cleave through his enemy who was laying on the ground. Black Star did a back handspring almost instantly and deflected the blade at the same time with Tara's gladius. He continued back stepping as Kai charged him and their blades clashed again, over and over. The ringing sounded through the night as metal struck metal, but nothing could be heard over the rain that drowned out even the sounds of sirens and horns coming from the street, no doubt originating from the emergency vehicles arriving where Piers's body had splattered against the road below.

Kai's aggressiveness had Black Star backed right up to the edge of the rooftop, his relentless strikes giving Black Star no time to recover. With few options Black Star performed an aerial between two of his strikes and leapt over his opponent's head, pulling the two shuriken out from within his sleeves at the same time. Still in the air, Black Star threw them at Kai, too close, he had thought, for Kai to deflect them, but he was wrong. He watched Kai's eyes track them and in one quick swipe of his blade, both projectiles went flying into the distance.

His reaction time is incredible, Black Star thought. He gained no advantage trying to get behind Kai, so he backstepped across their blood-stained battlefield once again. Kai took one deep breath, regaining composure, and pressed his advantage. He swiped as quickly as he could and Black Star dodged around him, striking from behind. Kai blocked his attack and retaliated, which was, of course, expected at this point. The second swing missed Black Star as he carried his momentum and moved away from Kai yet again, ending in another back handspring which launched him in the air, allowing him to throw his third and final shuriken at Kai. Kai turned, saw the shuriken glistening in the moonlight, and deflected the last projectile into the night sky.

For the two assassins it felt like hours as their blades rang against each other time and time again, sending vibrations throughout both of their bodies, weakening them with every blow. Black Star could feel what little energy he had left rapidly depleting and knew that he couldn't keep it up much longer. Kai felt less physically exhausted than Black Star, thanks to the Sicarii suit, but his mind was steeped in darkness, and he knew that if he let his mind wander even for a split second, he would die.

I need to do something, Black Star thought as he parried and dodged Kai's gleaming blade. *I need to end this fight as quickly as possible or I won't be able to make it home. Do I really have to go all out? Against this guy? No. I can't move that fast or I'll destroy this building and everything around us and I'll most likely kill myself in the process. He's tracking me at my fastest current speed with no problem. So maybe if I overclock, but just barely, it'll be enough.*

Black Star parried one of Kai's swings as hard as he could and then quickly back stepped twenty or so feet to put enough space between him and his black-clad adversary. Even with Black Star's eyes as keen as they were, through the downpour and the darkness of the night the only thing he could truly make out was the glistening of Kai's blade and the mask he wore, where the deep, red, glowing lines stared back at him, reminding him of the Phantom and the all-consuming darkness within himself. Truly, Black Star thought, such a mask would terrify even the sanest of men. But not him, his will was too strong to be broken by fear. He was stronger, more intelligent, and superior to his opponent, although he knew he had to admit that the man standing before him had been one of the greatest adversaries he had faced in a long time. Sure, Black Star was weakened by lack of food, lack of sleep, and acceptance of the darkness within himself, but he knew that Kai was an exceptionally strong assassin and warrior either way, because no matter how weakened he was Black Star never overclocked unless he absolutely *had to*. And right now, he *had to*.

Kai studied his opponent as he backed off. He wasn't used to fighting someone who was so quick, but he knew that the fight was just getting started. Black Star had more tricks up his sleeves than Kai could imagine, and he only hoped to survive the fight long enough to debilitate Black Star and get away. None of his swings had made contact, unfortunately, and even he was getting exhausted from swinging his blade over and over again. He was reminded of his fight with Gilroy and how strong Gilroy had been. Did Black Star feel as he had? Kai had thought.

Or is he just toying with me? The thought had crossed Kai's mind one too many times. Up to this point, the fight wasn't anything terrifying. He knew he had grown since his fight with Gilroy a couple of months back, but he couldn't imagine that he had grown so much. He knew Black Star had more speed in him, but how much was he preparing to release? How fast could he realistically go before destroying the things around him or exhausting himself? Kai figured that Black Star should be at least mildly exhausted, more than Kai himself, as Black Star had assassinated Vadim only an hour before and had fought and killed Squad Four as well. Kai glanced around at the bodies of his teammates. He felt sorrow, pain, and anger flicker within him, but he didn't have time to mourn, not right now.

Black Star was still standing twenty or so feet away from Kai. He dropped Tara's gladius and began stretching again. He could feel the hair on his arms and on the back of his neck stand up as he jogged up and down and then crouched and stretched his legs out from under him. The rain continued to pour around them, but the rain no longer reached Black Star as it evaporated right before it touched him.

"Kai," Eris spoke up, a tremble in her artificial feminine voice. "The atmosphere is changing. Look at him. Really look at him." Kai watched Black Star and saw steam forming around him where the rain was evaporating before it hit him. Smoke billowed off him, like he had just walked out of a hot shower and into a cold room. He was still stretching and as he continued Kai could see a faint blue spark jump from Black Star and into a raindrop.

"Did you see that Eris?" Kai asked, bewildered. "What was that?"

"Electricity. Kai, we need to go. *Now.*" Black Star stopped stretching and crossed his arms. He stared at them and as he did, he began speaking again.

"Look around us, look how your superiors treated your team. Discarded... and for what? I've spoken directly with a High Council member. You are all pawns in their game. You have to know that... so why, why fight for them? Why stick up for them?"

Kai had no answers.

"Well, I still have a trick up my sleeve. Something they never wanted you to know, I'm sure. Your squad was ordinary and I bet you think the world is too. But this world is fantastical actually... and I'll show you firsthand."

Overclock.

A surge of electricity burst from him and Kai's mask went dark. He was blind, even the artificial overlay was shot, and Eris said nothing. The helmet collapsed automatically and when it did Black Star was right in front of him, lightning surging around his body, flickering through his shaggy hair as it stood on its ends. His eyes flashed blue, just for a moment, and Kai was flying across the rooftop. He rolled and stood up just in time to block another flash kick from Black Star, this time with the flat of his blade, its point dug deep into the roof. Kai didn't have time to think. He could barely move. All he knew is that he was lucky he had his Sicarii suit on because that kick should have shattered most of his ribs.

Black Star had Tara's blade in his hand again and came at Kai. Somehow, Kai managed to block the strikes, but he couldn't move as Black Star had him pinned as he dashed around Kai, looking for any opening to strike. As he slid across the roof, the electricity coursing from Black Star's body evaporated the rain below him, releasing steam with every move he made, allowing Kai to track him just barely. Blades clashed and lightning surged and every single moment was a death sentence for Kai. He could feel the fear, the danger, the anxiety that at any moment he may slip up and be killed. He didn't know what to do. He had never faced something like this before. He had never faced raw power.

Black Star's ability was something to fear, and Black Star knew that the lightning flowing around him had to be threatening and ominous. As he continued his barrage of strikes he was certain this would show Kai their difference in power. He wanted Kai to understand that the Sicarii sent him on a suicide mission. Yet, for some reason, every strike was countered, every blow met with one of Kai's own. Black Star was impressed and tried to contain his excitement.

Swordsmanship like this is rare, Black Star thought as he took a single step. *It's like his body is reacting to me by instinct. He shouldn't be able to block me.* He took another step towards Kai. *I need to get rid of that blade.* Black Star was on Kai in an instant. Knowing Kai would block his blows, even if by instinct, Black Star targeted Kai's blade in the same place so that he would gradually chip away at the edge until it broke off.

Back, forwards, left, right, over and over again Kai spun his blade around him, unable to actually move the rest of his body. His blade swung three-hundred and sixty degrees around him, as if he had eyes in the back of his head, and he blocked every attack of Black Star's if only by luck. He knew he had one chance to pull off a parry and land a fatal blow on his opponent, because after that his stamina would be drained and he would slip up, which was the most likely outcome, or he would try it a second time and Black Star would see it coming, especially at the speed he was moving, reverse parry, and kill Kai. Gritting his teeth and feeling a burst of energy surge in him, Kai waited for Black Star to dash behind him. When Kai saw the vapor trail forming he swung around, before Black Star was even there, connected with Black Star's blade through a miracle, parried upwards, and to his surprise... his blade shattered.

The idiot did my work for me, Black Star smiled. He swung down on Kai's shoulder and if Kai wouldn't have jumped back in time the blade would've cleaved right through him. Instead, he was left with a cut on his left shoulder that ran down onto his chest. Black Star stood a few feet away from Kai, smiling as Kai dropped the remnants of Shatter. Black Star came at Kai once again and sliced left and right. Kai dodged some of the cuts, just barely, but others made slight contact as they scratched his skin and cut him in every direction. Kai could see Black Star moving towards his heart, so when he did Kai grabbed Black Star's wrist, twisted it, and slung his fist upwards into Black Star's elbow. Black Star knew that if Kai made contact, he would no doubt break his arm, so Black Star let go of the blade and as lightning surged through his body, he kicked Kai as hard as he could across the rooftop. Kai flew and smashed into the ground with a hard thud, knocking the wind out of him in the process. His shaggy hair, not dissimilar from Black Star's in length and color, was soaked by the rain. Black Star stood a couple of dozen feet away as lightning continued to trickle unnaturally around his body. The electricity wasn't surging. It wasn't looking for ground or for conduits. It was dancing around him, as if it had no better place to go. His hair had fallen a bit and was no longer standing on end, coursing with electricity. Kai saw this and wondered whether or not Black Star was losing power. As the thought crossed his mind he coughed up blood onto the rooftop - the kick had hurt him more than he hoped.

Yet again, not wanting to kick an opponent while they were down, Black Star waited for Kai to get up. He could feel the lightning surging through him, running through his brain, his muscles, and strengthening him both mentally and physically. He could feel the rest of his energy leaving him, but he knew he had enough left to kill Kai.

This is it, Black Star thought. *This is the end. I didn't want to kill him, but he left me no choice. He's been the greatest adversary I've had in a long time. Greater than D by far. Very few have the privilege of saying they made me Overclock. He's the only lead I have on the Sicarii. Should I kill him, adding another to the list of bodies I've already piled up and risk losing a source of information? Or should I keep him alive, risking my life and the lives of my sisters? We'll see how it plays out.*

Kai stood up and Black Star dashed towards him again and the lightning surged around him more violently. His hair stood back up on its ends as he jumped and kicked at Kai's head, but Kai blocked the kick with his forearm. His arm should have shattered, and he winced expecting it too, but it didn't. Black Star was taken aback just momentarily, but he continued his assault. Kai readied himself like a boxer, fists raised in front of him. Black Star came at him with more kicks, directed first at his torso and then his legs. Kai dodged left, right, and under at first, and when Black Star crouched down and swept his leg, Kai dashed backwards out of range, knowing that if he tried to jump over Black Star again he would surely take a hit. Black Star spun off the ground and used his momentum to kick at Kai's face again. Kai caught Black Star's leg as lightning surged around him and Black Star spun and broke out of Kai's grab. Black Star landed again and Kai came at him with punch after punch, swaying left and right to dodge Black Star's counter attacks.

A boxer, huh? Black Star thought. *Easy.*

Black Star moved to grab Kai's wrist and as he did Kai flattened his palm, dropped his arm, and brought his wrist back up, knocking Black Star's hand away. He hit Black Star in the chest with multiple palm strikes, as hard as he could, and every time he did he could feel the lightning course through him, buzzing from his fingertips to his toes. The strikes resonated through Black Star and he felt pain where he expected none as a surge of energy passed through him. He retaliated almost immediately, even through the pain, and struck Kai square in the jaw with a quick, electrical jab. Kai was stunned and Black Star followed up with body strikes of his own, hitting Kai in the chest, stomach, and with the final quick hit, Kai grabbed Black Star's left arm before it made contact. Black Star punched with his right and Kai grabbed that one as well. Anger brimmed in his eyes as they stared at each other only for a moment before Kai headbutted Black Star as hard as he could. Black Star stumbled backwards and Kai, now bloodied and bruised, punched him in the face once, twice, thrice, and Black Star's electricity flickered as he did. Kai stepped forward, turned his body sideways, used his momentum he generated, and struck Black Star in the chest with the weight of his whole body behind him. Black Star flew back a couple of feet and landed on his back on the wet rooftop.

No more. Black Star thought as lightning surged around him right before he hit the rooftop. The next few moments happened almost instantaneously to Kai, but to Black Star it seemed much longer. Black Star's mind was moving a million miles per hour, complete trains of thought ending within a millisecond at the most. He had already planned hundreds of moves ahead of Kai and so before his back made contact with the rooftop, lightning exploded out of him and he somersaulted in mid-air, rotating his body backwards so his feet would hit the roof instead. When he landed the rain around him evaporated immediately and he flitted to Tara's sword, grabbed it, ran to Kai, and impaled him in the stomach. What Kai had seen, however, was a flash of blue and then almost instantaneously Black Star was in front of him, eyes an electric blue, and the hilt of Tara's gladius was sticking out of him. A massive explosion sounded about the same time and the rain that was falling around them was pushed away, just for a moment, as the sonic boom caused by Black Star's speed displaced the air and rumbled the building they were on. Kai looked down at the blade and then up to Black Star. The electricity coursing around him had gone away, but it was too late. Kai knew he was dead.

Black Star pulled the blade out as Kai spit up blood and collapsed onto the wet roof, surrounded by the dead bodies of his teammates. He looked around at them, his vision blurring as exhaustion hit him and he began to bleed out. His face was beaten and bruised from Black Star's strikes, as well as the rest of his body, so he stayed motionless on his knees, clutching his stomach as blood poured through his hands. Black Star threw the blade across the rooftop and it came to rest near Amina's corpse. Kai looked up at his killer, realizing for the first time in his life he had been on the other end of the assassination. It was fitting, he thought.

"I didn't want to kill your team," Black Star said. "I didn't want to kill you. I don't know the Sicarii, but I know they killed my parents and I want them to pay. I've been looking for them forever. Tell me where they are. Tell me where I can find this High Council."

Kai could barely think straight. He had no friends left. No family. No one. His squad was dead. Alphonse was dead. Sohei was dead. The only person left was Haley and he barely knew her at all. And yet, his thoughts went to her and their meeting in The Coffee Shop. He had nothing left to hide, nobody left to serve. He would fall into oblivion and his mind would swirl into nothingness.

"I-sar-cii," Kai choked out as he collapsed onto the rooftop.

"What?" Black Star asked.

"Isarcii... Pharmaceuticals..." Kai said. Kai stared up at the rain as his senses faded out. He couldn't hear Black Star anymore, or the rain, or anything else. His last smell was of fresh rain and iron as he lay on the rooftop barely holding his bleeding stomach. He stared at the sky as the raindrops splashed against his face and he closed his eyes as his consciousness faded into the deep churning ocean within.

"If you live," Black Star said to Kai as his eyes closed. "I will find you." With that, Black Star looked around the rooftop and with sadness in his heart, moved towards the edge.

Black Star stood above The City. He had a pit in his stomach that something wasn't right. *I wish I didn't have to kill them. I'm trying to be a better person. This shows I've made it in too deep. I can't avoid the violence. I couldn't talk them out of this.* Black Star glanced around slowly at the cascading lights of purple, pink, and blue.

I should have seen this coming. I can't stop playing the game, not just yet. I have to finish it, but I don't see a finish line. The High Council has to know that I was the Phantom. Luckily, no one messed with that ego. However, I'm sure I'll have more people picking a fight. It is also worth noting that they are sending legitimate squads, not just hitmen. Maybe if I linger long enough the leaders will just come out, then we can get this over with. That's assuming, however, that there is only one group pulling the strings. It would be silly to think that in the corrupt world only one organization controls all.

Black Star took a step onto the ledge of the building when a pain shot through him, seizing up his entire body. He tripped over the ledge and began falling. He couldn't feel his body, couldn't control his movements. He knew he had no choice but to accept his fate. He was unsure if it was the toxins from Amina's vials finally taking effect or something else that he had overlooked, but either way death was imminent. Black Star closed his eyes and enjoyed the wind as it rushed past his face. He saw flashes of memories from his life - his mom, his dad, his sisters, his grandma and grandpa, even Makao, Gideon, Kito, and Cornelius. He saw the people he had killed, the mistakes he had made, and those he had hurt along the way.

Bittersweet, he thought. *A fitting end for a low-life assassin.* His thoughts trailed off as the filthy rundown alley came to meet him. Then, he hit the pavement, and the world went dark.

The Lightning Arc:
Book 2

ONE

NICO

Nico fell towards the dunes of the Iraqi desert as the light of the midday sun reflected off his armor, igniting him with the yellow and orange hues of fire. The red core of his warsuit shone just as bright, reinforcing the already violent color that penetrated through the evening sky. As he closed in on the sand, he ignited the wing-like thrusters on his back and scorched the sand as he landed, turning it to glass almost immediately. The landing was harsh, hurried, violent. The sand that wasn't liquified was thrust upward into the air as the ten-foot-tall armor crashed into the ground.

Just as it landed the front of the armor opened and Nico stepped out, clothed in boots and light gray robes, and walked towards the sand steps that led down into the ruins of the Akkadian temple face. After a moment, he arrived in the dark cave and turned on the generators, igniting the Black Seed on the front in a torrent of artificial light. Nico stared at it, unfazed, as it stared back into him, attempting to entangle a soul he had not. He walked around the dig site, weaving through tables and lights, searching for something, but finding nothing. He moved into the temple itself and scanned the darkened, sandy corners and around each of the beautifully carved pillars, but still, despite his efforts, did not find what he was looking for. As he moved deeper into the dark and up the steps towards the altar, he felt a darkness creep into him: someone was watching him. He could feel it. He stopped and turned, but when he did no one was there, as far as he could tell.

"Show yourself," Nico demanded in his sixteen-year-old voice. But despite his order, nothing or no one appeared. He walked up a couple more steps but yet again he felt as if someone was watching him, and this time they were closer, but when he looked around again all he could see was the dark. As he reached the top of the steps, he saw, sitting on the altar, a brown, leather-bound notebook covered in sand. He reached for it and when he did he felt the dark touch his hand, like he had stuck it in a cold pool of water. But he moved his hand through the deep and grabbed the book, as he was ordered. He opened it and covering every page from top to bottom, from side to side, was the Black Seed. It writhed and danced on the pages and screamed at him in a plethora of magnificent, terrifying colors, but he was mostly unfazed, albeit a little confused, and closed the book as quickly as he had opened it.

As he moved back down the steps, he still felt something watching him, but despite his slight paranoia he moved through the dark, back into the excavation area, turned off the lights, and walked back outside towards his Archangel armor. When he got within a few feet of it, the armor opened up and he slid the journal into a webbed pouch against the inside of the spine.

"Contact Alef," Nico said in his monotone voice as the sand danced around him. The speakers in his suit began ringing like a phone and after a few moments a man with a deep, but refined voice spoke.

"Did you find it?" Alef asked.

"Yes. The journal is in my possession," Nico answered.

"Good. Keep it for now. The Council is here, but we are besieged. Gimel's forces are attempting the coup."

"And yet they're still playing the fool?" Nico inquired, humored.

"Like the sons of Jacob," Alef replied.

"How long until they breach Headquarters?"

"Twelve hours at most, but the breach is irrelevant. The coup will fail."

"Metatron, Michael, and Helel are at your disposal," Nico said.

"I fear Helel has plans of his own, my friend," Alef replied. "Nevertheless, Metatron and Michael will suffice. Three of the Twelve are here as well, but their loyalty matters not."

"You're an arrogant fool as always," Nico stated, coolly.

"That may be, but no doubt less of a fool than others. Find

Jehoel. Bring her to me. I have matters to attend to." The line went dead after Alef delivered his order. Nico climbed in the scorched warsuit and it lit up the color of his core - a violent red. Nico's mind began buzzing and after a few moments of what would be excruciating pain for a normal person, a robotic voice spoke.

"Neural link finalized." Nico spread his wings and ignited the engines of the suit. The core burned brighter as the wing-like thrusters scorched the sand, and he left just as he arrived - a torrent of flame behind him. His mind was silent, as always, solely focused on his mission. He was a soldier, as he had always been. But more than that he was a slave - to Alef, to the world, and he knew it but he never really cared. He was incapable of it and he knew that too. He was but an echo of an imprint on the soul of the world and he was created for one singular purpose: to destroy.

■ ■ ■ ■ ■ ■ ■ ▪ ▪ ▪ ▪ ı

"How long until the army breaches Headquarters?" Gimel asked Alef as she stood leaning up against the High Council table. "And where is Sofia? She should be here protecting us." Her temper began to rise as it did whenever she sensed insubordination. Alef sat leaned back in his chair, smoking his pipe. Vav was sitting as well, too old, she felt, to move around like the others. Bet and He paced around the inside of the Council chambers, not doing much other than glancing at their phones and staring at the walls. Eventually, He found a place up against the wall and sat down on the floor, losing his war against boredom.

"Rough estimates by intel put the breach at 0600. I've sent Sofia to prepare for the invasion," answered Alef after taking a few more puffs from his pipe. He set it down next to his gold-plated flip lighter. It was empty.

"Ran out finally?" Gimel asked with a chuckle. "I don't think I've ever seen you finish off that pipe." Alef smiled. "Maybe it's time for me to finally quit after all these years." Vav looked at him and once they made eye contact, she looked away.

"How long do we have to sit in here?" Bet asked. "It's only been an hour and I'm already losing my mind. Isn't there somewhere else we can go?”

“How the fuck are we supposed to get out of the City, Bet?” He asked, irritated. “Every road is blocked off and whoever it is continues to scour the skies. Even if we wanted to, we can’t escape, and this is the safest place for us anyways. The chances of them getting to the Spire and then to us are slim to none. We have the Seraphim and there are at least two Squads currently in HQ, not to mention the anti-personnel systems that we have.”

“The chain guns won’t get us far,” Alef said. The four other Council members turned to look at him as he stood up. “It’s likely the invasionary forces know of our defense systems. They’ll disable them quickly, I assure you. Our defense relies solely on the backs of the Seraphim and Sofia, so let us hope they do their job.”

“And what about the two Squads that are here?” Gimel asked.

“Squads Six and Eleven will be dead by the end of the day,” Alef said. Gimel, Vav, He, and Bet glanced around at each other.

“I’m going to my chambers. I’ll be back out whenever something changes,” he stated as he turned and walked down the hall. After they had heard Alef’s wooden chamber door creak closed, Vav spoke up. Her hands were in her lap as she sat straight up in her throne-like chair on the far end of the table, opposite from where Alef sat. Her hair was in a perfect, white bun as it always was.

“He knows,” she said quietly.

“Impossible,” replied Gimel. “We’ve given nothing away.”

“And yet he knows,” replied Vav.

“How do you know?” whispered He.

“Because Sofia isn’t here.”

“Then we have to prepare for anything,” Bet said as he walked over towards the table. The gold chain that hung on his bare chest where his shirt had been unbuttoned glistened in the light of the Council chambers. “He dies *tonight*.”

Alef walked over to the wooden cart where a few bottles of liquor and two crystal glasses sat. He poured himself a quarter of a glass of gin in one of the ornate glasses and sat down in his tall-backed maroon leather chair. The heat from the fire licked the chair and his clothes, and he felt himself sink in the warmth of it. He brought the glass up to his mouth and took a sip of the gin. It burned as it rolled across his tongue and into his throat and as he sat it on the small, wooden table to his left, his hand began to shake. He breathed deep and exhaled deep. Again and again as if he had never breathed before. And with the final breath he drew, he exhaled like a deep sigh and finally opened his eyes. The warmth within him spread from his head to his toes and his hands stopped shaking. He looked around the room as if he had never seen it before. Every breath was fresh, every sight was new. And whenever he looked to his left, past his wooden side table and the beautiful crystal glass that sat upon it, he saw that his plant, a large peace lily, had died, and he smiled.

■■■■■■■■■■ ■ ■ ■ ▪ ▪ ▪ ▮

"Where is she?"

"Who, man?" the long-haired, bearded, scientist asked, terrified, as Nico stood in front of him, a handgun pointed at his forehead. Nico lunged forward and gripped the man's throat, lifted him up, and slammed him against the concrete wall, which made an audible "THUNK" as he did. The man's plaid shirt had been untucked after being lifted by Nico and on his left hip a faint, graying tattoo stood out. It was so small that most wouldn't even see it, but Nico recognized it immediately.

"You're an Engineer. Your tattoo proves it." Nico looked him up and down as he held him against the wall. His used-to-be white lab coat was stained brown around the collar and lapel where it had gone unwashed for God knows how long, and a blue and white name tag labeled "Brian" hung by a flimsy metal clamp from that same dirty lapel.

"Answer my question, Brian," Nico said as he looked at the name tag. "Or I'll pull your intestines out through your throat." Something about Nico's calm voice and the way he picked Brian up by one hand, even though he only looked sixteen, made Brian extremely willing to comply. But despite his attempt to form words, the lack of oxygen he was receiving only allowed him to express his blurry thoughts in the form of gurgles and gagging. Nico dropped him, ready to hear what the Engineer had to say, but as always wore no expression on his face, not even one of annoyance or anger.

As Brian collapsed to the floor he coughed uncontrollably.

"Fuck, dude," he said through coughs. He stood up slowly and came face to face with Nico who stood only an inch lower than him.

"I'll ask you again," Nico started calmly. "Where is the Engineer responsible for the creation of the artificial intelligence known as Eris?"

"Who? Elaine?" Brian asked, still terrified. "I-I don't know. I haven't seen her in over a year."

"Not good enough, Brian," Nico replied as he raised his handgun again.

"W-wait-wait-wait-wait!" Brian cowered behind his hands, doing everything in his power not to piss himself. "L-Last I heard she was staying in a run-down garage on the West side of The City."

"The Western Provinces are vast. I need more than that," Nico pulled back the hammer on his handgun and as he did Brian almost shit himself.

"Woah! Okay, okay, she's in the Western Provinces near Sunshine Alley. Her garage will be the only place without Sunshine junkies in front of it. They don't like the bright light out front."

"Good, Brian. Good. Thank you." Nico uncocked his pistol and holstered it. He began to walk away and Brian, sensing the threat had passed, stopped cowering behind his hands. When he was a few feet away and Brian was about to sprint out the nearest door, Nico drew his pistol and shot the hairy scientist in the head. His skull popped like an overfilled water balloon and brain and blood spattered the wall. Nico re-holstered his pistol casually, as if just finishing at the firing range, and walked away without even as much as a flicker of a conscience flaring up inside him. He had killed many more for much less and he had known no such luxury as a conscience even before he became the destroyer that he was today. Had there been any security guards left alive they would've surely came running at the gunshot but given that Brian was the last person alive in the lab at four in the morning, there was no one to help him or avenge his death. Nico had disabled the security cameras beforehand once he got within range of the building due to the constant signal blocker his warsuit emitted, so he was not worried that his presence at the lab would be noticed by Trytek Headquarters only a little over a hundred miles away in the Rocky Mountains.

But, when Nico stepped out of the white building that stood in stark contrast to the dry, war-torn plains of northeastern Colorado, he heard the faint, but distinguishable whooshing sound of a missile heading straight for him. As fast as he could he sprinted towards his warsuit, which opened as he lept through the air and into it. The port on the back of his neck received the neural link probe and as it made contact he whipped around as fast as he could, stuck his hand out, and the air-to-air missile collided with the suit with such force that the front of the laboratory was annihilated from the explosion, igniting the dark night in magnificent hues of red, orange, and yellow.

When the smoke cleared, the warsuit was left scorched which changed its already blackened frame little, but was otherwise unharmed, as was Nico. He looked around for a moment, trying to find whatever it was that attacked him, and after a few moments the Seraph armor locked onto a faraway black dot, surrounded by the deep dark of the night. In an instant the engines from the warsuit roared and Nico burst with wondrous speed, climbing to thousands of feet in mere seconds and moving towards the tracked dot. The artificial reality overlay of his helmet zoomed in and he could clearly see a stealth jet slinging through the air at what the suit tracked as Mach 13, sixteen thousand kilometers per hour, coming around again to fire on him.

"Fuck," Nico muttered as he spiraled upwards, the moon glistening off his blackened armor. His body couldn't withstand the gravitational force to give chase or even run away. He was dead in the water the way he was and he knew it.

"Flood it," he said aloud, calm as always even though he was staring down his own death. Without responding, his suit began flooding quickly with a light-blue liquid that glowed purple when combined with the red light from the suit's core. In a few seconds it reached Nico's mouth and he inhaled as deeply as he could, taking the liquid into his lungs. Had the liquid been anything but what it was, he would've lost consciousness and drowned in an instant. But the light blue hue of the liquid proved it to be heavily oxygenated, and when he took it into his lungs, he breathed it as if he was still in the womb. A memory flashed before his eyes, as it always did when he flooded his suit, and he felt a hint of emotion that he had not felt since, but it faded as quickly as it came.

The oxygenated liquid flowing through his suit and in and out of his lungs negated much of the gravitational force Nico felt as his thrusters ignited a bright white and pushed him well into the same speed range as the stealth jet that was hunting him. Within a few seconds, he caught up to it and a dogfight ensued with Nico chasing his adversary through the night sky. Had his suit not been tracking the jet, a feat which was near impossible for regular military technology, he wouldn't have been able to see it. No light was reflected on its stealthed body, not even the light of the moon or the stars, and so as they hurtled through the stratosphere the only thing that ignited the night besides the core of Seraphiel's armor were the tracers on the rounds that ripped from both machines' chain guns as they spiraled and danced around each other. After only a few seconds however, Nico overtook the unmanned jet, latched on to it, and ripped it in half. He tossed it away quickly as it self-detonated in order to preserve the technology within.

Another whistling sound approached him, and as fast as he could he pulled his airbrake, twisted, reignited his thrusters, and just barely pulled himself out of the way as the missile soared past his head. In the millisecond it took for the missile to pass him, he had already shot forward, further away from the explosive as it roared and curved back around towards him. It was a seeker, and although his suit had gathered that information as the missile passed him, he could tell by the roar and the chase it gave. Seekers were loud, their engines strong, and their targeting computers even stronger. Few things could outrun a seeker and it was the reason they were used in high-orbit conflicts. Unfortunately, his suit was not built for high-orbit, and he was not one of the few things that could outrun them.

On top of their speed and tracking, they could not be deceived by flares like traditional seeker missiles. Flares were so commonplace in the beginning of the War that countries had problems hitting enemy aircraft with the traditional heat-seeking variety. So, during the War non-heat seekers were developed and they were still just as dangerous as they were over twenty years prior. Nico remembered those days, the War, the Archangels, but he felt little purpose in ruminating on days that would never and should never return. Instead, he focused on the missile chasing him and how he was going to solve that mortal problem.

Only one thing to do, Nico thought as he soared over the blasted landscape below him. In the distance he could see the Rocky Mountains and shrouded deep within was his destination: Trytek Headquarters. One seeker he could deal with, multiple was a death sentence for him with his scouting loadout. The dual chain guns sitting atop his shoulder plates were powerful, but not powerful enough to deal with all-out war. He hadn't needed his Jacobian gear in a long time, and now he was wishing more than ever that he had it. Wishes were pointless however, he thought. Next time instead of wishing, he would be prepared, and he would rain death upon those that dare provoke him.

His shoulder-mounted chain guns spun around and spewed bullets behind him. His suit was doing it autonomously, but he was tracking them manually as well, as his internal visor was a current overlay of what was in front of him and behind him. Such a sight would sicken a regular soldier, but he had been seeing in double-vision for most of his life. This overlay could still be turned off however, and Nico only used it when absolutely necessary as it made combat, especially in all-out war, extremely difficult to follow. Inevitably, the rounds impacted with the missile and it exploded, sending a blazing sphere outward from it. Nico continued onward, towards Trytek, and as he closed in two more unmanned stealth jets flanked him. He dealt with them similarly to the last and danced with them through the night sky until they too ignited in a blazing fury. He grabbed a piece of falling debris from the jet and sped up towards Trytek.

The suit could see it now, just barely, nestled in the crevasses of the scarred Rocky Mountains. The anti-air batteries locked onto him - he could feel the ringing in his mind, like an instinct - one missile had launched, but that was all they would get. He used the piece of debris in his hand as a projectile and slung it at the missile like a frisbee, cleaving it in two. The explosion and smoke masked him, and once the artillery locked on to him again it was too late... he was too fast. This was the power of the Seraphim and the power of the Archangels before them. This was death incarnate.

Seraphiel ignited his reverse thrusters and air brakes just moments before smashing into a seeker gun and shredding it with the sheer velocity of himself. The gun ignited, as did the many missiles within it, sending a rippling effect to everything around it. He had gone straight through it and sunk deep within the earth, so he felt little of the explosion as it passed over him and ruptured the ground above him. With another burst, he shot up out of the ground, through the fire and smoke, and moved to the next gun, ripping through it with the explosive rounds from his chain guns and with his bare hands. It too ignited, but he was long gone before the explosion reached him. He moved to the next one, and then the next, a torrent of flame following behind him as he shot up in the air and came crashing down over and over again. His breathing became heavy and jagged as the oxygenated liquid, while scrubbed by his suit, began to wear on his lungs. That, coupled with the arrival of the mechanical reinforcements, told him his time was up, so as quickly as he arrived he left, but not without presents in tow.

A barrage of cluster missiles chased him upwards, high into the atmosphere as he flew east towards The City. The warsuit began slowing down, unable to keep up speeds above Mach 10, and as it slowed the missiles began catching up with him. He whipped around as fast as he could, while he still had his momentum, and manually tore through them with the remainder of his chain gun rounds. The explosion of a dozen of the missiles set off the rest, and it seemed, for a brief moment, as if the Sun rose a couple hours too early as the sky flashed white mixed with hues of yellow, orange, and red. His escape had been dicey to say the least, but he never flinched, never faltered, never worried. His expressionless face had never changed and he had never been taken over by anxiety or anger. His mind was blank and his success spoke of nothing to him except of adding itself to the incalculable proofs of his superiority. But he knew his 'greatness', if one could call it that, mattered not in any form. His success was a meaningless expression inside a meaningless world and that's all it would ever be. After he had flown for a time without any issue, he felt it safe to drain his suit, but as he began to slow and descend, a quiet hiss overtook him and a Spear missile collided with his back and he began falling to the forest below.

ABOUT THE AUTHORS

J. M. Coleman is the co-author of the dark sci-fi thriller series "The Lightning Arc". He is an author, teacher, and scholar, holding two bachelor's degrees in Theology and Secondary Education and one master's degree in Theological Education. He generally writes science fiction, horror, and/or fantasy, and spends his free time writing fiction and non-fiction, reading, and playing the few games he has time for.

L.L. Wirtz is co-author of The Lightning Arc. He has always had a passion for writing ever since he was kid making comics, a passion that has continued into adulthood and now takes the form of writing novels and poetry. His unique writing style is hard to replicate, and his creativity can be hard to match. When he doesn't have a pen in his hand it is often replaced with a frisbee or poi balls. He loves nature and pushing his body to the limit. When he is not exhausting himself outside during the spring and summer, you can find him inside playing a video game or watching his favorite anime. If he is not doing that he is juggling his friendships and meeting new people, constantly expanding his social life by creating new bonds - all in enough time to squeeze in an afternoon cat nap.